Meet:

SUSIE: Blessed with effortless beauty and charm and protected by an indulgent father, she suddenly has to face adversity and decide whether to leave her comfort zone and start over, completely.

JILL: Smart, poised, successful and generous. A pillar of competence and strength with a painful secret.

ANNE: Feisty, fearless and betrayed, can she allow herself to become vulnerable again?

SOPHIE: The emotional heart of her family and friends, who needs to rediscover her teenage self to help restore her husband's pride.

CHARLIE: The misfit outsider with hidden depths and, when it matters most, a steely determination to protect his friends.

Get to know:

KINGSBAY, LONG ISLAND: In this idyllic community of parties, pools and poker nights, the calm waters can be disturbed by minor eddies – and catastrophic tornadoes.

BARCELONA, SPAIN: Steeped in a vibrant history; a city of seduction, of great beauty, elegance and passion – just like its men and women.

GW00383916

BUNCO

BRIAN MCPHEE

Published by Entente Publishing

www.ententepublishing.com

hello@ententepublishing

1.001

for

SHEILA AND MARIANNE

IMPORTANT DISCLAIMER

Certain community events portrayed in this work are based very loosely on actual events. However, all persons portrayed are entirely fictitious and bear no resemblance to any persons, alive or dead. Any apparent resemblance to actual persons or places is entirely coincidental.

Considerable artistic license has been taken with public events that occur each year in Sitges, Spain. To ascertain the degree of license taken, the author recommends a personal visit.

ACKNOWLEDGEMENTS

Thanks to my cousin George Dunn and my wife Sheila, who helped with encouragement, corrections and suggestions.

Jackie Murphy, Jan McDade, and Sue Heyes were early readers who helped me avoid making even more mishtakes!

Allen Loates kindly proofread the final draft.

Victoire and Lucy recruited Estel Camprecios to help with the Spanish and Catalan translations. Moltes gràcies.

Thanks to my brother Stephen, who designed the cover.

Most of all, many thanks to my daughter and editor, Marianne, who provided invaluable comments and advice on every aspect of this story.

If you were to look for Dukes County on a map, you might find it between the northern parts of Queens and Nassau Counties on Long Island, New York. While not quite the Gold Coast, by any other measure, Dukes County would be considered extremely affluent.

Stirling Bayside in Dukes County is what is called a Census Designated Place - a loosely defined inhabited area that is not incorporated which, even more loosely, means that it doesn't have a recognizable town within its borders. Almost 40,000 people were recorded in Stirling Bayside in the last census.

Next door to Stirling Bayside, and also on the waterfront of Long Island Sound, is Jameston, a tourist-friendly, pre-Revolutionary town, population around 30,000 and proud home of Dukes College, one of the oldest liberal arts colleges in the United States.

Our story however, is chiefly concerned with the residents of Kingsbay, an extremely pleasant Stirling Bayside community of some 650 souls located on Broad Bay, an inlet of Long Island Sound. There are around 250 single family homes in Kingsbay, almost all very attractive spacious homes of four to six bedrooms on large wooded lots. Kingsbay also includes a few more modest homes, built before Kingsbay proper was developed.

Only in young and very wealthy nations with vast amounts of land could such communities exist. To the inhabitants of these neighborhoods in the United States, they are the very essence of the American Dream.

bunco

1. *(US, slang)* A swindle or confidence trick.

2. A parlor game played in teams with three dice, originating in England but popular among suburban women in the United States at the beginning of the twenty-first century.

PRINCIPAL CHARACTERS

The Smiths: Susie* *(née Linsley)* (25) & Andy (34)

The Petersens: Jill* *(née MacLeod)* (35) & Frank (37), their kids, Kevin & Lucy and Alejandra, their live-in nanny

The Coopers: Sophie* *(née Ramos)* (53) & Will (54) and their youngest son, Peter

Anne Murphy* *(formerly Johnson)* (61) and her partner, Ted Newberry

Charlie Crouch (21) and his grandmother, Betty (92)

The Andersons: Monica & Steve; now living in Spain

THEIR EXTENDED FAMILY MEMBERS

Astrid Casey - Frank Petersen's sister, her husband, Luke and their sons, Mark & John

Bill & Jean MacLeod - Jill Petersen's parents

Luis Ramos - Sophie Cooper's father

George & Rita Smith - Andy's parents

Paul & Mary Linsley - Susie's parents

NEIGHBORS IN KINGSBAY

The poker guys
(in addition to Andy Smith, Frank Petersen & Will Cooper)

Geoff Hooper, wife Caroline* & daughter Carol

Joe Levine, wife Pamela & son Joe Jr

Brian Russell, wife Pauline* & daughter Jenna

Pete Woods, wife Donna*

Others

George & Christine* Kavanagh, son Josiah and daughter Justine *(the Petersens' mother's helper)*

Cliff & Annette Walker and their adult daughter, Annemarie

Vivien Werner, widowed on 9/11

* Bunco Babes

IN BARCELONA

Sebastiá Xavier Domènech i Marti *(Javi or Tiá)*

His ex-wife, Magdalena Maria Bacardi i Meier *(Talena)*

Their son, Jordi Tomás-Maria Domènech i Bacardi *(Jordi)*

Javi's sister, Isabella *(Bella)*

CHRISTMAS 2010

Jill rang the doorbell. A few seconds later, a remarkably pretty young woman greeted her with a smile.

"Hello."

"Hi, welcome to the neighborhood. I thought you might be in need of coffee?"

"What great timing! Thank you. The place is beyond a mess, but come in anyway, out of the cold."

Susie led the way though the hallway, past several towers of packing boxes. Jill followed her into the kitchen, where yet more boxes covered every available surface.

"Just put the tray on top of any old stack. I'm Susie, by the way," she said, holding out her hand.

"Hi Susie, I'm Jill. Frank and I are your nearest neighbors. We're the Petersens. I can't believe you're moving in on Christmas Eve, how did *that* happen?"

"Just a sec, Jill, let me call Andy, before this coffee gets cold."

Susie walked to the foot of the stairs and called up, "Andy, there's a lovely lady here, with coffee and cookies."

She returned to the kitchen, "We were supposed to move in two weeks ago, but somehow our lawyer screwed things up, and so here we are. It's only because there wasn't much in Andy's apartment that the movers agreed to handle us this morning, otherwise we wouldn't have been able to move into our new home until after New Years, which would have been really disappointing."

As her husband came into the kitchen, Susie turned to him and said, "I was just telling Jill how we almost didn't make it in today. I hope I never see another lawyer for the rest of my life!"

Jill chuckled as she held her hand out to Andy, "Sorry to ruin your day Susie. I'm afraid I *am* a lawyer."

"So, what are the new neighbors like?" Frank Petersen asked when his wife returned.

"Really nice I think, and she's the most beautiful woman I've ever seen outside the movies. She'll cause a few flutters in the neighborhood I'm sure, although she's very young, mid-twenties I'd say. No kids. Anyway, you can judge for yourself tomorrow, I've invited them to have Christmas dinner with us."

"Why am I not surprised? Well, I guess two more will hardly matter."

"That's what I thought sweetheart. And you're *so* clever at managing all these unexpected demands, *so* competent, *so* all around wonderful."

Jill was laughing now.

He grabbed her around the waist and pulled her close, "Maybe I'll go check out our gorgeous neighbor myself. Maybe I'll be back in a few hours."

"In your dreams, big boy. Now kiss me and let me go, I've still to make up beds for the boys."

Frank's sister and family were coming for Christmas, as well as Jill's parents; but they both knew that Frank had more than enough food for the two extra mouths they would now be feeding. His sister Astrid had hosted Thanksgiving, and so it was Frank's turn to cook for the family. They were due around five this evening, and they were all going to Outback Steakhouse for dinner.

Jill's parents, Jean and Bill, lived locally, and would arrive tomorrow around two o'clock.

The afternoon passed in a flurry of preparations; Frank mostly in the kitchen and Jill making final touches to the guest rooms and the Christmas decorations. Nine-year-old Kevin came crashing in periodically, by himself, or with a friend or two in tow, looking for snacks or a catcher's glove or something else needed for their games.

Suddenly Kevin dashed in for the umpteenth time, and in a state of hysterical excitement. He yelled at the top of his voice "Dad, Dad, the Hutchins have got an ice rink! In their backyard! We're going to play hockey!"

"I want to play hockey too," piped up Lucy.

"But you can't skate yet Lucy. Maybe we can try the ice rink later when it's quiet, and we can start teaching you to skate. Would that be good? Plus, we haven't finished getting all the Disney princesses to write their letters to Santa."

Jill smiled as Justine Kavanagh, her thirteen-year-old mother's helper for the day, expertly handled her daughter, Lucy. Booking Justine for Christmas Eve had been Frank's brilliant idea; getting organized was much easier without trying to entertain an excited five-year-old at the same time. Their nanny, Alejandra, was home with her family in Puerto Rico for the holidays.

"Go back into the den with Justine and get those letters organized Lucy, they need to be sent by four o'clock if they're to get to Santa in time."

At 5:20 the Caseys arrived from Connecticut. Jill was very fond of Astrid and her husband Luke, and she enjoyed observing the closeness between Frank and his sister, who shared the same strong but gentle personalities. They were very at ease with each other. Jill hoped that Kevin and Lucy would enjoy the same togetherness when they were older. Jill realized that the success of Astrid and Frank's relationship had possibly been down to the sister being the older of the two as they were growing up. Certainly Kevin took little notice of his little sister, except to complain that she was no good at games. Perhaps things would change as they grew up.

There were hugs and kisses all round, although Jill smiled to herself, as she sensed that 16-year-old Mark was rather less enthusiastic about hugging and kissing his aunt these days. The two families sat in the family room with coffee and hot chocolate and caught up with the news since Thanksgiving.

After a few minutes however, Frank excused himself, "I'll be back in a minute."

He beckoned Justine out into the hallway. "Time for you to get back to your folks, Justine. Here's your money and a little extra for Christmas. You've been fantastic, we couldn't have managed without you today."

"Thanks Mr. Petersen, it was nice, Lucy's fun."

"Justine, just before you go, could you take Lucy up to her room for five minutes? Tell her she should bring one of the princesses to show her Aunt Astrid."

"Sure, Mr. Petersen."

As soon as Justine had shepherded Lucy upstairs, Frank returned to the family room. "Sorry to interrupt Luke, I just need to talk to the boys for a second while Lucy's upstairs."

He turned to address the three boys. "Boys, this is probably the last year that Lucy will believe in Santa and I don't want any of you spoiling her Christmas, especially you, Kevin. I'll be very disappointed if any of you give the game away. It isn't so very long ago that you all were her age, so don't try to be clever, OK? She's just a little girl and you're all supposed to be more grown up."

Astrid reinforced her brother's words, "And that goes for you two as well," she said, looking sternly at Mark, and especially at her younger son, John.

"Good timing Frank," added Jill, "I think I hear Father Christmas coming. Lucy! Come quick honey!"

Everyone grabbed shoes and ran out the front door to watch the Stirling Bayside fire engine drive slowly down the street with its klaxon blaring. Father Christmas was sitting atop the cab, waving and wishing everyone happy holidays. Meanwhile, his elves were throwing candy to the kids lining the sidewalks.

"That isn't the real Santa, is it, Mom?"

"No, Lucy, you won't see the real Santa tonight, he'll be too busy. Well, just maybe you'll catch a glimpse of him or one of the reindeer, or maybe you'll hear something on the roof if you're very, very quiet."

Kevin opened his mouth to say something smart, but a look from his mom changed his mind, "Yeah Lucy, but you have to be very quiet."

"OK everyone," announced Astrid, realizing it was time they got going, "let's go back inside and get our coats and we'll go to Outback. Lucy honey, will you come in the car with me, so you can tell me more about the princesses? Mark and John will go with your mom and dad and Kevin."

Astrid knew that Kevin idolized his older cousins, while they tended to ignore him, although she thought maybe Mark was beginning to enjoy the hero worship just a little. Once again she thought how complicated life could be with a 16-year-old.

Outback was a success, although the adults struggled to find many choices that were not calorie nightmares. Luke insisted that his sons shared one Bloomin' Onion between them, "Yes I know you could easily eat one each, but each one has nearly 2000 calories. No pretty girl is going to want to date someone who looks like that guy over there, munching on *his* Bloomin' Onion."

Luke knew how to appeal to Mark when it came to healthy eating; the guy he was indicating weighed well over three hundred pounds and flowed over his seat in every direction.

"OK, maybe I'll have something else."

"No Mark, you know you love it, we'll share one, like Dad said." John was still more interested in his favorite food than in girls, but only just.

"Thank God for grilled salmon," observed Astrid, "I'm not in the mood for another salad, and there's nothing else remotely in line with my diet in this place."

"You're absolutely right Sis, it's incredibly unhealthy. Now, who wants to share a salted caramel cookie dessert?"

They came out of the restaurant to a brand new world. It was snowing hard, and there was already over an inch on the ground. The youngsters were beside themselves. Even Mark forgot he was sixteen, as they ran around the car park, making tracks and throwing snowballs. Eventually everyone was corralled back into the two cars and they drove carefully back to Kingsbay.

"Who's going to help me with the luminarias?" asked Frank as they piled out of the cars. All four youngsters wanted to help. "OK, wait here you three; John can you help me in the garage please."

"The materials for the luminarias are in these two boxes, if you could give me a hand getting them down, that would be great. The waxed paper bags and the candles are in this one, and there's some sand for weighting them down in that plastic box on the next shelf. And John, as you're a bit older this year, can I ask you to look out for Lucy when the snowball fights start tomorrow? Kevin and his friends can be a bit boisterous and they forget how easy it is to hurt a little kid."

"Of course Uncle Frank, I'll keep an eye on her." John was delighted to be trusted by his Uncle Frank and he actually quite liked his little cousin, even though she was a girl.

Frank asked his brother-in-law to organize the luminaria work party, and soon the front yard and driveway were outlined by the warm glow of the candles inside the waxed paper bags. Everyone came outside to walk to the corner to see the entire curve of Linwood Drive beautifully illuminated, just like their own road and every other street in Kingsbay. The steadily falling snow completed the Christmas card look of the community.

They walked around the streets a while, greeting friends and neighbors, many of whom Astrid and Luke knew from previous visits.

"Aunt Jill, who's that across the street?" asked Mark.

"They're our new neighbors, Mr. and Mrs. Smith. You'll meet them tomorrow, they're having Christmas dinner with us."

Jill looked over at her sister-in-law and tried to suppress a smile. Mark was having trouble keeping his eyes off the stunning young woman waving at someone up ahead.

Before they could go over to introduce everyone, Frank appeared and announced that they had to get back to their house. "I can hear the carol singers; quickly now, we need to get ready."

It had become a tradition that the Petersen house was the pit stop for the community carol singers. So while the luminarias were being arranged, Frank had been warming the mulled wine on the stove.

Soon the twelve or so singers came up the Petersen driveway, singing *Silent Night*. Frank had set up a folding table by the front door to hold the warm wine and lots of cups.

"That was lovely singing, Geoff, thanks!"

"Thanks, Jill, and thanks for the wine, Frank. Very welcome. Perfect timing for the snow isn't it? Hi Lucy!" Geoff continued, "The snow's very good for Father Christmas isn't it? I think the reindeer prefer snow, don't you?"

"Yes, Mr. Hooper, I think they do, because it always snows at the North Pole, so they'll feel much more at home."

The singers moved on, and the two families retreated to the cozy house.

"Time for you to get upstairs Lucy, it's way past your bedtime. Say goodnight to everyone."

Lucy was about to protest, when Jill continued, "And then we'll hang your stocking on your bed."

Frank looked at his watch; it was just after ten o'clock, well past Lucy's normal bedtime. He looked over at his son; it was past Kevin's normal bedtime too.

Kevin anticipated his father, "Please Dad, it's Christmas Eve."

"OK Kev, since it's Christmas Eve and you kept your promise about Lucy. One more hour, then we'll all be going to bed. After we see Santa of course."

Despite her determination to listen out for reindeer on the roof, Lucy was sound asleep two minutes after her head hit the pillow. It really was way past her normal bedtime and it had been an exciting day. However, at 10:50, Kevin, in his Spiderman pajamas, woke her up.

"Lucy, Lucy, wake up, Santa's outside. Come and see!"

He took his little sister's warm hand in his own and led her through their parent's bedroom to the bay window.

"Look Lucy, there he is."

Through the snowflakes, falling in steady, heavy drifts, Lucy could see Santa with his big sack over his shoulder, walking down the middle of their street, toward her house. She could even see his white whiskers and bushy beard and the bright silver buckle on his considerable tummy. As she watched, spellbound, Santa came alongside her window, turned slowly, looked straight at her, and waved.

Lucy turned to look up at her brother, her eyes like saucers. Kevin looked at his little sister and held a finger up to his lips. And Lucy understood that this was their secret.

He took her back to her bed and came downstairs.

"How did it go?" asked Jill who was standing by the window watching, as Jack Emerson, dressed in his magnificent Santa outfit, turned the corner.

Too choked to speak, Kevin ran to his mother and wrapped his arms tightly around her waist.

Christmas morning dawned sunny and cold, with four inches of snow on the ground. The lines of luminarias were now little humps that defined the borders of front yards, like piped icing around the edges of so many wedding cakes.

Lucy, Kevin and John appeared around eight o'clock, but were kept out of the family room until everyone had assembled in the kitchen. At nine, everyone sat around the tree. Kevin read out the cards tied to each gift and Lucy delivered them to the recipient, and then waited impatiently to see what was inside the colorful wrapping paper.

Everyone loved their presents, although there was a moment of anguish when Kevin realized that the snow meant he couldn't ride his new bike.

"But, I'll get to ride my bike as soon as the snow melts, right Dad?"

Jill produced a carrot for a nose and demanded a snowman in her front yard that would be the envy of every home in Kingsbay. The four cousins pulled on boots and gloves. John gave Frank a meaningful look as he took Lucy's hand to go out the door.

"What was all that about?" asked Luke.

"I appointed him Lucy's protector in the snowball fights. It seems he'll be taking his duties very seriously."

At the same time that the snowman was being made, Bill and Jean MacLeod were setting out on the twenty minute drive to their daughter's house.

"Now drive slowly Bill, the roads will be slick with this fresh snow and no one's going to be plowing today."

"Sure Jean, but I have driven in snow before, remember?"

Jill's parents had only recently moved to Stirling Bayside from Colorado, following Bill's retirement from the Air Force. Bill was indeed an experienced winter driver, and in conditions much worse than this.

Unfortunately the same couldn't be said for everyone out driving that day. As Bill negotiated a junction, he looked to his right and threw his arm across his wife's chest, pushing her into her seat, as an out-of-control car slid slowly through a stop sign and gently, but firmly, pushed into Bill's car, luckily some way behind Jean's door. The impact finally stopped the other car, a small, ancient Chevy, which came to rest firmly against the MacLeod's Camry.

Both drivers got out to inspect the damage, which wasn't too bad, although Bill's rear panel would need some repair work.

"No real harm done son. Are you OK?"

"Yes, sir, I'm really sorry sir, the car just wouldn't stop, no matter how hard I pushed on the brakes."

"Well, son, in an old car like yours, that just what you mustn't do in conditions like this. Look up what you should do, or better still, get a newer car that will do it for you. Are you insured young man?"

"Yes sir, I am."

"OK, give me your details, and here are mine. I guess you'll be paying a little more for insurance next year."

A few minutes later the MacLeods were pulling in to the Petersens' driveway.

Bill embraced his daughter. "Your mom's a bit shook up, honey. I think a cup of camomile tea would be in order. Don't worry, we had a little incident, but everything is fine. Now, where are my favorite monsters?"

Just then Kevin and Lucy careened around the parked car, and threw themselves at their grandparents.

"Merry Christmas, Grandpa, Merry Christmas, Grandma!" their voices mixed together as one.

Lucy took her grandmother's hand, "Come and see what Santa brought me Grandma, you won't believe it."

Kevin pulled Bill's head down to his own level and whispered in his ear, "You have to be careful what you say, Grandpa, Lucy still believes in Santa Claus and we don't want to spoil it for her."

Bill nodded his head and put on a serious face, "Roger that, Kevin."

No matter how many times Bill had tried to explain that he had never flown a plane, Kevin remained convinced that anyone in the Air Force had to be a fighter pilot and, for now at least, Bill had decided to give up the struggle.

Jill settled her parents in the main guest room to unpack and quickly established that the crash had indeed been a minor incident and best ignored, or her mother would go on about it all day.

The arrival of grandparents meant more presents, including for the Casey boys, who were both surprised and delighted. And Grandma and Grandpa had to come out and admire the snowman, which, they all agreed, was without a doubt, the best in Kingsbay.

"It's a pity you don't have a scarf, Grandpa, because Dad won't give us one for the snowman, which is pretty mean if you ask me." Kevin was still not happy about the whole scarf issue.

"Kevin, I told you that I only have a couple of scarves and they're too good to be found in a puddle of melted snow in a day or so. If you stop going on about it, I might let you borrow one for ten minutes so you can get a photo of the snowman with his scarf on."

"Okkaaaayyyy, I guess."

While they were admiring the snowman, Susie and Andy appeared from around the corner.

"What a great snowman! Actually, I think he'll be warmer with this on."

And with that, Susie pulled the bright red scarf from around her shoulders and wrapped it around the snowman's neck.

Kevin looked at his father in triumph.

"Thanks, Mrs. Smith."

Kevin and Lucy had been coached with the new neighbors' name that morning. However, Lucy was comfortable with Susie immediately, and demonstrated this by commanding her, "Come and see my presents Susie, come on," as she grabbed Susie's hand.

"Just a minute young lady, we need to introduce Mr. and Mrs. Smith to everyone, and I think we'll do that inside."

"Oh Mom, that's *so* boring. Susie wants to see my new princess."

"I'm sorry Susie, she must have heard me mention your first name to Frank." Jill apologized.

Susie laughed and turned to Lucy. "That's OK, you can call me Susie, but only if you tell me your name."

Much to Lucy's disgust, introductions took a while.

"It's really incredibly nice to be invited to Christmas dinner, and on our first real day in Kingsbay." Susie continued.

Andy handed Frank two bottles of champagne, "We were going to drink these in our new house, but this is a much better idea."

Frank led everyone into the family room, where Lucy monopolized Susie to show her every present she had received.

Astrid offered to help Jill finish setting the table for their meal. When they were safely alone in the dining room, she turned to Jill, "I think Mark may just have a heart attack soon, he can't take his eyes off your new neighbor. In fact his dad isn't doing much better in that department," she finished with a chuckle.

"She is gorgeous, isn't she, and he's pretty dishy too, if you ask me."

"Mmm, he sure is. Is it just me, or does Andy look like Ben Affleck?"

"That's it! Ben Affleck. I've been thinking he reminds me of someone. He's even got the chin. Come on, let's get the first course on the table."

Christmas dinner at the Petersens was extra complicated because Frank insisted on cooking ham *and* turkey, "I know we just had turkey, but your dad likes his British Christmas dinner with turkey, Brussel sprouts and mince pies. No one else has to eat it."

"But Dad was only five when he arrived in California!"

"Yeah, but he told me years ago that they had a traditional British Christmas even when it was sunny and in the seventies in San Diego."

Of course she loved him for it, and for everything else he did to make Christmas magical for them every year.

There was one hiccup however, when Frank proudly produced the turkey and Lucy suddenly exclaimed, "That turkey looks just like a turkey."

"What do you mean honey, it *is* a turkey, just like the one Daddy cooked last month for Thanksgiving."

"But this one looks like the turkeys in our book about the first Thanksgiving in Miss Thompson's class, real turkeys."

"OK honey you don't have to have any turkey, have some lovely ham instead."

But Lucy was suspicious now. "Where does ham come from?"

Before anyone else could speak, Kevin answered his sister.

"From pigs of course."

"You mean pigs like Peppa Pig?"

Jill tried to save the day, "No, no honey, from farmyard pigs, they don't talk like Peppa Pig do they?"

"Peppa Pig is a pig. I'm not eating pig."

There were a few minutes of silence, while Lucy thought hard about this important issue. Finally she announced, "I'm a vegetarian, like Judy."

"Who is Judy, Lucy?" asked her Uncle Luke.

"Judy sits beside me in class, and her family are vegetarians and Miss Thomson explained what that means and that we weren't to tease Judy about it. Lots and lots of people are vegetarians. Like me and Judy."

So Lucy had no turkey and no ham and Kevin and John were quietly warned to say nothing as she cheerfully finished off half a dozen cocktail sausages.

Meanwhile Mark, who had made sure that he was sitting next to Susie, was quiet throughout the early part of dinner. Eventually Susie decided to get him talking, "What did you get your girlfriend for Christmas, Mark?"

Before he could stop himself, and to the astonishment of his mother, father and especially his brother, Mark replied, "I bought her a pair of gloves."

"Since when...?" began John, before his mother shushed him.

"Well, I want her to be my girlfriend. As soon as we get back to school I'm going to ask her to the Junior Prom. I hope she says yes, but she's very popular, so I don't know."

Mark's voice dropped as he finished, and he blushed with the realization that he had said much more than he wanted to in front of his family. He was afraid that he wasn't cool enough for the young girl who was the focus of his attention. Suddenly Mark looked quite distraught, and he wished he was somewhere else, anywhere where no one was staring at him.

Susie turned to Frank, "Excuse me Frank, I'll just be a moment."

She stepped away from the table and they heard the front door open and close. In a few minutes she returned, sat down and, when everyone else was once again talking, she turned to Mark, and handed him a small box, beautifully wrapped in gold paper.

She spoke quietly, "This is Chanel No. 5, Mark. It's the most sophisticated perfume in the world and every woman knows how special it is. My father sends me a bottle every year, but I haven't the heart to tell him I don't like it. You take it and give it to your girlfriend with the gloves, I'm sure she'll love it. Now tell me all about her."

The four women were in the kitchen washing glasses and loading the dishwasher.

"I saw what a lovely thing you did Susie, you handled my son so beautifully. You must have seen how he was looking at you earlier, but now he seems quite relaxed around you."

"Oh well, young men can be so confused don't you think? And Mark is a very nice young man. You must be very proud."

"And he has a girlfriend. I didn't see that coming!"

"Well, to be fair, she doesn't know that she *is* his girlfriend. I gather nothing has been said yet."

Astrid commented, "No one gave me Chanel No. 5 when I was sixteen."

"I'm a lot older than you Astrid, and no one's given me Chanel yet!" observed Jill's mother as they all laughed together.

While Astrid and Jean were taking the desserts into the dining room, Jill turned to Susie, "You know Susie, No. 5 is one of my favorites, I wear it on special occasions. If I'm not mistaken you're wearing it right now."

"But you won't tell him will you? And Dad really does send a bottle every year."

Jill smiled at Susie fondly and squeezed her arm, "No honey, I won't tell."

They were too many for Monopoly, so after dinner, two packs of cards were produced and they played Snap and Go Fish, with Lucy and Susie a team together. When they were bored with this, Susie turned to Andy, "Why not show the boys some of your tricks Andy?"

"Sure. Can you let me have the cards please, Jill?"

Andy separated the cards into their two decks and put one aside.

"OK," he started, "I'm going to need assistants. Let's start with Lucy."

Andy performed a series of card tricks, each time asking one of the younger kids to shuffle the cards, or choose a card or count for him. Andy really was a very good amateur card magician, and the adults were mesmerized as much as the kids.

After half an hour Andy announced his final trick, which involved finding a missing ace in the box that Lucy's latest princess doll had been in.

"OK that's it guys, bedtime for Lucy; Kevin and John can play video games for one hour in Kevin's room and then it's lights out!" Frank announced, adding, "But first you can say goodnight to everyone."

The children worked their way around the room, and when Kevin came round to Andy he asked him quietly, "Mr. Smith, could you teach me a card trick? It would be so cool to show my friends."

"Of course, Kevin. Come over any time and I'll show you how to do my best trick."

Bill and Jean departed with many warnings to drive slowly. Andy and Susie left for their second night in their new home, and the Caseys settled down in their guest rooms. Jill and Frank lay in bed, relaxed at the end of a very busy day.

Jill turned to her husband, "That went well honey, thanks again for everything; the meal was lovely, even for our new vegetarian."

"I hope that doesn't last too long! Andy and Susie are very nice, don't you think?"

"They're lovely. I couldn't believe how Susie handled Mark, she looks so young, but she's wise beyond her years I think. You know she was wearing Chanel?"

"Of course, don't you think I recognize it by now? I think I need you a bit closer to figure out what you're wearing tonight."

Meanwhile, in the house tucked behind the Petersens', Susie was putting out her bedside light. "What a great day, and what a wonderful welcome to our new neighborhood, I think we're going to be happy here, don't you sweetheart?"

"I do. Come over here and make me happy right now."

FOURTH OF JULY

Andy and Susie had been in Kingsbay for six months now, and Andy thought they had settled in well. Susie had recently joined the bunco group and seemed to have found a good friend in Jill. At some point he really had to find out exactly what the hell bunco was, he ruminated. For his part, he had been accepted into the Thursday night poker group; he and Susie were playing regular golf with some of the folks in the neighborhood; and next week was the guys' fishing weekend.

Meanwhile, it was Andy's favorite time of day; early morning just after dawn, when the streets were quiet and empty. He walked to the community marina where he kept his Catalina sailboat. Although

Susie often joined him, he liked to have a solo sail now and then, to clear his head and get his thoughts organized.

He could have done with Susie's help today, but he had left her sleeping. Susie had a busy day ahead, helping with all the prep for the Fourth of July weekend activities. This was her first big Kingsbay event and she wanted to be useful.

He was pushing the community dock cart carrying the brand new North Sail mainsail which had just arrived. It was pretty heavy and he had to get it on board without dropping it, and he didn't want to just throw it aboard. When he arrived at the marina he saw a young man walking along the path at the water's edge. Andy didn't recognize him and so as he came alongside the stranger, Andy politely challenged him.

"Good morning, I'm sorry, I don't know your name."

"Charlie," the young man muttered, "I live there, at the end." He pointed towards the far end of Bayside Avenue, "The yellow house."

The yellow house was a tidy little Cape Cod-style house, technically in Bayview Drive, but, as it was the corner house, it enjoyed the same waterside views as the big houses on Bayside Avenue.

"Good morning Charlie, I'm Andy. I'm pretty new to Kingsbay, so apologies for not recognizing you. Glad to meet you."

Charlie shyly shook the proffered hand. Andy noticed that the young man avoided any eye contact.

"Charlie, can I ask you for a favor? I have to get this on board that sailboat over there. Do you think you could give me a hand, it's kinda heavy?"

"Sure, no problem."

With Andy on board the yacht, and Charlie on the pontoon, it was a simple matter to pass the sail in its neat shipping cover onto *Susie Q*. Andy had bought the boat in March. Although four years old, she was in great condition, but he had known that the mainsail wouldn't see out another season as it was a transfer from yet another Catalina, and had to be nearer to fourteen years old.

Renaming the boat *Susie Q* was all part of his attempt to win Susie over to the idea of spending money on his toy. The Smiths were not nearly as wealthy as most of their neighbors, so the boat was a real indulgence.

"Thanks Charlie, that was much easier with two of us."

During their brief encounter Andy had become aware of how shy Charlie was. He suspected that the young man didn't have too many friends.

"Charlie, would you like to come out for a quick sail and help me break in this new puppy?"

He could see the indecision on Charlie's face, now looking straight at Andy for once.

"We'll only be out for an hour or so, max."

Charlie's struggle was written all over his open face. Eventually the lure of the water won out and he blurted out "Can I just run and tell Gran first?"

"Of course you can. I'll take this cart back to the dinghy store while you do that. No rush, take your time."

Andy had already fitted the new sail by the time Charlie returned.

"I'm really sorry, I had to help her go to ... I mean I'm sorry I ..."

"Relax Charlie. I'm not even ready yet. Come on board and sit over there please."

Initially, Charlie was uneasy moving around the boat, but as soon as they had cast off from the marina berth a change came over him. He became much more alert, engaged, and was soon full of questions. "What is this called? What is that for? How do you use this?" The young man was clearly loving what was apparently his first sail.

"Charlie, would you like to sail her?"

"Could I really? Do you think I could?"

"Sure. OK, see that big tree over there, across the bay? That's our target. Now slowly move over here and we'll swap places. Don't worry about the sheets, the ropes, until you're sitting. OK, now take the rudder in this hand and here, let me give you the sheet for the mainsail. Just keep us heading for that tree."

Gently, Andy introduced Charlie to sailing.

"Now we don't actually want to go to that tree, we want to go over there, to get out of the Bay." Andy pointed, as he watched the young man, shy no longer. "But the wind is over here, so we can't go straight for our target, because we need the wind to help us. In about ten minutes we're going to tack, that means we are going to aim for the other side of our real target."

Charlie was a fast learner. So much so that, by the time they turned for home, he was able to figure out when to tack more or less by himself. Charlie was shy and not very articulate, but certainly not stupid, Andy realized, quite the opposite in fact.

When they were back in the marina Charlie sat still on his bench, seemingly unwilling to bring the experience to an end. His eyes were shining, his face animated.

"Charlie, I sail at this time pretty much every Saturday and Sunday. Sometimes with my wife, sometimes alone, but whenever you see us, you're welcome to join us. Anytime."

"Well I think, if they can go off on fishing ..."

"... and golfing ..."

"... weekends, then we should have a weekend away too. I mean not counting the Broadway weekend, which some of the men come on anyway. I mean a *girlie* weekend. No men."

"I'm up for that. But where would we go? Not fishing that's for sure!"

"And when? Not during school term or they'll bitch about getting the kids off to school if we aren't there Friday and Monday and I want to have a *long* weekend."

"Vegas. I went there with my sorority once and we had a blast."

"Céline Dion is in Vegas, I'd love to see her. And Blue Man Group and Cirque du Soleil. Vegas is such a *great* idea. OK, who's all for Vegas for a long girlie weekend? Hands up."

Eleven hands were raised.

The Bunco Babes were meeting at Jill's house, but not to play bunco. They had volunteered as a group to take care of lunch on Monday. Traditionally the July 4th LobsterFest was run exclusively by the men of the community. But that was in the evening, and everyone had to be fed a lunch. So, to make a point, this year the Bunco Babes had offered to do a community BBQ, 'with no testosterone help thanks.'

They were slicing onions, lettuce and tomatoes and counting and splitting hot dog and burger buns and, it seemed, deciding on a trip to Las Vegas.

Christine Kavanagh tapped a fork against a glass, "Sorry ladies, but I have to back out of my bunco hosting night at the end of October. Does anyone want to swap?"

Before anyone else could respond, Susie called out, "I'll do it. I'll happily host it."

"But you're barely a Babe sweetheart, you don't have to host until next year. Trust me, hosting can be a pain in the ass."

A few heads nodded.

"But I'd like to host, please? You've all been so lovely to me, really."

Jill decided that her friend really wanted this, so she spoke up, "Well, I say if we have a willing volunteer ...?"

"OK Susie, you're it for October 26. And thanks. I owe you," said Christine, who continued, "Why is bunco on a Wednesday anyway? It's the favorite night for parent teacher meetings."

"Who knows?" someone observed, "Too late to change it now I imagine, we're all used to it."

"I know why," offered Sandra Taney. Sandra was the oldest in the group and had lived in Kingsbay for years and years. "Bunco used to be on Friday nights so we didn't have to worry about getting our kids off to school the next morning. Of course we drank a lot more then."

A few of the women looked startled. Sandra was not known for drinking much of anything.

"Oh yes, we used to get pretty hammered back in the day. Bunco was moved, because Dallas was moved from Sunday nights to Friday, and the first meeting after the change almost no one turned up for bunco, so we moved. Saturday was date night and some of the guys had Thursday for poker, so we settled on Wednesday."

"You're shitting us, Sandra," exclaimed Anne Murphy.

"No, Anne. It was after you arrived in Kingsbay, but before you joined bunco. You were still with Derek, my dear. A long time ago."

"What's Dallas?" asked Susie, to much hilarity.

"I've printed out a check list," Fred Simmons announced. They were meeting on his deck, the nine guys signed up for the following weekend's fishing trip. "I'm not going to read it, you can do that for yourselves. Are there any problems?"

"No problem Fred, just confirming that we'll be having the same boat as last year. She was dropped back in the water yesterday, and everything looks great. The new paint job is superb, and of course her bottom is like new, so we can expect three or four knots more cruising speed."

"Thanks Cliff, that's brilliant news. I thought we might have to go with the old boat, which rolls like a pig. Really great news!"

The meeting moved along. They sorted out cars, chill boxes, booze and designated drivers for the road home.

The annual fishing trip was in its sixteenth year now and was much anticipated by the participants.

The core group was constant from year to year, with occasional new recruits, like Andy this year. No one commented, or maybe noticed, that most of the new faces didn't return for subsequent trips. This may have been connected to the fact that the fishing group included most of the neighborhood's serious drinkers. They did plenty of fishing, it was true, but only because they had constitutions that allowed them to drink heavily all afternoon and all evening, and still function the next morning.

Conversation ranged over the prospects for the next week's fishing, to baseball and on to graphic comments about some of the younger women in Kingsbay.

"If I had a wife as drop dead gorgeous as Susie, I don't think I'd be leaving her at home alone for the weekend," said Cliff to Andy, with a leer on his face. Andy could readily imagine what they'd be saying about his wife if he wasn't there.

"God, why did I volunteer for this? I must have been drunk. Surely?" Carole was beginning to panic. She had agreed to coordinate the entire Fourth of July program. Which didn't seem such a big deal back in January; after all, she didn't have to actually do anything, just coordinate other people.

Of course that isn't how it worked out. Carole had spent the last two days checking out timings, recipes, allergies, music, deliveries. Thank God for

Susie, she thought. If Susie hadn't volunteered to be her assistant, she didn't think she could have coped.

And here Susie was in her kitchen at seven a.m. on July 4th. "How do you do it Susie? How do you look so good this early in the morning? Never mind, I'm just glad you're here. Can we run through the schedule once more?"

Susie read off her clipboard, "Twenty after eleven, the parade starts off from Fairlake Court. Calum O'Donnell is handling all of that. At noon we raise the flag and sing the anthem. The Boy Scouts and Girl Scouts are looking after all of that and the Rossi kids are playing their instruments. Bob Taney is leading the pledge of allegiance. It'll be lovely I think."

"Then the Bunco Babes are taking over for lunch. And Jill's in charge so it will be fine, Carole, promise. And Jill knows no peanuts anywhere, in any form whatsoever. And I have an EpiPen just in case. We're covered, we really are."

"Oh my God," shrieked Carole, "the sangria for tonight! We're supposed to have ten gallons ready and I..."

"Carole, calm down, it's all in hand. Andy found two five gallon containers and we made up the mix last night. We just have to add the Fanta and ice tonight and we're good to go."

"What's the recipe? I mean did you really get hold of it? He keeps it such a secret."

"Bob's a pussycat and he's on our side. Of course, Sandra helped persuade him. Four pints sugar syrup, eight pints each of Cointreau and vodka, eleven pints each of Fanta orange and lemon and twenty-four bottles of red wine and a ton of ice. Guaranteed to be excellent. The only things we have to add at the last minute are the Fanta and the ice, to keep everything bubbly and cold. And of course the usual LobsterFest team are handling everything else, and they've been doing it for a million years it seems, so I guess they know what they're doing."

"Yes, Sam is a really competent guy, so I'm not worried about the LobsterFest. Susie, you're a miracle! Let's have one more coffee and then we'll go see Calum. He's so young to be in charge."

The Independence Day parade was excellent, as usual. The youngsters rode their decorated bikes, babies were pushed in strollers streaming balloons, and everyone wore red, white and blue. The barbecue went well, the hot dogs and burgers were polished off, and young Carol Hooper was able to enjoy herself, safe from any exposure to peanuts, to which she was intensely allergic. No one was allowed in the pool, since the team was setting up for the evening LobsterFest, so there were more people than usual on the beach.

By late afternoon most of Kingsbay was at home, having a rest or getting ready for the evening. Except, of course, for the LobsterFest crew, the guys who would be cooking and the teenagers now setting tables, who later on would be serving.

Those teenagers who were not on the crew, would also be making good money, doubling and tripling up on babysitting assignments. There were never enough free teenagers to cope with the demand for sitters during major community events. So kids of similar ages would be brought to a neighbor's house and two or three teens would sit for four or five families, up to ten youngsters in sleeping bags in someone's basement, although the sleeping bags didn't see much service until long past official lights out time. Party-hopping from one basement to another was not unknown.

On these nights everyone in Kingsbay had a good time, except maybe the teenagers - who, however, made lots of money.

By six o'clock, guests with tickets for the first dinner sitting were arriving and being greeted by Sam Seawright, looking dapper in his tuxedo. On closer inspection, everyone could see that, under his tux, Sam was wearing that year's LobsterFest crew t-shirt. The design was a lobster on a plate, with a slogan underneath, *'Your Lobster, Our Passion'*, inspired by an ad campaign for a tire company earlier that year, *'Your Journey, Our Passion'*.

The first shift of volunteer bar men was soon hard at work, and Bob Taney's sangria was going down well. At 6:45 Sam called everyone to their tables and service began. Guests had submitted requests in advance for lobster, steak or surf 'n turf and had been issued with appropriate markers as they checked in, but, of course, there were a few last minute changes of mind which were generally accommodated, at least early in the evening.

By 10:30 everyone had been fed. Jill Petersen rose to propose a toast to the men of the community, who yet again had demonstrated that, *'once a year, men could not only cook a lovely meal, but also do the washing up afterwards'*. It was widely known that Jill rarely cooked or washed up, so her toast was received with ironic laughter. Jill finished her little speech by introducing the community rock band, Pale Purple, and the dancing started. Pale Purple was in the second year of performing in public, and was now a very good party band, playing classic rock and some current music. The band had four musicians, plus Marcy Johanssen, their excellent lead singer, all of them Kingsbay residents.

The combination of good music, great weather, and lots of drink, ensured a lively time. Everyone had a blast, including the teenagers, who joined in the fun after they had cleared the tables, a duty that offered lots of opportunities to sneak in a few drinks.

By two in the morning there were fewer than twenty people by the pool. The band was still around, although they had stopped playing an hour ago. They were catching up; they hadn't been drinking while they played. At some point, Joe

Levine, the drummer, looked over and saw Keith Wright and Annemarie Walker making out in the hot tub. Annemarie was the unmarried daughter of Cliff and Annette, and she was generally thought to be a bit of a problem. Like her parents, with whom she still lived at age thirty-six, Annemarie drank a lot, but the booze affected her much more than it did her father. Many people thought, rightly as it happened, that Annemarie also smoked a lot of grass. Keith, on the other hand, was a popular forty-something married man, who lived with his family on Kingswood Court, and who was one of Cliff's fishing buddies. The two were kissing passionately and Keith's hands were all over Annemarie's body, particularly her breasts. Joe looked around, and saw that he wasn't the only person who had noticed the action.

Joe walked over to them, "Keith, I don't think this is the place for this. Some of those teenagers watching, are friends of your kids. I think you should probably head home now, you too, Annemarie."

Keith had the grace to look guilty and embarrassed as he walked quickly away.

Annemarie moved more slowly, and as she passed Joe she looked at him with contempt.

"Prick," she hissed.

The ripples from Keith and Annemarie's antics spread though the community in the following days. Elaine Wright knew her husband was at fault, and she let him know in crystal-clear terms just how much trouble he was in. She forced him to apologize to the people who had seen him with Annemarie, or in the case of the teenagers, to their parents. She also made him sit down with their own kids and put him, and them, through a squirmingly embarrassing mea culpa. However, she also knew that hers wasn't the first, second or even third husband in the neighborhood to find a willing playmate in Annemarie Walker. As far as anyone knew, Annemarie had never had long running affairs; but it seemed that most neighborhood parties ended up with one guy or another making out with her, or worse. It wasn't because she was particularly attractive; her main appeal was her availability. Every teenage boy in Kingsbay somehow learned that Annemarie would be happy to initiate him into the mysteries of sex; she was catnip to many of them.

Elaine decided to talk with Pete Woods.

"It's not that I'm trying to excuse Keith, he was thinking with his you know what, and he'll be in the doghouse for weeks over this; but Annemarie is a problem. You know the Ropers moved home just to get their boys away from her? Annemarie is bad news for the community, and her father isn't much better."

This time Pete did not have a solution, "I don't necessarily disagree with you, Elaine, but I don't see what we can do about it. She lives here, they pay their dues and Cliff has quite a few friends in Kingsbay."

"Quite a few drinking buddies more like," sniffed Elaine. "Can't someone talk to her?"

"That's not a conversation I would want to have, Elaine, I don't mind telling you. If anyone was going to speak to her, it probably has to be a woman, and preferably a woman whose husband hasn't been involved with her. But I know the Ropers talked with her, and with Cliff and Annette, before they put their house on the market, but it didn't do any good."

In the end, nothing was done, and the problem of Annemarie Walker continued to fester in Kingsbay.

JILL

Jill MacLeod was not a standard issue military brat.

Her earliest memories were of the jets taking off and landing at Sunburst Air Force Base in Arizona. The life of peacetime military families generally involves a new house, new school and new friends every couple of years. Things were different for Jill. Her father, Bill, had gone to college in California to study computer science on an Air Force scholarship. By the time Jill came along, four years after his graduation, Bill was one of the Air Force's up and coming computer experts. When Jill was two, and her new sister Jane just three months old, Bill transferred to the new Systems Development Unit at Sunburst. When his time in Sunburst was almost up, the Air Force sent him for masters and doctorate degrees at the University of Arizona, only a few miles from the base. And so the family stayed put, and Jill got to stay in the same elementary school for six years: a luxury for a military kid.

Then things got even better. Bill was asked to carry out research and to teach at the Air Force Academy in Colorado, where he spent the remaining years of his distinguished Air Force career.

So Jill's childhood wasn't so different from that of a civilian; same house, same school, same teachers; although she did have a constantly changing group of friends. Because Jill was the constant fixture from year to year, and because she was pretty, athletic and fun, she was the acknowledged leader in pretty much everything. Which was OK, because, as a boyfriend from South Boston pointed out years later, Jill was also 'wicked smart'.

Jill went to college in Boston, where she soon had her first serious boyfriend, the Boston Southie. For a few months she thought it might be the real thing, but when they came back to start their sophomore year, she realized that, while she continued to mature, the boyfriend wasn't keeping up. Soon enough, he became the ex-boyfriend.

Jill stood out from her peers and attracted friends with her spontaneous, outgoing personality. She had an eye for vintage clothes and oversized costume jewelry and it was widely believed that she had never worn jeans.

Jill had inherited her father's striking green eyes and pale complexion. She had reddish hair, which she dyed a deep burgundy auburn in the summer before going to Boston. She was to keep this color for nearly forty years.

In her junior year, Jerry O'Hara, an Associate Professor in the English department, ran a seminar called 'Women in Shakespeare'. Jill signed up, and absolutely loved it. She loved the intellectual engagement with her teacher and she grew to enjoy their obvious mutual attraction.

He was in his early thirties; handsome, smart and single, she had just turned twenty-one, why shouldn't she get involved with him? So they went out for drinks a couple of times and enjoyed each other's company. Then Jerry took her to a drinks party held by another faculty member. There were a few graduate students attending as guests, but Jill was the only undergraduate in the room. A few of the faculty members gave them meaningful looks, but no one said anything. Soon several bottles of wine had been emptied and everyone was past caring much about pretty much anything. At one point the host left the room, and reappeared with an old-fashioned pewter cigarette box. When he opened it, they could see that it held seven or eight perfectly rolled joints.

"This is really great shit I brought back from Morocco. I mean, this is the best. Only one per couple, please."

The joints were swiftly passed around and lit. Jill was already slightly high from the wine and thought, *'what the hell, there has to be a first time, and at least I'm in good company'*. She managed not to cough as she inhaled some of the sweet smoke, although at first it burned her throat. By the third or fourth hit, Jill was feeling the effects, but it just seemed like more of the same pleasant feeling she already had from the wine.

Her next memory was of waking up, naked, in a strange bedroom. She had an ache between her legs but a much bigger ache in her head. She forced herself to stand, wrapped a blanket around herself and rushed to find a bathroom. When she came back, Jerry was sitting up in bed.

"Good morning," he said brightly, "not too sparky this morning are we?".

"What happened last night?" Jill asked.

"What happened? We had a blast sweetheart, and we had a pretty amazing time later; you're quite the little fuck bunny aren't you."

Jill was having trouble keeping herself under control, "I must have been high as a kite, I don't remember anything. I remember Toby, or Tony, or whatever his name is, handing round joints - and then nothing. You must have known I was out of it, you must have."

"Well, you were pretty far out there, but you said you wanted to have sex and I wasn't about to disagree. You said it loudly, in front of everyone by the way, so if it hadn't been me, I'm sure someone else would have obliged."

He could see the look on her face, "Oh come on, don't pretend you're some shy little virgin taken advantage of, you were totally up for it. And it wasn't your first time either."

"You shit. You complete shit. You knew I was totally wasted and still you took advantage. You're pathetic."

She found her clothes, pulled them on as quickly as she could, and left.

Two months later, she told him that she was pregnant, and was not really surprised by his reaction. He danced around the real issue, finally falling back on the excuse that if the pregnancy became public, it could cost him his job, any tenured job. He made it clear that he had no intention of jeopardizing his career over a fling with a student. Anyway, he pointed out, it was her fault. What woman her age wasn't on the pill these days, for Christ's sake?

This conversation happened just two weeks before final exams for the year. She bottled everything up, passed her exams and stayed in Boston that summer to recover from the abortion, and to hide from her family.

Her final year passed in a blur. Her friends noticed that she was more withdrawn, not quite the vivacious Jill they knew and loved. However they put it down to the fact that she was studying harder than anyone in her year. No-one was surprised when she graduated summa cum laude, and was accepted by New York University law school.

As part of her undergraduate degree, Jill had taken a class on the US Constitution and, much to her amazement, she had loved it. This had been the beginning of her decision to study law. Although throughout her time in law school she focused on corporate law, she never lost her interest in the constitution. And so, in November 2000, she joined an impromptu study group, established to follow and debate the controversies surrounding the Florida count in the presidential election, culminating in *Bush v Gore*.

Jill came from a Republican family and had voted the straight Republican ticket since she was eighteen. Her abortion experience had made her waver, given the strident anti-abortion rhetoric of most GOP politicians. However, by 2000 her disgust with the sex scandals around Bill Clinton had brought her firmly back to the Republican fold.

At the first meeting of the study group, Jill noticed a student who was part of the organizing team and who firmly, but graciously, managed the debate; reining in speakers who became too personal or offensive during the heated discussions. He was tall, well built and had a strong, handsome face that seemed always to be slightly amused at something. After the second meeting she asked around, and discovered that his name was Frank Petersen, and that he was graduating the following month. At the end of each meeting Frank summarized the debate and, when the final meeting was wrapping up, Jill realized that she had no idea where Frank stood on the issue.

She was considering how strange this was, given how passionate the debates had been and how prominent he had been in managing them, when a gentle tap on her elbow made her turn around, only to see him standing behind her.

"I hear that you asked for my name?" he said with a twinkle in his eye.

Jill blushed, but her discomfort vanished when he continued, "Espero que hayas estado disfrutando las reuniones. ¿Quieres un café? Invite yo." *'I hope you have been enjoying the meetings? Can I buy you a coffee?'*

"How did you know I speak ... " Jill began, "... oh," she finished lamely; he had obviously been asking around about *her*.

Jill had spoken Spanish since her childhood in Arizona, and at NYU she was part of a group that enjoyed debating legal issues in Spanish to maintain their fluency.

"Si, gracias, eres muy amable." *'Thank you, that would be very nice,'* she replied, as she was struck by how much she instantly liked this charming man with deep brown eyes.

Jill knew she was already hopelessly in love when, driving back to her apartment after only their seventh or eighth date, she felt compelled to tell him about Boston. She had not been prepared to talk to him about it so soon, but even then she wanted no secrets between them. She thought she could perhaps pass it off quickly, by telling him while he was driving. However, Frank pulled the car over to the curb, turned off the engine and took her into his arms and held her as she cried for the first time in four years. Jill wept for herself and for the baby that never was. Her whole body heaved as she was wracked with wave after wave of sorrow and guilt.

When eventually she stopped crying, completely drained, Jill could see the mess she had made of Frank's white shirt.

"If you bring this around tomorrow, I'll wash it for you," she whispered, trying to smile.

"It's OK" he replied, "I've got a few more. I'll keep this one as it is and we'll wash it together when we're married."

In later years, a family joke was that that first time was also pretty well the last occasion that Jill volunteered for a domestic chore. On graduating top of her class, she had a choice of offers from each of the top five Wall Street law firms, all with starting salaries of more than her father had earned in any three years of his life. By that time, Frank was working for Dukes County on Long Island and so when they married, a month after Jill's NYU graduation, the Petersens moved to a small condo development in Stirling Bayside, an easy commute on the Long Island Railroad for Jill and a fifteen minute drive for Frank.

Barely nine months after the wedding, Kevin was born, and, when Lucy arrived almost four years later, Frank arranged to take a twelve-month sabbatical to allow Jill to return to work. They were both comfortable with the fact that Jill was well on her way to a stellar career in corporate law, while Frank was earning less than a third of her salary. By now, Frank was the highly respected leader of the small in-house legal team in County Hall - so respected that the council had agreed to his unusual request for a year off work.

Meanwhile, after Kevin's birth they had looked around and found the perfect house for their growing family. Kingsbay was well established as a family-friendly community with an active social life for parents and kids. The community was on Broad Bay, near the western end of Long Island Sound, and boasted a community clubhouse, pool and marina. And it was in the best school district in New York State.

When Frank returned to work, he was helped by Alejandra, who became the family's live-in nanny. At Jill's suggestion, Alejandra spoke to the kids only in Spanish, while Mom and Dad spoke only English.

Except that was, for one week around Cinco de Mayo, when everything in the house, language, dress and food, became Latino. As the years passed, the kids' Spanish skills gradually surpassed Frank's. Even Jill, who thought of herself as fluent, began to suspect that Kevin was occasionally quietly swearing at her in Spanish when he had a complaint about homework or chores.

When Lucy finished kindergarten, Alejandra very politely and regretfully told them that she wanted to leave in the fall. With both kids in school most of the day, she realized that she would be bored and, in any event, she had decided to go to Dukes County community college to get her bachelors degree, so she could teach in kindergarten. A solution was found when Jill's parents agreed to move to Stirling Bayside to be home for Kevin and Lucy after school on four days a week. Alejandra would cover Fridays and other occasional sitting chores, in return for keeping her apartment above the garage, and use of one of the family cars to get to and from college.

Throughout all of these years, Jill managed to pursue her extremely successful career, while keeping almost every weekend free for the family. Soon after she had returned to work only two weeks after Lucy's birth, she had been made partner and her income had more than tripled.

A few years later, Frank was appointed head of the council's ethics committee, the consensus choice of politicians of both parties; an agreement over a sensitive senior appointment unheard of in living memory.

MONEY PROBLEMS

On his first day back at work after the Fourth of July break, Andy had arranged to start work at eleven a.m. At 9:30 he was sitting in a cafe, reviewing his notes once more. He had a complete analysis of their expenditure for the past six months. There was nothing outstanding in the numbers, no huge expenses, well, except for *Susie Q*, and that had been planned. And yet, the overdraft grew steadily every month. It was just ... stuff. Just one damn thing after another. Clothes for Susie, wine club deliveries, that crazy $4000 bid at the charity auction. What the fuck had he been thinking? A stupid bronze nude. Who needed it? He knew he had been showing off. $4000!

And Andy also knew that, buried in all those cash withdrawals, was maybe $1000 or $1500 each month that went to the bookies. He absolutely needed to stop this. He knew he was too prone to bet on emotion; he just couldn't place a bet against the Yankees or the Giants, whatever the spread. And he couldn't resist backing them to win. It had been an expensive year.

At ten o'clock he was ushered into the bank manager's office.

"Good morning, Mr. Smith. Thanks for coming in, I know you must be busy. The fact is Mr. Smith, we're worried. The bank is worried. If it wasn't that your wife has clear title to your home; well, without that, we would have had to call in your loan facility long ago."

"I know, you've been very patient. I've been through the data, and I think I can address your requirements. As of today, we will be reducing our monthly outgoings by $4000, well $3500 at least. This will bring the loan account down to $20,000 within twelve months. Will that be acceptable?"

"I'd be a lot happier with your wife's signature on this revolving loan agreement Mr. Smith."

"No; that's not happening. $20,000 in twelve months. That should be acceptable surely?"

There was a long pause. The manager shuffled his papers, clearly just buying time.

"Very well, Mr. Smith. But I want a schedule that takes us from where we are today," he looked at the top sheet, "$61,396 in the red. I'll send you a schedule to bring this to $15,000 in twelve months. There will be a 5% penalty every month that the schedule is missed. That is my best offer. Otherwise, I will have to insist on your wife's signature, and a charge on the house."

Andy left the bank and set off on the walk to his office. He was seething inside. *'Jumped up little prick,'* he thought. He had dropped that last $5000 just because he could. As if it made any difference. But he knew he had to meet the schedule. The little prick would just love to have Susie sitting opposite him, under his power. Well, it was not happening. Ever.

His thoughts turned to yesterday's call from his bookie. Another $9000 problem.

HALLOWEEN 2011

Every Monday evening when the weather permitted, there was a friendly but intense sailing race off Jameston's historic harbor. By the end of August, Andy and Charlie were competing as a team and steadily moving up the rankings, as they became familiar with each other, and as Charlie learned some of Andy's tips and tricks to help improve the performance of *Susie Q*.

Charlie had still never been sailing with Susie. Andy had concluded that he was just too shy, which was fine. Andy had figured out that, on the early weekend mornings Charlie had to be watching from some vantage point, to check whether Andy was alone, before coming down to the marina. Charlie was simply inordinately shy and Andy knew that Susie could be extremely intimidating to young men.

One splendid Sunday in September, Andy finally decided it was time to get to know more about his crewmate.

"So Charlie, I told you all about my job on Wall Street and I could see that you understood everything. Believe me, lots of people don't understand anything about what I do. So how do you know about securities and commodities trading?"

There was a long silence, which Andy allowed to continue until it became uncomfortable, until Charlie finally blurted out, "I trade with IDtrade almost every day. I've been doing it since I was fifteen."

"I'm impressed Charlie, I guess you're making money day trading?"

"I do OK. I trade pretty reasonable volumes and go for small percentage gains. It takes a lot of time, but I'm on the computer anyway and I enjoy it."

"What else are you doing on the computer?"

There was another long silence.

"I know you won't tell anyone, will you Andy?"

Andy shook his head. "Of course not."

He hoped Charlie wasn't going to confess something horrible.

"I'm part of a group, I guess you'd call us geeks or hackers. We break into large computer systems and leave stuff behind." He saw the look on Andy's face, "No, no, nothing malicious, although we could easily. No, we leave messages, telling the CEO or some civil service type or senior military guy that his systems have been hacked and how we did it and what they need to do to fix it. Then we go back in a month or two and break in again some other way. We drive them crazy. It's fun."

"You could make a career from this Charlie, companies pay to have their security tested."

"Oh we get paid. After the second or third break-in they usually leave us a message offering a consulting fee for a full-scale test of everything they've got online. They pay a lot of money, although we usually do the government stuff for free, or at least for not very much. We do a very good job. We get paid in bitcoins, although recently we've told some clients to give big public contributions to charity; Amnesty International last month and next month it will be Friends of the Earth. That usually ticks them off as well."

Andy looked at Charlie with new-found respect.

On the Wednesday before Halloween, Susie hosted her first bunco evening.

When Jill invited Susie to come to her first bunco night, as a substitute for a player who was on vacation, Susie was doubtful.

"I have absolutely no idea how to play bunco, Jill. None at all."

"Don't worry about that. There is absolutely no skill involved whatsoever. If you can roll three dice, you're a bunco expert. We'll have six tables of four. The host of table one will ring a bell and we start throwing dice. Let's say I throw first on my table. In round one, I get a point for every number one I throw. In round two I get a point for every two I throw. Round three, number three scores and so on. As soon as I throw and score zero, I pass the dice to my left and someone else has a turn. If you throw three dice all of the scoring number, you have to yell out 'Bunco'. That scores twenty-one points. Three identical dice of any other number scores five points. When someone on table one gets to twenty-one points, they ring the bell to end the round. Since you're a substitute you won't be asked to keep score. So all you have to do is throw the dice when it's your turn."

"Well that sounds easy enough."

"It's a lot of fun. After every round we figure out the scores and prizes, then you change partners and tables, so you get to spend time with everyone. You have to bring a wrapped prize, costing no more than ten dollars. There are prizes for the most points, least points, most buncos, most wins, most losses. Lots of prizes. Everyone drinks a little too much and eats way too much. You'll love it!"

That was nine months ago. After just a couple of months, several bunco players moved out of Kingsbay and Susie became a fully-fledged Bunco

Babe, playing every two weeks. She was very lucky. Some people had waited a year to join, and in fact since Susie had become a member, only one more new Babe had joined. And now she had hosted her first bunco evening.

Afterwards, Jill and Anne assured her that it had been a great success. Her friends had stayed behind to help with the considerable clean up. All twenty-four women had turned up, with no substitutes required except for Christine, who should have hosted, but instead was attending her daughter's PTA evening.

In the ten months since Susie and Andy moved in, Anne Murphy had become one of Susie's good friends in Kingsbay. At sixty-one, Anne was quite a bit older than Susie, but her quick wit and willingness to try anything at least once, made her great company. Susie also admired Anne's strength and independence. Jill told her that Anne had kept using her married name, Johnson, until her youngest child had left for college. The following day an email went to everyone in Kingsbay, announcing that, from now on she was once again, Anne Murphy.

There had been the usual laughing and yelling when someone won a prize, and as bunco rules ensured that almost everyone won something, that had meant lots of noise. Which is why, on bunco nights, the husbands and kids of the host headed for pizza and the movies. In Andy's case, Frank had taken pity on Andy and invited him to join him and the kids for dinner and Pick Up Sticks. As it turned out, Andy spent a good deal of the evening teaching card tricks to Kevin and, after the kids had gone to bed, to Frank as well.

Back at Susie's, the three women cleared the last of the folding tables and stacked them in the garage to be passed on to the next host.

"Time for one more adult beverage I think," announced Anne, collapsing onto the sofa in the family room.

"Works for me," echoed Jill.

"And for me, and here's a bottle of wine hardly touched. I've barely had a drink all night. But it was fun as well as hard work."

Susie brought the bottle and glasses over, and poured wine for each of them. "Cheers, and thanks ladies, I would have hated to face that mess in the morning."

"Best of all, you don't have to do it again for years, just think about that!" Jill reminded her.

Bunco met every two weeks and, with twenty-four members, Susie's turn at hosting wouldn't come round again for quite a while.

"So, are you all set for Halloween, Anne?" asked Jill.

"Yes, honey, I'm all set. First Halloween I've really looked forward to for years. I'm drowning in candy!"

Susie and Jill knew that this year, Anne's daughter, Joanne, was coming from Chicago for Halloween, bringing her husband and Anne's grandkids, aged six and eight.

"I'm surprised the grandkids didn't want to stay in their own neighborhood for Halloween," Susie offered.

"Are you kidding, honey? Remember, Joanne was only a year old when we moved here. Pete and Donna and the Emersons used to babysit her and my other two. She knows about Kingsbay and Halloween. You've never seen Halloween here have you? Well, sometime Sunday night, leave Andy to man the fort and take a walk around. You're in for a treat."

"But Halloween isn't 'til Monday," exclaimed Susie.

"Yes, but trick or treating is better when it isn't a school night, so we move it to the nearest weekend night."

"Gosh, I'm glad you told me!"

"Oh, you'd have noticed on Sunday afternoon honey, never fear. I just hope the rain holds off long enough for the trick or treating to be over."

Everyone had been obsessively checking the online weather forecasts for the last two days. Hurricane Sienna had devastated some of the Caribbean islands and then tore up the east coast of Florida. The storm carried on northwards, parallel with the coast, but was predicted to turn sharply east into the Atlantic, somewhere around Delaware or Atlantic City. Although they should miss the storm's center, it would still dump plenty of rain on Long Island.

Jill thought that Susie was looking tired, "I'd better go and send your husband back home Susie. Thanks for a lovely night. Come on Anne, we need to let this girl get to bed, she must be exhausted."

"OK Jill. Good night Susie, great job, well done tonight, I know it's a bit intimidating the first time you host one of these things. Hell, it never stops being intimidating when you've got awesome bakers like Chrissie coming over!" They all laughed, while Anne continued, "One piece of advice, honey. I don't know how much candy you've bought in for Sunday, but I recommend you go to the store tomorrow and buy the same amount again."

"Good night both of you, and thanks again. And don't forget what we agreed earlier, Jill; Sophie and I'll be round Friday night to help with Kevin and Lucy's costumes."

There was no way that Susie would have missed that Sunday was the day for trick or treating. All afternoon, in almost every front yard, people were out stringing lights, setting up displays or hiding loudspeakers behind bushes.

By 5:30 it was dark, but still no one knocked on the Smiths' door. Suddenly their phone rang and Jill's voice urged them from her cell phone, "I forgot you don't know. Hurry down to the corner with Linwood."

Susie and Andy jogged the 100 yards or so to the corner and arrived just in time to watch a headless horseman trot by on a magnificent black stallion. The effect was fantastic. The tall rider (they learned later it was Herman Gottfried) wore a huge greatcoat that ended in a very realistic empty shirt collar apparently rimmed with bright blood, while in his arm he cradled his severed head complete with bulging eyes and blood covered neck. A very close study revealed the grey mesh square at apparent chest height, allowing the rider to just about make out where he was going. It was an amazing start to the evening.

"Now it's back to the house," called Frank as they all hurried home.

Susie lost count of the number of kids who arrived at their door, in costumes ranging from the professional, to a few teens who had made barely any effort; they were too cool for costumes it seemed. But they still wanted candy. Kingsbay's reputation had spread over the years. Susie realized there were lots of kids she had never seen before.

When, finally, there was a lull in the arrivals, she asked Andy if he would mind managing alone for a little while, so she could have a look around.

As she walked around Fairlake Court, Susie was completely blown away by the terrific displays she could see everywhere. One house had a graveyard in the front yard, complete with headstones announcing uniformly gruesome deaths; all illuminated by green spotlights and with an occasional owl hooting from a dark corner. In another yard stood a gibbet with a corpse swinging on the noose.

At the corner with Kingsbay Road she caught up with the Petersens.

"Come with me, Mrs. Smith, come on."

Kevin had grabbed her hand and now dragged her back in the direction he had just come from. She realized that she was entering the Woods' driveway. Suddenly, to her right, in the middle of the Woods' lawn, a coffin slowly opened with a loud creak and a white-faced Dracula figure slowly sat up. He had a thin line of blood on one side of his chin. Slowly, deliberately, he raised a single hand tipped with long sharp nails and then dropped it and complained "Kevin Petersen, you've been here twice already. No more candy for this one, Donna!"

Kevin just laughed and yelled, "Bye Mr. Woods!" and hustled Susie back down the driveway. "Isn't that great Mrs. Smith?" He didn't wait for an answer, instead looked at her innocently and asked "Would you like a drink of snake blood? Come on, over here."

He led her up another neighbor's driveway, although Susie wasn't sure whose it was. There was a yellow sign at the end of the driveway, just like at the Woods' house she recalled. At the top of the driveway stood a trestle table with red paper table cover, which fell to the ground on all four sides. A sign advertised *'Genuine snakes' blood, good for growing children'*. When they got closer she could see a final word that had been crudely crossed out, *'in!'*.

Susie walked up to the table, "Kevin says I should try your dr..." At that point Susie screamed, as a bloody hand lunged from beneath the table and grabbed her ankle.

"Oh my God," she stammered, "you scared the bejesus out of me."

She was laughing now at Kevin who was rather dramatically, rolling on the ground, breathless from hysterical laughing. A face appeared from under the table, and she recognized John Alexander.

"Sorry Susie, I didn't know it was you. Who ..., ah, young Kevin, you rascal. You should have stopped me, Liz."

"I know, but Kevin was standing behind her, begging me not to."

Susie turned to Kevin, "Come on monster, let's find your folks. Bye John, bye Liz."

As they left the Alexander driveway she asked Kevin, "What are the yellow signs for, Kevin?"

"Oh that means no little kids, because they might get too scared. Lucy can come here next year. And thanks for our costumes Mrs. Smith, they're really neat."

They could see Jill and Frank ahead, "That's OK, Kevin, I just helped your dad a bit with the sewing."

She walked back to her house, admiring the various displays and sounds along the way.

"You should go out and have a look around, honey, the neighborhood is amazing. I really think you should, because we'll need to up our game next year for sure. Go take a look, you'll see what I mean. I'll look after the candy. But don't be too long, the grown up party starts at nine and we need to change."

The community rule was that trick or treating had to finish by eight and the rule was strictly enforced, signs were even put up at the entrances to the community.

By 10:30, Kingsbay clubhouse was absolutely packed. It had started to rain heavily thirty minutes before, so no one was hanging about outside. The Halloween party was fancy dress and, as with every other social event of the year, Kingsbay went for it with maximum enthusiasm. The unspoken rule was: be boring, be expensive or be outrageous. Most people ended up in the boring category; ghosts, vampires, sixties hippies, glam rockers and the like. Expensive meant buying or hiring complete ensembles from theatrical outfitters; pirates and their wenches, Cinderellas and princes, cowboys and Indians, popes and nuns. Outrageous involved either showing lots of flesh, or wearing something utterly politically incorrect.

In previous years the latter category had included people in blackface, Osama bin Laden, death row inmates and, memorably, a group effort portraying victims of a car crash with lots of gore, blood and fake internal organs, all organized by a Vietnam vet in the community exploiting the fact that he had lost half a leg to an anti-personnel mine.

There was also a small minority of the community who wore masks to this annual event.

One year in the early 1990s someone had proposed that the Halloween party, which in those days had a theme, should be inspired by Venetian Carnevale. This involved wearing elaborate traditional Venetian masks. That year's party developed legendary status. It turned out that in those pre-web days, every reference to Carnevale that anyone could find focused on the revealing Regency period costumes and the sexual license encouraged by the anonymity of the masks. Kingsbay, or at least a good part of Kingsbay, went at it with its usual gusto. The weather that year was unseasonably warm, and so the revelers could move outside in search of a secluded spot. People still talked about that party. Part of the legend was the suggestion that two marriages broke up as a direct result of the goings on.

Some people had obviously enjoyed the famous evening and still felt nostalgic about it, since they persisted in wearing their Carnevale costumes, which were, in truth, often spectacularly beautiful.

Although Susie was reasonably adept at sewing, she and Andy had chosen a moderately expensive route, because they just assumed that that would be the norm in Kingsbay. They appeared as Sandy and Danny from the final scene in Grease. Andy was in full leathers and slicked back hair, and Susie wore Sandy's off-the-shoulder skintight top and satin pants.

By eleven o'clock the temperature of the room had risen by at least ten degrees, and even more flesh was on display. There was a lot of more-or-less harmless flirting going on; a few spouses would have some explaining to do in the morning. Near midnight Andy found himself in a slow dance with Vivien Werner. Andy knew Vivien reasonably well, she attended most community social events and she certainly wasn't the kind of woman he would miss. She was a striking brunette who managed to look good all the time. She didn't dress especially provocatively, but there was no hiding that she was an extremely desirable woman. She was dressed as the Penelope Cruz character in that summer's Pirates of the Caribbean sequel. Andy had never met Al, Vivien's late husband, who had been killed in the attack on the Twin Towers on 9/11.

"You know I never dance like this Andy?"

"Like what?"

"In a holding dance. Oh, I get asked all the time, but there's enough tension between me and the Kingsbay wives already, so I'm very careful about who I dance with, and how I dance. Doing the Twist with Jack Emerson is fine; although I think Josephine might still give him a hard time afterwards."

They both laughed, Jack was in his eighties. Vivien continued, "Susie is too beautiful to be insecure, so I can enjoy this with you."

Suddenly the mood between them shifted. His arm around her waist drew her in a fraction more and now the entire length of her body lay against his. He was very conscious of their hips moving together, her breasts against his chest and the intimate warmth of her breath on his neck. *This is a very sexy lady,'* he thought, enjoying the moment.

At more or less that same moment, Susie found herself struggling to cope with Cliff Walker.

She had been dancing with a group of women until the tempo changed to a slow tune and they headed back towards their respective tables for their drinks. As Susie passed by, Cliff caught her arm and pulled her close.

"Guess who?" he slurred, muffled by his brilliant red mask.

"Oh I know its you, Cliff," she replied, choking back the temptation to add, 'from your awful whisky and cigar breath and your pot belly'.

He had a hand on the small of her back and was holding her far too tight. She could feel him rubbing himself against her and she was finding it hard to push him away. The situation deteriorated very quickly indeed; one moment she was trying to pull her hips away from him and the next he had slid his free hand, which had been clasping her shoulder, down onto her breast, accidentally or deliberately pushing down the thin fabric of her top. She twisted herself violently out of his grasp and tried to think of something cutting to say, but realized that her top had torn and her breast was exposed. She clasped her arms around herself and ran to the ladies room.

Anne had witnessed the final moments of the episode and she had seen a couple of women hurry after Susie and so, in the shocked stillness that briefly fell over that part of the room, she strode up to Cliff, reached up and pulled off his mask.

"Cliff Walker," she called out, in a voice loud enough to carry over the music, "you are a revolting, obnoxious piece of shit. It is a never-ending mystery to me why you would imagine that any woman, would choose to spend one fucking minute in your presence. You are a complete waste of space and you need to leave here right now, this minute. Get lost, asshole."

With that, Anne picked up a nearby glass of beer and threw it over him.

At this point a few people applauded and then a few more, until Cliff had no option but to slink pathetically off.

Anne went to find Andy. "You need to go to the ladies room and attend to your wife," she instructed.

Susie and Andy arrived home soaking wet. The rain was really coming down now and the wind had picked up.

"Oh, Andy it was horrible! He was all over me and when he grabbed me and pulled down my top, oh God, I felt so humiliated; everyone could see me. He was so awful."

"Come on, Susie, you're fine, nothing happened. You did well sweetheart, you stopped him before anything serious happened."

"'Anything serious?' Are you deaf, Andy? He grabbed my breast, he thought he could paw me because he controlled me." Susie was yelling now.

"Calm down, honey. A guy tried to feel you up. It happens. You're OK. Let it go."

"Calm down? How can you be so, so, so insensitive, so unbelievably fucking *stupid!*"

Susie was now angrier with her husband than she was with Cliff Walker. Andy should have worked that out, this was the very first time he had heard Susie swear.

But he carried on. "Susie, you're upset, I get that. I understand why you're upset, but sometimes guys like Cliff who've had a few dr..."

Susie stopped him with a raised hand. She was now icy calm. She stood, still dripping, in the middle of the kitchen, "Andy, you have absolutely no idea what goes on in these situations. Do *not* try to excuse him because he's drunk. Drunk or sober, Cliff Walker is an animal, a creep, a loser who preys on women. I know he's your fishing buddy, but he is a horrible, evil, disgusting son-of-a-bitch. Now I am going to bed, and you are sleeping right there." She was pointing at the sofa.

Susie had a very restless night. At two a.m. she was still tossing and turning, as the events of the disastrous evening replayed over and over in her mind. Suddenly there was an insistent beeping sound in the room and she realized that the bedside alarm clock was dark. They were having another power cut. These weren't uncommon, so much so that she and Andy had talked about installing a wired-in gas-powered generator beside the garage, but they were expensive and so far they hadn't taken the plunge. In reality, cuts generally lasted no more than ten or twenty minutes, and most no more than twenty or thirty seconds.

The silence that followed seemed more profound than usual. The HVAC had stopped working and so the background sound of circulating air had stopped, but it was more than that. Susie swung her legs off the bed and stood up. The silence was broken by a low rumbling sound, almost inaudible, but she could feel it through the soles of her feet. And then, as suddenly as it had started, it stopped. The sound of the rain returned, louder than she remembered. She was nervous now, uncertain whether she should get back under the covers. She was very aware that Andy wasn't with her. She was debating with herself whether to go down to wake him, when a new sound began. It was like the whistle of an old-fashioned train in a black and white movie, but lower pitched. And it was becoming louder every moment that she stood there. She decided that she needed her husband, and she groped for the hallway and the stairs.

Susie had reached the landing half way down the stairs when the storm arrived over the house. The noise stopped her in her tracks and she had to sit down on the cool steps. The volume of the storm was suddenly incredible. The entire house shook and she could just hear Andy yelling from the family room. He was looking for her, but he was disorientated by the blackout and the unbelievable violence of the storm. His voice galvanized her, and she bumped her way down the final few steps on her butt. She still couldn't see a thing. She raised her hand before her eyes and saw nothing. Susie was really scared now. If only she had her phone, she would be able to create some light, but she was in her nightdress and becoming disorientated herself.

The noise kept growing louder and louder, until it seemed that the storm must surely be inside the house. Just when she thought it couldn't possibly get any louder, there was an enormous boom, as if a thundercloud had erupted right above them. Over the storm she heard the faint sound of glass exploding and, as quickly as it had started, the noise eased, but only to the level of a tropical storm; it was still raining torrentially. At that moment, Andy found her and they held each other tight.

"I'm so sorry, Susie, I was a thoughtless idiot."

"Never mind, what was that noise? And I heard glass breaking, exploding really. Andy, do we have a flashlight?"

"Yes, in the laundry room. Stay here and I'll feel my way to it."

In a couple of minutes he was back, preceded by the welcome beam of a large flashlight.

"Come on, let's put on some clothes and go find out what the hell just happened."

They dressed quickly and went from room to room, but there was no sign of any damage.

Susie grabbed Andy's arm. "Let's go check on the Petersens."

They went tentatively down their driveway, stepping around a mess of branches and a broken garden chair that wasn't one of theirs. Just before they came to the sidewalk, they veered left towards the Petersens' house. As Andy played the light over their neighbors' home, they saw two figures standing with their backs to them. It was Frank and Jill, wearing nightclothes with jackets on top. They ran over to their friends.

"What happened, Frank?" asked Andy.

"I'm not certain, but I think maybe a tornado touched down between our properties. Is your house damaged?"

"We only checked from the inside, but no broken windows, I didn't think to check the roof though. What about you?"

"As far as I can tell, the storm blew out the extension. All the windows have just disappeared, and there's a hole in the roof. The rest of the house is fine."

"Where are the kids?" Susie was standing with her arm around Jill's shoulder.

"They're fine, a bit shook up, but Alejandra is with them. Look at the trees."

The trees between their two properties were all down, lying in strange shapes. All this time they were standing in a downpour and almost complete darkness, it seemed that all of Kingsbay was dark.

Frank suddenly spoke, breaking the spell, "Let's get inside, come in with us for a minute, I've got a portable generator, so we can get some lights on at least, and I wouldn't mind a hand to get something over these windows Andy."

Andy replied, "Of course, but you guys go on, I want to quickly check our roof."

In ten minutes they were all in the Petersen family room, where the temperature had already dropped dramatically. Frank had rigged up some lights, but there was no heat, and the ruined extension was open to the entire ground floor.

Susie took charge. "Jill, I think we should gather up Kevin and Lucy and Alejandra over to our house. We've no generator, but we do have candles and our house will stay warm far longer than yours. Andy can stay to help Frank if they want to try to do anything tonight."

It took a little while, but eventually the two women got everyone settled in bed, although Lucy insisted on sleeping with Alejandra and for once, she was allowed. Kevin was already treating the entire episode as an adventure and opted to sleep on the sofa in the family room 'in case anyone tries to get into the house in the dark'.

Meanwhile, Frank and Andy were trying to come up with an action plan. They had held onto the generator to give them light in the kitchen and to power some tools. But they had nothing to put over the empty windows, and the wind and rain was coming in remorselessly.

"Let's go over to Ross Fisher, he's been finishing his loft to make two extra bedrooms for the kids. I bet he's got some flooring plywood around, and he's got every tool known to man. If we cut through your property we can call by Vivien's to check that she's OK. We should have done that already, she's on her own."

Vivien was fine, and grateful they had thought to call on her. When they got to the Fisher house it was, of course, in complete darkness, just like everywhere else. No-one's cellphone had a signal, so they had no choice but to bang on the front door. At least they were dressed for the weather now Andy thought, as they stood in the driving rain for what seemed an age, before Ross opened the door to them.

"Who is it?" demanded Ross.

"Oh sorry, Ross," Frank realized that he was shining his flashlight straight in Ross's face. He turned it to illuminate Andy and then himself. "Ross, I'm really, really sorry to wake you at this ungodly hour, but I have a bit of a situation."

Frank quickly explained their position and what he needed. By five o'clock the three men had successfully boarded up all the shattered windows and patched the roof, although by then the kitchen and office were well and truly ruined. But at least now the house could be heated, if the power ever came back on.

In the end, the power was out for four days. The Petersen family stayed with Susie and Andy throughout the outage. Frank and Andy rigged up the generator, and another one that was delivered by

Frank's brother-in-law, Luke, on the second day. With both generators running, they could power all the lights in the house and could heat two rooms with portable heaters, plus at any one time they could choose between the coffee maker or the microwave or a TV.

"So the TV stations are just out in the air everywhere?" Kevin was excited by this new idea as Frank and Andy tried to get a watchable picture using an old indoor antenna, as the cable service was still down.

"Yes, and it's completely free, not like cable," his dad confirmed.

"You mean we pay for TV?"

"Yes, Kev, we pay for TV, we pay for electricity, we even pay for water."

"You're kidding me again, you're just treating me like a stupid kid who'll believe *anything*. As if anyone would pay for water, that's just ridiculous! Oh you forgot air, you forgot to say we pay for air!"

Frank appealed to Andy, "Andy do you have a water utility bill handy? This kid thinks everything in the world must be free since he never pays for anything, not even the candy he eats."

Andy found the latest bill and sat next to Kevin on the sofa. "There you are, see, right here: $142 for water and another $46 for sewer service, that's all the waste."

Susie joined their conversation. "I suppose we should have told you about your bills before you agreed to stay here, Kevin. There's water, and I notice you drink a lot, but since you hardly ever wash I guess that's OK, and gas for the generator, and laundry charges of course and meal service. If you stay after the power comes back your bill will really go up, 'cause there'll be more heat, more lighting, more everything. What do you think Andy, should we say $21 a day for Kevin?"

"Sounds about right to me, how do you want to pay Kev? We take cash or credit card but no checks."

Kevin looked at Susie and back at Andy. His dad was facing away from him, so he couldn't see his face.

"Don't look at your dad, Kevin, he's got his own bill to worry about, and your mom's. Not sure who's picking up the bill for Lucy."

It took at least a minute's silence for Kevin to figure out he was being teased again. "Oh Mr. Smith, you're just as bad as my dad. I didn't believe you for one minute, not one second, not even one millionth of a millionth of a second."

Later they regretted showing Kevin the water bill. He began waging a campaign, terrorizing his sister into reducing her water use to close to zero. This led to several bouts of tears as he tried to stop her using water to clean her teeth and insisted she completely finish every drink of water she started.

ANNE

When Anne Murphy graduated from high school, she stood five feet nothing and weighed ninety-eight pounds. She bought many of her clothes in the junior department, but nevertheless always looked good.

Anne's mother had been even more petite than her daughter, a blessing for Anne in her childhood and teenage years, as her mom had a good idea of the challenges her daughter was facing.

Her mom drummed her life lessons into Anne from her early years. Don't back down, don't be condescended to, don't ask for allowances and don't accept them if offered. Never be afraid of anyone or anything because of your size. And most of all, there is nothing small about your brain, use it. But don't try out for basketball.

Anne learned her mother's lessons well. She refused to be paired up with younger girls at sports. She insisted on attempting every challenge, even those she was doomed to fail.

When Anne was fifteen, her mother bought her a coffee-table photo book full of images of Audrey Hepburn.

"This is your style guide sweetheart. Look at what she wears; look at *how* she wears everything, clothes, sunglasses, hats, bags. And especially look at how she conducts herself."

Anne thought Audrey Hepburn looked fantastic. She did adopt Audrey as her style icon. But Anne knew she would never be as demure, as compliant as Audrey. Anne thought Eliza should have told Henry Higgins to go screw himself.

Anne's enthusiasm for crew turned out to be more important than she imagined when she had taken it up back in her freshman year. In her final year she coxed and captained the most successful men's crew in the history of Dukes College - which was a pretty long history, as it was one of only ten colonial era colleges in the United States. She was cox largely because of her size; she was captain entirely because of her smarts and her irrepressible spirit.

Her last ever race was the final of the National Championships, where Dukes was matched against the reigning champions, and the home team, the University of Texas. In a thrillingly tight finish, Dukes College won after a photo review. At the celebratory dinner that night, Anne was seated next to the Texas captain, Derek Johnson, six foot six and 210 pounds, all of it muscle. As the meal progressed, Derek became more and more conscious of the huge difference in size between them and he couldn't imagine how they could dance a waltz with any semblance of dignity, never mind elegance. "You know we have to lead the first dance together?" he asked during dessert.

"Yes," Anne replied, "but don't worry, you'll do fine."

Traditionally the first dance was a waltz, led by the home team captain and his date; but Derek's girlfriend was still caught up with finals and wasn't at the meet. The coaches decided that, to mark the unique achievement of a female captain winning the title, Anne should partner Derek in the first dance. When a very nervous Derek led Anne on to the dance floor, the band started up *'Boogie Woogie Bugle Boy'*, and Anne led them through an energetic jive. She had had a chat with the bandleader before dinner.

They spent the rest of the evening talking, and discovered that they enjoyed the same books, the same movies and the same music. Derek had mentioned his girlfriend a couple of times in connection with that first dance and so when they parted, it was with a handshake and vague intentions to get in touch at some point in the future.

In fact, almost eighteen months passed before Anne's phone rang early one Sunday. It seemed that it had taken Derek almost six months to realize that he was thinking about Anne more than was healthy for his existing relationship, and so he had ended it. He still didn't contact Anne, although he had tracked her down via the Dukes College yearbook. By then he was working in Seattle, and wasn't much interested in a long distance relationship with a woman in New York. However when he was invited to lead a special interest group at a week long IT conference in Manhattan, he decided that the opportunity was too good to waste. He called her and asked if she was, by any chance, free the following weekend? If so he planned to fly in late Friday before the conference started Monday afternoon.

Anne could indeed be free, and when she discovered that Derek had never visited New York, she offered to be his tour guide for the weekend. She took him to her favorite places. Derek squeezed himself into a table at the Brooklyn Diner for Saturday brunch. Saturday night he enjoyed his first proper curry, in Nirvana, overlooking Central Park. And he was squeezed again, this time into a packed Serendipity, for Sunday afternoon hot chocolate and ice cream.

When they weren't eating, they walked and talked and talked some more. On Sunday evening, an hour before sunset, they took a round trip on the Staten Island ferry. On the return journey they watched Manhattan light up before them and they kissed. On Monday after work, Anne brought an overnight bag into the city, and moved into Derek's hotel room.

"I choose to recall that I've known you for eighteen months. Sounds better than admitting we're having sex on our first weekend." Anne rationalized.

She was a reverse commuter to Long Island for the rest of the week.

The following Saturday was Derek's final day in New York and Anne brought him to her small apartment in Port Washington, financed with her biochemist's salary from BioPharm Solutions in Garden City. Derek found it hard to believe that this picturesque waterside village could be thirty minutes from Manhattan. He realized that he was falling for Anne, and for New York.

Six months later, after hundreds of telephone calls, eight weekends and a wonderful week together in Sedona, Derek found a position with a start up software company working out of a loft in Tribeca, and moved into Anne's small apartment.

Another squeeze.

They married and had three children by the time they were thirty. Anne had suspended her career -- by the time the last baby came along she had three children under five years old to handle and it was simply impossible to manage the kids and her job. She enjoyed being a mother, but she subscribed to every major biochemistry journal, and had every intention of getting back into the workforce at some point.

Meanwhile Derek's career had prospered. The small software company grew, steadily at first and then explosively. From programming, Derek gravitated to project management and then found himself spending more and more time recruiting staff to keep up with the rapid growth of the company. In the year that baby number three came along, he was made vice president of Human Resources and could afford to move the family into a five-bed waterfront property in Kingsbay. He was thirty and, on paper at least, a millionaire.

On the other hand, he was home less and less. The company culture embraced twelve hour days. Eventually the management team decided to open a second technical center in Utah to avoid New York rents and salaries. This meant Derek had to spend one week in three out west, recruiting staff and setting up HR systems and support services. Utah offered wonderful outdoor attractions summer and winter, but not much in the way of nighttime entertainment.

Derek took to livening up endless, monotonous nights in his hotel with the company of a succession of young women. At first he restricted himself to failed job candidates, offering to discuss their interview skills over a drink in the evening. However, in time he had a succession of flings with a series of cute girls from the help desk or the western region sales team.

In 1982 Anne and Derek's eldest child, was five. Derek missed his daughter's party because he was dealing with what he thought of as his 'situation'. Emily, a 20-year-old help desk intern from Utah State, announced that she was pregnant, that Derek was the father and no, she wasn't having a termination. Furthermore, her father had pointed out that Derek would certainly lose his job if the affair came to light. Derek was, after all, head of HR and the affair had broken at least four different rules in the company's code of conduct.

Derek had no intention of leaving Anne to marry the girl, and eventually he sat down with Emily and her father to negotiate a settlement. Emily's dad knew she had a strong hand, and the best deal that Derek could arrive at was $150,000 to buy a house for mother and baby and $15,000 a year for twelve years, so Emily could employ a full time nanny, finish her studies and start a career. And, of course, he was to have no contact with the baby.

In his heart of hearts, Derek knew that he could never keep this mess from Anne, but that didn't stop him trying. He somehow managed to keep the initial settlement secret. Oddly enough, guilt made him become a more attentive husband and father. He traveled much less after he insisted that the company finance a senior deputy to run his department in Utah. For a while it seemed that he would get away with his 'situation'.

Emily had her baby, a little boy she named Joseph. Unfortunately Joseph was born with acute respiratory problems, which necessitated a lot of specialist medical attention. Emily and her nanny coped pretty well until Emily graduated. At this point she suddenly realized that she, and more importantly Joseph, could no longer be covered by her father's health care insurance. Indeed it had been an anomaly that Joseph had ever been covered. In any event, neither mother nor child was now insured, and Joseph needed regular access to expensive preventative and emergency treatments.

Emily's letter to Derek was sent via their respective attorneys, as she had no wish to risk unmasking him by writing to his work or home addresses. Her letter was extremely reasonable. She didn't want more money, she just wanted Derek to add Joseph to his health insurance, which she knew would cost him little or nothing. When she was established in a good job with medical benefits, the arrangement could end, but until then, they needed his help.

The problem for Derek was that Anne dealt with all their insurance paperwork, and all the other household bills for that matter. With three toddlers requiring inoculations, treatment for childhood illnesses and minor bumps and bruises, there was lots of paperwork to be dealt with. So he had to tell her, and in the telling, Anne glimpsed the degree to which there had been previous Emilys.

Much later, Anne thought that she might have forgiven him if he had told her on day one, but the weight of the hundreds of lies that he must have told her, and would have gone on telling her, all bore down on her and she knew she could never see past them. He told her on a Friday night when the kids were in bed, and on Saturday she told him he had to move out.

On Sunday Anne completed the paperwork to get Joseph insured.

TEMPTATION

The Mergers & Acquisitions team of Dover Securities was based on the same floor as Andy's trading group. Dover Securities wasn't a big firm, but it did OK, handling second and third tier transactions, and the partners were ambitious for bigger things.

Alan Davidson was the rising star in M&A, and he was working on a deal that would get him either a partnership or a job offer in one of the prestige finance houses.

"Let's go guys," he called, clicking the print icon on his screen.

But when Alan stopped by the big printer on their way to the conference room, there was nothing there. No document, no flashing warning lamp, nothing. He checked the paper bin, but there was lots of paper.

"Fuck it! Fuck it! Fuck it! Never mind, I've got it on my laptop. Let's go, don't want to keep Napoleon waiting."

And he immediately and completely forgot all about the failed print job. And with that, many lives would change a great deal.

Because three minutes later, Andy sent a print command to the same machine, and again it failed. However, unlike Alan, Andy had time to reboot the printer. When eventually he collected his document, he was at first irritated to find five sheets of garbage on top of his presentation.

Except that the pages weren't garbage. He realized that they weren't garbage even before he returned to his desk. He was perhaps helped, by the header on every one of the five pages - 'IN STRICTEST COMMERCIAL CONFIDENCE'.

Andy knew he had to stay cool, and he did. He knew he had to finish out the day behaving completely normally, and he did that too. But when at last he was in his basement office area at home, he allowed himself a 'Holy shit, Batman!'

The five pages were a summary of the game plan between today, and exactly one week from today, when Dover Securities' client, AllMedia Corp, would announce an agreed bid for GarageGuys Inc. The bid would be $15 a share and Andy had quickly established that GarageGuys had closed three hours ago, at $12.25.

Andy struggled to breathe. This was it, the chance he had been subconsciously looking for. The kind of chance that had made all those rich fuckers rich, was now his. He'd always known that the super rich had got that way with this kind of inside information, passed around their la-de-fucking-la clubs and alumni societies. Even after he had joined a Wall Street firm, a part of him continued to believe that the market was rigged to make sure that people like him would never make a big score.

And now he held the key in his hands. His own fucking hands. But how to use it? And not get caught? The members of the rich bastards' club looked after each other, but he knew that if he screwed up, no one would bail him out. He had to be clever, really clever.

The good news was that the offer date was a week away. He had time. Meanwhile he had to act normally. And he had to figure things out. One thing he knew above everything else; he would not be like his loser father, forever chasing a dream that was always just out of reach. He would grasp his opportunity. He had the nerve, the balls, to take this chance and use it to create the life he knew he deserved.

After some cancellations and a few new recruits, fourteen Bunco Babes flew to Las Vegas for a four-day Memorial Day weekend. It had taken nearly a year to get husbands to agree and dates coordinated, but here they were, at last.

On Thursday, their first night, they went to see Blue Man Group and took two huge stretch limos back to the Bellagio.

"Here's to Charlotte!" someone proposed when they had settled back in one of the hotel's many bars.

Charlotte was a travel agent and a Bunco Babe, and she had used her connections to get them agent rates at the Bellagio, much less than half the rack rate. They were in truth, a little awed by Charlotte's seemingly endless connections, which had also produced deeply discounted tickets for everything they wanted to do.

"The reality is, girls, I send maybe 600 comfortably off guys here every year one way or another. So of course everyone here loves me. Forget discounted tickets to Caesars Palace showroom; if anyone fancies an eighteen-year-old hooker, I can probably arrange that for 50 cents. Sorry, I'm being cynical."

On Friday night the Babes were scheduled to see Cirque du Soleil. First however, there was the 'all you can eat' brunch and some fun at the slots. Unfortunately, by five o'clock Susie was feeling very poorly, with a constant need to run to the ladies' room. She called Jill's room to explain that she would have to miss the show. Within twenty minutes, Jill and Sophie turned up with the hotel doctor in tow. After a swift examination, he announced that Susie had a mildly elevated temperature and possibly a very slight case of food poisoning or, more likely, a food intolerance reaction. A quiet night with no alcohol and lots of water would quickly restore her to health.

After some discussion, and over Susie's futile protests, they decided that Sophie would stay with Susie.

"To be honest, honey, I'm not so sorry to be staying with you. There's talk of going on to a piano bar after the show and I really don't feel like another late night. So relax, we'll have a nice visit, and a quiet night."

By eight o'clock Susie was feeling much better, well enough for Sophie to call room service to order green tea and toast for Susie and a salad and glass of white wine for herself.

Susie and Sophie were already friendly, but they hadn't spent any significant time together before Vegas. Susie thought that Sophie was very nice, very gentle and a real calming influence on everyone around her. She also observed that Sophie had a nice figure, lovely pale olive skin and a strong, attractive face. However as Sophie told her some of her story, and Susie realized that Sophie had three children all a good bit older than herself, she was astonished.

"You must have been so young, how did you have the strength, the nerve, to do so much when you were so very young?" she asked.

"To tell the truth, Susie, when I look back now, I don't know what helped me to do some of the things I did when I was really just a kid. Maybe growing up without a mom? I don't know, but I do know that I was always aware that my father lived every moment of his life for me. Every decision he made was for me. I guess that could be a burden for some kids, but for me, it made me feel strong. If my papí thought so much of me, maybe I was somebody worthwhile."

She took a sip of her wine and continued, "You know I'm Mexican? Well, not me exactly, but all of my family is Mexican: my mother and my father, my aunt and uncle. A lot of the time people don't know or forget. Hey, I forget myself sometimes. Bet you didn't know that I was baptized Julieta Sofia? But then someone will say something and I'll be reminded. People in Kingsbay are too educated to talk about wetbacks, but they'll make sweeping statements about lazy immigrants. Let me tell you, no one worked harder than my father, no one."

"I've had such an easy life, Sophie, I'm becoming more and more aware of just how lucky I've been. The fact is that my father always gave me anything I needed, and I guess I've always known I was ..."

"Beautiful?" suggested Sophie, with a gentle smile.

"No, no, but, well I never had acne or zits, and I've watched girlfriends try to straighten their hair, or curl their hair or dye their hair or whatever their hair and I never had to worry about any of that. Oh dear, I sound just awful, don't I?"

"No, you're just being honest."

"But I know what you mean about names and insults. I remember once listening to my father talk with some of his friends, they were talking about their golf club. And Mr. Roberts, one of my father's friends, commented, '*at least we don't have any Canadians in the club.*' I was mystified, and later I asked my dad why Mr. Roberts didn't like Canadians. I mean, we lived in Vermont, so we knew lots of Canadians. My dad explained that, actually, Mr. Roberts didn't like Jews, but it wasn't polite to say so out loud, so this code had developed and people said, 'Canadians' when they really meant Jews. I guess I was about ten or so and it was the first time I realized that not all grown-ups were nice. Later on, it occurred to me that it was odd that my parents would have Mr. and Mrs. Roberts over to dinner now and then. Why were my mom and dad friends with horrible people? To be honest, I still struggle with that one."

The two women talked on and grew closer to each other as they did. By the time Susie was fading, it was almost eleven p.m.

"Good Lord, Susie I'm supposed to be looking after you, and here I am keeping you up all night!"

"It's been a lovely evening Sophie, I'm glad we had this time to chat. Thanks for sitting up with me. But you're right, I do need to get some shut-eye."

"See you in the morning," said Sophie, as she headed for her own room.

SOPHIE

Sophie was not supposed to be an only child. Indeed, she wasn't supposed to be a Sophie.

Julieta Sofia Ramos was born in San Diego in 1958. Her father, Luis, was from a small village in Sinaloa State in Mexico, in a village Luis had hated for as long as he remembered and which he left when he was sixteen, never to return. Luis worked hard, and became an American citizen, thanks in part to two years service in the Navy. When he was honorably discharged, Luis immediately found a well-paying civilian job on the huge naval facility in San Diego. He was now able to send for Margarita, his childhood sweetheart, who had waited steadfastly for almost six years, never seeing or talking to each other all that time. Instead, throughout the years, they had exchanged weekly letters, discussing plans for their future and finding new ways of expressing their love for each other.

Those plans included at least four children, whose names they had already chosen, four boys' names and four for girls, just in case that was the way things worked out.

Luis' older sister Alicia, had also escaped their home village, and she lived with her large family in Queens, New York, in Elmhurst. So this was where Luis and Margarita were married. They could have gone back to their home village in Mexico for the ceremony, but they were both fixated on being American and they wanted an American wedding. Barely twelve months later, and much to their delight, Julieta Sofia was born.

Years afterwards, when Julieta asked her father what had happened to her mother, he explained that when he and Margarita were growing up in rural Mexico, they saw maybe three or four cars in a year. Perhaps this lack of familiarity made Margarita careless that Saturday. They were walking beside the park; Luis was pushing the stroller, when Margarita stepped off the sidewalk to allow a young man in a wheelchair to pass them. She stepped directly in front of the side mirror of a bus coasting to the nearby stop. As Luis told the story, no one was to blame, not the bus driver, not the young man, just bad timing and bad luck.

Luis was twenty-four, sick at heart and with a ten-month old baby to care for. Fortunately, he was a well regarded employee in the Navy base, and a friendly boss, and a compassionate senior officer, facilitated his transfer to Fort Hamilton in Brooklyn. Luis and Julieta Sofia moved to be close to her Aunt Alicia, Uncle Francisco and her five cousins.

With no memories of her mother, Julieta grew up happy in a warm family environment where she was loved, cherished and spoiled by her slightly older girl cousins, who seemed to think that this baby had been sent as a wonderful toy for them to dress up and play with. Francisco was a carpenter, with a well-equipped workshop he had built himself at the end of their long narrow garden. Julieta grew up with the idea that if you needed something, you went down to the workshop and made it. Toy forts for the boys, dolls' houses for the girls and all the soldiers and tiny furniture they needed. When the children were old enough to graduate from hand made wooden tools to the real thing, Francisco patiently guided them to make their own toys and carts. Meanwhile from her aunt, Julieta learned to cook and to bake and to understand that nothing should go to waste.

The only cloud in Julieta's young life was her father's pain. Luis never fully recovered from the shocking death of his beloved Margarita. Although he tried his best to hide his grief, every now and then a pall of sadness would descend over him and Julieta would feel her father's sadness. She learned that if she climbed on to his lap at these moments, she would be cuddled for the longest time and then papí would smile again.

As Julieta moved through grade school, one by one her cousins entered middle school and then high school, and Luis realized that his nephews and nieces were living entirely Latino lives. They spoke Spanish at home and among their friends; and their English, although fluent, was heavily accented. The only recurring source of friction between Luis and his daughter was his insistence on speaking only English with her and constantly correcting her pronunciation. Time and time again he reminded Julieta that he and Margarita had come to America to be *Americans*, not to be lifelong Hispanic immigrants. It also seemed to him that his nieces and nephews were not being challenged enough in school. There was more TV than homework in the evenings and he didn't much care for changes he was seeing in the neighborhood. Eventually Luis decided that he wanted a different, better, environment for his daughter and he began to investigate alternatives.

For almost a year Luis explored areas of Long Island that he had never visited. He learned that Dukes County had the best public schools in New York State, but had housing costs to match. But Luis was a saver. He was paying very little rent in Queens because he and Julieta lived in a tiny apartment; not a major problem as they ate nearly every meal and spent every weekend at Alicia's home. He figured that, with care, he could live for a year on his savings, even with the higher rents in Dukes County and in particular in Stirling Bayside, which boasted the best public high school in the county.

Luis was well aware that any move would be a huge disruption for Julieta, who had been part of her warm, slightly chaotic Mexican family for all the life she could recall. He would have to be more available to his daughter, especially at the beginning. One year should be enough to establish himself in a new job or business that would allow him to be in the house when his daughter came home from school each day.

And so it was done. Amid tears from his daughter and after some very harsh words with his sister, Luis and Julieta moved to a small rental in Stirling Bayside.

The night they moved in to their new home, Luis sat his daughter down for a very serious conversation. He reminded her that she was now a young woman and she needed to act in a more grown up way. In particular, he wanted her to start using the name Sophie. She was an American girl and she would have a better life if she acted and sounded American all of the time. In truth Julieta, or Sophie as she now was, had already realized that her complexion was much lighter than her cousins and she knew that she could easily pass as an Anglo. Luis had anticipated a major row and for weeks he had been dreading this conversation. But to his amazement, his daughter had simply replied, "OK, if that's what you want papí. I mean, Dad."

Luis would have been less surprised if he had only known that, at that particular juncture, Sophie thought the coolest person on the planet was Marcia Brady, the pretty and popular oldest sister of the Brady Bunch. Season two was just about to start on TV and Sophie figured that, if she was going to be cast as Marcia's best friend, she had better be an all-American girl. Maybe papí would let her dye her hair blonde?

It didn't take Luis anything like a year to establish himself in business. During his years in the Navy he had supervised many construction and engineering jobs, mostly routine maintenance, but some involving new build projects costing a few million dollars. He used this experience to develop a project management business, organizing residential and small commercial construction jobs for clients too busy or too rich to handle the tasks themselves. He won his first client by doing a job for free, and grew his business after that through word of mouth from grateful clients, impressed with the negotiating skills that ensured their projects were completed on time and below budget.

Sophie never did become a blonde, Luis wouldn't go that far, although he did finance retainers, despite the shock of seeing the orthodontist's initial estimate. She settled in at Stirling Bayside Junior

High and then Senior High. Sophie was a popular girl with average grades except in Spanish and in home economics, where her cooking skills allowed her to shine. She occasionally went back to Elmhurst to visit her aunt, uncle and cousins, but Luis never once accompanied her. He and Alicia had not spoken since they had moved. Alicia thought that Luis was ashamed of his Mexican family and heritage.

At Sophie's high school, the only juniors who could attend the Senior Prom were those going as the date of a senior class member, and even then they needed written parental permission. Obviously therefore, getting asked to the prom was an obsession among juniors from Christmas onwards.

From the beginning of her junior year Sophie had been watching one particular senior, Will Cooper, and she knew that he had also noticed her. Will had a reputation of being very nice but painfully shy. In other words, he was just the kind of boy who would be a prime target for senior and junior girls worried that they would never be asked to the prom, and who knew that they would have to take the initiative and do the asking. Sophie found out where Will lived and pre-empted her rivals by knocking on his door on December 27th during the Christmas break.

"I just thought I should tell you that, if you come round to my house in person tomorrow evening, say around six o'clock, and ask my dad, I'm pretty sure he'll let me be your date for the prom. And don't worry, I'll be there too, and he's really, really nice. Honest." And Luis was really, really nice and agreed that she could go to the prom with Will, subject to a midnight curfew, which, after much pleading, was later extended to one o'clock. He recognized a good young man who seemed to like his daughter and he was pretty sure that Sophie would be able to handle him.

Will and Sophie became an item and dated every Saturday night, all that Luis would allow. By the time the prom actually came around, they were in love. Luis relaxed his dating rules a bit more during their summer break, but by then the young couple both had vacation jobs that kept them pretty busy, especially Will, who was working on a construction site. One Sunday late in August, Will announced to Sophie that he wasn't taking up his place in college in the fall, but going into business with a friend he had made on the site.

"Most of the building guys are really lazy and a lot of the work is really shoddy. Mike and I figure we can do better work, faster and cheaper. And to be honest, I'm not so good at hitting the books."

Sophie immediately replied, "You need to talk to my dad."

And so Will and Mike started their little construction firm with lots of guidance from Luis, who was able to give them their first commission. Luis's own honor code meant that he had to explain the position to his client, a Mr. Fredericks. Yes, it was his daughter's boyfriend and yes, they were very young. But it was a small job, a home extension for a bar and pool table, and Luis promised that he personally would pay for the entire project if Mr. Fredericks was less than 100% satisfied. In the end, Mr. Fredericks was delighted when his new recreation room was completed nearly two weeks ahead of schedule.

On the day of the handover, and at the urging of Sophie; Will and Mike had arranged a little ceremony. Luis and Mr. Fredericks were invited to inspect the finished job. Then to the surprise of both men, Will quietly announced, "Mr. Fredericks, you know you are our first client. We wanted to thank you for giving us a chance. We have had something made to go with your new pool table."

At this Mike lifted a dust sheet to reveal a beautiful cue stand. Obviously hand made, it could hold six pool cues, a set of balls and it had a custom made triangle cleverly built into the design. It was a beautiful piece of incredible craftsmanship.

"Where on earth did you get this?" asked an obviously moved Mr. Fredericks.

Will took a deep breath and remembered what Sophie had coached him to say.

"From this man, Mr. Ramos's brother-in-law."

When Francisco came into the room Mr. Fredericks shook his hand and then stood back bewildered, as the brothers-in-law tearfully embraced.

When Will had told Sophie about the new business's first client and his pool room project, she had quickly conceived of a way to begin to heal the rift between her father and his sister's family. And now, her plan was working, and very soon her father and his sister were as close as ever once again.

With Francisco doing the immaculate finishing carpentry, the team soon became sought after by the wealthy inhabitants of the Gold Coast who wanted high quality small construction projects: gazebos, pool houses, extensions, beach houses, boat houses and the myriad follies and toys of the rich.

A year later, Sophie sat Luis down, and he knew he was in trouble when she started "Papí," She only called him papí now when she was set to wheedle something out of him. "Papí, I want you to buy a house and help Will fix it up. Just a small one that I've already seen. Will won't ask me to marry him because he thinks that *you* want me to go to college first and because he thinks he needs to have lots of money and security to look after me. But of course I'm not going to college, I'm going to help Will and Mike and Uncle Francisco run the business. I'll manage the bills and the supplies and the employees and so on, because the firm is going to get bigger and bigger. So, you help him to fix up the house, then I'll ask him to get married and he'll get a mortgage and pay you back and that will be that. What do you think? Oh, the house is in Kingsbay by the way, near to John F. Kennedy Elementary."

Sophie knew how important school districts were to her father and she also knew that he worshipped the memory of the first Catholic president.

Just as when she organized Will to take her to the prom, and organized Uncle Francisco to make the pool cue stand, Sophie saw no reason why she shouldn't just organize people to do what she wanted when it was so obviously a good idea for everyone involved. Somehow this didn't make her selfish or spoiled or manipulative - well maybe a little manipulative with her father, but then what daughter isn't, she reasoned? She really did see that most people just didn't push on with life because they persuaded themselves not to try.

Luis agreed to go with her to see the house. On the south side of Bayview Drive the houses were much smaller than in the rest of this affluent community. In fact, these were the original homes that pre-dated the main phase of construction of the Kingsbay community in the late 1960s. Small Cape Cods with two bedrooms and small yards; some were in poor shape, although others had been completely renovated and were extremely attractive. And of course the community was well known as the most family-friendly community in Stirling Bayside.

The house for sale was in dreadful condition, with boarded up windows and a sagging roof. As they stood looking at it, a lady walking her dog passed by, and told them that the house had been empty for years, while some complicated legal problems were resolved relating to the previous owner, who had died overseas with no immediate family. It seemed that a distant cousin had now been traced and wanted the house sold quickly.

Within seventy-two hours Luis agreed to buy the house, with a bid of two-thirds of the already low asking price, as he could close quickly and would do so without an inspection. He allowed Will and Mike to assume that the house was for himself and he told them that, while he didn't expect a discount, he did expect their very best work. Francisco was in on the secret and consulted with Sophie before installing a clever, compact kitchen that they designed together; a small deck in the back yard and a covered front porch, complete with swing.

When the house was finished, Will took Sophie to admire the team's workmanship and Sophie asked him to marry her. Will, of course, said yes.

And the house was their wedding gift from Luis, who thought that his beloved Margarita would be very happy.

SURRENDER

With Susie in Vegas, on Saturday morning Andy figured he could sail for as long as he wanted; and he was in the mood for a good long outing. The weather was perfect, sunny skies and a steady wind to carry him swiftly out into Long Island Sound. He had a lot to think about, but he wasn't quite ready to focus on what he was going to do about the deal. Instead he found himself musing about his time in Kingsbay. They had lived here for a year and a half now, and Andy had become increasingly aware of just how wealthy some of his neighbors were. It wasn't that they were quick to show off their wealth, quite the opposite in fact. But, without any comment, someone would suddenly have a new boat, always bigger than their last boat, which was in any case only three or four years old. Or it might be a new Jaguar or Mercedes for their wife. Just recently, one of the guys in Pale Purple had built an extension onto his four bed house, so the band could have a dedicated rehearsal space and recording studio -- and this was a couple with no kids, just the two of them in a four bed, four and a half bath home with a finished basement, now doubled in size for the band.

Andy was doing OK at Dover Securities, but he wasn't remotely in this league. Susie helped out at the local elementary school but he didn't want her in full time work, and in any case she had no training in anything likely to bring in big bucks. Of course thanks to Susie's father, they had no mortgage, but even so. In January they had gone to Aspen for four days skiing with Jill and Frank, the Petersens' first vacation without the kids. Jill and Frank were the least ostentatious people imaginable, so when Jill offered to have her office travel group book everything, Andy had quickly agreed, not anticipating first class flights, limo transfers and a five star chalet with fabulous service. But he realized that the Petersens just took it all for granted, and so for that matter did Susie. The trip had put a big dent in his finances, and now Susie was talking about Europe as a vacation idea. She had reminded him how much he talked about his student trip to London, Paris and Barcelona; wouldn't it be neat to visit those places again and he could show her the sights?

The Aspen trip had derailed his efforts to meet the loan schedule with the bank. For eight months, he had succeeded in lowering his loan account every month. It had been a pain in the ass. He missed the adrenalin rush of the bets on the Yankees and, especially, every Sunday on the Giants. But he had done it. And then Aspen came along and blew a two month hole in one, admittedly great, week. Thankfully, a new manager had taken over at the bank three months before. He had agreed to extend the deadline by three months. But Andy was becoming really sick of feeling like the poor kid on the block again. He had had his fill of that when he was a kid.

And now this Vegas trip. When Susie told him that she had put her hand up for the trip he couldn't stop himself commenting on how expensive it would be. "There'll be flights and hotels and shows and gambling money Susie. Where do you think it's all coming from?"

She was immediately contrite. "I'm sorry Andy, I guess I just didn't think. You're right of course, I'll tell the girls I've changed my mind. Sorry, honey."

But he soon calmed down and insisted that she must go, but maybe in future she could talk to him first about major expenses?

In any event, he thought, the AllMedia deal would start to put things right. How to get it done?

He knew quite a bit about Securities and Exchange Commission rules, certainly enough to know that this would be insider trading and the SEC was really clamping down on that these days.

Charlie would be key. As soon as he had read the document, Andy knew that Charlie would be his shield. Charlie had been day trading for years, he was completely unrelated to Andy or to Susie and, he realized with mounting excitement, Charlie even lived in a different zip code, making their connection even less obvious. Andy remembered the realtor explaining that a new zip code, 11505, had been carved out when Kingsbay was developed, while the old houses where Charlie and his gran lived were still in 11039. The realtor claimed that there was a price premium for a 11505 property, which Andy decided was BS. The newly developed properties were two, three or four times the size of the old houses, so of course they were more fucking expensive.

Still, he didn't want to take any chances, there was no need to be too greedy, he would be making plenty; plus the germ of a bigger idea was developing. If he made a serious effort, he was pretty sure he could get transferred into the M&A group, even though it would mean a short term drop in salary. With Charlie as his secret weapon, he could exploit future insider opportunities just as easily. He had to talk with Charlie tomorrow morning.

Andy felt for the wind and set a course to bring him back to Broad Bay and Kingsbay marina.

It was almost two o'clock before Andy secured *Susie Q* in her berth. He wanted to swing by Charlie's house to make sure the young man joined him for a sail the following morning. As he passed the community pool, Vivien Werner waved to him and he walked over to greet her. They hadn't talked since their intimate dance at the disastrous Halloween party. She was lounging by the pool, looking exceptionally sexy in a bikini which drew attention to more than it covered. The pool was quiet at lunchtime, with only a dozen or so people swimming lazily to and fro or sunbathing on the loungers. Andy acknowledged a few greetings as he crossed to Vivien.

"I saw you come in. Have you had any lunch?"

"Nope, I was just wondering what I might find in the fridge."

"Have a sandwich; as usual, I brought too many. There are beers and sodas in the clubhouse, it has just been restocked."

Andy found himself a cold beer in the clubhouse fridge and signed for it on the sheet on the door. Every adult in Kingsbay had a key to the bar area.

"So, Vivien, how are you doing? You didn't go to Vegas?"

"Bunco's not really my thing Andy, and Vegas is a Bunco Babe event."

"I only figured out the game when Susie hosted an evening last year. Can't say it's my thing either. But you still haven't told me what's happening with you these days."

"I'm good. Mary had a good freshman year at college and will be back home in six weeks. She's spending time with her roommate and her family until the middle of July, and then I'll have her to myself until she goes back at the beginning of September. I've missed having her around this year, the house seems very quiet. How about you, you're looking very ... I don't know ... very pleased with yourself."

"Oh my God, that sounds awful! No, I've just had a great sail out into the Sound. Perfect sailing day, you should come with me some time."

As soon as he said the words, the atmosphere altered. They were both back in the memory their dance, before Anne had hauled Andy away to tend to Susie. Vivien lowered her head just a touch and looked up at him with a smile, "An offer a girl can't refuse."

He blushed just a little, but he also smiled. He allowed himself to look down to her bikini top and the swell of her breasts, knowing she would see him. They chatted for a while longer, until Vivien said, "If I don't get out of the sun I'll fry. I've just started on my tan and I do *not* want to be a lobster." She gathered up her things. "Andy, come round for a drink tonight," she added quietly, holding his gaze.

"I can't tonight Vivien, sorry, already confirmed for poker, but how about tomorrow night? Around 9:30 maybe?" he looked at her very carefully. By 9:30 it would be completely dark.

"That would be great, and please, call me Viv."

She wanted him to know she had understood. "Come to the back door, it's much faster."

They parted and went their separate ways along Bayside Avenue, Vivien to her home and her excited thoughts about their conversation, Andy towards Charlie's house to arrange to sail with him the following morning. He didn't think about Vivien again at all until the following day.

Thursday night poker had been moved to Saturday this week because so many wives were in Vegas and the guys wanted to break up the weekend and have an excuse to book a sitter for Saturday night. The same seven guys formed the regular group, with other players coming and going from time to time. Andy and Susie's arrival in Kingsbay had come a couple of months before one of the long term poker regulars left the neighborhood. Andy had been delighted when Frank invited him to join the group.

They played for points, which Joe Levine kept a record of. Except once a year, on the Thursday of Super Bowl week, each player brought $100 and they played until someone won the pool.

The previous week Andy had been asked to confirm his sign-up for this year's fishing trip and found himself making an excuse. He realized that he wasn't really all that keen on the fishing group, especially after the Halloween fiasco with Cliff and Susie. He much preferred the couples they played golf with, and he especially liked being a regular member of the poker group. He had come to understand that, while there may only be one or two poker guys on the Kingsbay committee in any year, every aspect of community business was casually discussed while they played cards, and whatever conclusions were arrived at on Thursdays, invariably became committee policy at the next meeting. The poker personalities were in reality the informal leadership of Kingsbay.

They had played half a dozen hands and Andy was only half listening to the discussions about community business. He had nothing to contribute, and, slightly to his own surprise, he found himself telling them about his upcoming trade, not in detail, but in the broadest terms. In hindsight, he understood that inviting them into the trade was an attempt to cement his relationships and raise his status in the group.

"Guys," he began a little nervously, "on Tuesday I'm going to buy some leveraged options on a company stock. I can't tell you much, really anything about the deal, but trust me, it's a fantastic opportunity. If any of you would like to participate, just let me know before I leave for work on Tuesday morning."

"Can't you tell us anything at all about the deal Andy?" asked Geoff Hooper.

"Sorry Geoff, it's really hush, hush. That's why it's going to be a great deal, and why I need you guys to keep it to yourselves. I guess I can tell you that it revolves around a small tech company."

Frank Petersen responded immediately, "Jill looks after all our investments Andy, I'm afraid I'm the wrong person to ask. Your deal, Pete."

And so the evening progressed and nothing more was said about Andy's invitation until, as they were leaving, Brian Russell came up to him, "I'll walk with you Andy." When they were alone, passing along The Crescent, he asked, "How much money are you talking about for this deal Andy?"

"Well, Brian, to tell the truth it could be anything, but I think it would be more equitable and avoid future problems if we each put up the same money. I think this particular deal, which involves a pretty small company by the way, could probably only stand about $100,000 in total. So depending on who wants in, say $25,000 each or so?"

In the end only Brian wanted in, and they agreed to put up $45,000 each. On Monday morning Andy sent Brian an email with the details of his bank account and Brian made an expedited bank transfer first thing Tuesday morning.

Kingsbay had lots of 'flag' lots; homes that were hidden behind street-front properties and accessed via extra long driveways that passed between two houses. The Smith's home was on a flag lot. They were located behind the Petersens' property. Their respective driveways ran parallel until the Petersen's garage, where the Smiths' ran on until it opened up onto a wide lawn area in front of their home.

By chance, Vivien's property was on a similarly shaped lot close by, so although her address was Kingswood Court, hers and Andy's properties had a shared rear boundary, albeit one crossed by a community footpath.

At 9:30 on Sunday night, Andy quietly stepped out of the screened porch at the rear of his house and made his way through the grove of oak trees onto Vivien's property. He quickly crossed her slightly overgrown backyard onto her deck and porch. The French door to Vivien's family room was unlocked and he quietly let himself into the house. He stopped to look at her in the warm glow of the candles illuminating the room.

"I thought it best not to have the lights on," she started.

"Shhh," he responded, walking slowly towards her.

She was wearing a short, figure-hugging summer dress with oversize buttons down the front, the top two undone. He closed the distance between them and looked at her. In his mind's eye he could see the toned shapely body he had admired at the pool. Vivien's eyes sparkled in the candlelight and he saw the rising and falling of her breasts. Her lips were full and slightly parted. He kept his eyes locked on hers, as one by one he undid the dress buttons down to her waist. He placed a hand on each of her shoulders, then slowly slid his hands down over her breasts, opening her dress to her waist, then slipped his arms inside the fabric and around her back. He drew her to him. They kissed, tentatively at first and then she felt his tongue open her lips and she responded. She sighed as his hand found her breast once more and caressed her.

"Upstairs," she urged.

As they lay together afterwards she whispered, "Ten years is a long time."

"Why now? Why me?"

"I don't know, lucky timing I guess. Our dance at Halloween, the way you looked at my body yesterday morning. You've no kids, which is important to me. You were walking along the road at the right time. Who knows? And stop fishing for compliments," she teased. "I've never had a toy boy before." In reality, of course, Vivien knew that there was only seven years between them. She slowly drew her nails lightly down his body and felt him grow hard again.

That first night he stayed until she fell asleep. Around two in the morning he made his way silently back to his own house and slept soundly for the first time that weekend.

Memorial Day was yet another sunny day in the neighborhood. The community kids who were members of the Stirling Bayside Boy and Girl Scouts led the procession to the flagpole beside the community clubhouse. At eighty-one, Jack Emerson was the oldest man there, although he made a point of acknowledging Charlie's grandmother who, at ninety-two, was the oldest inhabitant of Kingsbay. Jack had been leading the Memorial Day ceremony for more than fifteen years.

He looked at the youngsters and their parents arranged before him in a loose horseshoe. "I've been doing this for a few years now, and I hope to keep on doing it for a few years more. I want to thank the Scouts for leading us here, and I want to talk in particular to them and the other young people who join with us today to honor those who have served our country and who serve it still, all around the world."

"Let me start, by reminding you young folks that Betty Crouch is with us today." It took a moment before everyone realized that he was referring to Charlie's grandmother, who sat in her wheelchair in front of her grandson. She was looking down at her hands, which trembled a little in her lap. Betty Crouch was rarely seen outside her home. Most of the young people had no idea who she was.

"Exactly seventy years ago, in 1942, Betty volunteered to serve her country. Did you know that Sally?" Jack was looking kindly at Joe Levine's five-year-old daughter who was standing in the front row shaking her head. "Yes, she did. She volunteered and she became a nurse and she went France to look after our soldiers in the war. I bet you didn't know that did you Josiah?"

"No sir, I didn't" replied the older Kavanagh teenager.

"You should ask her about it one day. But although she's a remarkable woman, I don't want to talk about Betty Crouch today. Earlier this year Frank Johnston died. Many of you won't have known Frank, he left Kingsbay around fifteen years ago, maybe sixteen. Frank was poorly for many years before he died in March. And do you know why he was poorly Emma O'Donnell? Well, Mr. Frank Johnston was poorly, because for sixty-seven years he carried a piece of German artillery shell in his head and there were times it hurt him pretty bad. That artillery shell isn't hurting him any more. In a moment, we're going to recite together our Pledge of Allegiance and I would take it very well if all you Boy Scouts and Girl Scouts and all you other young people, were to think about Mr. Frank Johnston and what it means to have a painful wound for sixty-seven years and not to mind it none; because Frank always said that the pain only reminded him that he was alive, not like so many of his friends who died when they were not much older than some of you are today. Think of them while you join me now. 'I pledge allegiance ...' "

Andy had missed the ceremony because he and Charlie were out in the Sound on *Susie Q*.

"Charlie, can I ask you a favor?"

"Of course Andy, anything."

"Would you execute a couple of trades for me? I'll give you the funds in advance of course, and you would only hold the position for three or four days, maybe less."

"Why don't you do the trades yourself Andy? You must get better dealing terms than I do."

"Because I can't." He took a breath. "Charlie, do you remember telling me about your online hacking and consulting group? Well, this is a bit like that. I need to trust you with something that would embarrass me or maybe get me in trouble if you told anyone. But I don't think you would."

He looked closely at the young man in front of him.

"Andy, I guess you know that I don't have any friends in the real world. I've never figured out how to just get along with people. I would never tell anyone anything you tell me."

"I know, Charlie. So, the fact is, I saw some information that I wasn't meant to see, and I want to make some money from it. You can too if you want. On Thursday, AllMedia Corp will announce an agreed bid for GarageGuys Inc. The bid will be $15 a share and GarageGuys is trading at $12.25, although there's very little trading volume in them. How much do you pay for option contracts Charlie?"

"Forty cents."

Andy knew he could buy options through his company for maybe fifteen or twenty cents on a deal this size. No matter, he had in any event decided to make this deal a trial, which is why he limited the size of the transaction when he spoke with Brian. He needed to see this all working and then gradually work up to bigger deals. Andy could be patient when he had to be, and he was now set on getting moved into the M&A group where he knew more opportunities would come along.

"It's an agreed tender, so it will go through quickly for sure. Here's my plan - we buy options on GarageGuys and spend the same amount buying a couple of closely comparable stocks. That way we will disguise your trade when it gets checked out."

"The trade will be investigated?" asked Charlie with a grimace.

"Every trade in AllMedia or GarageGuys for a month prior to the deal will be looked at. However, you'll check out without a problem. You're already an active trader, you'll have bought other stocks in the sector in the same trading session and you've no traceable connections to any of the principals."

"What about connecting me and you?"

"I'm not officially involved in the deal, and in any case they'd never connect us; no family connections to me or to Susie and it so happens, we don't even share a zip code. I've thought it through and I'm pretty certain we're good."

Andy kept quiet and allowed Charlie time and peace to think it through for himself.

After a while Charlie asked, "How much do you want to trade?"

"$90,000: $45,000 in GarageGuys and the same split between any two small cap tech stocks you want to choose. I think they'll all get a little bump on this news."

"Can I think about it Andy?"

"Of course you can, just not too long. Could you call me this evening?"

"Alright, I'll call you by ten."

At eight o'clock Charlie called and confirmed that he was ready to go and would put $15,000 of his own money into the trades.

At five a.m. Wednesday morning, Andy was logged onto his computer in his basement office. He confirmed that Brian's money was in his account and he committed an immediate transfer of $90,000 to Charlie's account. He sent a text to Charlie's mobile, "Let's do this! $$$$"

The following Thursday most of the usual faces were at poker night. As soon as everyone sat down, Brian Russell called for silence. "Guys, I just want to tell you that we have a certified genius among us, a certified freaking financial genius. All I want to say is, next time you should listen to Andy. Just listen and take advantage of his ideas."

"I guess you guys did OK?" ventured Geoff.

"OK? We did way better than OK. Guys, I gave Andy $45,000 and four days later he deposited almost $175,000 in my account. The fastest, easiest $130,000 I'll ever make!"

Will spoke up. "OK Andy, I admit it, I don't understand how you do it. How can you make so much money?"

"It isn't a dumb question Will. I can do it because of option contracts. These allow me to buy the right to acquire a stock in a few days or weeks, but at today's price. It's easier if I give you an example. Let's imagine a stock called Kingsbay Securities, and it's trading today at 4 bucks a share. Now I have a hunch that Kingsbay Securities will be trading at $6 next Thursday and I have $100 to spare. I could go out and buy 25 shares at $4, and next week I'd sell them for $6 each, which is $150, I've made 50% on my money and I'm happy, right?"

Will nodded, and Andy continued, "But say I could have bought option contracts for ten cents each? So for $100, I buy 1000 options to buy the shares next Thursday, but at today's price of $4. I only pay ten cents for each option. I haven't bought the shares you understand, just options to buy them later. If I don't buy them, maybe because Kingsbay

Securities falls to $2, then I lose all my $100. But, and here's the beauty of it, next Thursday when Kingsbay is trading at six bucks, I have the right to buy 1000 shares at the old price of $4, so my profit would be 1000 times the increase in price from $4 to $6, which is 1000 times $2, which is $2,000. And I never have to actually fund the purchase, I simply buy and sell at the same time and bank the proceeds of $2,000. And remember, I only risked $100."

"If it's that easy, why does anyone buy shares then?" Will continued.

"Well, options are more risky that's why. If I had just straight out bought 25 shares at $4, and in fact the price drops to $3, I still own $75 worth of stocks, and the price might go back up again one day. In the same situation, if I had traded options, I would end up with nothing - I would have lost my entire $100."

"So it's higher rewards for higher risks, just as usual?"

"Well, yes, but as long as you can afford to take the loss, the rewards can be fantastic. And, if you are certain that the price will go up, well it's a no-brainer."

No one asked the question on everyone's mind, *How can you be certain that the price would go up?* because, of course, everyone knew the answer.

ANDY

George Smith had failed at every job he ever held, and he had had many over the years. He had failed at every business venture he launched, and there had been more than a few of those. The strange thing was, these failures were never George's fault. Often it was his son-of-a-bitch boss, sometimes a crooked competitor who paid off clients to win business. Occasionally it was just George's rotten luck. His wife had stopped listening to his complaints years ago. Which was fine with George, because he sometimes thought Rita was just another part of the problem.

He had to admit though, she still looked great, especially on her back. Even after the kid had come along four years ago, she had kept her slim figure and her great tits.

George had now decided that if he was to turn things around, he needed a fresh start and he resolved that the best place for that would be England. He reasoned that sleepy olde England would present easy pickings for a dynamic American like himself. His father had been English and George figured he could get an English passport. He went off to the library and discovered that he could indeed get a British passport and that the kid could get one too. He had been amazed to discover that England and Great Britain weren't quite the same place. Go figure.

Rita was less than enthusiastic. In fact she thought George was crazy, but took little notice, confident that this scheme would come to nothing, just like all the others.

However this time George pressed on. He gathered the necessary paperwork, and was mildly surprised to discover that the kid, Andy, was actually a year older than George remembered; but then he wasn't great at birthdays and anniversaries and stuff like that. He took everything to the British Consulate in Manhattan. Three months later, two British passports arrived in the post. They arrived too late for George however, as he was by then, three weeks dead of a sudden, massive heart attack. As Rita observed, this time George's luck really had been rotten. The passports were thrown in a drawer.

Rita had little education and had never worked. She married George during one of the rare periods when one of his schemes was actually making pretty good money. It folded a year after the wedding.

Rita was however still glamorous with a knockout figure. She attracted men like bees to a honeypot. She had only occasionally exploited a man's interest during her marriage; and then only when George was really down on his luck and had no money to take her dancing or buy her nice things; neither of which she was prepared to go without for any length of time. However when George died, Rita quickly realized that she could make good money without having to leave the house.

Andy learned to close his ears to the sounds coming from his mother's bedroom. Monday to Thursday, between six and seven in the evening, Rita's bed was almost invariably host to a client. Friday was payday, so happy hour extended to eight or nine o'clock. Saturday mornings and afternoons were also busy, although Andy was usually out of the house then. The packing plant front office and accounts staff were paid on the first Friday of every month. Rita charged extra that weekend. He closed his ears, but he knew what was happening and he hated it. He hated the men who, if they noticed him at all, would flip him a quarter as they left. And Andy really hated his mother. When he became a teenager he hated her even more, for the unsettling feelings she aroused in him when she walked around the apartment in her skimpy underwear or in one of her 'special' outfits; low cut dress, push up bra, extra high heels.

When Andy was sixteen, he persuaded Rita that it would be better for business if he wasn't around, which was true enough. So she agreed to pay the rent on a crummy studio for his final two years of high school.

Andy moved out at the start of his junior year. He never saw his mother again. She mailed him a check every month for two years. Afterwards, if anyone asked, he explained that both his parents had died in a car crash.

Andy worked hard, first at La Guardia Community College and then at Queens College, and earned his degree in business and finance. He excelled to the extent that, in his senior year at Queens, he was awarded a scholarship to finance a semester at the London School of Economics and a summer traveling through France and Spain. He had kept hold of his British passport and had it updated to use for his European trip, except that when he went to Student Affairs he was told that he couldn't use it.

"Well, you could leave the US on it and get into Europe with it, but you wouldn't get home. You don't have a visa," the lady explained.

"But I'm American!" Andy protested, and told her how he came to have the British passport.

"It's OK, honey, we've got plenty of time and we've done this lots of times. Here's the form to fill in and this sheet will tell you what you need to do. First off, get over to the library and fill this in, and there's a photo machine over there too. Then go the Dean's office; they have someone who can witness all your paperwork. Then come back here with a check. We already have a notarized copy of your birth certificate and we'll send in your application with the others. That way they'll process it faster. You'll have your American passport in good time, don't worry. But take that British passport with you to England, it could come in handy in Europe; for a start it would let you work if you wanted to."

Andy loved Europe. He couldn't have pointed to any one aspect of the trip that affected him more than any other. Somehow the entire experience had a major impact on him. He was particularly impressed with Spain. The friendly, laid-back people seemed less pressured and less competitive than Americans. Whatever the reason, the vivid memory of the trip stayed with him.

Andy was very handsome and women were invariably attracted to him. He always had a girl friend, but few lasted more than a couple of months and none managed a year. He could be fun to be around, he was an excellent lover and there were occasional moments of kindness. He was however, prone to sudden explosions of temper, which could be provoked by seemingly trivial incidents; but he was never physically violent.

When their affair was over, his ex-girlfriends realized that they knew very little about him.

He had no male friends.

When Susie's father raised concerns about her proposed marriage, she pointed out that it was thanks to him that she had met Andy. When Susie graduated from St Michael's College, her father had financed a week's vacation in New York for Susie and her roommate, Jo. They had a suite at the Plaza, tickets to the Met and two Broadway shows. He arranged for them to have a dedicated limo from ten in the morning until midnight every day (he didn't want them reliant on cabs, far less public transport). And they had enough spending money to do just about anything they wanted in the city.

On Sunday after breakfast, they crossed Central Park South and walked into the park. It was a glorious June day and New York was at its best. The park was full of people walking, cycling, roller blading, jogging. Young couples pushed strollers, and lovers of every age walked hand-in-hand. On a small rise, the two girls stopped to watch the chess guys take on all comers at speed chess. The regulars almost always won. The girls were about to move on, when a very handsome young man took a seat and tried his hand. He started off reasonably well, but the chess guy was too experienced and just too good for him.

He handed over his ten dollars and came right across to the girls. "You know I think I might have won if you two hadn't been distracting me. I think the least you can do to make it up, is to let me buy you ice-creams."

Andy's relationship with Susie was completely different from that with any girlfriend he had had before. For one thing, they didn't have sex, which he found pretty astonishing. Of course this wasn't Andy's choice, but he was strangely accepting when Susie told him early on of her plan to wait until she was married. She explained that initially it had been a religious issue; she and her family were Roman Catholic. But even as her faith had waned over the years, she had decided to stick with her youthful resolution to be a virgin when she married. Abstinence was made easier by distance. Susie continued to live in Vermont, teaching grade school, and of course Andy was in New York. He had occasional encounters with one of the married women he worked alongside, but felt no guilt about this.

He told Susie his lie (which by now he almost believed) about his parents dying together when he was young and Susie decided that it was obviously a painful topic, and never again asked him about his early years. As the months went by, Andy came to appreciate her kindness and how calm he felt whenever they were together. Susie never pressured him about anything, and while he didn't analyze his feelings too much, he discovered that her quiet determination not to have sex before she married was strangely appealing. And of course, her extraordinary beauty captivated him. They were in truth, an extremely striking couple.

When he proposed and she said yes, he was not entirely surprised when Susie's father Paul arranged for them to have a man-to-man chat over a beer.

"Susie has probably told you that we were a little uneasy about you guys at first. You're a good bit older than Susie and we know nothing about you, about your family. No, no, hold up there." Paul held up his hand, palm toward Andy, who was about to react. "All that's in the past. We're happy now that you two are tying the knot. I'm only raising this by way of explaining that what I'm going to say now is not about you, it's about how I feel about my daughter. The fact is that Susie's future is all I think about these days. I know that one day I won't be here to, well to be around for her. That will be your job I guess. Anyway, here it is. I've told Susie that I'll pay for a house for you both. I've told her the budget, which I think you'll find is pretty generous, even by the standards of New York property values. And I wanted to tell you man-to-man that the house will be in Susie's name. Life can throw us curve balls and I want this house to be her security, I hope you'll be OK with that."

The wedding was in Susie's hometown in Vermont. Since Andy had no family, it wasn't a huge event.

Nevertheless, between Susie's family and college friends and Andy's work colleagues, most of whom were surprised to be invited, it was a respectable sized crowd, that filled the smaller function room of the hotel. Even the best man was surprised to be asked. He only met the bride-to-be two days before the wedding.

After dinner and the obligatory speeches, the band played and the drinks flowed. Andy was feeling pretty good as he worked his way slowly back to his table after a visit to the men's room. Everyone seemed to be dancing, which was good, but as a consequence, it was hard to move around the room. He was working his way along the wall furthest from the top table when pressure on his shoulder turned him around. He was instantly intrigued to recognize the very sexy woman he had noticed earlier.

"They're all real," she said as she reached an arm around his neck, "and this is nice, don't you think?" As they began to dance, he was aware that she was moving them through the crush to a quiet corner of the room.

"What do you mean?" he asked.

"Oh come on, I saw you looking when we were introduced. Just to remind you, I'm Gillian, Jo's stepmother. And my tits are all natural. Looking is OK, you're welcome to do more than look if you like."

Jo was Susie's bridesmaid. Andy and Gillian danced and he quickly realized that this was the most sexual or sensual, he wasn't altogether sure what the difference was, woman he had ever encountered. She pressed herself against him and breathed into his ear. "I'm enjoying this, aren't you?" Without waiting for an answer she guided his hand over her breast and continued, "Actually I can feel your cock swelling, so I guess I know the answer to that."

"I live in the city. I'm putting my card in your pocket. Anytime you want to fuck, just call. Lunchtime or five o'clock, whenever you like, I'm always ready." She pushed herself against his erection one more time and then released him. "Always," she breathed and walked off.

Andy couldn't quite take in what had just happened, in full view of a room jammed with people. However, as he looked guiltily around, he realized that no one had noticed anything at all. He slid his hand into the pocket of his tux and felt the card. It had happened then.

Six weeks after his honeymoon he called the number on the card. She answered after three rings.

"Gillian, it's Andy Smith"

"Ah, Andy, the bridegroom. When?"

"Today, around five or a little later."

At ten after five he walked into the lobby of her building and pressed the button for the eighteenth floor. She was waiting to guide him to her corner apartment. "I'm so glad you decided to come. Let's have a drink, champagne OK?" she asked. He nodded his agreement as he watched her, spellbound. She was wearing a loose, silk dress with spaghetti straps. She turned back to him with a glass of champagne in her hand, and with the other she eased off her dress and allowed it to slide to the floor. Underneath she was completely naked.

"Enjoy," she said, slowly pouring the chilled wine over her breast.

As it turned out, Gillian was both sexual and sensual and Andy enjoyed being with her once a week or so. The most amazing thing about her, apart from the mind-blowing sex, was that it didn't matter when he called. He could see her on Monday, and she'd be ready to see him again on Wednesday. But if it was three weeks later, that was OK too. She was the perfect sex partner, available almost every time he called, with no questions asked.

Gillian had established a set of rules at their first meeting. They were lying in bed after vigorous sex that had satisfied them both. "I'm going to give you a key. You must always call and speak with me before you come over, but if I'm out shopping or whatever and you arrive before me, you can let yourself in. If I tell you I can't make it, don't whine and don't ask why. Don't call until you are ready to leave your office, I don't want to hang around waiting. I'll be available to you Mondays through Thursdays but I don't want any questions about what I do or who I see when I'm not with you. And

I never want to hear anything about you and your wife. Ever. Next time, bring a spare shirt and shorts and I'll send them out for you, so you always have a change when you leave here. I don't want you found out any more than you do. And don't ever tell me you love me; we're fuck buddies, that's all."

For six months she was the perfect mistress, until one day he called, confirmed that she was at home, and thirty minutes later, let himself into her apartment. He found her sitting on a sofa, talking with a ridiculously good-looking young man.

She introduced him, "This is Giovanni, I was his very first woman four years ago when he was a 15-year-old virgin." She pretended to pout, "He abandoned me, but now he's back to study at Hunter College for four years. Isn't that great?" She went on, "Now I can have my two favorite men to enjoy."

Andy wasn't so sure, but Gillian was clearly aroused as she continued. "We've been chatting, and Giovanni is absolutely up for a threesome. What do you say darling? I so want to have both of you. Together. This is what I want."

Andy felt that he had no choice but to agree and so he nodded, but his heart wasn't in it and, it soon became clear, neither was his body. Embarrassed, he tried to leave unnoticed, but the final humiliation was hearing Gillian call out, "Leave the key on the table darling. Giovanni will need it this week."

He never called her again.

CHANGES

Although Labor Day marked the end of summer and the start of a new school year, Long Islanders could usually count on another six or eight weeks of great weather, and so it proved as Homecoming weekend approached for the Marlins of Stirling Bayside Senior High. This year the game was with the Jameston High Minutemen and the entire school was caught up in preparations for Friday night. Everyone turned out after classes on Wednesday for the pep rally and bonfire. There were no homework assignments the entire week, and all classes were suspended from lunchtime on Friday.

Kingsbay had reserved its usual area behind the bleachers for the pre-game party. For the past few years, the fishing trip regulars had taken charge of the barbecue at Homecoming, using the two huge community grills; while the golfers organized the cold food and the drinks. Ever since an unfortunate incident in 1985, when some of the fathers of the two teams started fighting during overtime, both headmasters and their successors had enforced a complete ban on alcohol on the school grounds, so fruit juice, water and sodas were all that was available, although a few of the grill chefs kept suspiciously tight grips on their insulated, and seriously outsized, travel mugs.

There was a great turnout of around 150 adults from Kingsbay, and almost every high school age kid for miles around was also attending, but they were in a different section, with their classmates.

Almost 4000 people attended the game, which Stirling Bayside won 24-21, having been down 18-21 with 90 seconds to play. Josiah Kavanagh scored the winning touchdown in his first Homecoming game.

On Saturday afternoons the Kingsbay golf group played at Stirling Country Club. Susie and Andy were regulars, as was Anne. Normally one of the guys whose wife didn't play, teamed up with Anne to make a foursome. She was a sought after partner because she was amazingly consistent, if not the longest off the tee. However there was a lot of interest when this particular week, Anne turned up with a partner of her own. She led him over to Susie and Andy, "I thought we could play with you guys today?"

"Absolutely," replied Andy.

Anne made the introductions, "This gorgeous creature is my dear friend Susie, and this almost equally gorgeous creature is her husband, Andy. Guys, this is Ted Newberry, a friend of mine."

"A friend, a *friend*," he complained, "I've only been trying to get her to marry me for six months and she calls me a friend!" He was smiling broadly as he put his arm around Anne's shoulder.

Anne blushed, "Well, I've decided to give him a trial run," she said turning again to Susie, "Ted's moving in with me next week."

"I'm beginning to think she only wants me for sex, ouch!"

Anne had stomped on his toes, but not too hard, "If I wanted someone for sex, I'd have picked someone young and handsome, not an old fool like you."

The affection between them was obvious.

"Well, Anne Murphy, you're certainly the quiet one," exclaimed Susie, "not a word, not a single word."

Anne linked her arm with Susie's "I know honey, and I'm sorry, I really am, but the truth is, I only met Ted six months ago, he proposed on our second date you see. I didn't want to jinx it until I was sure." She raised her voice a little so Ted and Andy could hear, "Not that I'm sure yet, I've never seen him play golf for instance. Or load a dishwasher."

It turned out that Anne didn't have to worry about Ted's golf. He was a good player with an outstanding putting game and they enjoyed a great round of golf. Ted was funny, always kind, and quick to poke fun at himself.

"I'm not real smart Susie," he confided at one point, "my home room teacher once told me 'Ted Newberry, if you got another brain, it would be lonely.' And I guess she was right. But I was a great salesman, I could sell just about anything. I enjoyed selling, never wanted to do anything else once I started."

Anne wasn't letting him get away with that. "Don't believe a word that comes out of that man's mouth Susie, do you know what he sold? He sold analytical and containment equipment to laboratories, that's how we met. Trust me honey, it means selling technical shit to technical people. 'Not real smart' my ass! When he gives you a line like that Susie, he's about to sell you something. I want to sign him up for Amway."

Susie and Andy laughed so much that they both fluffed their next strokes, which gave Anne and Ted an unbeatable lead in their game.

"You cheated!" Andy said as they headed to the clubhouse, "You came out with the Amway line just to put us off."

"Sore loser," returned Anne, "just for that I'm ordering a large one, Andy, and you're buying."

They entered the busy clubhouse bar, and spotted the long Kingsbay table against the window. Andy detoured to the bar to order their drinks. Everyone was eager to be introduced to Ted and no one was interested in the brief conversation between Andy and Vivien, also at the bar ordering drinks for her foursome.

"Mary is coming home next weekend." Vivien spoke quietly, but she didn't have to whisper, there were noisy conversations going on all around her.

"So I won't come round on Wednesday?"

She looked at him intently, "I'm afraid not. She suddenly announced that she was coming home for fall break because she split up with her boyfriend, who was going on the same trip Mary had scheduled, and she just couldn't face going, poor thing."

"OK, I understand," he replied, "I'd better get back."

After that first night in May, Andy had gone to Vivien's house every other Wednesday night, fifteen minutes after Susie left for bunco. It had been Andy's suggestion, 'bunco goes on until eleven or sometimes twelve o'clock, so we could have a few hours together.'

And that is how it worked out. They would be together from seven until ten every alternate Wednesday night. They would be in bed and making love within ten minutes of Andy's arrival. While the affair drew them closer, it was still essentially a physical relationship. Vivien had come to terms with this the previous month. Mary was home from college and Vivien explained to Andy that this meant their Wednesday nights would have to stop until her daughter went back to college in the fall. But on the last Friday of August she had phoned Andy at work. "Hi Andy, it's Viv, are you free for lunch?" she asked. "I could come up to the city."

"Of course, that would be great. I'll book somewhere and send you a text. I'll choose somewhere near Penn Station."

Fifteen minutes later Vivien had called him back, "Andy, to hell with lunch, book us a room."

He had taken the rest of the day off and they had made love all afternoon. The sex was more intense than ever, something about checking into the hotel for a few hours made it all seem more exciting to Vivien. She came up to the city once more before Mary went back to college, and they were able to resume their own special bunco nights.

That Sunday, the word was spread by community email and by old-fashioned jungle telegraph;

Kingsbay was having a neighborhood tailgate party before the broadcast of the Giants' evening game against the Cowboys, in honor of their very own Josiah Kavanagh and his winning touchdown. The party would be held in Fairlake Court, with a dozen or so big SUVs providing the tailgates and the community grills on hand to cook burgers for everyone. Around fifty or sixty people turned up and made a great fuss of Josiah.

A small group of men were standing around Ross Fisher's huge Nissan truck, each with a cold beer in hand, as they watched the build up to the game on a portable TV, sitting just inside the back of the truck. They were helping themselves to salted snacks with their beers.

At the end of Fairlake, where it met Kingswood Dr, two teams of teenagers were throwing a football back and forth. An errant throw landed at Andy's feet and he picked up the football and tried to return it to Al or Jason Chambers, he never could tell the two apart. However, he was out of practice, and he overthrew and the ball bounced crazily down Kingswood into the middle of a bunch of younger kids, being kept well away from the tailgaters by mothers and hired sitters. Little Carol Hooper was first to the ball; she collected it up in her arms and tried to throw it back. The ball travelled maybe five feet before bouncing harmlessly against the curb, with three or four kids in pursuit.

A few moments later Carol stopped running, and stood still as she began to wheeze and very quickly began to have real breathing trouble. Within seconds she was in clear distress. Just moments before Carol picked up the ball, her mother had gone home to use the bathroom, taking the rescue EpiPen with her.

As the little girl slowly sank to the ground, Ted ran to her, caught her in his arms and laid her gently on a nearby lawn. He arranged her carefully in the recovery position and spoke quietly to her, reassuring her that all would be well. Meanwhile he pulled his phone from his pocket and called 911. He looked around and, seeing that everyone was frozen, he fixed his eye on the nearest adult, "Get her mom, now!"

Despite Ted's efforts, Carol's breathing slowed and then stopped completely. He began rescue breathing for her, pausing only for a second or two when Caroline Hooper came running with the EpiPen in her hand and calmly injected her daughter in her left thigh. Ted resumed breathing for the little girl. After a few seconds there was a little gasp and Carol started breathing by herself. Someone turned up with a comforter and Ted and Caroline wrapped the small figure in it. Ted picked her up and gently placed her in her mother's arms.

As Caroline was walking slowly back to her house, her daughter cradled in her arms, the EMS team arrived and took charge, giving the little girl another shot of ephedrine, which they had determined she needed.

"We'll take her to Jameston General now ma'am," said the senior paramedic, "they'll take care of her. You can come with us, or follow in your car if you prefer."

Andy, clearly agitated, approached Ted and grasped him by the shoulders, "God Ted, I'm glad you were here, you really stepped up man. It must have been me, handling the ball after eating peanuts for twenty minutes. I should have been more careful."

"Don't beat yourself up, Andy, it was just one of those accidents that happen. I'm sure she'll be fine now."

The two men walked slowly back to the tailgaters, but stopped short to finish their conversation.

"We just shouldn't have any peanut products at an event where there will be kids," proposed Andy.

"I think you're right, it's impossible to keep track of who's got an allergy and who hasn't at these events. How do things like that get sorted in the community?"

"It would go the committee and if they agree, someone will send out a community email and probably an announcement will appear in the next monthly bulletin. Although be honest Ted, if I mention it at poker on Thursday and Pete and the guys agree, it will just happen."

"The poker players run the community?" Ted asked in surprise.

"Not exactly; it's just that Pete Woods is kinda the go-to guy in Kingsbay, just because everyone likes him, respects him. He and Donna have lived here forever and they know everyone. Did you know that Vivien is their daughter? And Simon over there is their son. And the other poker guys, Frank, Brian, Will, Joe and Geoff are all well regarded as well. I hear them casually chat about something, and next thing you know, whatever it is winds up being debated and agreed by the committee. This year Geoff Hooper and Brian's wife, Pauline, are on the committee. I think there's pretty much always at least one poker player on every year. It took me a while to figure it out."

"Nice that they invited you to join them. So how many of you are there? Seven? Strange having an odd number."

"Yea, that's something else I just figured out. The eighth seat is like a guest seat - usually they just like having a fresh face at the table; but sometimes it's so they can invite someone else if they're discussing some Kingsbay issue and need another opinion or an expert or whatever. It means they can be well prepared before raising things with the wider community."

"Smart guys."

"Hey, I don't want to make it sound like the Mafia or something. Why not come along one week and meet them? You'll like them, it's very relaxed, not too serious at all."

"I'd like to do that one of these days."

The following Friday, Andy's boss called him into his office and told him that, as he had requested, he was being transferred to the M&A group.

EASTER 2013

On the morning of Easter Sunday it was as if someone had thrown a switch. The windy, wet weather vanished as if it had never happened. Suddenly it was spring. Andy joined many of his neighbors at the marina as they spent the day getting their boats ready for the season.

Around ten a.m., Pete Walsh called out "Socks?"

There was an immediate response in favor, and so by seven that evening all of the Kingsbay sailors, many of their wives and a few non-sailors who liked to party, assembled on the Kingsbay beach. The 55-gallon oil drum had been rousted out of its space behind the dinghy storage racks and half filled with kindling and a tiny amount of gas from someone's outboard. At 7:15 precisely, at the dramatic conclusion of a spectacular sunset, a match was thrown into the drum and the fire started. Each sailor in turn approached the burning drum and threw in a sock, thus committing himself to wear no more socks until the fall.

On Easter Monday, Andy and Susie headed towards the marina. They had planned a full day's sailing along the northern shore, with a hazy plan to stop off somewhere for lunch. As they approached the dock, Susie excused herself, "Andy, I think I'll visit the restroom before we take off." She turned into the clubhouse to use the ladies room.

And so it was that Susie finally met Charlie. He had emerged to help Andy prepare the boat, and was on board when Susie trotted down to their pier.

"Sorry honey, I bumped into ... oh hi, you must be Charlie." Susie leapt easily aboard and reached out her hand to the discomfited young man.

"Hi," Charlie managed.

Andy quickly assessed the situation. "Charlie, this is my wife Susie, she'll be coming with us today, but don't worry, Susie will be happy to have you share the sailing with me. Right Susie?" he looked over to his wife.

"Of course I will. Andy tells me you two have become quite the sailing team. I'm looking forward to watching you guys at work."

Charlie was trapped. It was too late to get off the boat, but he was incredibly uncomfortable to be so close to this beautiful young woman he had seen around the neighborhood. He thought she looked like a movie star.

However, as they sailed out of the bay into the Sound, Susie was so friendly and so interested in whatever he did, that Charlie soon found himself relaxing and enjoying the day.

"Charlie, do you think we could make it into Oyster Bay? There's a great place there for crabs, and they have a pontoon that will easily take *Susie Q*. What do you think?"

Well, Charlie was damn well determined that they would make Oyster Bay before one p.m. and he used everything Andy had taught him to sail *Susie Q* as fast as she could handle, and brought them alongside the crab shack at one o'clock precisely.

Susie had been genuinely impressed by Charlie's handling of the boat "Charlie, that was fantastic! Really! I loved every minute. Thanks," and she just naturally reached out and linked arms with him as they walked up the pontoon to find a table.

They had a wonderful day, eating crabs washed down with cold Yuengling beers and feeling the first heat of the season from the spring sunshine. On the trip back, they competed to see just how far into the wind *Susie Q* could sail before whoever was skipper was embarrassed as the wind spilled out of her mainsail and they came to an abrupt and messy stop.

When at last they returned to Kingsbay, Susie took charge, "Andy, we're leaving you to tidy up here; Charlie is going to introduce me to his grandmother. Yes, you are Charlie, and there's no point in making a fuss about it, let's go." She took Charlie's arm again and marched him along Bayside Avenue until they reached Betty Crouch's house at the corner of Bayview Drive.

"Susie, can I just go in and tell her you're coming? Please? We don't get many visitors and I wouldn't want her to ..."

"Of course Charlie, you go ahead, I'll just sit on this bench until you come get me. And there's no hurry, I'm not going anywhere,"

It was twenty minutes before Charlie came to collect Susie. He opened his mouth to apologize, but before he could speak Susie placed a finger on her lips. "Don't apologize Charlie, don't say anything, it's fine, it really is. Now let's go visit your gran."

Later she tried to explain to Andy just how good Charlie was with Betty, how attentive and gentle. And it was clear how much the old lady depended on her grandson, "Charlie is really great with his grandmother you know, he really is a saint." Andy listened, but she knew that he wasn't really grasping her account, or maybe she wasn't telling it properly. In the end she gave up and they went to bed, but Susie lay awake for a while thinking about the young man and his challenging life, restricted by his chronic shyness and the demands of caring for his elderly grandmother.

Meanwhile, Charlie was having an equally restless night. His thoughts were full of Susie, her beauty, grace and kindness. He had had more fun today with Susie than with any girl he had ever known, which in truth wasn't saying a lot. By the time they sailed back to Kingsbay, Charlie was in love, but not in any way that a typical 22-year-old might be in love with a beautiful young woman only a few years his senior. Charlie adored Susie rather than desired her.

He had thoroughly enjoyed every minute of their time together sailing and having lunch; but he became quite besotted when she came to visit Gran. For many years now, his grandmother had left her house less than once a month. In all that time, the minister from Bayside Presbyterian was the only person to cross their threshold, which he did every two or three months. Today Susie had sat with Gran for over an hour, instructing Charlie to please make them coffee.

Charlie finally fell asleep thinking how lucky he was to have Andy and Susie as friends.

Almost a year had passed since the GarageGuys deal, when Andy suggested to the poker group that another opportunity was about to arise.

Joe was still not interested in the slightest, Will and Sophie were off on a short vacation and Frank had flu and so missed that poker game. Pete was tempted, but in the end only Geoff Hooper decided that, in view of the success last time, he wanted in with Andy and Brian. So after the game, the three of them sat down in Geoff's basement.

"OK Geoff, Brian and I are putting up all our proceeds from the last trade, so its $130,000 this time. Same rules, we're all in it together."

"I know, Brian and I talked it over after you guys made out so well last time. Count me in."

So between them they had $390,000. Charlie came in with $60,000 to make it a nice round number. On this occasion it was a software play, another agreed acquisition, this time of a Dover Security client, MXD NetSoft; but the execution was just the same. Andy and Charlie spread the money over three stocks and this time one of the stocks dropped in price, and so those options were not executed.

Nonetheless, it was a happy night two weeks later at another poker evening, another one that Frank had to miss.

"OK guys, each of the three of us put in $130,000. I can tell you that tomorrow morning, almost $600,000 will be deposited in each account, meaning we are each about $470,000 better off."

Pete Woods was first to speak, "Jesus, Andy, I had no idea you guys were making so much money, did you Will?"

"No, I didn't Pete, and I'm beginning to feel like a friggin' idiot for not getting on board with it."

"Hold up, Will, and you too Pete. I've told the other two not to spend their money, or at least not all of it. There's going to be another opportunity, I think before the end of the year. However that may be the last, at least for a fairly long time."

Will had persuaded Sophie to sit down for a moment, "Honey, Brian and Geoff each gave Andy $130,000 to invest and a few days later he deposited $600,000 in their accounts. They made almost half a million dollars each Sophie. In Brian's case he really invested nothing this time, because he had already made $130,000 profit on the first deal Andy offered us."

"I don't know Will, it seems too good to be true, which usually means that it is. Are you sure this is legal?"

"Well, honey, normally I'd agree with you, but this may be the exception. It seems on the up and up. And it's Andy for God's sake, I mean we've know them now for well over a year and they seem like pretty good people don't you think?"

"I have to say, Susie is really nice. I don't know Andy as well as you do, but he seems OK. Can we discuss this with my father? I'd like to get his take on it."

"Andy made us promise to keep all this to ourselves; but I guess Luis would be OK."

They sat down with Luis, and told him about the trades. Will added, "We don't know for certain that there will be another opportunity. Andy did say that there could be something by the end of the year, but maybe there won't be."

Luis was very cautious, but in the end, Will's enthusiasm won him over and he eventually agreed that it did seem to be too good an opportunity to ignore.

"Why don't I come in with you Will? That way if anything goes wrong, you won't be out so much money, and if it goes well, the profits are in the family anyway."

Will understood what his father-in-law was really saying, that all his money was really Sophie's.

"Thanks Luis. I'll call you whenever Andy brings up another deal."

ENDINGS

Alan Davidson was now Andy's boss in the M&A group at Dover Securities. All things considered, he wasn't a bad boss Andy thought, for sure he had had much worse. This morning however, Alan was not a happy camper.

"The sons of bitches at the SEC have decided to audit us. Apparently there were masses of unusual trades in MXD stocks in the couple of days before the announcement. It's a royal pain in the ass I can tell you, these fucking audits can take weeks, months even, and we'll be up to our necks in paperwork, you'll see."

"What are they looking for?" asked Andy, impressed with himself for sounding so calm.

"Actually, Andy, you're off the hook on this one. They'll be looking at our history, to see if there are any similar patterns in the quiet periods before all of our deals for the past year or so."

"Why us?"

"Oh it won't just be us. The lawyers, the other advisors and of course the principals will all be checked out. But since this was your first deal, you've no history to review. You're in the clear. The SEC enforcement guys take the view that there is never a first time for advisors, they always look for patterns over time. It's different for principals, they might only get one chance to make a score. Think about me and the rest of the team on Sunday, while you're watching the game and we're wading through file boxes. We'll probably be in here the entire fucking long weekend."

Andy knew he had a lot more to worry about than Alan knew. Andy realized that, when the SEC spotted Charlie's two trades, red flags would be raised, no matter that the trades were camouflaged with other transactions. As he sat on the LIRR train going home on Wednesday evening, he ran over every aspect of the deals. He was still confident that they wouldn't connect Charlie to him. He was going to enjoy his long weekend. July 4th fell on a Thursday this year and, like millions of Americans, Andy had decided to stretch it into a four-day holiday.

And tonight was bunco night.

Once again, Mary wasn't coming home until the end of the third week of July, so Andy could look forward to at least two more Wednesday night trysts; after that he supposed they would spend the occasional afternoon in a Manhattan hotel. This week Andy was in the mood for something different. Before he left the office he called Vivien's home number.

"Hi, this is Vivien."

"It's me. How about a little outdoor fun tonight? It's going to be a great sunset."

"Sure, where?"

"Meet me at the junction of Middle Neck Rd and Sands Point Rd; there's a closed down restaurant where you can park. I'll be there about 7:15. Bring a picnic rug and maybe some cold wine."

"See you there."

Three minutes after the door closed behind Susie, Andy drove out of their driveway. Fifteen minutes later he pulled alongside Vivien's car in the deserted lot. She stepped out, went around to the trunk and lifted out a rug and a small wicker basket, which turned out to contain a chilled bottle of champagne and two glasses. As she walked towards his car, Andy saw that she was wearing a silk camisole-style top with no bra, and white linen shorts. He could clearly see the shape of her full breasts through the fine material. She had dressed to turn him on, and it was working.

When she had slid into her seat, he reached over and kissed her, and traced the curves of her breast with his hand.

"You look very ... desirable," he finished, rather lamely.

"The look I was going for, was extremely fuckable."

She blew him a kiss and continued, "It's a perfect evening for it, isn't it?"

"It is now," he smiled back.

Vivien sat back in her seat and reached for her seat belt as they moved off.

"So where are we going?"

"Just down here there's an old Jazz Age mansion that's been closed for years but hasn't been redeveloped. Do you remember the tornado two Halloweens ago?"

"Of course. That was after our dance. You and Frank Petersen came to check up on me. Little did I know then," she teased, "that one day you'd come checking out something else."

"It touched down here as well. The tree people who came out to clear up the mess in Kingsbay also did work up here; I got talking with one of the guys, who told me about some of the damage."

At that point Andy pulled off the narrow road he had been slowly driving along and they got out of the car. They retrieved the rug and basket and he locked the car. Andy took Vivien's hand and led her into the trees, angling towards a high wall they could occasionally glimpse through the greenery.

"It should be around here," Andy muttered, "ah, here we are."

They had arrived at the nine foot high wall, except they were looking at a section totally destroyed by a huge fallen tree. The oak had been on the other side of the wall and when it collapsed, it had taken out a section eight or ten yards long. The odd thing was that all of the broken branches on their side had been neatly trimmed in line with the boundary, and all of the wood and what must have been a ton of broken masonry had been carefully removed. But on the other side, there was a jumble of tree limbs and shattered stonework.

"The tree guy told me that no one knows who owns the estate now, so there was no one to order debris removal or pay for it, so everything was left the way we see it. The property on this side is owned by a bird protection trust, so they had their mess tidied up. This means we can get into the old estate, which apparently has a private beach that hardly anyone knows about. Come on, let's go."

They picked their way carefully around the fallen giant and were immediately in their own private world. The grounds were overgrown, but they could still see the outline of formal gardens stretching up to a huge house that stood more or less intact. They headed to their left and soon found themselves on the driveway that swept majestically to the enormous porticoed entrance. Still further to their left, Long Island Sound sparkled in the evening sun.

Hand-in-hand they strolled up to and all around the imposing building.

"This is real Gatsby stuff, isn't it, Andy?"

"I had a quick look online this afternoon, but I couldn't pin down the name of this estate, so I don't know who owned it. But I did learn that there were dozens and dozens of houses this size. Quite a few are still standing, although none are private homes any more. Must have been quite a scene back in the day."

When they had walked all around the house and arrived back at the entrance, they found a smaller path that seemed to be headed to the waterside. It soon started to dip, as the gardens fell away towards the water's edge. They passed an overgrown tennis court, and off to their right they could see a crumbling, but still impressive boathouse, bigger than either of their homes. The boathouse arch framed a perfect view of the Sound looking towards the Connecticut side. A single sailboat leaned gracefully by, making for home.

"If it rained, we could make love in there," suggested Vivien with a wicked smile.

They had arrived at the beach. It was around fifteen yards deep and stretched off on either side to where the land bent back towards the house. It faced almost due west, and it was completely deserted and completely still. It was still forty minutes before sunset: distant sails were dotted around the Sound. Andy spread out the rug and opened the bottle. They sat side-by-side sipping the cold wine and pointing out occasional landmarks as they recognized them. The Throgs Neck and Whitestone Bridges were already lit up towards distant Manhattan on the horizon.

"Did you know, Andy, that when you sail out of the Sound, between Fisher Island and Plum Island, you are at exactly the same latitude as the gap between Corsica and Sardinia in the Mediterranean *and* the point where you would enter the Black Sea after sailing past Istanbul, which is the gap between Asia and Europe *and* the gap between Honshu and Hokkaido, the two biggest islands of Japan. All these gaps at the same height on the earth; for some reason I find that interesting."

Andy was somewhat less intrigued by this information. Instead he came around and knelt behind Vivien. He stroked her bare shoulders and she tilted her head away, offering her neck to be kissed. She leaned back into him and he reached around to run his hands over the thin silk of her top. He savored the sensation of her nipples responding to the caress of the fabric moving under his fingers. She gave a small moan and turned her head to find his lips.

"Take off your clothes, Andy."

While he undressed, she peeled off everything except her flimsy top. She looked at his body and he could see her desire.

"Lie down on the rug, I want to be on top, facing the sun."

Andy lay down on his back and she lowered herself astride him. She moved on him slowly, easily; not yet in a steady rhythm. One by one she undid the tiny buttons on the front of her camisole. Finally, it slipped off her shoulders; and he watched, mesmerized, as her hands outlined and then cupped her breasts; then ran languidly over her belly and hips. Her eyes were closed, her skin and her hair, tumbling around her face, glowed in the last fiery rays of the setting sun. She leaned forward, placed her hands on his chest, and found her rhythm.

Afterwards they dressed and sat a while longer, watching the lights of the distant planes taking off and landing at La Guardia ten miles away. At last it was time to leave and Andy drove her back to her car.

Two days later, the fifth of July was unseasonably grey, with heavy skies threatening rain later; suitable weather for a funeral.

A former Kingsbay resident, Cal Everett, had died suddenly, aged only sixty-four and he had requested that his funeral service be held in First Baptist in Stirling Bayside.

His brother Eddie came up from Florida for the service and to offer a eulogy.

"It's easy to describe someone as 'unique', a 'one-off', a 'lone wolf'. Let me tell you just some of the ways that my brother Cal was truly a one-of-a-kind guy."

"He was the first member of our family to graduate high school; he was the only guy in his college class to volunteer to serve in Vietnam; he remains the only recipient of the Distinguished Service Cross to be awarded an Oak Leaf Cluster after being busted to a lower rank. He is, surely, the only born and bred New Yorker to have supported the Red Sox since he was ten and he was, without question, the greatest frisbee master that Kingsbay ever knew. At least, that's what I've been told."

There were a few laughs and then Eddie continued, "Our parents were born of immigrants. Our father's family were English and our mom's people came from Germany. They were both of them raised on the Lower East Side, long before Delancey St became trendy."

Eddie told stories about his brother; about growing up in New York and especially about his remarkable service in Vietnam. He wound up with a few more recent tales of events during Cal's time in Kingsbay. Peter Cooper recognized some of the later incidents, even though the stories were being somewhat embellished. Peter was thirty-two, the youngest of Sophie and Will's three children, and he remembered Cal as one of the fun adults when he was growing up. Cal was often the umpire for their summer softball games. Whatever his job was, it seemed to allow Cal plenty of long afternoons for having fun.

Peter lived in New Jersey now but had felt strongly that he should attend the funeral. He felt that he was representing all the kids who had been encouraged and umpired by Mr. Everett.

The seating at Bayside Presbyterian was arranged in an arc and Peter's attention was drawn to a striking young couple sitting opposite him and his parents. He would ask his mother about them after the service, he thought.

However, Eddie talked for so long about his brother, that Peter realized that he was running really late. As the congregation finally stood to leave the church, he turned to his father and spoke softly into his ear, "Pops, I really need to dash, can you give me a ride to the station? I don't have time to call a cab."

"Mom, I need to fly," he continued, taking Sophie's arm, "Pops is going to take me to the station, he'll meet you back at Fellowship Hall in twenty minutes. Say hi to Mrs. Everett for me, and tell her I'm sorry I couldn't stay. I'll call you at the weekend." He kissed Sophie's cheek and urged his father quickly to the car.

Saturday morning Charlie was waiting by the marina as usual.

"Good morning, Charlie, it's just you and me today, Andy's playing in a big golf tournament this morning. Is there anywhere in particular you'd like to head for?"

Charlie was happy at the thought of having Susie to himself for once and he couldn't have cared less where they went, except ... "How about trying for Bayville or somewhere around there?"

Bayville was at least a four hour sail, even with good winds.

"OK, there's a crab shack just this side of Bayville where we can have lunch. We'll work her hard to get over there and have a leisurely sail back. How does that sound?"

That sounded just great to Charlie and so they set sail out of the bay into the Sound, then turned east and tacked their way along the coast. After an hour or so of companionable silence, Susie asked, "How is your gran, Charlie? I must come visit her again."

"She's good Susie and she'd really like it if you came to see her again, she enjoyed meeting you last time."

"She's an interesting lady. How old is she Charlie? I didn't want to ask her."

"She's ninety-three, she was born in December 1919. Her father came back from fighting in the First World War, he had been injured so was one of the first to return. He and Gran's mother were married right away and Gran was born ten months later. She was born right over there." Charlie was pointing to a spot inland, off their bow.

"Really! So she's lived around here all her life?"

"Yes, she has. She was born in Winfield Hall, her mother was a maid working for Mr. Woolworth."

"Mr. Woolworth of Woolworth stores?"

"Yep. Actually she only worked for him for a couple of years. Mr. Woolworth built Winfield Hall and then died two years later. He was already six months dead when Gran was born, and a few weeks later the house was closed up and they all had to leave. But by then, Gran's father had found a job as a gardener in Westbury and that's where Gran grew up. Her mother eventually found work there as a maid."

Charlie was enjoying Susie's rapt attention and so he continued.

"Gran's father died when she was just nine, his wounds from the war never healed properly I guess. Then, when Gran was sixteen, her mother took off. Seems like she had wanted to leave for a long time, but the man she took off with didn't want a young girl around. So she had persuaded him to wait until Gran's sixteenth birthday; and the next day, they left. She left Gran a note, but she never has told me what's in it. Anyways, Gran took over her mother's job and that's what she was doing when Mr. King saw her."

"Mr. King?" asked Susie.

"Mr. King. People think that Kingsbay is named after the King of England. I mean we're in Dukes County, and that for sure is named after King James of England, and there's Jameston and all; so it stands to reason, right? But actually Kingsbay is named after Mr. Adolphus Cleveland son-of-a-bitch King. Sorry."

This was the first swear word Susie had ever heard from Charlie. "No need to apologize, Charlie."

A silence descended on board *Susie Q*, but this time no one would have described it as companionable, it was tense.

Eventually Charlie continued, "My gran never married, she grew up in Westbury and when she was sixteen, she started to work there. By 1941, Gran was twenty-two; King was thirty-three. Gran had been sent into Jameston to buy some things for the cook. King must have noticed her and seen how pretty she was; because the next thing, word came that there was a better paying job going in a new house in Broad Bay just built by rich New Yorkers, Mr. and Mrs. King. Long story short, Gran got the job and went to work for the Kings. According to Gran, the first few weeks in the new job were fine, but soon Mr. King was after her. He would send for her when his wife was out visiting or shopping, and she had a lot of trouble keeping him off of her. She had finally decided that she would have to leave when Pearl Harbor happened, and King went off to Washington and she didn't see much of him for a few years. She had a sweetheart then, a young man from town called Joe Dawson. In 1943 Joe was called up for service and he went to Europe. And that's where he was killed, in Normandy during the invasion. Gran doesn't speak of him much, but she never had another boyfriend and she never married, so I guess Joe was her true love. His picture is on the wall in her bedroom. When Joe died, Gran volunteered for the Red Cross and went to France herself. I think it was her tribute to Joe."

Charlie paused at this point. This was the longest speech Susie had ever heard from Charlie, but she knew that the story wasn't finished.

Sure enough, after a while he continued.

"When King came back two or three years after the war ended, Gran's troubles started up again, so she made some excuse and she quit. She worked in a few of the other big houses on the North Shore, but after the war the big estates started to close, and service jobs became harder to find. In 1954 she ended up back working for the Kings; she felt that she was too old for Mr. King to bother her anymore. And in fact he didn't, so things were OK for Gran."

"Like most of the owners of the big estates, King had started to build houses on the edge of the property. Those are the houses on the south side of Bayview Drive."

Charlie stopped speaking for the longest time now and they both concentrated on sailing the yacht in silence. Susie sensed that Charlie was upset.

"Charlie, you don't need to tell me anything more, you know."

"No, I want to," he replied. "In 1956 King raped Gran. His wife was away in New York for a few days and the second night King came to Gran's room and raped her. He told her that he had sold the estate to be pulled down for more houses, he'd be moving out in a week and he'd been determined to have her ever since he'd seen her all those years ago."

"Gran knew the police would do nothing. It would be the word of a housekeeper against that of a rich man. But she knew that his wife would believe her, because King had chased other girls over the years. So she went to Mrs. King when she returned, and Mrs. King did believe her; and she made King give Gran the house we live in, which is where my mother was born the next year."

"Oh dear," exclaimed Susie, "that must have been hard for her."

"It was, but she managed. Mrs. King got to hear about the baby somehow and she arranged for Gran to have a little money every year until my mother was sixteen. Gran says that Mrs. King was a saint. Anyway, I'm sure you know the rest of the story Susie; everybody in Kingsbay knows. My mother never married, but one day she was pregnant with me. Of course it wasn't so bad as when Gran was an unmarried mother, but still."

By now Charlie's voice was so low, Susie had to lean towards him to hear. His last words were no more than a whisper, "And then my mother died having me, and Gran looked after me and now we kind of look after each other."

Susie straightened up and looked away so she wouldn't see Charlie's tears. After a while he dried his eyes and she gave him a gentle smile. "Thanks for telling me Charlie, I know it must have been difficult, I feel very special that you trusted me."

After a pause, Susie smiled at Charlie again, "Now how about lunch?"

They sailed on, and soon after noon *Susie Q* was tied up at Jake's Crabbe Shack. Susie and Charlie worked their way through a dozen crabs, washed down by a couple of cold beers. By mutual unspoken agreement, they kept the conversation light and soon they were laughing at Susie's tales of life in a Catholic girls' school. After a particularly funny tale, Charlie noticed a few of the other customers looking at them and smiling.

'*They think we're a couple*,' he thought, and he had a moment of enjoying the guys being jealous of him with his beautiful girlfriend. Just as quickly however he had another, much deeper insight; '*Susie would never be my girlfriend*', but she was his very good friend and he loved her and he felt great about that, really great.

The lighthearted mood stayed with them during the pleasant sail back to Kingsbay where they arrived just after six o'clock. Susie was aware of a subtle change in Charlie; he seemed more relaxed, more at ease, even teasing her at one point when she misjudged the wind when she was bringing the boat about. She guessed, wrongly as it happened, that it had to do with getting his story off his chest.

For the rest of the summer Susie made a point of calling in to visit Gran Betty, as she took to calling her, at least once every two weeks. She told Charlie that she would be happy to sit with Gran if Charlie wanted to go out of an evening, but he never took up her offer. Still, he was happy enough to leave Gran when they went sailing, although Susie learned that he always prepared a lunch for her before he set out.

In time Charlie told Susie about his computer hacking activities and gave her a lecture on her own computer security. He wasn't convinced that she was paying enough attention. So one day, before they went sailing, Charlie sat Susie down on the top step of his front porch, dropped down beside her with his laptop and, while she watched, appalled, he broke into her Facebook account, her email account and then brought up a profile of her that was available for purchase, showing her online shopping history and her record of parking and speeding tickets, the last one still unpaid. "Do you want me to get rid of that for you?" he teased.

"Yes, please; no, no, no, what am I thinking? Of course not. My God, Charlie you're frightening me!

OK, show me again about good passwords. Could you really cancel the ticket?"

When Susie came into the house after that first sail with just her and Charlie she called out, "Hi Andy, I'm home!" There was no reply. He wasn't in the kitchen or the family room or out on the deck. Eventually she found him in his office in the basement. "Hi honey, what are you doing down here, come sit on the deck with me, it's a lovely evening. How was your game?"

Andy swung round in his seat, "I just need to deal with a work thing for a few more minutes honey, I'll be up shortly."

It was actually over an hour before he emerged and he was very withdrawn when he did appear. However, he assured her that it was nothing, just work stuff and a bad day on the golf course. He had lost his match on the last hole, after holding a four hole lead with only five to play. He had lost each of the final five holes.

They watched TV after dinner until eventually Susie announced that she was tired and ready for bed.

"You go on up, I'll be up in a while, I'll just go down and finish off an email."

Susie decided to leave him be. If he wanted to talk about it, he would.

In fact Andy was totally stressed. He had been walking to the fourteenth tee while his opponent took a quick comfort break. He had nothing much on his mind except that if he could win this hole, the match was over. Suddenly, from nowhere the fully formed thought came into his head, *They'll look at Charlie's bank account and see my transfers in and out.'* He was completely unsettled, and of course could not get the thought out of his mind, nor the thought that he had been incredibly, unbelievably stupid not to think of this before.

He stumbled through the final holes, losing them all badly, and rushed home. He sat in his office trying to figure out what to do. Nothing came to him, he couldn't change the past. He tried to imagine the steps the SEC guys would go through. The key question was whether they would look behind Charlie's transactions. By the time he went back to his office after having stared at the TV for a few hours, taking in nothing, he was beginning to calm down. All of his initial thoughts were still valid. Even if Charlie's name came up as being on both lists of traders in the suspect stocks, so what? They still wouldn't link Charlie to him. And why look at Charlie's bank account anyway? The source of the money wasn't an issue, after all the transactions had been tiny by Wall Street standards.

But, if they did get to Charlie, how would he react to pressure? Would he tell them about his good friend, Andy?

He finally went to bed after two in the morning, but lay awake the rest of the night. No matter how he tried to persuade himself, there was always a tiny doubt, a small voice in his head telling him that it would all come out.

On Monday he went back to work, alert to any sign of suspicion, but everything was completely normal, at least as far as he was concerned.

On Tuesday just after noon his mobile rang, it was Vivien, she was in the cafe opposite the front door of his office. He went down to join her.

"Andy, I came to say that I don't want to see you again, I mean, to be with you again."

"What the hell, Viv? What's happened? Last week was great wasn't it?"

"Wednesday was amazing, but that has to be the last time. I need to stop this before it goes any further. Anyway, Mary comes home in a couple of weeks."

"But you can come into the city surely?"

"No, Andy, I mean it, no more."

He kept on at her for five minutes, but Vivien was adamant; the affair was over. Sure they'd see each other in the neighborhood, and she hoped that they could simply be friendly, but no more time alone, no more sex.

"I need to go Andy, I just wanted to tell you face-to-face."

Vivien leaned across the table, kissed his cheek, and left.

CRUISE

A year earlier Andy had explained to Susie that his income would drop when he took the new job in the M&A group, but that it would be a much better opportunity in the long run. She was content with that, and realized that she had to help keep their budget under control. So late in January she had hatched a plan for a summer vacation that would be fun and cheap. Over dinner she explained her idea to her husband.

"Andy, I've been thinking about the summer and I have an idea for a vacation," she saw the look on his face. "Listen, I think you'll like it, I think you may love it actually. Why don't we have a sailing holiday? And not just us. We could organize two or three other couples and take a couple of boats all the way to Montauk, or Sag Harbor, or even round to the Hamptons, but we'd sleep on board, so it would be really cheap and I'm sure we'd have a great time. What do you think?"

"I think that is a really brilliant idea honey. Really great. Who did you have in mind?"

"The Petersens of course, and then I thought we could invite Sophie and Will and maybe Anne and Ted. I think Anne would really appreciate us all getting to know Ted better; I think she's going to accept his proposal one of these days, and you seem to get on well with him, even if they are a bit older. I would suggest some of your poker friends, but other than Pete, they all have kids, which complicates things; they don't have Alejandra and the MacLeods on permanent sitting standby."

"I think they're all great choices Susie, I'll mention it to Pete, but I don't think they'll come. Perhaps we could invite the others to meet us for an overnight somewhere nearby, on our way back - I mean with all the kids. That could be fun."

"Great, I'm glad you like the idea. I'll try to get the main group organized and then you can ask the others about the overnight trip. I'm aiming for September, when it might be a little cooler."

It turned out that in August, Andy explained that he had to attend a two-week intensive summer training program on international securities practices to help him with his new responsibilities. So

Sophie's choice of September for their vacation was very convenient indeed.

As Andy had predicted, Pete and Donna declined to join the sailing trip; everyone knew that Donna got seasick just thinking about sailing. But everyone else had loved Susie's idea, and dates were quickly organized. They decided that they would sail in the Petersens' 45 foot Island Packet cutter '*Luckie*' and Ted's lovely Swan 47 he had named '*My Office*'. The only change was that they would spend one night in a luxury hotel on Shelter Island where they could enjoy a long bath and a blowout dinner. Even Andy was happy with this alteration to the plan.

From the minute they cast off from the marina, it was clear that they were going to have a wonderful trip. Sophie, Will and Anne were novices, but all of the others were experienced sailors, so swapping crews was easy and after the first day they could even change skippers without a problem. One lovely, lazy day followed another. They had decided to find a decent restaurant for lunch or dinner each day, otherwise they would grill something light, usually fish, and make lots of salads. Each crew took turns hosting onboard meals, so everyone had lots of downtime to lie back, admire the views and join in the desultory conversations about life, the universe and everything. '*My Office*' was more luxurious and a much faster yacht, but '*Luckie*' was more forgiving and more spacious below decks, so everyone was happy to be on either boat.

They spent four or five hours ashore each day, either after a long lunch, or before dinner. Between the four couples, they knew most of the good eating places and cute villages on the Long Island shoreline. Will was able to point out some of the luxury waterfront mansions where his company had installed pool houses, boathouses, gazebos or other projects.

"We're thinking of getting into shoreline protection. The climate change guys say there will be more storms and they'll be stronger. I've been looking at buying a small quarry, so we could have our own supply of rip rap boulders."

"You guys seem to keep busy," observed Ted, "I see your trucks around a lot."

"Yes, we're lucky. But since Uncle Francisco retired, we've struggled to find someone to take charge of our finishing teams. It isn't easy finding real craftsmen who will teach their skills to others. But we'll get there, right Sophie?"

"We always do, thank God." She made a quick sign of the cross, "What about you Andy? Susie tells me you've been really busy for a couple of months now, since before your course in August."

"The course was a killer. I'd get home at ten and head straight to bed, exhausted. I've been working on a deal in London. The time difference is murder. I'm usually at my desk by 6.30 in the morning and a couple of times we've hung on until 2 a.m. to have a call with the Brits coming in to work in the morning. The good news is that it will be over soon and I can sleep for a week."

"Well, it's good that the economy is picking up at last," said Frank. "We're seeing an uptick in zoning requests, so more construction for you Will," he teased.

Ted added, "I heard Cliff Walker is buying a big new boat, so I guess his landscaping business is doing OK. He sold Happy Hours III for a good price and is buying Happy Hours IV at the Miami spring boat show." Ted was not aware of the history between Cliff and Susie. Anne filled him in later that night.

They were almost half way through their cruise, and Frank decided they should sail northeast of Plum Island before turning for Shelter Island. As they passed Plum Island, Andy couldn't help showing off to Frank and Ted who were on '*Luckie*' with him.

"Do you know, if you fired a bullet due east from us right now, it would pass through the gaps between Corsica and Sardinia, between Asia and Africa at the Bosphorus and between Honshu and Hokkaido islands in Japan."

"Wow, cool trivia Andy!" exclaimed Ted.

When they checked into their rooms at the hotel on Shelter Island, there were polo shirts on their beds.

On the right breast there was an image of a stylized sailboat against a setting sun with words around the image, *'My Luckie Office Cruise 2013'*. They all appeared for dinner in their new shirts. It was Ted's doing, but he brushed it off, "They were happy to do me favor. In my business I must buy a thousand of these shirts every year. They owed me."

Still he flushed and smiled when Jill, Sophie and then Susie came up and kissed his cheek. "It was a lovely, lovely thought Ted, thank you." Jill spoke for everyone.

They had arranged to meet up with Brian, Geoff, Joe and their families off Hobart Beach Park, in Northport Bay, an easy sail for the kids. The MacLeods would also be on one of the boats with Kevin and Lucy. The five boats anchored close to each other and a bunch of inflatable toys appeared. Eventually everyone assembled on the beach and Geoff and Joe rowed an inflatable dinghy ashore with coolers full of food and drinks, charcoal and a portable grill. While everyone was eating, Joe Jr. came up to Frank with a very serious look on his face.

"Mr. Petersen, I'm sorry to tell you that you've spelled the name of your boat wrong, it should be L-U-C-K-Y. Sorry Mr. Petersen."

Frank smiled and called his son over, "Kevin, can you explain to Joe Jr. how *'Luckie'* got her name?"

"When we decided to buy a new yacht, my mom said we were very lucky to be getting one, and Dad decided *'Lucky'* would be a good name for our boat. Before we actually got it, I realized that if we called it *'Lucky'*, Lucy would think it was her boat and not mine, 'cause it would have nearly her name. So Dad said we could spell it L-U-C-K-I-E, which has three letters from Lucy and three from Kevin. Dad's good at stuff like that."

A little later the adults could see that all nine kids were having an apparently serious conversation, well, serious for all of them apart from Margaret Hooper who was only three and sitting contentedly on Jenna Russell's lap having her hair braided.

"I wonder what all that's about," mused Anne.

"I think I have an idea," said Susie, "I overheard a couple of them earlier. I hope Ted has another favor to call in." she added mysteriously.

After a few more minutes the kids came over to the adults, with Jenna in the lead.

"Mr. Ted," she started. The neighborhood kids struggled with the idea that Ted wasn't 'Mr. Murphy' and so had spontaneously decided upon 'Mr. Ted', which was fine with him.

"Mr. Ted, I've been telling them that they shouldn't worry, you've probably arranged for our shirts to be back in Kingsbay, right? I mean we're on the cruise too aren't we?" She smiled sweetly, looking Ted straight in the eyes.

"Quite right Jenna," Ted stifled a laugh. "The second batch are being delivered to our house next

Tuesday I think. I wasn't sure about sizes for all you kids, so maybe you could write them down for me?"

"No problem, Mr. Ted. See guys, I told you." They all ran off, cheering.

"How the heck did they even know? I mean there are only three of us wearing the shirts today. And how did they know it was Ted? How do kids figure this stuff out so quickly? Did you tell them Susie?" Anne was mystified.

"No, I swear," insisted Susie, "I heard Joe Jr. asking Jenna if she had noticed the shirts, that's all."

Ted was smiling as he observed, "A born salesman that young woman. You'll notice she didn't even have to ask for the shirts. When she said, 'See guys, I told you', I don't think she meant *I told you he had ordered our shirts*', I think she meant, *'I told you I'd get him to buy us all shirts!'* "

THANKSGIVING 2013

Andy had not been exaggerating when he complained about how busy he had been; he really was working all hours of the day. Susie had become used to barely seeing him in the morning, as he left while it was still dark; and most nights he came home around ten o'clock, sometimes later and sometimes not at all. He had taken a couple of clean shirts into work so he had a change for the nights when he just didn't come home.

"Don't worry honey, it won't be for much longer, then I'll never pull these kind of hours again. Promise."

So Susie was surprised and a little hurt when Andy told her that he would be making an effort to get home in time for poker night the week before Thanksgiving. However she was mollified when he explained that it was because he had invited Ted to play for the first time, and Frank wouldn't be there, thanks to some conference he had to attend.

"I feel I really need to go with him, since he is my guest, and we talked about him playing with the group way back in July."

Andy called Ted in the afternoon and told him that he would pick him around seven o'clock.

As they walked around to Geoff's house, Andy surprised Ted by telling him about the first two trades.

"I needed to tell you Ted, because another deal is about to close and tonight I'll be asking the guys if they want in. I didn't want you to be sitting there with no idea what we're talking about. And of course, you're welcome to join in or not as you prefer. It's all the same to me one way or another."

"Is Frank part of the investing group?"

"No, and neither is Joe or Pete. Will hasn't been in before, but he's told me that he and Sophie will be in this time along with Luis, her father. Brian and Geoff will both be in again."

When he felt the moment was right, Andy set out the third deal.

"OK, guys, after the success last time, the ante for this deal is $200,000."

There were a few intakes of breath and then silence.

Then Brian spoke, "Andy, I don't want you to think I'm not grateful, and I understand why you wanted us all in for the same stake, so there would be no hard feelings. However, I've been in from the start and I think we should be able to reinvest our profits, even if that takes us over the base amount."

Andy looked around, "Does anyone have any problem with that?"

No one did. In the end Brian came in for $600,000, Geoff for $500,000 and Will and Pete agreed to put up $200,000 each. Ted had intended staying out, but he was influenced by Geoff and Brian upping their stakes, and by Pete participating at all. He decided to risk $200,000.

Joe continued to decline and Andy didn't even look for Frank later on to ask him.

"OK, everyone, please get your funds to me by Tuesday first thing. I'll send my bank details to those who need them."

On Saturday morning, Andy and Charlie were prepping *Susie Q* for a sail when Cliff Walker appeared at the marina.

"Andy, could I have a word?"

Cliff was standing on the grass and clearly wanted Andy to go over to him.

"Thanks for coming over Andy, I didn't want that fucking weirdo kid listening to us. I think he's probably a fag. Look, I noticed you and Susie missed the Halloween party again and I feel bad about that. It could be that she misunderstood me a couple of years ago and that's why you guys are staying away. Do you think I should talk to her, tell her she was mistaken, everything is cool and she should come to the parties again?"

Andy pretended to think about the question. The truth was that he was having a moment of clarity: He absolutely detested Cliff Walker.

"You know Cliff, I don't think I would. Why not leave it with me and I'll talk to her when the right moment comes along. You know how you have to pick your moment with women."

"Too true, OK I'll leave it with you." He turned to walk away and Andy made an on the spot decision.

"Cliff, walk with me a minute, no this way, away from the clubhouse. I hear you'll be buying a new boat in the spring?"

"In February at Miami, she's a beauty, brand new and built to my exact specs."

"That's what I thought. Cliff, can I tell you something in complete confidence, a total secret?"

"Sure," Cliff was, of course, intrigued.

Andy laid out the deal for him, first explaining how much they had made on the first two deals.

"Cliff, you're one of the big men in Kingsbay, it seems to me a good idea to ask if you want a piece of the action this time around. I have to tell you that other guys are in for between $200,000 and $600,000."

Cliff's face flushed, "Is Brian Russell in your group? I bet he is, he's been like a dog with two dicks lately. I bet he is."

Andy said nothing.

"I'm in for $600,000 Andy, and thanks, I won't forget it."

Andy worked all day on Sunday, and on Monday morning he gently woke Susie up.

"Are you awake honey?"

Susie shook her head slowly, "No," she moaned.

"Listen honey, I can't come with you to Vermont on Wednesday. I have to work all through the holiday. They don't have Thanksgiving in London, who knew?" He said with a wan smile.

Months and months ago, they had arranged to spend Thanksgiving with Susie's family and had bought plane tickets back in August.

"You should go anyway, I mean I'm not going to be home much at all, but the deal closes on Friday and I'll be done with this work, work, work crap. Promise."

"Oh, Andy, you really can't go? Everyone will be disappointed; I'm disappointed."

"I know sweetheart, I know, and I'll make it up to you. Maybe we could go to Vermont for Christmas this year. Would that be good?"

"That would be great, I'd love that ..."

After some hesitation, and another apologetic smile from Andy, Susie conceded, "OK honey, I know you've worked really hard on this, so I'll forgive you this time."

She kissed him slowly and deeply.

"No, you hussy! I can't, I've been waiting an hour to wake you up, I've got to go. I'll see you tonight. I'll try not to be too late."

He kept to his word and wasn't too late coming home. They had a simple meal and afterwards they made love on the sofa.

On Tuesday he came home at 9:30 p.m. As soon as he came into the family room he asked her, "Susie, why didn't you answer the phone? I tried calling, like six times."

"The phone didn't ring once. You should have tried my cell, I have it right beside me." She held up her iPhone.

"Call the house number, honey."

Susie dialed the house number on her cell and held it to her ear.

"It's ringing," she said. But obviously it wasn't, the house phone was silent.

"Shit, there must be a fault. I'll call it in from the office tomorrow, but I don't suppose they'll fix it on the holiday."

On Wednesday morning first thing, Andy purchased the options. He then went to find his boss and reminded him that he had to leave at noon to take Susie to the airport.

"Don't worry Andy, you've earned it. No one has put in more hours over the last couple of months."

"Thanks, Alan, but first we've got the conference call with London and Frankfurt at ten."

Andy made it home with time to spare. He helped Susie with some last minute packing, and at 2:30 he threw her cases onto the rear seat of his car and they set off for JFK. Even though it was the day before Thanksgiving, they were early enough to miss the worst of the traffic.

In good time, Andy drove into the yellow car park for terminal 5 and made his way up through the levels, "Look honey, we must have led good lives, a spot right opposite the skywalk."

He grabbed Susie's bags and wheeled them through to the JetBlue check-in area. It looked like chaos. This was the busiest travel day of the year, and it showed. However the staff were used to it and the apparent chaos was in reality under some control. Eventually Susie was checked in and they walked to the security area.

"OK honey, this is where I leave you. Have a great time, give everyone a hug and tell them I'll see them at Christmas."

"I'm sorry you're not coming. I love you."

"Love you to, honey," he held her tight and crushed her lips with his kiss.

"Hey, easy there! I'll see you in a few days."

"Call me when you get to your folks."

Susie joined the line to pass through security and Andy backtracked to the skywalk.

In less than ten minutes, Andy was back at his car. He drove out of the car park and fifteen minutes later drove into a different car park, this time a tired looking, off-airport facility offering long-term covered parking. He carefully backed into a spot, not backing up too far. Before cutting the engine, Andy opened the driver side window fully. Then he got out, popped the trunk and took out a large suitcase and a carry-on.

As he walked away, he looked back. The BMW projected a couple of inches in front of its neighbors, not enough to be in danger, but enough to be visible. The key was still in the ignition, the window was open and the doors unlocked. It looked exactly like a car waiting to be stolen for its insurance money.

He walked to the waiting elevator and pushed the button for the first floor. He found the line for the shuttle to take him back to JFK.

He glanced at his watch, he had plenty of time.

REALIZATION

When Susie finally walked into Arrivals at JFK a few days later, she was ready to get home as quickly as possible. The drive from her parents' home to Burlington Airport had taken almost two hours in driving snow, then there had been all the usual security hassles; her flight took off forty-five minutes late and there was a long delay before she could collect her checked in bag. In other words, a typical twenty-first century flight.

As she came through the automatic door, she was intently scanning the waiting crowds for Andy. She walked slowly past the line of hopeful looking drivers lifting up iPads or cardboard signs with names of passengers, hotels or unlikely sounding conventions. Could there really be a '23rd Annual Symposium on Conference Title Etymology'? she wondered. She couldn't see her husband. She retraced her steps back along the line with the same disappointing result. Now she was becoming a little agitated; surely he wasn't late? He couldn't have forgotten, they had talked only this morning. She found a quieter space to stand, took out her cellphone and called his number. It didn't ring, but went straight to voicemail. She tried the house, but it just rang and rang, which didn't surprise her, she was pretty sure the home phone was still not working.

She called his cell again; straight to voicemail again. Now she started to worry. Could he have had an accident? If he had run out of gas or had a flat or something stupid, he would surely have called and left a message. She checked her own voicemail just in case, even though she had no missed call message. Nothing. Now she wasn't sure what to do. Should she hang around the airport in case he showed up, or go home and wait? She decided to have a coffee and if he still hadn't appeared, she would take a cab home.

Nearly three hours later, Susie's cab pulled into her driveway. She paid the driver and let herself into the house. Almost immediately, she spotted a folded piece of paper on the kitchen table. She opened it up and read *'Susie, I've gone away. Don't bother trying to find me. Sorry, Andy'*.

She read it twice, trying to take it in.

Susie looked at her watch, it was just gone eight o'clock. She called Jill, "Jill, it's Susie, can you come over for a moment please?" She went through the hall and opened the front door a crack so Jill could come straight in.

A few minutes later, Jill pushed through the door, "Hi there, it's me! How was your trip?"

Susie was still sitting at the kitchen table in her winter coat, still wearing her woolly hat. As Jill came towards her, Susie silently reached up and handed her the note.

"Oh my God! When? How?"

"He wasn't at the airport to pick me up. I waited over an hour then took a cab; I came in and found this. I spoke with him this morning."

"Wasn't Andy in Vermont with you?"

"No, no he couldn't make it; he cried off on Monday, too much work. He's been working incredibly long hours for weeks, months even. But we spoke every day; we spoke just this morning. Did I just say that?"

"Here, take off your coat, let's have a drink, and I'll call Frank."

The three of them sat in the family room, Jill had poured a generous brandy for Susie and smaller measures for herself and Frank.

"We thought he was with you. I haven't seen him all weekend, but then I didn't expect to." Frank continued, "Did you guys fight recently maybe? Was everything OK?"

"Everything was fine. I had come round to accepting the ridiculous hours he was working. We didn't even fight when he told me he wasn't coming to Vermont. He said we'd go up for Christmas. Jesus, Frank, he talked with my folks on Thursday to wish them Happy Thanksgiving!"

"Look, Susie, it sounds like maybe work got to him, too much stress and he just flipped out. I admit the note is kind of weird, but he may just have driven off to clear his head." Frank didn't sound too convinced himself. The note could easily have said, *'Need a break, be back in a week'*. He could have signed it with love, but he hadn't.

"I think you should call his boss in the morning, and get a handle on what was happening there."

"Do you want me to sleep over, honey?" asked Jill.

"No, I'll be fine. I am fine. To be honest I feel like I'm in a movie, that this isn't really happening. Maybe I'll feel different in the morning."

But in the morning she felt just the same. She had slept well; her first waking thought was that Andy had gone, but she still didn't feel any real emotion. She looked through his closet and his drawers and saw that some clothes were missing. His passport was still in the drawer with his belts, so that was something, a part of her brain processed. Around ten she called his office, and eventually found herself talking with his boss, Alan.

"He's been working crazy hours, Susie, that's true, but so has the whole team; although Andy was particularly keen on this deal. He had a big role and I assumed he was hoping for a promotion at the end of it, and he could get one I think."

"When did you decide to work on Thanksgiving?" she asked.

"We didn't work on Thanksgiving. We worked on Wednesday, although Andy left early to take you to the airport, and the rest of the team worked Friday, which was closing day for the deal. I must admit, I was surprised when Andy didn't show up Friday, but his part of the paperwork was finished anyway. I assumed that he had just crashed. But I'm the only one of the team in today, everyone was told to come back Wednesday."

This new information began to crack Susie's composure. On Thursday morning, Andy had told her that he was calling from the office, she clearly recalled him talking about how the room with the coffee machine was locked, and everyone was bitching about it. That meant he had been lying to her for days.

Alan had nothing else to tell her, "Maybe he just got stressed out, I'm sure he'll be back Wednesday with everyone else."

On Monday evening Frank called Brian Russell.

"Hi Brian, can I come over for a minute?"

"Yeh, sure. What do you want to talk about, Frank?"

"I'd rather explain when I see you."

When they were sitting in Brian's basement, Frank asked him, "Do you remember the stock deal you did with Andy last year?"

"Of course, worked out great. And the next ones too."

"Ah, that's what I was going to ask you, so there were more deals?"

"Two, one is still on, it should close by the end of the week."

"Dammit!" Frank Petersen *never* swore; Brian knew this had to be bad. "Brian, I have to tell you, Andy's missing, he's gone off somewhere and Susie has no idea where he is. He's been gone since, well probably since last Wednesday, but for sure since yesterday."

"Christ! I gave him $600,000 on Tuesday. And I think Geoff maybe gave him the same, or close enough. And the other guys all gave him money. Jesus, what a mess; what a huge fucking mess."

Now it was Frank turn to be stunned. "$600,000! Really! Six hundred? Good God, Brian, what were you guys doing?"

"Come on Frank, you saw how it was, Andy had a tip I guess, I don't know. Anyway, it worked out the first time, I made like $130,000, which I gave to

Andy for the second deal and that one made another four hundred and something, so I gave him all of it on Tuesday."

"Who else got into this?"

"Geoff was in for the last two and Pete, Will and Ted all got in for the last deal, for $200,000 each I assume."

"Ted? OK, we need to get on this right now. Let's get them over here."

They were all at home and within thirty minutes they were in Brian's basement and they all knew that Andy was missing, and they had a growing feeling that their money was too.

"I said no, twice; why the hell did I go for it third time?" asked Pete, with his head in his hands, "Donna's gonna rip me a new one over this when she finds out!"

"OK guys, who all knows about this?"

Will answered first. "I discussed it with Sophie and Luis, Oh God, Luis! Half of the money was Luis's."

"Brian?"

"Yeah, Pauline knows."

"Geoff?"

"No, Frank, I was going to tell Caroline when we hit the jackpot with this third deal."

"Well, I think you all need to talk to your wives and lawyers and then we should meet again and figure out what we do next."

"Lawyers? Why should we talk to our lawyers?"

"Geoff, I know you didn't know exactly what Andy was doing with the money, but a prosecutor could argue that you had to have a pretty good idea he was trading on inside information from his job. I have no idea if you guys broke any laws, but I'm pretty sure Andy did. And I hope you all reported the money to the IRS. Meanwhile I think it would be best if we didn't discuss this with anyone else."

After hearing Frank's shocking news late Monday night, Jill called Susie from her desk first thing Tuesday morning.

"Susie, you need to go online or call your bank and find out how much money is in your account. Do it now, honey. I'll be home early and I'll come by."

Susie went online to discover that they were overdrawn by almost $400,000.

She called the bank and wasted half an hour trying to talk with someone intelligent who knew anything about their account. She called her father and told him what was happening. He arranged to fly down the next day. Then she called Jill back and asked her to bring a recommendation for a lawyer when she came to the house later. When she finished her call, she realized that she was still using her cell phone for all her calls. She called the phone company and discovered that no fault had been reported, and someone would be out in two days to look at her installation. In due course she discovered that Andy had deliberately unscrewed the line to disconnect them.

Jill called again at four, to tell her that Sophie and Anne would also be coming round, probably about 5:30 and would bring pizzas. Susie thought to herself, *'They're already forming a support group'.*

However, when the four women sat down to tackle the pizzas, it soon became clear that Anne and Sophie had come, not just to support Susie, but to tell her yet more terrible news.

Sophie had appointed herself spokeswoman. "Susie honey, I'm afraid that there's more bad news, but we want you to know, really know, that it doesn't affect anything at all. OK?"

Susie had no idea what she was talking about, but said nothing.

"Susie, Andy stole money from other people as well as from you."

Jill had obviously passed on the information about the overdraft, which surprised Susie, until Sophie continued. "He took money from Brian Russell, Geoff Hooper, Pete Woods ... and from Will and Ted."

This was finally too much for Susie to bear. She pushed herself away from the table and ran, sobbing, up the stairs. The other three sat for a few minutes and then Sophie stood up.

"I'll go," she said quietly and followed the sound of Susie's sobs to her bedroom.

Twenty minutes later, Susie and Sophie reappeared. Susie was a bit of a mess, but seemed to be over the worst of her tears.

"I've explained to Susie that no one was blaming her even before they knew that Andy had cleaned her out as well," Sophie told the others, "and, a piece of good news, Susie's dad is coming here tomorrow."

Jill spoke up, "That's great news Susie. Here are the details for Bobby Ronconi. He's a friend, and the smartest personal lawyer in the city, he'll be a great help. Honey, when does your dad get in tomorrow?"

"At three, at La Guardia."

"Good, that's easier than Kennedy. Listen, why doesn't Frank meet your dad and bring him here. Frank can explain the situation while they drive here. He knows all about the involvement of the poker club Susie, although neither he nor Joe Levine gave Andy any money."

Now Anne spoke up, "Susie, you should also know that everyone affected has agreed to keep all of this quiet, at least until we understand better what happened and what's going to happen. And Pauline and Caroline are just as sure it's not your fault as we are, they wanted us to tell you that, they didn't come tonight because, well just because."

"Because you three are all the friends I could possibly ask for? Sophie, you were lovely again upstairs, thank you. And as for you two..."

"Don't worry about thanking us, we're all in this together. Now listen, I've had another idea. Are you happy to talk with Bobby Ronconi?"

"Of course Jill."

"Then I'm going to call him now, he's probably on his way home. I'll ask him to come here tomorrow about 4:30, then you and Frank can brief your father and Bobby at the same time and you won't have to go through everything twice. What do you think?"

"I think you're all wonderful."

By seven the following evening Bobby Ronconi and Paul Linsley knew everything that Susie and Frank knew about the situation: the poker games, the phone company and the daily calls to Vermont. Andy's note was now in the possession of Bobby, and Susie had told them about her conversation with Andy's boss and about the overdrawn bank account. Paul told them that he would clear the overdraft in the morning.

Bobby intervened, "Please don't, Paul, not just yet. Before we give the bank any money, I need to put them on notice that we don't yet accept that Susie has any responsibility for the debt. She didn't sign anything; I'm not sure I see how the overdraft can have been properly authorized. Let me get something to them to that effect first thing in the morning, and then you can clear the account, so Susie can get on with her life. I'll have the bank ensure that Andy has no further authority over the account."

"Good advice Bobby, thank you."

"You don't have to thank me, I'm Susie's attorney, she expects me to take care of these things, right Susie?"

She smiled weakly and nodded.

Paul had been very impressed indeed by Frank during their conversation in the car, and now he was sure that his daughter had a good attorney on her side. He would stay with Susie for a few days, but he was feeling better just knowing his daughter had good people on her side.

Following Bobby's instructions, Paul cleared Susie's overdraft and set up a monthly transfer to keep his daughter in funds until she resolved her long term future. He had decided to return to Vermont on Monday, but first he was looking forward to meeting Susie's friends for a potluck dinner on Saturday night.

Anne and Ted, the Coopers and the Petersens turned up at six with their contributions for dinner. They all sat around Susie's dining room table enjoying the good food, good wine and good conversation. Susie learned some things about her father that she had never heard before, including stories about girlfriends he had before he met her mother.

"Dad! No more, I don't want to hear!" Susie could barely speak for laughing after a particularly implausible story involving a five star hotel, a conference of evangelical Christians and Paul and his date being caught skinny-dipping in the hotel pool. "How will I face Mom again?"

"Oh, you'd be surprised at what your mom knows. I was seven years older than Mary, she didn't think she was dating a monk."

Just then there was a series of loud bangs at the front door.

"I'll get it," said Will as he rose from his chair by the hall entrance.

They heard the door open, then Will gave a yell and Cliff Walker was standing at the entrance to the dining room. Will followed him in, rubbing a red mark on his cheek where the door had hit him.

"Where is he, where is the little shit?" Cliff yelled. His face was flushed and he smelled strongly of whisky.

Before anyone else could move, Paul Linsley had his face one inch from Cliff's.

He spoke quietly and with real venom, "I don't know who the hell you are, but get the fuck out of my daughter's house before I throw you out on your ass!"

Cliff opened his mouth to speak again, but Paul grabbed his wrist and twisted him around, forcing Cliff's hand up between his shoulder blades. He nodded to Will to open the front door, and frog marched Cliff outside. He gave him a push and Cliff crashed down the entrance steps to the ground.

"When I go back in there, I'll be calling the cops. You can expect a visit from them tomorrow. You'll also be hearing from Susie's attorney. If you set foot on this property, or go near my daughter again, I'll make it my business to see you in jail. Are we clear? Now get your sorry ass off this property."

Paul turned to go back into the house and saw Susie staring at him, open-mouthed, from the doorway.

He smiled gently at his daughter, "Close your mouth sweetheart, it isn't a good look for you."

"I think I need to have a word with your friend, the bishop, about your language, Daddy." She hugged him, and they went back to her friends.

When Paul and Susie returned to the dining table, Frank had been talking. "I was just saying, Susie, I guess we can add Cliff Walker to the list of people stiffed by Andy. I wonder if there are any more?"

But no new victims emerged that week, or later.

The next day was Paul's last full day before he went home.

"There's one more of my friends I'd like you to meet Dad, but I need to see him by myself first, he doesn't know about Andy yet I don't think."

It was now just a week since Susie had come home from the airport to find Andy's note. Without anyone seemingly having had a conversation about it, word was slowly spreading in Kingsbay that all was not well with the Smiths. However Susie was pretty sure that Charlie wouldn't know anything yet, and she wanted to tell him herself. She knew he was close to Andy and that the whole business would upset him.

"Why don't you make a few calls on Cliff Walker's account, while I go see Charlie; then I'll bring him round for a coffee and you can meet him."

As expected, Susie found Charlie at home with Gran. After some innocuous chat, she asked Charlie to take a walk with her down to the marina. They climbed aboard *Susie Q*.

"Charlie, I have to tell you something, it's not very nice I'm afraid."

She told him the story, omitting unimportant details, but telling him about the series of deals, Andy's thefts from their friends and the note he left her. When she was finished, they sat in silence for maybe three minutes, although to Susie it felt much longer.

"Did he steal money from you too Susie?" Charlie finally asked.

"Yes, yes he did Charlie,"

"I can get it back for you," he calmly, but confidently, assured her.

She rested a hand on his arm, "Oh Charlie, you're such a great friend. Thank you honey, but it's OK, my father is pretty well off and he already took care of me, but it means a lot to me that you would offer. But I want you to promise that you won't try to get money for me Charlie, really. All I need to know is that you're OK and that we're still friends."

He looked startled, "Of course we are Susie, you're the best friend I have in the world."

She looked away for a moment and wiped a tear from her cheek.

"My father has been staying with me this week Charlie, but he goes back to Vermont tomorrow. I told him I'd like him to meet a special friend before he left. He's expecting us for a coffee. Would you come?"

"Sure Susie, I'll come. I've never been in your house."

Susie looked at him, surprised. "Do you know, you're right. How strange. Well, let's go fix that right now."

"That young man worships you Susie, you do know that?"

"I guess I kind of do know that Dad. But the strange thing is that it isn't, you know, difficult? And I'm really very fond of him."

"Yes, I could see that. You seem more like his favorite big sister I guess. But just be careful Susie, for his sake. I think he's quite vulnerable."

"Maybe one day I'll tell you why Dad, but not now. Let's call it a day shall we? Are you packed? I expect Mom will be glad to have you home."

"I sure hope so, honey."

INTERNATIONAL RELATIONS

Andy's business class ticket gave him access to the airline lounge at Arrivals in London. He had a shower, changed his clothes and enjoyed an English breakfast. Then he found an empty cubicle in the business center and lifted his carry-on bag onto the desk and opened it. His first thought was that buying a proper briefcase would be high on his shopping list. He took out a plastic carrier bag holding a one-inch thick stack of papers. All of his preparations were documented in these papers: the Panamanian company registration; Luxembourg, Swiss and UK bank details, and the short-term rental agreement for his London apartment, or flat as he needed to get used to calling it. Finding the flat would have been much more difficult if he hadn't spent time in London all those years ago and had at least some ideas about different sections of the city. He took out his cell and ordered a car to take him into the city.

Three weeks later, Andy was completely settled in London. He was enjoying his flat in the heart of Mayfair, he had settled on three favorite restaurants, and he had found a sports bar near the American Embassy in Grosvenor Square that had American sports on TV all day. That afternoon he had an appointment with one of the top realtors in London, or estate agents as they were called here. He took a black cab to the agent's office.

"£8 million, in a portfolio of properties with good rental yields and reasonable capital growth prospects. I'll be buying through a Panama company if that matters. Can you put something together for me to look at?"

In forty-eight hours it was all arranged, in two weeks it was completed. London really did feel like the easiest place on the planet to invest money with no questions asked. He celebrated by walking across the street to a yacht brokerage. In even less time he, or rather his Panamanian company, was the owner of a one-year-old Hinckley 59 adapted for single-handed sailing. He decided to celebrate and headed for Nobu, one of London's best Japanese restaurants. He was early, so decided to have a drink in Nabokov first.

Nabokov could have been in LA or New York or Paris. It catered to the expensive tastes of rich Russians, one or two of whom had made their money legitimately. The oddly tanned, overweight men with no visible necks, were outnumbered two to one by impossibly thin, surreally gorgeous young women who could have stepped out of a lingerie ad, and in some cases had. Andy stood out in this crowd. His jacket was a little rumpled, his shoes were designed for a boat, not a cocktail bar, and his nails had never been tended by a manicurist. Most of all, he failed to exude the slight air of menace which was obligatory in the Nabokov milieu. However, he was young, slim, and very handsome, and it seemed that he could afford to order his drinks without first checking the price list.

Valentina was bored, really bored. She had been nursing a glass of Crystal while listening with half an ear to the inane chatter around her. This was her life these days and she was B-O-R-E-D. She spotted Andy and, although she knew it was a crazy move, she walked up to the bar.

"Would you like to buy me a drink? Or we could go somewhere else?"

"Please don't misunderstand me," Andy replied, "but are you a professional?"

She laughed, "No, but thanks for the compliment. I'm bored. And hungry."

"What about the food here?"

"Terrible; pretend Russian, expensive."

"OK, let's go round the corner."

He decided Nobu was too close to Nabokov in spirit, so he led her around the corner to Langan's. Mostly unchanged since the 1970s, Langan's served very good, very traditional food in an understated, unpretentious atmosphere. Andy was pretty certain that Valentina would never have crossed its threshold. He was right.

"I've never been here before. That's nice. By the way, my name is Valentina."

"Hi Valentina, I'm Andrew. This is a very nice restaurant, I hope you like it."

The waiter gave each of them a one sheet menus and they looked it over.

"It's so cheap! How can it be so cheap, this is Mayfair?" Valentina wanted to know.

They ordered, or rather, Andy ordered for both of them. Valentina was regretting her decision as she looked around the faded walls covered with interesting, but inexpensive looking art.

The food arrived and, against her better judgment, Valentina tried some of it. It was surprisingly good. She looked around again, slower this time. To her amazement, she started to recognize a few of the other diners. An actor who had a part in the last Bond movie, with a very striking girl whose face was frustratingly familiar, although Valentina couldn't quite place her. A woman that she had seen when she watched a political program on the BBC. Valentina was not really as stupid as she sometimes chose to pretend.

"There are famous people here aren't there?" she asked.

"I have no idea. I like Mayfair and I like the food here. This is my favorite local restaurant."

Much later a waiter explained that Langan's was a low-key refuge for celebrities who wanted to get away from the glitz and glamor of most of the restaurants in Mayfair.

The relationship between Andy and Valentina was unusual on several levels. They asked no questions of each other, no questions about the past, the future, about why they rarely called each other. They spent three or four nights together each week, but never inquired about the other nights. They seldom talked on the phone. The barman in Langan's was their go-between. Andy just had to accept that there were many nights when she couldn't see him. Sometimes he discovered this via a text while sitting at the bar waiting for her. But when they were together they had fantastic sex. Neither of them was much interested in theater or concerts or galleries; they were very compatible in that regard. They took in new movies when they opened, they watched TV and they had lots and lots of sex. Andy never saw the inside of Valentina's flat, and she rarely slept over in his.

They never went back to Nabokov's, or to any other hangout of the Russian expat community. Valentina insisted on eating at Langan's almost every time they went out for dinner.

"I like it, we know people there now, the staff are nice and there are no big, fat, stupid Russians."

Andy and Valentina had been seeing each other for almost three months when one evening, seemingly out-of-the-blue, he surprised her while they lay in his bed.

"I'm leaving London, leaving for good."

Valentina was nestled in his arm.

"For good? You mean like forever?"

"Yes, forever; I may come back for a few days now and then, but I won't be living here."

"Where are you going?"

"Spain, where it is warm and sunny and not so crazy."

"I'll come with you, take me with you." As she said this, Valentina realized that she was serious, she really did want to go with him. She turned over to face him, leaning on one elbow. "Look Andrew, I'm not going to pretend. We're not crazy in love, but we get along OK, no? And it's fun in bed, no? So why not take me? Why not?"

"It's not going to be first class Valentina, not even business class some of the time. I'm not sure that this is what you want."

"How do you know? I hate London now, except when I'm with you. It's just the same bars, the same clubs, the same party that goes on forever. Why not give me a chance?"

They talked it over for a week, on and off. In the end, he agreed. She wasn't Einstein, but then neither was he. She was easy company and the sex was fantastic.

He took her down to Portsmouth to see the yacht, which had been delivered the previous week. All of the modifications he had ordered had been done perfectly. Her new name '*Aywol*' had been written in an elegant script across the stern and at the bow.

"So, do you think you could live on this for two months?"

"Two months! Wow. That is a long time. Yes, I could live here with you for two months, it could be fun. I'll have my Kindle; I'll learn Spanish and I'll bring lots of box sets. Yes, I could do this."

Departure was set for ten days time.

"Can we leave in the afternoon Andrew? I would like to come down from London and just leave. Would that be OK?"

"Sure, that's fine, we don't need to worry about tides here. Don't bring too much stuff Valentina, it all has to be stowed. No suitcases, bring soft bags that can be folded up. We can buy you some new clothes in Spain. I'll be coming back down in two days and will spend the week getting everything ready and putting some supplies aboard."

From his arrival in London, Andy had taken to introducing himself as Andrew. He had a natural tendency to mimic the accents of people around him, and after just three weeks, his accent had become Mid-Atlantic; to an American he sounded vaguely uptown, probably an Easterner. Meanwhile to an Englishman, Andy sounded oddly dislocated - perhaps like one of those Scandinavians who speak perfect, unaccented English. Now and then he would use an American term which would reveal his true nationality. Of course Valentina simply assumed that he was what he seemed; a vaguely wealthy, attractive Englishman. Andy was on his way to forging a new identity. He surprised himself at how little he thought about his life in America. In a year he would be fully European, except perhaps for his continuing absorption with the Giants and the Yankees.

He had taken the new yacht out on his own a couple of times. He was delighted with how she handled and pleased with the modifications he had ordered. The only real challenge was docking by himself. So far he had been lucky, there had been knowledgeable sailors on the pontoon on both of his returns, ready to take his lines and make them fast quickly and with no fuss. He wasn't looking forward to arriving at a deserted marina in poor weather, but he would cross that particular bridge when he encountered it. Maybe Valentina would be a help after all.

Their departure was on a good sailing day; overcast, but with a steady wind from just the right quarter. They sailed past Gosport and out into the Solent where the wind freshened. They passed the Isle of Wight to starboard and soon they were in the English Channel proper. Valentina sat watching intently, gradually understanding some of the various ropes; sheets, Andrew called them, what they did and how he used them to control the boat. She was determined to make herself useful during their voyage.

Andy had decided to take it easy for the first few days until he was well and truly familiar with the yacht. So his aim that first afternoon was simply to come around the Isle of Wight to Ventnor on the south coast of the island. He planned an early start the following morning to cross over to Cherbourg in France.

Cherbourg was one of the primary Channel ports in France, and since the UK was not part of the pan-European customs union, arrivals on UK registered yachts were subject to more bureaucracy at their first port of call. The Cherbourg Capitainerie even had digital scanners to record passport details. However as they both had UK documents, everything was very casual. Before they left London, Andy had established that Valentina had UK nationality, but she was vague about exactly how she had obtained her status. Andy didn't press the matter. As this was their first landfall in France, they were told that the Customs Office would send someone over for an inspection.

In less than fifteen minutes, the Customs officer arrived. He asked to see their documents once again, looked at their small supply of alcoholic drinks and confirmed that there were no firearms aboard. It was all very relaxed and soon over.

The days passed without much incident. Valentina developed a routine: reading in the morning, practicing her Spanish in the afternoon and watching DVDs with Andy in the evening. She had taken over cooking and was gradually extending her range, which had been limited in the extreme. She had had the foresight to buy a thick Jamie Oliver cookbook and this became her bible. Andrew had told her that they would sail around Ushant, an island off the bulge of Brittany, and then stop for a few days in Concarneau, which his pilot book said was very pretty. She was looking forward to shopping for some ingredients that Jamie called for in many of his recipes.

Concarneau lived up to its billing; a working fishing port with a separate marina in the heart of the walled town. They arrived on a Tuesday afternoon. Their first stop was the Capitainerie, where they presented their passports and ship's registration certificate. Andy had bought a strong metal briefcase in London, to keep his important papers. Valentina had asked him to keep her passports with his own documents. She had become aware of how careful Andy was to always spin the combination locks every time the case was opened and closed, but she displayed no curiosity or interest in its contents.

While they sat on deck enjoying a glass of wine that first evening, Andy suddenly announced, "I think we need a break from sailing for a couple of days - well, to be honest, I need a break."

Andy had done more solo open water sailing this past week than in any one year in his life, and he was tired.

"Let's hire a car and see a bit of this part of France. What do you think?"

"That sounds great. Let's look online and see where we should go."

They spent a couple of hours with online maps and tourist sites and decided to head for St-Malo via Quimper. They would put off any further plans until they were ready to leave St-Malo.

The next morning after breakfast, Andy prepared to set off to the local car rental office to pick up a car.

"Andrew, you've done all the sailing, why don't I at least share the driving? I'll come with you, then we can both drive the rental car."

But he was insistent. Valentina should stay behind and pack a bag for four or five days, while he went alone to the office. In fact, they had a minor row before he left. Valentina felt she had been, in every sense of the word, a passenger for the past week or so and she wanted to be more useful. But Andy was oddly adamant and, in the end, he forced her to concede.

Quimper was less than fifteen miles from Concarneau, but on the tight winding roads of Brittany, it took over half-an-hour to cover the distance. However, by the time they parked in the center of the old town, they had gotten over their argument about driving. They enjoyed walking around, admiring the timbered buildings and agreeing that the magnificent medieval cathedral, with its famed vaulting, almost twenty chapels and hundreds of stained glass windows, was best enjoyed from the surrounding streets, where they found a very nice restaurant for lunch.

St-Malo was a three-hour drive from Quimper, and they wanted to find a hotel for the night before dark. Lunch had taken longer than expected and so Andy drove a little faster to make up time.

He didn't see the two gendarmes until they were less than 100 yards away, as they had been hidden by a tall hedge. However, he couldn't miss the signal to stop. The car came to rest alongside the nearest policeman who was indicating that Andy should lower his window.

"Carte grise et permis de conduire, s'il vous plaît, monsieur." He looked at Andy's blank face. "English?" he sighed.

"Yes."

"Driving license and your rental agreement. No, don't get out of the car, monsieur."

Andy had started opening the car door, but now had no choice but to open his wallet in the car and fish out his New York driving license and put it into the hand of the gendarme as he reached into the car. He found the rental papers in the door pocket and handed them over as well.

The policeman took the papers to his car, which Andy could now see was parked well into the driveway of a farm, and completely invisible to anyone approaching from Quimper. The policemen's colleague stood for a long minute on the passenger side of the car, frankly admiring Valentina, who never went out in public looking anything but fabulous. Eventually he forced himself to join his partner in the blue police car where they did whatever cops all over the world do in these situations.

"You have an American driving license, you are an American!" Valentina was clearly incredibly excited by this development. "You are, aren't you, American I mean?"

"It's no big deal. Don't go on about it."

The gendarmes returned. By prior arrangement they swapped sides, so that the older cop could have a chance to enjoy looking at Valentina. The younger policeman addressed Andy.

"We will let you not pay a payment this occasion, monsieur, but you must drive more slowly, no? This is not America; our French roads are very beautiful but no so faster as in your America. And you have not taken wine with lunch, no?"

Andy shook his head.

"Excellent! Tonight you should have cider, not wine."

He leaned into the car and held out his hand to Valentina. He tried his best Clint Eastwood accent, "Have a nice day, lady."

Both gendarmes laughed loudly at this; they clearly enjoyed their own humor. Cheerfully, they waved them on and Andy drove away, careful to abide by the speed limit.

Notwithstanding their brush with the gendarmes, they had no trouble finding a comfortable hotel in St-Malo. Valentina had checked out online reviews and had been able to call ahead and book their room in a hotel in the heart of the walled old town.

She was bubbly and excited as they walked from the car park towards the imposing entrance.

"This looks very nice, don't you think?"

"Yes, it looks fine," he replied, with less enthusiasm. He was still ticked off about the driving license incident. He had argued with Valentina about the rental car just to avoid a situation where she would see his US driving license, and now his secret was out.

They approached the reception desk to check in. The clerk asked for their passports.

"So, you are both British I see."

Immediately, Valentina cheerfully informed him, "Actually I'm also Russian, and he's also American. So we're a little bit of everything," she smiled pleasantly.

He handed them their plastic room keys and pointed to the elevators. As soon as he closed the room door behind him, Andy exploded. "What the fuck do you think you're doing, telling him I'm American? Who gave you permission to tell everyone my fucking business. Well? Well? Fucking idiot!" He was right in her face now, little flecks of his spit hitting her cheeks. For the first time since she had met Andy, she was scared.

"I'm going for a walk. Stay here and don't talk to a fucking soul."

The door slammed behind him.

He walked around the streets of St-Malo for an hour, although if he had been asked, he would have said that he didn't notice anything of the ancient city. He knew he had overreacted, but he was so angry, with himself, with the gendarmes, with Valentina. He had been so careful, but he had no option but to stick with his US license. He had never become an official resident in England, and so could not have tried to exchange his US license for the UK version. Anyway, that meant taking a UK driving test and he wasn't sure he was up for that.

He was beginning to understand how difficult it was going to be to maintain his invisibility when he was with someone else. He had already told Valentina that he wanted no reference to him on her Facebook page or her Twitter feed. She seemed to grasp his wish for secrecy immediately and, he had to admit, she appeared to be very discreet. He had looked at her social media accounts and sure enough, there was no reference to a boyfriend or their trip, although she had initially maintained a steady stream of comments on other people's posts, birthday wishes to online friends and other meaningless chatter. A few messages asked where she was. Someone, a man it seemed, was apparently asking around to find out where she had disappeared to. She had been ignoring these questions, and he had noticed that the rate of her postings was slowing dramatically.

He trudged back to the hotel and went up to their room. Before he could say anything, Valentina's arms were wrapped around his neck.

"I'm sorry, Andrew, I'm really, really sorry I made you angry. I was excited. My dream since I am five years old is to live in America. It is still my dream. I was just excited to think that I am with someone who is American. I thought you were English, but I see now that you are like me, with two nationalities."

"OK, Valentina, it's just that I like to be private, to keep my business to myself."

"I understand, I do, really I do. I understand being discreet, being private. Some of the people I knew in London were *extremely* private I can tell you." She paused. "Andrew, do you think we might go to America one of these days?"

"Perhaps," he lied.

The next day they went out to explore the town. As the day progressed, Andy's mood improved. They explored St-Malo thoroughly and ate in one of its really great fish restaurants. Andy treated Valentina to some new clothes more suited for sailing than her existing wardrobe. The only continuing problem, from Andy's perspective, was that she now wanted to quiz him on his life in America. And this was a huge problem. He didn't want to just refuse to talk about it, this would only make it a mystery and even more intriguing. Against this, he couldn't tell her anything about his life in Kingsbay without quickly getting into areas best left unexamined. And, by this point in his life, he was ashamed of his early years, his loser father and whore of a mother. As a consequence, he told her a lot about his college years, which was safe territory, and he told her a lot of lies about everything else. Lies which grew more complicated with each telling.

They decided to cut their tour short and head back to Concarneau and the yacht. They bought some provisions and Valentina bought ingredients for several meals. Their next major stop would be Arcachon, 250 miles as the crow flies, but, of course, a much longer sail for '*Aywol*', as they would hug the coast and call in somewhere near La Rochelle for a break. Although Valentina was a willing student, Andy was still doing all of the sailing and he didn't relish too many long passages. Nevertheless, five days later they sailed into the shallow, calm bay of Arcachon and reported once again to the Capitainerie.

Andy was becoming seriously concerned about Valentina's American obsession. And it was an obsession. He was certain that she was thinking about it all day. Certainly it had become her sole topic of conversation. Whenever they picked up wi-fi or cellphone signals, she had started to look up American recipes, thinking that this would please him. She planned to shop at Arcachon for ingredients to make cheesecake and was currently stressing about finding the French equivalent to Graham crackers. It was wearing him down, and it was worrying him as well.

On the other hand, they were having more sex and the previous morning she had announced that her period had started, but he wasn't to worry. Right then, again that night and again this morning she had gone down on him and given him enthusiastic oral sex. He realized she was trying to make herself the perfect partner, perhaps the perfect American wife, and sex was her only currency.

A PEN

On a Thursday afternoon towards the end of May, Susie had just made a cup of coffee and was heading for the deck to enjoy it, when the phone rang.

"Hello, Susie speaking."

"Is that Mrs. Smith?" The voice was a man's, pleasant, with a very slight accent that she couldn't place.

"Yes, that's me," she replied.

"May I speak with Mr. Smith, Mr. Andy Smith?"

"I'm afraid not, he's not here at the moment."

In the six months since Andy's disappearance, Susie had learned to be careful about what she said about Andy before she understood who she was talking to.

"Perhaps you could give him a message? I have good news, we have found his pen, his Montblanc pen. I do not know if he would like to collect it, or I could mail it to him if he prefers. May I give you my number and he could call me at his convenience?"

"I'm sorry, I don't understand, you have a pen of Andy's?"

"No, it is I who is sorry, perhaps I should explain. My name is Gallo, Dr. Javier Gallo, I was Andrew's Instituto Lingüístico tutor in August last year when he lost his Montblanc pen, and now it has been found."

Susie was struggling in every sense. She found it hard to understand a couple of the words the caller had said and she was perplexed about the entire conversation. She did remember Andy's Montblanc pen, she had helped look for it a couple of times when he left it lying somewhere around the house.

"Dr. Gallo, please excuse me, I'm struggling to grasp what you're telling me. You say you were Andy's tutor? At the Institute...?" she couldn't remember what he had called it.

"The Instituto Lingüístico, in Brooklyn. Andrew came here for a two week, intensive one-on-one Spanish course, he did very well, but towards the end of the course he mislaid his pen. He and I spent fifteen minutes searching for it, but with no luck. He was quite upset and so, when the builders found it yesterday, I remembered clearly to whom it belonged."

Susie was thinking as quickly as she could, Andy was at a two-week intensive course last August, but it was about international finance or something; something about his new job. Since he vanished, she had become adept at buying herself time to think when challenging situations arose.

"Dr. Gallo, you say you are in Brooklyn? Perhaps I could drive over and collect the pen?"

"That would be fine, if you wish. Is tomorrow convenient, in the morning?"

"I could be with you at ten o'clock without dealing with rush hour traffic. Can you give me your address please, and perhaps a telephone number just in case?"

She took his details and confirmed their appointment in the morning.

His office was on the third floor. As Susie walked along the hallway she could see evidence of construction work everywhere. There were dust sheets in neat piles, and here and there old-fashioned heating radiators were propped up against walls. She arrived at Room 352; 'Dr. Javier Gallo' was painted neatly on a wooden plaque beside the door. She knocked and the door quickly opened.

"Mrs. Smith? Do come in." He was much older than she had expected, at least seventy she thought, although from his voice she had been expecting someone closer to forty or maybe fifty. "Please, take a seat."

The office was pleasant and quite large. Apart from his desk, there was a large table that could seat six or eight, and bookcases, many, many bookcases crammed with books and binders. Against the far wall was a huge model town on a table, it must have been eight feet long she guessed.

"I see you have observed my town?" he said with a smile. "Please take a look. I call it Tierrarota."

Susie thought that Dr. Gallo moved with an elegant gracefulness and spoke English like a Lord in an old black and white English movie. She had seen the word 'courtly' used in novels, now she knew what it meant. She joined him in front of the model, which was an incredibly detailed miniature town with houses, shops, factories, a railway station. The town was surrounded by farms and woodland on three sides, with a beach at one end and a hillside at the other.

He began to point and to speak slowly and very clearly, *"La casa, mi automóvil, la estación de tren, los caballos, mi granja, la escuela.* You see? I use it to teach everyday vocabulary. Students seem to remember better this way, rather than just looking at words in a textbook," he waved his hand to indicate the bookshelves.

They took their seats again.

Susie had come prepared with a story about them planning a long vacation to South America and Andy deciding to learn Spanish before their trip, but she was instantly comfortable with Dr. Gallo and decided the truth, or at least some of it, was the best policy.

"Dr. Gallo, I'm going to tell you the truth. My husband Andy disappeared six months ago. I have no idea where he is, if he is even alive. And I had no idea he was learning Spanish. So you see, this is all somewhat confusing for me and I would appreciate any information you can give me."

"Oh! Well I am very sorry, Mrs. Smith, I had no idea. I hope I have not caused you any distress? Perhaps I should not have called?"

"No, no, not at all. Any information that might help us find him would be a blessing."

Dr. Gallo studied the young woman seated across his desk. His first thought was that when husbands disappear, it is generally to get away from their wives, but this lovely young woman didn't look like someone one would run away from, quite the opposite. Still, he was old enough to have learned that outsiders never really knew what went on in marriages.

"Well, I fear that there is little to tell. Your husband signed up for an intensive two week Spanish immersion course with me." He could see that she hadn't looked at the institute's web site.

"Basically Andrew and I spent the entire day together from nine in the morning until nine in the evening. We spent an hour or so in here with the model, then we would go for a walk around the streets until lunch, which would be in the Spanish restaurant around the corner. Then we returned here for grammar and more vocabulary in the afternoon. Around six, we repaired to a local tapas restaurant for dinner. And all day we spoke nothing but Spanish, from the moment he walked in the door on Monday morning. It is very hard work, very exhausting, but the fastest way to learn a language."

"How good was Andy's Spanish at the end of the course?" Susie was intrigued.

"When he first arrived, he had very little Spanish, remembered from middle school. Two weeks later he could carry on a very simple conversation using the simplest verb forms for past, present and future. He could shop, order food and drink, ask for and understand directions, pay bills and so on."

"Wow, that's pretty good! Dr. Gallo, did Andy ever tell you *why* he was learning Spanish?" Susie asked and sat forward on her chair; her breathing had stopped.

"He said only that it was for work. He wanted to move to the international division of his company and they required that he had some competence in another language. He had some very basic Spanish, he could count to ten and say hello, thank you and so on; so he chose Spanish rather than French,

German or Chinese which were his other options, apparently."

Disappointed at hearing nothing but more lies, Susie thought some more.

"And did he give you any idea where he would be working, I mean in Mexico, Argentina, anywhere specific?"

"No, not as I recall."

"Or perhaps you discussed the culture or customs of a particular place? Can you think of anything at all that would help?"

"You know, now that you mention it, I do recall a conversation we had in the last few days of his course. But not about Spanish, about Catalan. He asked about the use of Spanish in the Catalan region."

"The Catalan region?" Susie was baffled again.

"Here we are." He went to a bookshelf and found a large laminated map of Spain, "This is Barcelona, the second biggest city in Spain. All of this area from south of Barcelona to the border with France, all this is Catalonia. The people of this area are Catalans, with their own traditions and their own language. The area is called Catalunya in the Catalan tongue. As I explained to your husband, everyone in Barcelona and the rest of Catalonia can, and does, speak Spanish. However, in everyday life most people prefer to speak Catalan. There is some overlap between the two languages, but many significant differences. Catalan is not a form of

Spanish, it is a separate language, like French or Italian."

"So they don't speak Catalan anywhere else?" Susie followed up.

"A little further south to Valencia and in the islands, but nowhere else."

"And Andy was interested in this language?"

"Yes, I would say he was, we probably spent well over an hour discussing it. I speak only a little Catalan myself, so I could only show him a few verbs and discuss some simple vocabulary; but yes I would say he was very interested. I recommended a couple of books that he could refer to."

Susie couldn't think of anything else to ask, "I should go now Dr. Gallo, thank you very much for your time. If there is anything else you remember later that might help me trace my husband, perhaps you would call me again."

"Of course, Mrs. Smith. One thing, I do not know if it is important. One day, at Andy's request, we spent a few hours on vocabulary relating to sailing and sailboats. He had brought in a sailing magazine, and we worked through some photographs of yachts and drawings of layouts and so on. I sail myself, so I must say it was quite interesting, he is obviously a very keen sailor."

"Yes, he is." Susie rose to her feet, shook his hand and started walking to the door, she was on the verge of becoming upset.

"Thank you again, Dr. Gallo." She said, with her hand on the door handle.

"Mrs. Smith, don't forget the pen."

Six months previously, Susie would have left Dr. Gallo's office in tears; but six months of dealing with the aftermath of Andy's deceptions had toughened her up, and so she held her tears in check until she got back home. Dr. Gallo had stripped away her last hope, that Andy's decision to leave her was a last-minute panic, some kind of breakdown brought on perhaps by the thought of being in trouble over his financial misdeeds. She had clung to the thought that he hadn't planned to rob their friends or to abandon his wife, but had simply been overwhelmed by the fear of humiliation and maybe prison.

As Frank had told Jill when they discussed the disaster, people will cling to any straw when the alternative is to accept that they had been living a lie for weeks, months or even years. "The head of contracts in West County ran off with his secretary and $4 million he had skimmed off over six years, and was never seen or heard from again. His wife went to her grave convinced that he had been framed and killed by gangsters despite hundreds of documents to the contrary. She just could not accept that she had been duped for so long."

Susie made herself a coffee and tried to keep her emotions under control. She sent a text to Jill asking her to come round for a drink that evening after dinner. She thought of Sophie and how strong she had been when she was much younger than Susie. She decided to give her a call.

"Hi Sophie, it's Susie, are you by any chance free for lunch? I'd really like to chat to you about something." Sophie and Will's company occupied three units behind a mall on Northern Boulevard, no more than fifteen minutes by car.

"Sure, that would be great. Why don't we meet at Casa Sicilia at 12:30, would that work?"

"Perfect, see you there."

Susie arrived early and asked for one of the booths with high glazed walls on three sides of the table. They could talk with some privacy at least.

As soon as Sophie was seated, they ordered iced teas and the daily special. Susie told her about her meeting that morning with Dr. Gallo.

"So he'd been planning this for months Sophie, months!" Susie's eyes were blazing, but she wasn't crying.

"Do you realize that when we were having those lovely days on our trip to Shelter Island, he was already figuring out how to leave me and steal your and Will's money? How could anyone be so contemptible? I tried to tell myself that it had been a last-minute decision, a panic when he thought he'd be in trouble with the insider trading thing, but now I know better."

Their food arrived and Susie began pushing her food around her plate, she had no appetite at all.

"I feel so guilty, Sophie."

"Come on, sweetie, we've talked about this before. No one blames you for anything, and this doesn't change that in the slightest. Andy deceived you more than anyone, all he took from us was money, but we all know that he took so much more from you. We've all lost enough already, let's not lose any more by jeopardizing our friendships."

She reached over and placed her hand over Susie's, "That would be the biggest loss of all, don't you think?"

"Thank you, Sophie, I don't know how I would have coped these past months without you and Jill and Anne, I really don't."

"You don't look like you're going to eat that, so here's what I suggest; I call the office and book out the rest of the day. We have some retail therapy and then we get Jill and Anne and we sign them up for a girls' night. Sound good?"

"Sounds great, I already invited Jill to come round after dinner, she has Kevin and Lucy to see to."

"OK, I'll call the office and you call Anne. I'm thinking Chinese for tonight?"

The two women took a cab along Northern Boulevard to Americana Mall and window shopped the luxury stores. By unspoken agreement, they avoided any serious subjects, which allowed Susie's brain to begin to sort out her emotions without her conscious participation. They went into Armani, Susie's favorite dress shop, but she had no enthusiasm for buying anything. The fact was, that other than bunco, and nights with her three friends, she hadn't been out in the evening for months, and certainly nowhere that called for Armani.

In the window of Burberry, Sophie saw a dress on sale, reduced by 60%. She couldn't resist going in to try it on.

"I almost never buy anything in this mall, it's so expensive. But 60%...," she trailed off. "Oh why not? It fits me perfectly, and I can't remember the last time I bought myself something really nice."

"It looks great on you Sophie. The color is perfect."

Sophie bought the dress.

Buying herself an expensive treat obviously put Sophie in a reflective mood, because, as they walked past Agent Provocateur, she surprised Susie by commenting, "If I could give my younger self one piece of advice, it would be to wear as much sexy underwear and as many bikinis as possible. After a few years and a few kids, you'll think back wistfully to those years when you had the figure to carry it off."

Susie responded, "If I look as good as you when I have three grown up kids, I'll be very happy Sophie."

After a few minutes, Susie continued, "I'm not sure I should say this, but one of the thoughts I've had since leaving Dr. Gallo, is how can I get a divorce from Andy if I can't find him?"

A PLAN

By six o'clock, Sophie and Susie were in Susie's kitchen, warming plates and chilling wine. At 6:20, Anne rang the doorbell and came in carrying Susie's post, "I guess you forgot to pick these up, honey."

"Thanks Anne, just put them down on the countertop please. Now what do you want to order? I've got to tell you, Sophie and I are ravenous!"

They worked out their order and called it in to the local Chinese and then opened a bottle of wine. They chatted inconsequentially while they waited for their meal to turn up. Susie picked up her post and casually glanced through it until she suddenly stood up holding a letter. The color drained from her face. "Oh God, oh God, it's from England! Maybe it's from..." Susie peeled open the envelope and her two friends watched as her shoulders dropped.

"It's only a wedding invitation from an old friend from college."

The food turned up and they enthusiastically attacked the Chinese dishes. Still no one raised the issue that they were here to discuss.

At last Jill arrived and the group could come together to talk about the new information. The first task was to bring Jill and Anne up to speed.

"So you think he's in Spain, in Barcelona?" asked Jill.

"Well, I think so; but I have his passport so I don't see how he could have got there."

"Maybe he ordered a replacement passport?" offered Anne.

"So why do that when he had a perfectly good passport in his drawer?" Sophie wondered.

"Well," started Susie, "if he was worried about police or investigators, maybe he thought he was buying some time? I mean if he had no passport, he had to be in the US, right?"

"Wait a minute," Jill insisted, "he wasn't just buying some time, he was buying his future. He had covered all the bases. What were the odds that his damn *pen* would turn up? I mean, come on, that was an unbelievable break."

"A break, Jill?" asked Anne. "A break for what? A break for anyone trying to catch the asshole? Sorry

Susie, but he is. Nobody is even looking for him any more, the SEC guys don't care enough to really go after him. They would be interested if he turned up on their doorstep, but otherwise, he's in the clear as far as I can see. Don't get me wrong, I'd love to think Andy could be found, I keep thinking about our Shelter Island trip and how all the time he was planning to shaft us. And of course what he's put Susie through." The others were amazed to see a single tear escape and roll down Anne's face before she shook her head. "Fuck'im, I'm not going to spend the rest of my life thinking about Andy Smith. What else is new with you guys?"

"Quite right Anne." Sophie responded, "Well, don't forget, Susie's been invited to a wedding in England."

"Really, Susie, when did that happen?" asked Jill.

"It was in the post today, I didn't see it until Anne brought it in this evening."

"Who's it from?"

"An old college friend. Alan was on the ski team with me. He spent a semester in London and met an English girl there and it seems now that they're going to be married. Of course I'm not going; I'm not going to London on my own and anyway, it would cost a fortune."

Her friends knew that Susie was living on help from her father far more than on the tiny salary she made from her part-time school job. Sooner rather than later she was going to have to do something about her situation.

"When's the wedding Susie?" Jill asked.

Susie went into the kitchen to find the invitation again. While she was out of the room, Jill turned to the others, "Girls, support me when she comes back, I'm taking her to London, she needs a break."

Susie walked back in holding the card invitation, "It's in August, the sixteenth. At Highclere Castle, which sounds very grand. But I'm *not* going!" Susie laughed.

"You are kidding, right? Let me see that invitation."

Susie passed the card to Anne.

"Oh my God, it is, it is. Do you know what this is you ditzy woman? That's only Downton Abbey you've been invited to! How can you *not* go?"

Susie looked perplexed, "What are you talking about Anne?"

Anne, Sophie and Jill all looked at her. Sophie spoke first, "Susie, have you really never watched Downton Abbey? It's a British TV show on PBS. It's awesome, you have to watch it."

Anne butted in, "It's all about this English noble family and their servants, and their home is Highclere Castle. I mean it's Downton, but in real life the whole thing was filmed in Highclere Castle, rented out by the poor aristos who actually live there. And now Susie is going to be inside it, at a grand wedding no less. I would *kill* to be there."

"But I'm not going, although it does sound pretty cool."

Jill looked Susie straight in the eye, "Yes, you are, sweetheart, or rather we're going, you and me, to London and to the wedding. You can take me as your date. And it's my treat, no arguments, you know I can easily afford it, so please don't be boring."

"And before you start arguing Susie, if you don't go, I'll make her take me," announced Anne, to much laughter. She held the invitation behind her back, "And we'll use this invite to gatecrash your precious wedding, and tell Lord Alan that you sent us to embarrass him because he wouldn't have sex with you on the last ski trip."

Eventually they wore her down and it was agreed that Susie and Jill were going to England for a week in August to take in the wedding and the sights of London.

"Thank you, Jill, this is really is generous of you. It'll be fun, and Alan is really cool; and although I have never met his girlfriend, I'm sure she'll be nice."

"At least we know she's loaded, or at least her dad is," commented Anne.

Jill turned to Susie, "Come on, let's get the tickets now, so you can't change your mind. I'll get the office people to sort out a hotel, but let's get our flights booked, August will be busy. Where's your computer Susie?"

"I'll bring it down," she replied.

They were soon crowded around the laptop on Susie's countertop. She opened Google and started to type, but as soon as she entered 'Bri', the search history suggested '*British Airways*'. Sophie noticed, but didn't think too much of it.

Susie hit 'enter' and they arrived at British Airways' home page. "OK Jill," she muttered, "the wedding is on Saturday, August 16th. Shall we fly out on the Thursday so we can get over our jet lag?"

"Yeah, and talking of jet lag, we'll be flying business class, no way we're squeezing into coach for seven hours. So just select that over here," she was pointing at the box for flight details.

"Just a minute, Susie, hold on." Sophie was pointing at the top right hand corner of the screen, "Look at this."

In the top corner the screen said: '*Mr. Smith*' and underneath: '*My Frequent Flyer Points: 8645. My Tier Points: 140*'.

"That's weird," said Jill.

"Not necessarily," replied Sophie. "Hold off on booking your flights for a second Susie. Can I use the computer? I've got a funny feeling..." her voice tailed off as she quickly navigated to the members' section and the record of recent flights and there it was. Andy had flown New York to London on

November 27th last year, at 9:50 p.m., just four hours after Susie's flight to Burlington departed.

"Oh dear God!" whispered Susie.

"But how could he fly overseas without..." wondered Anne.

"Just a moment." Sophie found the page for personal details and, under the section 'Advance Passenger Information', she found what she was looking for. She spoke very quietly, "He has a British passport."

Sophie looked up at Susie, "I'm sorry Susie, really I am."

Sophie stepped away from the computer and hugged her young friend, who was by now quite numbed by the tsunami of information she had been dealing with all day. Her entire life with Andy now seemed to be a lie, all of it. First, the knowledge that he had been planning his theft and departure for months, then, the idea that he had put her on a plane to Vermont at Thanksgiving and almost immediately boarded a flight to England and now, they discover that he had a British passport. It was all too much.

"Let her go, Sophie." Sophie was surprised to hear the tone of Jill's voice, not exactly sharp, but firm.

Jill took Susie's hand and led her back to the family room and the sofa.

"Listen to me Susie, this is important, honey. I know it seems like it's been a terrible day, I get that;

but it hasn't really. Nothing happened today that hadn't already happened; you just found out today. But your life isn't worse than it was this morning, you knew he was gone, you knew what he did, you just hoped maybe he wasn't quite the shit he seemed to be. Well, he was and he is, but you're stronger than you were when he left and you'll get stronger every day. And we're all here to help, right girls?"

"Right."

"For sure."

Susie looked at her three friends.

Jill was right, as usual. All that happened today was she had been forced to accept reality. Andy may have loved her at one time, but for whatever reason, he had stopped loving her. The fact that he had also stolen from their friends told her that she wasn't to blame, there was something wrong with Andy, not with her. She would be strong.

"Let's get those flights booked, Jill." She smiled at her friend, who nodded back.

"Just a minute you guys," Anne spoke with a hand in the air.

"You're going to London and we know shitface went there, maybe still is there. Or maybe he did go on to Barcelona, whatever. Why don't we try to find him? Maybe we won't, but shouldn't we try? Wouldn't it be awesome if we could find the son-of-a-bitch and spoil whatever life he has established?"

Sophie wasn't convinced. "That seems pretty crazy, I mean, where would we even start? Maybe he's in England, maybe in Spain. He could be British or American. He is a needle in an *enormous* haystack."

"No, he'll be British no matter what," interrupted Jill, talking almost to herself. "He's a citizen of the European Union too, if he's British. That means he can travel around pretty much under the radar. He can get healthcare, buy property, get a job, or whatever, in Spain, in Italy, wherever. No visas needed. If he was still an American, his life would be much more complicated."

Jill had dealt with plenty of EU citizens in her career; she knew how it worked.

"And we know quite a lot about this particular needle."

Susie found herself suddenly keen on the idea of finding Andy, and disrupting his comfortable new existence. She went over to a cupboard, found a writing pad and a pen and sat down again prepared to write. "He speaks basic Spanish, he likes to sail - don't forget his teacher said they spent time on Spanish vocabulary about sailing. Oh, did I forget to tell you that? Well, it didn't seem important, but now I'm not so sure."

Anne joined in, "He likes to play golf, so we could look for him at the golf courses. What else would he be doing Susie?"

"He loves sports, the Giants and the Yankees, I can't imagine him not keeping up with the games."

Sophie looked over to Jill with a question in her eyes. Jill nodded forcefully.

"He'll look for women." Sophie added quietly, looking directly at Susie.

There was total silence.

"Sophie, you didn't, I mean he didn't?" Susie stammered.

"No, of course not, but he had at least one affair here in Kingsbay, and so I'd assume he had more."

"He had an affair *in the neighborhood*?" Susie thought she had heard everything by now. "In the *neighborhood*? Who with? When? Why?"

Before Sophie could reply, Anne interrupted with real feeling, "Hey, this is the first I've heard of an affair, but I can tell you, some men just can't keep it in their pants no matter what. There is no 'why', it's just the way they are. Trust me, I know."

"OK, but I still want to know. I promise not to do anything, but I want to know, Sophie."

"It was with Vivien. I don't know when it started, but it ended in July, I'm pretty certain."

There was silence for what seemed an age. Until Susie came out of her trance.

"Vivien! Vivien Werner! Well, that explains something that's been bothering me. A couple of months ago, I invited Vivien to come over for a coffee. I mean, we're basically the only single women under fifty in Kingsbay. I thought we could maybe go to a movie or a show together. Anyway, she put me off a couple of times and I stopped asking. I couldn't figure it out, I always thought she was nice. I guess she has a guilty conscience."

"How do you know all this Sophie?" asked Anne.

"Someone saw them, and told me because he knew I was Susie's friend. Please don't ask who told me Susie, he didn't know what to do when he found out; he did the right thing I think, telling me. And I'm sure he told no one else. And I told Vivien to put a stop to it and I think she did."

Anne was looking at Sophie with admiration, "People think I'm ballsy, but you just went up to Vivien and told her to stop screwing Susie's husband, and she did what she was told?"

"Oh, it's not too hard to get people to do the right thing when they know what the right thing is. Sometimes they just need to be pointed the right way."

The information about Vivien snapped the final bond for Susie. She knew for certain she would never miss Andy again; she would have no regrets about his departure. In fact, maybe she should just let the whole thing go. She said as much out loud.

Jill responded.

"Since this is a night for secrets and surprises, I'm going to tell you one now, all of you. I've never told anyone this, except Frank, but when I was in college, I had an abortion. It happened because an Associate Professor I was dating, took me to a party and gave me my first and last joint. I got high as a kite and woke up pregnant. Of course it took a while before I knew I was pregnant, but when I told him, he walked away from the entire situation. And I let him. I let him avoid any consequences and I bet some other girls went through some similar crap after me, all because I didn't have the guts to take him down. I would have been humiliated, but he might have been stopped. And I've regretted it ever since. Now, maybe we can't make Andy face his consequences, but we can try. If we fail, you'll at least know you tried your best and you can let it go and get on with your life."

There was complete silence as they digested Jill's bombshell.

After several minutes Susie topped up everyone's wine glass and said, "Let's drink to the future - with consequences." They laughed, a little uneasily, sipped their drinks and finished off the second bottle of wine.

Anne proposed that they meet again the next Sunday to start to plan the search for Andy. Everyone agreed and they each hugged Susie in turn and headed to the door. When it came to Jill's turn to say goodnight, Susie gave her an extra hug and whispered, "Thanks for giving me courage."

Sophie had the last word "Susie, before you go to bed tonight, go online and order the Downton Abbey box set, and get caught up quickly!"

The four women met at Susie's again on Sunday afternoon. The others had to smile when Susie led them into her dining room. She had set it up like a meeting room. Instead of a place setting, there was a pad and pen at each seat.

"Well," she said, "we need to be organized. This is going to be difficult and we need a plan."

"Quite right, Susie, we do," agreed Anne.

They started by going over the ideas they briefly raised on Friday. They had three ideas that might help narrow down the search, sailing, golf and his two sports teams. They would look for Andy in marinas, golf courses and sports bars. His interest in women seemed too broad a clue to be of much help.

"How can we look for him? If he sees us before we see him he'll know we're looking for him, and he can just take off for a few months. We can't stay in Europe forever. Actually Susie, how long are you prepared to stay away?"

"I don't know, Sophie, I guess I haven't thought that far." She paused. "I think I would stay two months, if we can't find him and get the money back in two months, it could take two years, and I'm not giving up two years of my life," she decided. "I'll resign my position at school. It isn't a real job and, one way or another, it's time I moved on. Even if we don't find him, I need to do something with my life."

"Well, that gives us a target." Sophie observed, "Say we do find him, what then? What will we do with him? How do we get the money back?"

"We beat him black and blue until he hands it over," proposed Anne.

Susie answered her, "Seriously Anne, this isn't the movies. I can't see any of us attaching electric leads to Andy's privates to torture the money out of him - tempting as that may be. How about we simply threaten to hand him over to the police? The US authorities may not be actively looking for him, but they'll for sure act if we hand him over."

Now Sophie spoke up. "Will is worried that he and the others might be in trouble if Andy is brought to trial. The attorneys have said that it isn't clear whether the people who gave Andy money could be charged as accessories. It isn't only that Will doesn't want the authorities involved, but that Andy probably knows this too. He might call our bluff, thinking we won't go through with our threat."

They mulled over this thought for a while until Jill thought she might have the answer.

"What if he knew for certain that Will and the others were in the clear? What if they already had immunity? Say they had done a deal with the prosecutors, to give evidence against Andy and in return they don't face charges? Then Andy would know there is nothing to stop us giving him up."

"Would they actually do that?" asked Anne.

"They don't have to. All that matters is that Andy believes they did. I've dealt with the District Attorney's office lots of times. I have dozens of letters from them. I'll bet someone good with Microsoft Word," she said, looking at Sophie, "could easily copy the letterhead, and I could come up with the text of an agreement. How would Andy know it wasn't the real thing when we show it to him?"

"Wow, that's great Jill. You're one smart lady!" Anne continued, "But what about the problem of him spotting us while we look for him?"

Jill spoke again, "Anne, Sophie, do you remember the Andersons, Steve and Monica?"

Anne answered first, "Of course, they lived on Fairlake, nice couple."

Sophie joined in, "I know what you're thinking. They moved back to Europe, to Spain, we still exchange Christmas cards. They live in Marbella."

"I'm not sure I understand, what are you thinking, Jill?"

"Well, Susie, you don't know Steve and Monica, they left Kingsbay a few years before you arrived. They're really nice people and are still good friends of ours, I saw them in London about eighteen months ago. Steve and Monica are English, and they lived here in Kingsbay for about ten years. When Steve retired they moved back to Europe to be nearer their family; both of their children had already moved back to Europe. They wanted a warm climate, so now they live in southern Spain. I think they would help us find Andy, and of course he doesn't know them."

Sophie spoke again, "Peter will help."

She saw Susie's blank look.

"My son, Peter, he'll help. He was so angry when Will told him what had happened, and I think he can recognize Andy, though Andy won't know Peter."

"But how Sophie? Did he ever meet Andy? I mean, I'm pretty sure I've never met Peter."

"No neither of you ever met him, but he saw you at Cal Everett's funeral. He asked me later who the good-looking couple was sitting opposite us in the church."

Susie blushed.

Sophie laughed, "Oh no, not you this time, Susie; Peter is gay, he was more struck by Andy."

"Don't worry honey, I'm sure he thinks you're cute too." Anne was highly amused by Susie's discomfort.

"Anyway, trust me, Peter will jump at the chance to visit Europe, especially if his father is picking up the tab." Sophie smiled. "And I'm going to come over as well, with Peter. I have an idea that might work," she added mysteriously.

They spent another hour talking, trying to come up with a plan.

They provisionally agreed that Jill and Susie would fly to Barcelona on Tuesday, August 19th, after they had their time in London for the wedding.

As they prepared to pack up for the day, Anne raised a question they had all been thinking about. "I'm still worried about the plane ticket to London. Why not fly straight to Barcelona if that's where we think he's headed? We could be wasting our time in the wrong country. Is there no way we can confirm for certain which country he is in?"

"There might be," offered Susie, "can we leave it until we meet next week?"

They had decided to meet each Sunday afternoon to review their plans and, hopefully, their progress.

A NEW RECRUIT

Whether it was the support of her friends, or the idea of the trip to London or just contemplating going after Andy; for whatever reason, Susie felt better than she had since Andy had left. Her natural resilience had kicked in and she was, to a large extent, over the emotional trauma of his disappearance. This didn't mean she had forgiven or forgotten, quite the opposite. She was determined to try her best to find Andy and do something to balance the score. But she was rational, even dispassionate now and her mind was full of ideas on how they could find their needle in a haystack.

She had an idea that Charlie could help.

She walked round to the house on Bayview to talk with him. The house was too small to afford any privacy, so they walked along the shoreline. Susie started by asking Charlie for his phone number and email address, "It's crazy that I have to walk round here every time I want to talk to you. And it's too cold!"

"When we get back to the house, I'll write them down for you. Now what did you want to talk about Susie?"

"Can we go back to my house? I'm freezing! Will Gran be OK?"

"She'll be fine for a couple of hours. Come on, race you."

They ran back to Susie's house, and were at least warmer when they sat at the kitchen table.

"Actually, let me make us coffees while I tell you what's been happening." Susie pushed back from the table and went around the island worktop.

She filled Charlie in with developments since they had last talked. As she recounted things, even she was amazed at how much had come out the day she went to Brooklyn.

"And so Charlie, we've decided to try to find Andy, although I'm not exactly sure what we'll do if we do find him. But I know I want to get back the money he stole from everyone else."

By now Susie was accustomed to the fact that Charlie liked to take his time thinking. At the beginning, she thought he was just a slow thinker, but she had quickly come to the realization that he was in reality, a deep thinker, who rarely had to change his plans once he had figured things out.

"Do you want me to try to find Andy, by tracking him online?"

"That's exactly what I was thinking Charlie! I knew you'd be our secret weapon! Are you up for it?"

"Yes. You know I liked Andy and thought he was my friend, but he betrayed you and those other people. And now I think he used me too."

He told her about his involvement with the first two trades. Susie was appalled.

"Charlie, you could be in trouble. We need to get you to talk to Bobby, my attorney, first thing tomorrow."

"No Susie, don't worry about me. The SEC won't come even close to me, I guarantee it, and I know what I'm talking about. I'd rather you didn't tell your friends though, would that be OK?"

"Of course honey, you were just being used. But if there is even a hint of trouble, we're calling Bobby, OK?"

"OK, but don't worry. And Susie, I like to come to your house, and you've got my phone and email details now, but you know, we could have had this conversation in front of Gran. She would love the idea of catching a guy that betrayed his wife."

When Anne, Jill and Sophie came round the following Sunday they were surprised to find Charlie already at the table.

"Everyone, I think you know Charlie. Charlie, this is Anne and Sophie and Jill, my friends."

They all smiled at him, obviously confused. For his part, Charlie took confidence from Susie and smiled back.

"I've told Charlie everything and a few days ago I asked him to help us find Andy."

The others looked at each other, clearly mystified at this development.

Finally Jill spoke, "I don't think I understand. No disrespect Charlie, but how do you think you can help?"

By way of an answer, Charlie reached into the backpack sitting on the floor beside him. He took out a small pile of papers, sorted in five clear plastic folders. He passed them around so each woman had a folder.

"These are the SEC's files on Andy. This is what they've been able to discover so far about the money. As you'll see, they have no idea where he is. The money was transferred to a bank in Panama, but went out again the same day and the Panamanian banks deliberately don't keep records of where they transfer money to. So essentially, it vanished."

"Holy shit!" Anne exclaimed, "How the hell, I mean, where did you get this?"

Susie answered for Charlie.

"I swore on all our behalf, that we would never tell anyone about Charlie's help. Charlie is an internet whiz. He tells me that the only computer systems he can't get into are the one's he and his group have been paid to secure. And given time, he could probably get into most of them again if he had to."

They all turned and looked at Charlie. This was the misfit kid who hardly anyone ever saw, who some people assumed was perhaps backward in some way. And in a few days he had hacked the government to help them.

Jill spoke again. "My apologies Charlie. I'm an attorney, so I'm going to forget what Susie just told us. Remind me never to ask you where you get information from in the future."

Susie was of course, delighted. She had had no idea if Charlie would have anything for them so quickly. "Charlie, you've had time to look at this, what does it tell us?"

"As near as the SEC can figure, Andy left with around $15 million, but as I said, there has been no sign of him since he left here. They don't know about his British passport, so they have assumed that he is still in the US. But he hasn't rented or registered a car and he hasn't used a US credit card."

He continued, "They have two theories. One, is that Andy has a completely new identity and is living with it now. This would explain why there's no trace of him. However, it's difficult to turn up out of the blue in the US with $15 million. So he would have to be abroad, traveling on a new passport in another name. They don't really believe this, largely because there is nothing in Andy's past to suggest he has the knowledge or contacts to pull this off."

"Theory number two, is that he left the US via Puerto Rico, or more likely, the US Virgin Islands. You don't need a passport to travel to either one, a driver's license will do. From there it would be fairly easy to charter a private yacht and enter any of the other Caribbean islands. Some of them wouldn't ask too many questions about where his money came from, and he could have opened a bank account before he left here. And with $15 million available to him, he could quickly establish the contacts to get a new identity. This is their primary theory."

The $15 million number had stunned everyone. They had been thinking in terms of the money he had stolen, which came to one to two million, depending on how they counted the profits the others had made and then handed back to Andy.

Charlie could see their confusion.

"He made most of it on the final trade, that's where most of his money came from. Of course he hasn't paid taxes on it, so the IRS is after him as well." He passed around a much thinner file. "I didn't make copies because it really says nothing new. And you really don't want to have these anyway." He looked meaningfully at Jill.

Anne looked at him carefully.

"Charlie, could you get my IRS file if you wanted?"

The hurt on Charlie's face was so transparent and so painful to see that they all looked away.

"I would never do that to a friend of Susie."

"I'm sorry Charlie," said Anne, "I really am, please forgive me, please?"

"Anne is my friend Charlie, if she says she's sorry, it's because she means it." Susie interjected.

"OK, no problem, Anne. Just so you know, I've started to show Susie how to keep herself safe online, I'd be happy to help anyone else."

"Sign me up," announced Sophie immediately.

Jill wanted to move the conversation on. "Charlie, did Susie tell you how we found out about Andy's passport?"

"Yes, she did. I've checked, and he hasn't applied for a replacement US passport. I'll keep an eye out to see if he applies for one, he could report his old one lost or stolen."

"Should we tell the authorities about his English passport?"

"That won't be necessary, although it couldn't hurt I guess. I discovered that Andy's UK passport had been scanned on arrival at Cherbourg."

"Where's Cherbourg?" asked Sophie.

Charlie confessed, "I had to look it up. It's a port in France, just across the English Channel. So we can be pretty sure that Andy is sailing to Spain."

Anne spoke again, voicing what they were all thinking. "My God, Charlie. I can't believe how much you've discovered in a couple of days. It's actually kind of spooky."

Susie was delighted with her friends' reaction to Charlie's involvement, but she wanted to cement his role even more.

"Charlie, why don't you explain your other idea? About the District Attorney."

"OK. Susie told me your idea about the immunity letter, Jill, which is excellent. But what if Andy thinks the letter is a forgery? Imagine if he reads the letter, then denies it's real, what would you do? Suppose you could tell him to look in the web site of the New York District Attorney and he finds the press release from say, June, one announcing the details of the agreements. I think that would be completely convincing."

Sophie looked at him, now completely amazed. "You could do that? You could put a fake release on their site? Wouldn't they find it and take it down?"

"They would find it, and they would take it out, but not fast enough. Someone in Spain would call me, ten minutes before you show Andy the letter. I would plant the release then and pull it out again thirty minutes later. If you were talking with Andy at nine o'clock in the morning, it would be three o'clock here in the middle of the night, and there's no chance anyone would notice a thing."

By the end of the meeting, the women were feeling much more confident, even exhilarated. Charlie's achievements and astounding capabilities had given them all a boost, and somehow had been the final act in bringing them together as a real team. They were no longer three friends reaching out to help Susie, but a single group with a shared goal.

They decided that the next meeting would be in Jill's house.

BAY OF BISCAY

Andy was giving serious thought to handing Valentina some money and putting her off the boat before he left Arcachon. Her whole American fixation was just too much. It was clear to Andy that Valentina was now a woman on a mission; to marry him and move to the US. There was no way either of these things were happening, and he had to put an end to the conversations before she made a mistake and talked to someone else about her hopes and plans.

However, before he found an opportunity to have the conversation with her, she gave him something else to think about.

They were having dinner in a seafood restaurant overlooking the huge oyster beds, when Valentina looked at him very seriously, "It's nice being together, just the two of us. And it's so much easier to be private, not like in London, surrounded by other people all the time, where I could make a mistake and give something away."

After a pause, she carried on talking about how much she hated London and how much she would prefer to live in America, in the suburbs like those she had seen in countless movies.

While she prattled on, Andy wondered if her remark about privacy had been innocent, or was it a subtle hint about what might happen if she was back in her old life? Valentina sometimes surprised him with glimpses of a smarter and tougher woman under the sex kitten facade.

He didn't put her off the boat; but he was even more seriously concerned about her now.

A few days later they set off again, with San Sebastian their next goal - which meant a twenty-four hour sail. Valentina insisted that she could take a watch in the night if no change of course was required. They had set off early in the morning and by midnight, Andy could see that they were making good time. The wind was steady and the forecast was for more of the same. Andy decided to take a break.

"OK Valentina, let's see if you can stand a watch by yourself. I'm going down below for a couple of hours rest. If I haven't come up by 2:30, come and wake me. If you see anything at all, come and get me, OK? The autopilot's on, so you don't have to touch anything."

"OK Andrew, I'll be fine, go get some rest. I'll call you right away if anything happens."

Andy went below, took off his shoes and lay on top of the bed. He didn't think he would sleep, but he wanted to rest his eyes and relax, although the problem of Valentina was still monopolizing his thoughts.

He woke with a start; he had been having a very vivid bad dream. He was sitting in an uncomfortable wooden chair that kept shifting under him. He was watching Valentina explain to Susie how they could all live together without a problem. Susie seemed to be agreeing, but she wondered where Valentina's four babies would sleep in the tiny studio apartment. And who would pay the bills, as they had no money and couldn't find work?

He was shaken. He reached for his iPhone, touched the screen and the phone told him it was 3:23 a.m. He padded silently through the salon into the cockpit. In the moonlight he could see that Valentina was sound asleep. She had pulled her feet up onto the port side cushion and had been semi-reclining, facing aft with a pile of cushions supporting her back. Her head nodded slowly with the gentle swell of the ocean. Andy looked at her for a minute, then, with little conscious thought, he turned and went below, into the crawl space in front of the engine. He found the roll of spanners, opened it and pulled out the largest, which weighed three or four pounds he guessed. He returned to the galley, picking up a towel as he moved into the salon and up to the cockpit. Before he could have second thoughts, he swung the heavy tool and smashed it as hard as he could onto Valentina's head.

The flat side of the spanner took her just behind the ear. For a split second, he thought her eyes had flickered open, as her head snapped forward and she fell, motionless, onto the decking. He had expected blood and was prepared to wrap her head with the towel. However, there was no blood that he could see, except in her hair in the immediate area where he had hit her - and even that wasn't much. He felt her neck, but couldn't detect a pulse. He put his ear to her mouth, but he couldn't hear her breathing. He pushed up her sweater, there was no movement of her body, no sign of life that he could see. She was dead.

Valentina had been wearing jeans and a bright red woolen sweater against the night air. Andy grabbed a short length of rope and tied it tightly around her narrow waist, cinching it as tight as he could. He tied the other end securely to the small outboard motor that was fixed to a nearby storage bracket. First unclipping the safety lines on the stern, he dragged her limp body by the feet, until her hips were barely on board the yacht. He came around to her head, knelt down and, placing a hand on each of her shoulders, he slowly pushed her overboard. She bobbed about for a few moments and eventually settled, floating behind the yacht, gently tugged by the rope around her waist. He freed the outboard and dropped it over the transom. It plummeted through the dark water like a stone and, with a sharp tug, Valentina's body followed it.

Belatedly, he looked around; there was nothing to see, no lights visible in any direction. He knew they were about fifteen miles from shore, so he hadn't expected to see anything. Quickly he went below and found Valentina's two folded kit bags. He emptied her drawers and closet and gathered up the innumerable jars and tubes that seemed to be everywhere. Everything went into the bags. He had to get one of his own bags from its stowage space; she had more clothes now than when she first came on board. He found her Kindle, iPhone and laptop. He opened his briefcase and pulled out both of her passports. He looked through the galley and the salon for anything he had missed. The only thing he turned up was a lipstick. He was satisfied that he had found everything, although he would have another, more leisurely search when he made port. He opened the largest bag again and slipped the entire roll of spanners, including the tool used to kill her, inside the bag and zipped it shut again. He securely tied the three bags together by their handles, before dropping them into the sea.

Finally, Andy sat down in the cockpit and checked his course. Everything was fine.

Suddenly the enormity of his action washed over him. He had killed someone. His began to picture Valentina's body, cold, still, white, at the bottom of the ocean. Fish and crabs would ... "STOP!" he yelled aloud, his voice echoing over the silent sea. Reaction set in and he wept silently. He hadn't planned to kill her. Yes, he had thought about it, but he hadn't actually planned it. Seeing her asleep on her watch, maybe the echo of his dream, most of all her comment, perhaps threat, about privacy - somehow everything had combined in his head and he knew that he would be only be safe without her.

Why did she have to see his license? She would probably still be alive. If only she hadn't looked.

Andy stayed two nights in San Sebastian. During this time he cleaned the boat from bow to stern, inside and out. He found nothing more than a couple of minor items of make up. He figured that he should have a couple of women sleep aboard as soon as he got to Barcelona. This would be his cover if anything else ever did turn up.

With another overnight effort he made Santander. Here he asked for assistance in the Harbormaster's office, and they found him a young sailor, Antonio, who would crew with him all the way round to Barcelona. He promised Antonio a healthy bonus if they could make Barcelona in under twenty days, and they made it with three days to spare. They had sailed night and day in all but the worst seas. By the time they tied up at the marina in Barcelona, Andy was exhausted, physically and emotionally. He paid off Antonio, checked in with the Harbormaster and went back onboard, intending to sleep for most of the next two days.

It was the twentieth of July.

A NEW LIFE

Once he had caught up with his sleep, Andy began his exploration of Barcelona. He was delighted to discover that the city was even more beautiful than he remembered, although also more crowded. He decided at once, that while he wanted to live downtown, he didn't want to be in an area popular with tourists. He found a realtor he liked and began visiting properties in various parts of the city.

He started to build a life for himself. He visited the major sports bars in the city and settled on Wards Sports Bar as his regular hang out, as they showed lots of American sports. A long chat with a barman assured him that, during the season, there was an NFL game on a big screen every Sunday night. Baseball would be much more difficult; games took too long, they were on too late and there were too many of them. He would need another solution to keep up with the Yankees.

He also visited the golf courses around Barcelona. Although not the closest, he eventually decided that the Terramar Club was a nice course and seemed to have the friendliest staff and members. He had been told that there would be no problem joining the club. The club secretary would be happy to introduce him to other expat members who would in turn, sponsor his application after they had played a few rounds.

If he was going to play golf, Andy needed a car. He visited the nearest BMW dealership and ordered a BMW 650i convertible. The dealer found one in Madrid that was close enough to his specifications and within the week it had been transported to Barcelona, detailed and made ready for its new owner.

Best of all, almost everyone he met spoke English, although they appreciated his stumbling efforts with Spanish.

But no matter how hard he tried to forget, at least two or three times every day he thought about Valentina. Every time he saw an attractive girl who looked even vaguely Eastern European, Valentina popped into his consciousness. If he passed a car repair shop, he thought of the spanner and the terrible dull sound it made against her head.

He had planned to live aboard *'Aywol'* until he found an apartment. In just a couple of weeks however, he found that he wasn't comfortable on board. There were simply too many memories. He moved into a hotel and soon realized that he didn't want go aboard his yacht anymore. He would have to sell it.

He wasn't going crazy. He didn't obsess about Valentina. Most nights he slept OK. Nevertheless, while he surprised himself with how little he thought of Susie, he was hacked off that, even in death, Valentina was intruding into his life.

THE REAL DOWNTON

By the time Charlie had traced Andy to Cherbourg, it was too late to cancel the London part of the trip. Susie had sent an email accepting her invitation, explaining that she would be bringing her friend Jill and emphasizing how much she was looking forward to seeing Alan and his new wife.

Plus, the Downton effect had kicked in.

London was a revelation to Susie. She had expected history and she wasn't disappointed. What she hadn't anticipated were the green spaces and the wildly colorful ethnic neighborhoods. Their first day was a bit of a blur. Jill had been in London lots of times and she wanted Susie to see a real picture of the city. Jill felt that the inside of museums wasn't the best reflection of anywhere. They checked into their hotel, unpacked, freshened up and then met in the hotel lobby. Jill's office had organized a private tour, and, as it was a lovely sunny day, the organizers sent a convertible. The two friends settled in the back seat and their driver took them past the sights familiar from a hundred movies and TV shows: Buckingham Palace, Big Ben, Trafalgar Square and Piccadilly Circus. They passed Green Park, Hyde Park and St James's Park. Susie was amazed by the peace and tranquility of the parks, surrounded by the hustle and bustle of the vibrant city.

Then Jill asked the driver to take them through Regent's Park, past the zoo and on up to Hampstead. They got out of the car and walked through the historic village just four miles from Piccadilly Circus. They looked over the 800 acres of Hampstead Heath and window-shopped the antique shops and galleries set among the Georgian houses and Victorian apartment blocks.

"Are you OK for one more stop before we go back to the hotel?" Jill asked.

"Absolutely, I feel fine."

So Jill had the car bring them back through Camden Town and Market. Again they got out to walk, this time along a canal. The Market was jammed with an incredibly diverse crowd of young people shopping the stalls of artisan products, antiques, vintage clothes and, it must be said, a lot of junk. The costumes and the people wearing them were from Asia, Africa, the Middle East and every corner of Europe.

Susie decided that she had to visit an English pub. The one they chose sold beers brewed in the adjacent brewhouse. The barman poured them small samplers of each of the beers and explained how each was made.

"What do you think?" Susie asked.

"To be honest, I'd rather have a glass of good white wine," replied Jill.

Susie laughed, "You must admit though, you've rarely seen such a variety of people in a bar in Jameston."

It was true. Even the bar staff were a cosmopolitan group. The barman who had served them was a huge black man with extensive piercings. His colleagues behind the bar, were an elegant young Chinese girl who worked with quiet efficiency, and a bubbly girl with a strong Italian accent who made up for her total lack of efficiency by charming everyone with her non-stop chatter.

The customers were even more varied.

"Are there ghettos in London?" asked Susie.

"I'm not exactly sure," replied Jill. "I've been in areas where everyone seemed to be Nigerian, or Pakistani, or Polish or whatever, but the areas are much more mixed up than at home - London's a real patchwork quilt of a place. In America there's an African-American culture, but in London there are

Jamaican, Kenyan, Nigerian, Ethiopian and a dozen more black communities, and they don't have much in common with each other."

"But then again, my friend in our London office tells me that there's still lots of informal discrimination in England - they're just more polite about it."

After the pub, they decided to have an early night, so settled for a plate of sandwiches in the hotel bar, accompanied, at Jill's request, by a glass of good white wine.

On Friday, they wandered the streets of London. They discovered the Victorian arcades off Piccadilly, the designer stores in Old Bond Street and the upscale neighborhood streets and pubs of Mayfair. Without realizing, they walked many of the same streets that Andy had been enjoying just weeks before. In the evening they went to a West End show.

On Saturday morning their car met them at ten o'clock for the drive out to Highclere Castle. They deliberately left early, so that they could avoid taking the freeway out of London. They drove past Windsor Castle, through part of Surrey and into Hampshire.

Highclere Castle lived up to expectations. They enjoyed seeing the settings familiar from Downton

Abbey. Alan was delighted to see Susie again, and his bride, Louisa, was the quintessential English rose.

The only sour note was a guy at their table for the wedding meal. It seemed that Giles had nothing good to say about America, or rather about Americans. Americans, he insisted 'had no culture, no subtlety, no flair.' Sure they had 'money, guns and great teeth,' but were altogether inferior in every way to sophisticated Europeans, 'no offense intended of course'.

Just when Jill in particular thought she couldn't take any more, Alan saved them. He came over to their table and pulled a chair up between Jill and Susie. When Giles went off to the restroom, Alan apologized.

"Has Giles been a pain in the ass? I thought so. I'm sorry, we should never have put you on his table. He's Louisa's cousin and he goes on and on about the States every time I see him, which is rarely, thank God."

"He's not alone though, lots of the English think just like him, but most are too polite to say so to our face. Some of it is down to the obnoxious Americans they sometimes encounter and a lot of it is a complete disconnect when it comes to some particular issues - mainly guns, religion and a few of our politicians."

"Mostly though, I think it's envy. It pisses them off, that the world they live in gets more and more American every year. The best TV, the biggest movies, the most popular writers are American. Amazon, Facebook, Google, Apple, nearly all the web sites and lot of the coolest technology they use is American. The Brits in particular don't like the fact that no-one much cares what they think about anything anymore."

"On the other hand, lots of Brits visit the US every year and love it. But I apologize for Giles."

"The meal is almost over, I promise the speeches will be short and then I want a dance with each of you. Meanwhile, pick up your things and I'll introduce you to some of our friends who are a bit more laid back."

Other than the odious Giles, the day was delightful. The food was excellent, there were some interesting guests with less of a chip on their shoulders than cousin Giles. Plus they got to dance in an amazing setting, although Jill missed having Frank to partner her. There was a member of staff on hand to take groups of six or eight at a time around the house and gardens, visiting places where particularly memorable scenes from Downton Abbey were filmed. They also saw the collection of Egyptian antiquities collected by an earlier Earl of Carnarvon, who helped discover the tomb of Tutankhamun.

"Sophie and Anne will be so jealous." Susie remarked after their own tour.

By eleven p.m. they were ready to leave. They both fell asleep in the car on the drive home.

They enjoyed the rest of their visit to London. They took a trip on the London Eye, had a curry in Brick Lane and did some shopping in Harrods. Tuesday morning found them in Heathrow Airport boarding their plane for Barcelona. Susie was becoming nervous. London had been fun, but Barcelona would be work, or something like it. As they flew high over France, she began to worry that they were crazy to imagine that they could find one man in a huge city, a man who didn't want to be found.

BARCELONA

At the same time that Susie and Jill were standing in line at immigration at Barcelona airport, Andy was viewing what would become his new apartment. He made an offer on a twelfth floor apartment in the Illa Del Mar complex, a new high-end development, more or less on the beach in the Diagonal Mar section of the city. It was a beautiful apartment, with wrap around terraces overlooking the beach. The sparkling blue Mediterranean filled most of the view. There was a park next door and a shopping mall on the far corner of the broad boulevard. The surrounding streets boasted lots of restaurants and fashionable bars. The apartment complex itself had pools, a gym and a tennis court, and Andy had seen lots of young mothers around in the daytime. He was confident that there would be opportunities there too. He had decided that, for the moment at least, he would have no attachments. Safely married hot young mothers, one-night stands and, if necessary, the occasional professional would have to take care of his sexual appetites.

It was a perfect apartment in a superb location; and so of course it was expensive, at 1.2 million euros, but he could afford it.

The women took an airport taxi to their hotel near the Ramblas and the Plaça de Catalunya. Jill wanted to unpack and call home before they went to find somewhere for dinner, so they agreed to meet an hour later in the bar.

When Susie entered the bar, she saw Jill at a corner table.

"Well, Susie, it's going to be an interesting evening in Kingsbay."

"Why's that?"

"I talked with Frank. He has to go to Albany this afternoon to talk at a committee meeting tonight. Unfortunately my folks have theatre tickets for this evening, so they can't sit for the kids."

"Alejandra must have watched them a million times surely?"

"Of course she has, this is Frank making mischief. He phoned Charlie and asked him to sit with them."

"Charlie! Sitting? What was Frank thinking about?"

"I told you, making mischief. He knows very well that Alejandra will be home shortly after my folks leave. He could have taken them over to Justine for half an hour. He's match-making."

"I'm not sure about this Jill. Charlie's, well he's very shy, very quiet."

"The kids love him. Kevin thinks he's some kind of computer game genius and Lucy doesn't know anyone else who can actually predict what patterns she'll get from Spirograph. Neither do I, come to think of it. Since you started bringing him round when we were meeting in our house, they've really got to know him, and they like him."

"I know, but Alejandra?"

"I don't know, but Frank must know something. They have met after all, quite a few times. Frank must have seen something, he wouldn't mess them about."

"No, he wouldn't, I guess."

"I'll find out tomorrow how it all went. Let's go eat."

The few remaining days that Jill would be with Susie were to be used organizing an apartment and getting a handle on the search.

First stop was an apartment rental agent they had found online from the US. They had an appointment for ten a.m. on their first morning. They wanted a three-bed apartment in the city center, and the agent had only one candidate to show them. At 8:30 they met for breakfast in the hotel dining room.

"How did it go with Charlie and Alejandra?" Susie asked as soon as she sat down. "I've been thinking about them since I woke this morning."

"Well, apparently - at least according to Frank's email. Frank didn't get home until around eleven and they were sitting together in the dining room. They had phoned for Chinese and were looking at something on Alejandra's laptop when he arrived. Frank was dead on his feet, and so he emailed me, then went straight to bed and left them to it. I don't think he knows what time Charlie left."

"Oh my God, it would so great if they got on, Charlie needs a friend his own age, never mind a girlfriend. I'm going to call him in a day or two to see how he feels."

"Shouldn't you just leave him alone to handle it?" asked Jill.

"One thing I've learned from Sophie, is that people sometimes need a bit of help doing what they know they should."

At ten o'clock they were ushered into the agent's office.

"It is the height of the season," he explained, "all I have is this one cancellation, and it is only available because it's rather large and quite expensive."

The flat was right around the corner from their hotel. It was on the third floor of an old-fashioned building, constructed around a central courtyard where some residents had parking spaces. There was no elevator. However, the flat itself had high ceilings and featured air conditioners in every room. There were four large bedrooms, all with private bathrooms with showers and tubs. And it was indeed expensive, but, with no choices open to them, and not in the mood to trail around other agents, they took it. They would be able to move in on Saturday afternoon.

Susie rented a car and they drove out to some of the golf courses surrounding the city. They had decided that there were six reasonable candidates that Andy might be interested in, all 18-hole courses with proper facilities. They didn't get out of the car, they were simply forming a general impression of the golf clubs. Six courses didn't seem too intimidating to check out properly.

Before leaving home, they had identified the main sports bars in the city, but there was nothing they could do by way of preparation about them, without the risk of being spotted by Andy.

They found six marinas in Barcelona itself and could see that there were many more to the northeast and southwest of the city. They couldn't think of any quick way to find Andy or his boat in a marina. Perhaps Charlie would think of something, otherwise Susie would have to cover a lot of ground, making enquiries.

In the weeks leading up to their trip, they had all got to know Charlie and all came to appreciate his unassuming personality and his incredible ability to uncover information online. They also permitted him to exploit his skills where they could see no moral dilemmas. For example, Charlie rearranged the room assignments in their hotel to get Jill and Susie rooms next door to each other, near the top of the hotel and with the largest balconies. Sometimes he didn't consult them, like when he flagged everyone for upgrades on their flights.

On the evening before Jill was scheduled to fly home, Steve and Monica Anderson arrived in Barcelona after a long drive from southern Spain. They had planned to break their journey with an overnight stop around the halfway point, but last minute commitments got in the way and, by the time they arrived at seven o'clock, they had been on the road almost twelve hours, more or less non-stop.

They all met for a light supper in the hotel dining room. Jill performed the introductions and she and Susie filled the Andersons in on what little they had learned since leaving New York. The Andersons were in their early sixties, with a single daughter living in Paris and a married son in England, who had so far produced two grandchildren, with another on the way.

"We really enjoyed living in Kingsbay, Susie," Monica explained, "but I wanted to be closer to Jeffrey and Lisa when the first grandchild came along. Now it's so easy to fly to Birmingham for just a few days if we want to see them, or even if they want me to babysit for an overnight event."

The following day Jill was leaving for home. Susie called her room at 7:30 in the morning. "Can I come to your room?"

"Sure, I'm just packing."

Susie arrived with a big smile on her face.

"Charlie and Alejandra are going on a date tonight! Can you believe it?"

"Susie, what have you been up to?" Jill had a pretend stern look on her face.

"Hardly anything. I called Charlie last night before I went to bed, so it was five o'clock for him. I asked him how he had got on with Alejandra and he went on and on about how great she was: so interesting, so nice, so cute, blah, blah, blah. I asked him when he would be seeing her again and he said, 'whenever Mr. Petersen asks me to help with the kids I guess'. I mean, Jill, he would be *hopeless* left to himself. I suggested that it might be a good idea if he didn't wait, but called her up right then and invited her to a movie or dinner or both. Fifteen minutes later he sent me a text saying they were going out tonight and about ten smiley faces. I don't know where they're going, but who cares, right?"

"Well done you."

"Oh, and Jill, I asked Charlie to think about how we could find out if Andy had recently brought a boat into one of the marinas. He promised to work on it. I guess when he's not dating Alejandra that is! I'm so excited about them, I hope it all goes well. Charlie will be twenty-four this year and he's never been on a date before, can you believe it? I could cry for him sometimes."

Susie insisted on coming out to the airport with Jill. At the entrance to the security area, she hugged her friend. "Thanks for everything Jill; for a lovely trip to London and for helping me to get organized in Barcelona. I'll email you regularly and we can Skype too."

"You take care of yourself and don't let it get you down if you don't find him."

"Oh, we're going to find him Jill, don't worry!"

Susie returned to the hotel to collect her bags. She had already checked out before driving to the airport. She met up with the Andersons in the hotel lobby and they made their way around the corner to install themselves in the rented apartment. Steve drove them to the nearest supermarket and they bought all the supplies they could think of. From now on, Susie wanted to eat in as much as possible to keep her budget under control.

"You know, Susie, we should return your rental car, we really don't need two cars and when we go to England, you can use ours."

The Andersons had a long-standing arrangement to visit their son and his family in Birmingham. When Jill had called them back in May, they had changed their plans and agreed to drive up to Barcelona to help for five or six days, after which they would fly to England from Barcelona and then drive home again.

So while Monica and Steve unpacked the groceries, Susie drove to the nearest Hertz office and handed back her Seat Ibiza. She meandered back to the apartment, enjoying the busy streets full of locals heading home from their jobs or doing last minute shopping before the stores closed for the day. Many of the Barcelona streets were really boulevards, broad handsome thoroughfares with extremely wide sidewalks that accommodated lots of seating and tables for the innumerable bars, cafes and restaurants in the city. She was beginning to get used to the Spanish schedule of dinner at nine or ten at night, but she was hungry by the time she let herself in to the flat.

"Perfect timing Susie," announced Steve, as she walked into the living room. "I've opened a bottle and Monica just put dinner in the oven: it's a casserole and needs two hours to cook."

Steve led the way onto the small balcony, where they could just about squeeze in three kitchen chairs.

"We know you want to get started right away Susie, but we thought we'd mix in some fun with the search tomorrow if you're up for it." Monica looked at her while Steve continued.

"Tomorrow is Festa Major in Sitges, an important local festival that draws people from all over the region. We should get up early and head down the coast, it's about an hour's drive. I'll drop you two off in town, go on to the golf club and make some enquiries, then come back and find you."

"Honestly, I can't tell you how grateful I am that you guys are helping us out, it's so generous of you. And of course you need to have some fun as well, I plan to enjoy being in Barcelona myself. There is only so much we can do to find Andy, and when we're not doing that, we need to relax."

Monica wanted to know more about the specifics of the plan, if they did spot Andy. "Say we do find him in a bar or playing golf or whatever. What then? At first I thought you were just going to call the cops, but I gather you have something else in mind."

Susie tried to collect her thoughts. "Getting the cops involved is our last resort. If we have to do that, I don't think any of my friends will get their money back for years, maybe forever. I want to offer Andy a deal: he hands over all the money he stole and the money he made and we let him go. That way he doesn't get to benefit from what he did, and everyone gets back what they lost. The money left over we can give to charity."

She continued, "So we have to grab him and stop him from running away while we try to persuade him. If he agrees, he has to stay with us until the money has been transferred. Then we'll let him go, with enough money to live on for a month or so. If he doesn't, we call the cops and the US consulate, and they can deal with him."

They sat watching the people pass below them, getting to know each other in the balmy evening, before going in to enjoy Monica's excellent dinner.

SITGES

Nothing could have prepared Susie for the fun of Festa Major. By the time Pete dropped the two women off as close to the center as traffic was permitted, it was 9:30 a.m. and the first priority for Susie and Monica was to get something to eat.

That remedied, the two women followed the river of people to the main square, which was soon jammed to capacity. Suddenly, strange flute music started up and the crowd grew quiet. As always, Susie's looks made her stand out in the crowd and sure enough, a crowd of young men called them over, took them by the hands and gently pulled them up to join them on the back of an open truck. The men explained that they had parked the truck in the square before the police closed the roads. One of them had a cousin in the police who had made sure that it hadn't been towed. So now they enjoyed the best view in town, and so did Susie and Monica.

Susie craned her neck and could see that, in the center of the crowd there were two roughly circular groups of people, mostly men, but with a few girls. One group wore red shirts and one blue, all wore white cut-off cotton slacks with black sashes and bandanas. Soon some men near the very center of each circle were hoisted onto their comrades' shoulders, a great cheer went up and the music picked up tempo. Now the elevated men linked arms around each other's shoulders and a second group clambered up on top of them. The towers were now the height of three men, with the guys at the bottom bearing the weight of their fellows. The levels were not hollow rings Susie could see, but solid masses of men. At a signal that Susie missed, large groups of similarly uniformed men started to push in and she realized that these were acting like buttresses, helping the bottom layer take the strain. Now four teenagers climbed up the linked figures and Susie spotted a couple of well built young women among one group.

Things were moving fast now. Before the fourth group had even finished getting themselves properly linked up, four more youngsters were clambering carefully up the growing tower. Now she could see that they were all barefoot, to improve their grip she supposed, and to cause as little discomfort as possible to whoever they were standing on top of. A sixth level was now climbing and Susie was surprised to see that these kids were only nine or ten years old.

"Aren't they too young?" she gasped, scared on their behalf.

"Look, senyora. At the bottom." One of the young men on the truck directed her gaze. Now she could see a ring of adult men who were not supporting the base, but had their hands free. "They could catch them, but they won't fall."

The race would be close, but the reds were ahead.

Susie turned to her guide, "The red team will win, yes?"

He smiled. "Watch, senyora, it is not just about being fast."

A single figure was now climbing each tower, or *castell*, as she was corrected.

"These are the *enxanetas*, the riders to the top. They are both seven, the blue is the daughter of my neighbor."

Susie held her breath as the two final youngsters climbed, swiftly at first, and then slowly, to pull themselves carefully on top of the sixth level. When they stood erect, each raised four fingers proudly to the sky. There were cheers and the music reached its climax. It seemed that the red team had won by a few seconds.

"Look, senyora, it isn't finished, they have to all come down, and the blues have a surprise for you."

The *enxaneta* of the red team made his way down quickly and the next level started to dismount as soon as he passed them, but Susie could see that the little girl atop the blue tower hadn't moved. And yet people below her were dismounting.

"The blues are trying an *agulla,* a needle, senyora, they will try to leave just one person on each of the top four levels before they finally dismount."

Susie could barely stand the suspense, as the needle of four levels emerged from the center of the blue tower. Soon the little girl on top was able to raise her four fingers again, this time in assured victory. Quickly, but gracefully, she dismounted, followed immediately by the nine-year-old who had held her on his shoulders, and the rest of their team safely dismantled their tower.

"That was absolutely fantastic," Susie said to the group around her, "wonderful, amazing, thank you!"

They asked Susie and Monica to join them for the sardana that would follow soon, but they declined with smiles and laughter and eventually the young men consented to lower them carefully to the ground.

"That was absolutely terrific Monica, I've never seen anything like it."

"Apparently they sometimes go up to ten levels, if you can believe it."

"So Monica, what is the sardana they wanted us to go to?"

"Ah, well, if we just follow the crowd we'll get there. The sardana is a communal dance, a circle dance, where everyone holds hands and moves slowly around the circle. It's easier to understand by watching rather than me try to explain it."

They came to the space, a triangle formed by three streets coming together. There was more of the strange flute music, but now accompanied by drums, accordions and more woodwind and brass instruments. The dancers had formed a circle and were dancing with slow, but complex, steps. People from the crowd were welcomed in, or invited to help form new circles. Susie and Monica watched for a while and then Monica indicated that they should move on.

"Let's have a cold drink," she suggested, "before the giants and the devils turn up. And I need to give Steve somewhere to aim for."

They found a sidewalk cafe table and Monica ordered *granizados* for them both.

"Before you ask, it's something between a shake and a fruit juice. They're very refreshing. Let me call Steve and tell him where we are."

Susie looked around, while Monica called her husband. The town was very pretty and she was looking forward to walking along the promenade she had glimpsed several times down side streets. They were sitting on the main shopping street that ran parallel with the beach, about two hundred yards away.

"He'll be here in ten minutes. Then we can find somewhere to watch the end of the procession. If we walk up a block and turn left, we can get ahead of the crowd and be in the plaza when the head of the procession arrives."

Fifteen minutes later Steve finally arrived. "Sorry I'm late. It's tough walking against the crowd. Not much luck at the golf club I'm afraid. It's a nice place, but most of the staff are off work today because of the festival. The club pro wasn't there, or the manager. We'll have to come back again another time, next Monday I think. According to the only person I could speak to, there's a British expat group who play every Monday, but not tomorrow because of the holiday."

They left the cafe and walked quickly to the next street away from the beach and turned to outflank the procession which they could hear noisily, but slowly, making its way through the town. The plaza was in reality just an irregular shaped intersection where several roads met. There were already people standing around waiting for the parade to arrive. Susie and the Andersons found the last table in yet another cafe, this time on the upstairs open terrace. Their table was at the rear of the terrace, but Monica pointed out that, as soon as the parade arrived, everyone would stand along the front balustrade.

They waited nearly half an hour before loud noises and drifting smoke signaled that the head of the procession was arriving. They moved to the front of the terrace and Steve urged Susie to stand in front of him to get the best view.

The procession was led by young men dressed as devils. They had painted their faces red, with jagged black designs over the red color and they wore black horns. They were wearing what looked like sacks, with cutouts for their head and arms, and they all carried three foot long sticks, from which dangled strings of firecrackers that were constantly renewed and lit. In the tight confines of the plaza, the noise was deafening. The performers, and the spectators, were constantly beating out little burning sparks that cascaded everywhere, but no one seemed to mind. It occurred to Susie that, between the firecrackers and the tower builders, she had seen grounds for a hundred health and safety lawsuits back home.

The devils were only the opening act for the main body of the procession, a group of six papier-mâché giants, each ten or twelve feet tall. The giants were hollow, with a strong man inside each figure who could lift the giant, walk or dance a few paces and then lower it again to give him a moment's rest.

"The first two are the King and Queen, then the Moors and then the Americans." Steve called over the incredible noise as the band started up again and the giants danced a sardana.

"Why Americans?" Susie shouted.

"Actually they're Cubans, come back home with money they made from rum. Did you know that the Bacardi family came from Sitges?"

"I had no idea." Susie yelled back.

They gave up trying to talk as the noise increased yet again when the firecrackers reached their finale and the giants began to slowly make their way out of the square.

When the crowd had thinned a little, they left the terrace and made their way down to the wide promenade and walked slowly towards the picturesque church that stood on a small promontory, dominating the view of the coastline.

"You guys seem to know Sitges pretty well," Susie observed.

"It's one of our favorite places," Monica replied, "we love visiting Barcelona and always have a few days in Sitges when we come up. We come for Carnevale, for this Festival or for Corpus Christi at the end of May."

"What happens in May?"

"Six or eight streets are closed to traffic, and local groups and clubs compete to make the most beautiful flower carpet. So you have a mural, maybe a hundred yards long, but on the ground, made up of tens of thousands of flowers and leaves and fruit. It's just incredible to see. The carpets are laid in only a few hours in the early morning and then you can walk along the narrow walkways left on each side to admire them. It's amazing."

They reached the end of the promenade and walked up the broad stairway to the church, where they turned to enjoy the vista back along the beach curving gracefully along the bay. Every one hundred yards or so the beach was broken by a low wooden wall that ran down to the sea.

Steve explained, "They're to stop the sea washing the sand away. A lot of the sand is imported, the Mediterranean isn't rough enough to make really fine sand, so it has to be renewed every year. And the walls also mark out the different beaches."

He could see that Susie didn't understand. "There are family beaches, gay beaches, nudist beaches, mixed nudist beaches, beaches where you can hire jet skis and so on. Each group has their own space."

The church was closed to visitors that afternoon so that the fireworks could be set up on the roof and in the belfry.

"They use this lovely old church as a platform for fireworks?" Susie was aghast.

Monica laughed, "I know, it seems crazy doesn't it? But it's the most prominent site in town and they would point out that they've been doing it for over a hundred years and no harm has been done."

Susie wasn't convinced and shook her head in disbelief.

They wandered past the church into the heart of the old town. They visited the small museums founded by Sitges's artist colony before the First World War. Then they dropped down into the other, smaller beach where they carried their shoes and walked along the water's edge. Soon after seven o'clock Monica announced that it was time to walk back into the old town to have a drink before dinner.

"We'll eat earlier tonight, because we have to be out of the restaurant by 10:30 for the fireworks. I booked a table at our favorite restaurant, I hope you like fish."

The restaurant had a small bar in an open courtyard and they ordered a bottle of cava, while Steve and Monica told Susie more about the town.

"A few decades ago, Sitges was one of the few destinations that welcomed gay people, so the community really flourished here, helping to open lots of great restaurants and clubs and cute boutique hotels. But now the gay community has more options, which is great of course, but it means that they don't come to Sitges quite so much, and it's becoming more of a family resort. Unfortunately this means less money in the town, so it's becoming a little less stylish each year, sadly."

They had a lovely meal. The highlight was a whole sea bass baked in a mound of sea salt that was cracked at their table to reveal the perfectly cooked fish inside.

Just after 10:30 they left the restaurant and joined the stream of people heading onto the promenade and the beaches, from where they could look back to the church and the old town. The bay was crowded with a large flotilla of yachts anchored to watch the show.

Precisely at eleven o'clock the fireworks began and went on for thirty minutes. It was on the same scale as the Fourth of July display in Manhattan, but against the backdrop of the lovely old town. Susie's favorite was the row of perfect palms trees that appeared from the roof of the church, and glowed for what seemed a very long time, before changing into a solid wall of flaming sparks that tumbled down the wall of the church.

"Thanks for a wonderful day guys. Sitges is one of my new favorite places." Susie said this as they approached Steve's car to set off for the drive back to Barcelona. "I think I'll come back next Monday, to try the golf course and to see the church."

As they emerged from the tunnel on the freeway, Susie knew she would be too tired to phone Charlie if she waited until they were back at the apartment. "Guys, do you mind if I make a call?"

She called Charlie's number, "Hi Charlie, it's me. How did last night go?"

"Great, we had a great time. We went to movie and then we went to the Italian place you told me about. It was really nice. I took your advice and didn't order spaghetti."

"What did you see?"

"We saw a movie called 'The Hundred Foot Journey', it was really good. I saw on a forum somewhere that it was a good date movie. Alejandra said she enjoyed it too. It was quite funny, very sweet and no one had a limb torn off. You would have approved." He laughed, and continued, "I thought of you afterwards. I looked it up when I got home, the movie was made in France, just three hundred miles from where you are right now."

"Well, I'm glad you're thinking about me, but I wouldn't mention that to Alejandra if I was you."

"Why not? Anyway Susie, I've been thinking about Andy and marinas. It seems that new arrivals are supposed to register with the Harbormaster and fill in a form with their details. I haven't found out yet what happens to the information. It must be entered in a system somewhere, otherwise why collect it? I've put out a request for information in my network, someone will know I'm sure. Then I'll be able to find him. Oh, and can you send me a photograph of Andy, one that shows his face clearly? I'm hoping you have one on your phone or your laptop."

"I'm sure I have Charlie, but why do you want it?"

"I have an idea, I'll tell you if it works."

"OK. Good night Charlie, well, it's good night here anyway, well after midnight. Look up Festa Major in Sitges if you want to know what we've been doing today."

"I will, good night, Susie."

As soon as they ended the call she realized that she hadn't asked if he was seeing Alejandra again. She would send him a text tomorrow.

THE HUNT REALLY BEGINS

On Monday morning the Andersons took off to investigate two golf courses north of Barcelona. Susie sat down and opened her laptop. She had been too tired the previous night to check her email. There was a long message from Bobby, her attorney. It seemed that Cliff Walker was trying to sue her to recover the money that Andy had stolen. Bobby assured her that his case was groundless and would never get to court. Apparently Cliff had to try four lawyers before he found one to even take the case. Bobby asked her to call him when she had a moment. She calculated that she should call at three in the afternoon, which would be nine a.m. for Bobby.

Charlie had set up a private online area for them to share information, especially when Susie was in Spain. Although she had nothing much to report, Susie felt she should make a start on using it. She summarized the list of marinas and golf courses they had identified and the sports bars around the city that claimed to show American sports. For the benefit of Sophie and Anne, she described the apartment and gave her impressions of Barcelona. Although it made her feel a bit guilty, making it seem as if all she was doing was enjoying a vacation, she described as best she could the events in Sitges. Then she went through the images in her phone and found a photo of Andy taken when they were out sailing on *Susie Q* and sent it off to Charlie, wondering again what he wanted it for. She took the opportunity to clear out the store of photos, transferring some to her laptop, and deleting the rest.

When she finished, she went out for a walk through the medieval section of the city and then crossed the Ramblas to find the main market, *La Boqueria. La Boqueria* was a food paradise. Around three hundred stalls of mouthwatering displays of perfectly presented fruits, vegetable, meats and fish and delicatessen items, like olives and olive oils, cheese, breads, candied fruit, nuts and everything else one could imagine. Most stalls specialized in one category of produce, but what set them apart was the consistently high quality of every item offered for sale, and the amazing variety and breadth of choice on display. The stallholders were all enthusiasts, eager to explain the unique qualities of their products. She stopped at one stall selling dried, salted and preserved fish: anchovies, boquerones, banderillas.

"Here senyora, try this, please."

The vendor passed her a small paper square with a sliver of pale fish.

"This is Bonito del Norte tuna. Every year the fish swim north to the Bay of Biscay. They eat and eat and grow fat off the coast of northern Spain. Just when they are about to move south, my uncle and the other fishermen catch them with fishing rods. The day they are caught, they are cooked in seawater then packed by hand in the finest olive oil."

Susie put the morsel in her mouth, where it immediately melted, leaving the smooth taste of the ocean. She bought some for her lunch.

Without being aware of the time passing, Susie spent almost two hours wandering around the market, buying small portions of whatever took her fancy. As she was leaving, she was given a tiny sample of cured bellota ham and thought it might be the best meat she had ever tasted.

"This is Black Label, senyora, the finest category, from a pure-bred Iberian pig that lives in the oak groves and eats only acorns during the *montanero*, the winter. This is the finest ham in the world."

That too was bought for her lunch. Susie looked at her watch, and realized it was time to get back to the apartment for her call to Bobby.

"Bobby? It's Susie Smith, you asked me to call."

"Hi Susie, how is Barcelona?"

"Fantastic, Bobby, I may never leave. I've just bought enough amazing food for four meals, and I only went into the market to browse."

"I thought we needed a quick chat. I told you that Cliff Walker is bringing a case against us. He's found a low-life, ambulance-chasing lawyer without a reputation to lose. The lawyer figures that a fair percentage of people prefer to pay something to settle a dispute in order to avoid a court case. His thirty percent of $100,000 wouldn't be a bad return for a few letters. I suggest you refuse to settle. As soon as the court date comes close, he'll drop Cliff in a New York minute."

"Whatever you say Bobby."

"The reason I wanted to talk to you, is to tell you *why* Walker is hell bent on suing."

"It turns out that he boasted to some of his cronies about the huge score he was going to make with Andy. So he was utterly humiliated when the news emerged that Andy had run off with his money. And it gets worse. With the money gone, Walker couldn't fund the purchase of his new boat; he lost his deposit of $250,000. To add insult to injury, Andy seems to have wanted to really screw Walker for some reason. All the money from Geoff,

Will and the rest was pooled with yours and invested in Andy's name. However, for some reason he kept Walker's money separate and traded in Walker's name, although he steered the profits to his own account. A few weeks ago the IRS received an anonymous letter, giving them details of the Walker trade. So now they're after him for tax on his profits, which in theory were about $2 million, even though he never saw the money. Walker doesn't have the cash apparently. I have an idea that Andy sent the letter, or arranged to have it sent, it was postmarked New York."

Susie tried to take it in. Andy had apparently decided to get Cliff Walker. Was it because of the Halloween incident almost three years ago she wondered?

Bobby continued, "The SEC seem to have thrown in the towel. They have no leads at all on Andy and he is small fry and they have bigger fish to go after. I don't think we'll hear anything from them. And, I've saved the best for last. The bank has agreed that they didn't follow their own procedures in allowing Andy to run up the overdraft. They're going to offer a settlement in a day or so. Do I have your permission to settle for say $50,000, if they agree to write off the balance, which is just over $340,000?"

"That would be awesome, Bobby. Excellent work. Thank you, on behalf of my father. Interesting news about Cliff Walker too."

After her call with Bobby, Susie decided it was time to try her first visit to one of the city center marinas. She was nervous about this, because she was afraid of being seen by Andy. She was aware of a slight tension every time she was out in public in Barcelona. It wasn't that she was afraid of a confrontation, rather that he would see her from across the street without her noticing and then he might take himself off for a while. But, if they were going to find him, she would have to take some chances.

She walked across the city to Port Olympic. She quickly found the Capitania and psyched herself up to play a part.

"Hello, I wonder if you could help me. I'm looking for my brother Andy, Andrew Smith. He may have arrived here in the past four or six weeks. He's been, well, we haven't seen him in three years, and now our mother is very sick. I'm afraid she's dying, and she wants to see her son one more time."

The man across the counter clearly wanted to help. "Do you know the name of his boat senyora?"

"No, I'm afraid not. It's a sailing yacht, that's all I know. He told a friend that he was making for Barcelona from the south of Spain. Andrew Smith is his name. He is thirty-seven years old and has a British passport."

"One moment, senyora, I will check."

He disappeared into a small office and she could see him checking his computer. He spend almost ten minutes looking and came back shaking his head.

"I am sorry senyora, he has not been here. There are many other marinas in the area. Perhaps one of those? If he comes here, I will be sure to tell him that you are looking for him. A man should see his mother before she dies, I think."

"No, please don't, he may run away again. He and my father..." Susie allowed a single tear to escape. "If I could give you my number, perhaps you could call me. I will arrive immediately and talk with him."

"As you wish senyora. Good luck, families are very important, yes?"

Susie thanked him once more and left. It hadn't been too bad, she thought. However, on balance, she thought it likely that the guy would, for the best of reasons, tell Andy about her if he ever showed up. It was a risk they would have to live with.

ENCOUNTER

On Tuesday, the Andersons visited two more golf courses, again without any sign of Andy. That morning, Susie spent several hours in the Barri Gòtico, the Gothic Quarter, guidebook in hand. She walked the labyrinth of small streets, visited the Cathedral and some of the other churches, and saw the Roman ruins. In the afternoon, she called into another marina and went through her story once again, with exactly the same result.

On Tuesday evening there was a big soccer match on TV that Steve wanted to watch. Monica and Susie decided to go out and have a stroll down the Ramblas.

The two women wandered slowly through the busy thoroughfare, stopping to admire the artists and caricature painters and the occasional living statue. Some of the caricaturists were really good. Susie decided she would get Jill to send her photos of Kevin and Lucy and have them painted. There were hundreds of people doing exactly the same as them, wandering in no hurry, with no particular destination in mind. They arrived at the bottom of the Ramblas, near to the monument to Christopher Columbus, turned and made their leisurely way home.

Halfway back up the busy boulevard, Susie noticed a huge NBA themed bar on the second floor of a building on the right hand side of the Ramblas. They stopped to look at it, wondering if this was somewhere Andy came to watch sports. Suddenly Susie felt a sharp tug on her shoulder and, quick as a flash, a man was running away with her purse. He had cut the strap with a craft knife and bolted into the crowd. Before she could react, there was a shout and crash, as someone stuck out a leg and the thief fell into an artist's easel and he, and the easel, clattered to the ground. The man who had tripped the thief stomped hard on the fist clenching the purse. The thief screamed, as a couple of his fingers were broken. The Good Samaritan reached down, pulled the bag from the damaged hand and walked towards Susie and Monica. He was tall, elegant and very handsome.

"Senyoras," he said reaching out his hand with the purse. "English, American?"

"American," responded Susie automatically.

"Senyora, I apologize for my city. This man is not from Barcelona I think. He is from the east, perhaps Romania. I hope you will not hold this against us?"

Susie was enthralled. He was the most sophisticated looking person she had ever seen. He was wearing cream linen trousers with soft leather moccasins, a beautiful white silk shirt with a pale blue cashmere sweater draped over his shoulders. And he had a voice like honey.

"Not at all," she replied, "we love your wonderful city."

"Excellent! I am delighted. Perhaps I may buy you a glass of wine to make it up to you?"

Susie was about to politely decline, when Monica broke in, "That would be lovely. What about him, what should we do?"

She was pointing to the would-be thief who was trying, without success, to extricate himself from the street artist and some of his friends, who clearly expected him to pay for the ruined easel.

"Oh, forget about him. They'll find all his money and take it. The police will show up, but won't be too interested. They arrest these people and they come back the next night and go back to work. Hopefully, his hand will stop him causing trouble for a few weeks. May I introduce myself? I am Sebastiá

Xavier Domènech i Marti." He smiled, "but Javi will do, however."

They introduced themselves and he led them to a small bar nearby. As soon as they entered, the barman, who turned out to be the owner, came from behind the bar and embraced Javi, welcoming him. Javi introduced the two women, and they were led to a small table at the rear of the bar.

"Now what would you like to drink? Something long or something short?"

"Long for me," replied Susie.

"Perhaps a short drink for me, may I have a vermouth?" Monica requested.

"Dues sagries i un vermut per favor Josep."

Javi turned back to the two women, looking at Monica. "I must say, you don't sound like an American, Monica."

"No, I'm not, I'm English, but I live in Spain, in Marbella."

"Entonces, ¿eres uno de los expatriados británicos se han instalado en España?" *'So, are you one of the British expats who have made a home in Spain?'*

"Sí, llevamos viviendo en España casi ocho años, nos gusta mucho." *'Yes, we have lived in Spain for almost eight years, we like it very much.'*

"May I congratulate you on your Spanish, Monica, it is very good. It seems many of your countrymen never learn Spanish, no matter how long they live here."

"Thank you, but my Spanish is nowhere nearly as good as your English. Where did you learn to speak it so well?"

"I went to school in England, to Winchester, and then I attended Harvard. So I have no excuse not to speak fluently. And you Susie, do you also live in Spain?"

"No, I am only here for a month or so I'm afraid. I come from Long Island, in the community where Monica and Steve used to live, so we have mutual friends."

They talked about their day in Sitges and Javi recommended some places worth visiting for the rest of Susie's trip.

Meanwhile, Monica finished her vermouth as quickly as she could, while Susie had barely touched her tall glass of sangria. Monica stood up and, before Susie could react, she announced, "I think I'll get back to the apartment Susie, Steve will be wondering where we've got to. No, you stay here, I'm sure Javi will be happy to walk you home."

She turned to Javi and held out her hand, "A great pleasure to meet you Javi, even under such circumstances."

He took her hand and replied, "I will be happy to escort Susie home, and thank you for your company. Buenas noches, Monica."

Susie and Javi sat for another thirty minutes and then walked slowly back to the apartment. When they arrived at her building, he asked her, "It is a good building. Which floor are you on?"

"The third."

"The American third?"

She laughed, "Yes, the American third, so for you the second. I learned about that in England, after making two mistakes, trying to follow directions."

"Well, I'll leave you now. It has been a great pleasure to meet you, Susie. I am sorry about your bag, but delighted that it gave me the opportunity to meet such a lovely lady. I hope you enjoy the rest of your visit to Barcelona."

He held out his hand.

"Thank you Javi, for my bag and the drink and for your advice on what to see in Barcelona. You live in a lovely city."

She reached for his hand and was surprised when he lifted hers and brushed the back of her hand with his lips.

"Bona nit, Susie."

And he left.

Susie climbed the stairs and let herself in to the apartment. Monica was waiting for her.

"How did it go? Isn't he gorgeous? Did he ask for your number?"

"You are dreadful Monica," Susie said without much conviction, "leaving me with a stranger. He is very nice, and no, he didn't ask for my number.

Thank goodness," she ended, with even less conviction.

Susie lay in her bed, unsettled by the evening's events. In the few years of her marriage, when she was completely uninterested in anyone but her husband, many men had tried to hit on her. And now the one time when, she admitted to herself, she had badly wanted a man to ask to see her again - nothing. She also recognized that she was not used to being dismissed, and she had the grace to be a little embarrassed by the thought. She had a fitful night's sleep.

The next morning, the three of them were having breakfast when there was a knock at the door. They looked at each other, bemused; no one knew them in Barcelona.

"I'll go," said Steve, walking into the hallway.

He opened the door to a youngster of nine or ten. The boy looked at Steve and, after a tiny delay, he held out a beautifully wrapped parcel, "For senyora Susie, senyor, from my father."

And with that, the boy turned and skipped back down the stairs.

"For you it seems, Susie," Steve said, handing her the parcel.

She opened it carefully. Inside, was a soft cotton slipcase protecting a beautiful off-white shoulder bag made of the softest leather she had ever handled.

Silently she handed the bag to Monica, who looked at it very carefully.

"Do you know what this is, Susie?"

Susie shook her head.

"This is a *Talena* bag, this is made from ostrich leather. This bag retails for over $5000. If you can get one that is."

She handed the bag back to Susie. "You should look inside."

Susie unzipped the bag; sure enough, at the bottom was an ivory colored calling card. In traditional flowing script it announced, *'Sebastiá Xavier Domènech i Marti'* with a phone number below. On the back, in a strong copperplate hand, was the message, 'Please have dinner with me this evening, Javi.'

She showed the card to Monica. She had yet to speak a word since the knock on the door.

"Well, I'd say you were a hit, Susie. I wonder where he got this bag? It's barely nine o'clock in the morning, the shops aren't open for another hour. Do you suppose he has a stock of these in a cupboard, just in case he meets a beautiful woman whose bag has been stolen?"

"What do you think I should do Monica? I don't think I can keep this if it's so expensive. What do you think Steve?"

Steve answered first, "Of course you should keep it. He gave it to you, didn't he? I assume he can afford it, so I wouldn't worry about the cost. Anyway, maybe it's a knock-off."

Monica dismissed him, "Why did I marry a man without a romantic bone in his body? Of course it isn't a knock off. Only a hopelessly unromantic Englishman could suggest that. He had way too much class to send her a fake bag, for God's sake. Anyway, see this tiny number stamped on the zipper? You can enter that number on the web site and it will tell you the model, year and color of the bag, the name of the man who cut the leather and the woman who sewed it together and the place where the animal was reared. And of course Susie needs to think about whether to keep the bag. I suggest that Susie accepts his invitation and decides at dinner whether to keep the bag or not. It all comes down to whether she'll want to see him again after tonight, right Susie?"

"Yes, that's it. If I'm not going to see him again, I can't keep the bag. I must admit though, I'm glad he got in touch."

She telephoned the number on the card and accepted his invitation, but she didn't mention the bag. He told her that he would pick her up at nine p.m.

As Susie ended her call, Steve suddenly remembered, "I almost forgot, the kid who delivered the bag said it was from his father. I should have mentioned that earlier, it quite slipped my mind."

Monica and Steve were planning to check out two marinas well to the north of the city. They would use the same story that Susie had dreamed up, but now Andy would have a married sister. The two marinas were the most remote that Andy would conceivably use, they thought, and the Andersens had good friends in the area they wanted to visit. They would be gone for the entire day and evening.

Susie decided to take a walk through the city to the furthest of the city center yacht clubs. While she strolled through the bustling streets, she thought back to how well dressed Javi had been, and about the cost of the bag. She guessed the restaurant he was taking her to might be very smart, and the only smart outfit she had with her, was the summer dress she had brought for the wedding, completely unsuitable for this evening. When she was done at the marina, she would go shopping.

It took her an hour of steady walking to reach the yacht basin. She found the Capitania and told the man on duty her sad tale, by now very familiar to her, and more believable with each performance. This time however, the result was quite different.

"Senyor Smith, of course, I remember him very well. He was here for two weeks. He was not very happy with the berth we gave him, it was a little exposed and perhaps a little uncomfortable. But as you can see, we are very busy and I was not able to offer him anything else. He left when he found another berth, further from the city. Perhaps

Castelldefels or Sitges, I'm afraid I was not working on the day he left; I don't know which marina he went to. Just one moment please."

Susie was ecstatic. This was final confirmation that Andy was definitely here in Barcelona. The young man returned in a few minutes.

"His boat is called *'Aywol'*. A very nice yacht by the way. Good luck, senyora. Would you like me to telephone the other marinas to the west?"

"Oh, no thank you, I would rather find him myself. Thank you, you have been very kind."

She called Monica and told her about the marina discovery. The Andersons could relax and just enjoy the rest of their day with their friends.

It was too early to call the US, so Susie went shopping.

She didn't want to waste too much time, so she did a quick search on her phone and found the address of the Armani store in Barcelona. It was on Passeig de Gràcia, which she knew was just the other side of Plaça de Catalunya. So, feeling rather brave and adventurous, she worked out how to take the Metro to the Plaça station, and walked to the store.

She quickly realized that she had struck lucky; there were loads of designer shops all along both sides of the wide boulevard. She hurried on to Armani and spent a pleasant hour trying on cocktail dresses, until she found an elegant midnight blue dress that fitted her perfectly and highlighted her eyes. She decided that she would break the habit of a lifetime and not carry a purse that evening. The thief had ruined her nicest bag and she felt that buying another would send the wrong message in the circumstances. So she had a free choice of shoes.

Conveniently enough, the Jimmy Choo store was also on Passeig de Gràcia, just a short stroll away. She found a pair of 'Lucy' high heel pumps that she liked and smiled at the thought of showing them to Lucy Petersen when she went home. Susie had never needed anyone to style her hair, but she decided a manicure was called for. She looked around the girls serving in Jimmy Choo's.

"Hello, I've been admiring your nails. Is there a manicure salon near here by chance?"

It was her lucky day, she decided. The Nail Concept salon was nearby and the sales assistant had given Susie the name of her favorite manicurist, after she had called from the store to make an appointment for Susie. Susie had explained enough of her story for her new friend to persuade the manicurist that this was an emergency, and Susie had to be fitted in between appointments.

So it was a happy Susie who stood in the shower back in the apartment at 7 p.m. She realized that she was acting like a teenager going on a first date. Heck, she *felt* like that teenager again. She took her time applying a minimum of make up and tried to calm down with a small glass of white wine from the open bottle in the fridge. She took her glass out onto the balcony and called Jill to tell her the news about Andy.

On the stroke of nine, Javi knocked at her door. Susie opened it and he stood frankly admiring her.

"I know you hear this a lot," he said, "but you are incredibly beautiful. Thank you for accepting my invitation, and thank you for..." He gave a wave of his hand to indicate her outfit, her look.

She blushed a little as he offered her his arm and they went down into the street.

"The restaurant is only about fifteen minutes away, if you don't mind walking; or I can call a taxi?"

"No, let's walk, it's a beautiful evening."

"It is just off Passeig de Gràcia, so we will pass Casa Batllo, have you visited it?"

Susie had been smiling at the mention of her new favorite street, "No, although I have walked along Passeig de Gràcia, but I was focusing on the shops, not the buildings."

"Ah," he said, "I understand; new shoes."

"How did you know?"

"Those are Jimmy Choo's I think, 'Lucy' is a new style this year. I just guessed."

"I'm not sure I like being with a man who knows more about shoes than I do." She laughed and then became serious.

"Since we are talking about shoes, can I ask you about the lovely bag your son delivered?"

"Of course."

She told him Monica's theory of the cupboard full of bags.

Now it was Javi's turn to laugh, "Not a bad idea, but no, I don't have a supply. My ex-wife helped me out."

Susie abruptly stopped walking, incredulous. "You mean you gave me a bag that belonged to your ex-wife?"

"No, no, of course not. You know perhaps the bag is called 'Talena'?"

"Well, to be honest, Monica knew."

"Talena is my ex-wife. Are you ready for another Catalan name? My former wife is called Magdalena Maria Bacardi i Meier, Talena to her family and friends. When I left you last night, I called her and asked her to meet me at one of her shops early this morning, so I could buy your bag."

"You called your ex to open a store early so you could buy a bag for another woman?" Susie's voice betrayed her astonishment.

"Talena is my best friend, Susie. Well, actually she is married to my best friend. Talena and Mateo are my best friends I should say. She designed your bag and she owns the company. I see you are not using the bag tonight. Wrong color?"

She explained her dilemma about accepting such an expensive gift. He made no comment, except to say, "Perhaps I can explain more over dinner? Look, we are at Casa Batllo."

They had stopped outside an amazing building that did not have a single straight line as far as Susie could see. It looked as if it had grown out of the sidewalk.

"It was designed by Antoni Gaudi, Barcelona's most famous architect. It is also known as the *Casa dels Ossos*, the House of Bones. Do you see how the building has a skeleton? The roof is a dragon's back. I would like to bring you back to see inside before you leave."

They walked on, Javi pointing out some of the other unique buildings along the street.

Soon they arrived at Lasarte, the restaurant he had chosen. Once again, he was greeted warmly by name, this time by the maître d'hôtel. They were shown to their table and the maître d' spoke to Javi again, "I'll let Martin know you are here, Javi. Will you be having the tasting menu?"

"Would that be OK with you Susie? Is there anything you are allergic to perhaps?"

"No, nothing, and yes, I'm happy to be guided by you, you seem to be familiar with the restaurant."

She looked around and was glad she had shopped, even if she had spent almost $1500. The other guests were all very chic indeed and there was a lot of discreet, but very expensive jewelry on display. She also noticed that there were no empty tables.

"Since Monica isn't here, I'll ask on her behalf, how did you get this table, Javi?"

It was his turn to look bashful.

"Well, I took a chance to be honest. I came here last night after I left you. This is where I called Talena from. They always keep a table until the last minute, just in case. I took a chance that you would accept my invitation."

"Just in case?"

"Just in case a regular customer calls."

"And if I hadn't accepted?" She smiled, teasing him.

"Talena and Mateo would have had dinner on me, that was my deal with Talena for opening the shop. Now you know all my secrets."

"Tell me more about Talena and your son."

"We were married very young, too young in hindsight, only twenty-one. We had our son Jordi, but a few years later we discovered that, while we loved each other, we weren't in love. Do you understand Susie?"

"I think so."

"We divorced, and then Mateo, my best friend since we were six, told me that he had been in love with Talena for years, but of course had hidden his feelings. He asked my permission to talk with Talena and after a year or so he persuaded her to marry him. They have twins now and they are very happy. Oh, and that's why I know about shoes; when you live with someone in the fashion business, you pick up a lot."

"And Jordi?"

"He lives between us. When the twins were tiny, he lived with me most of the time; he said the smell of diapers made him sick. Now he moves between us; Talena or I text the other every evening to check him in. By the way, he's not very happy with you at the moment."

"Why not?" *'This could be a problem,'* thought Susie.

"Because you didn't open the door this morning."

He was smiling. "He got dressed up especially, and then Monica's husband opened the door. He was hoping to see the beautiful American woman, and of course he thought the man might be your boyfriend, so he told me."

Susie had a sudden rush of emotion at the thought of the conversation that must have transpired between father and son that morning.

Just then, the first course arrived.

The meal was unlike anything she had experienced. There were eleven courses before coffee, each more delicious than the last. Some were no more than a single mouthful, none were more than two or three. Every dish featured one dominant taste combination, complimented by perfect accompaniments. And with each course they were served a very small glass of a wine carefully selected to complement the food.

Before the final two courses were served, the chef owner appeared at their table and pulled up a chair. He explained to Susie how the desserts were made and stayed to watch her enjoy them with a glass of sweet sherry.

"This is made from Pedro Ximénez grapes," Martin explained, "see how you like it."

It was intensely sweet and utterly delicious.

Finally, their exquisite meal was finished, and they went to the door.

"I asked them to call for a taxi. One way is enough walking in those heels I think."

The taxi dropped them at her building. They stood for a moment until Susie spoke.

"Thank you Javi, for a wonderful evening; everything about it was magical, including the company."

He brushed her lips lightly with his and asked "May I see you tomorrow?"

"Please."

"Bona nit, que dormis bé, Susie."

She looked at him with a question in her expression.

"Good night, sleep well."

"Bona nit, Javi."

GETTING ACQUAINTED

Susie woke up the following morning and stretched luxuriously. The previous night had been like a dream, and the dream would continue today, he had said. What she really wanted, was to lie in bed and relive every minute of the evening; but she worried that he might call and suggest something before lunch, so she forced herself to get into the shower and get dressed.

Sure enough, as she moved into the kitchen to make herself a coffee, her phone rang.

"Bon dia, Susie."

"Bon dia, Javi."

"Have you had breakfast?"

"No, I was just about to make some coffee."

"Leave the coffee, I'll be there in ten minutes."

"No, sorry, Monica and Steve are leaving this morning to go to England, I must say goodbye. Could we meet at ten o'clock perhaps?"

"I will be there at ten."

Monica appeared, "So how was dinner?"

Susie tried to explain how extraordinary her evening had been.

"You certainly are traveling first class Susie, Lasarte is the hottest restaurant in Barcelona. It's tipped to have the first three Michelin stars in the city."

"Monica, I can't thank you and Steve enough. You've made the start of this project so much easier for me, a complete stranger."

Steve was just coming into the room, "We're not strangers now Susie. We'll see you again in a week or so."

"Have a great visit."

They said their goodbyes. Susie felt a little guilty, she couldn't properly concentrate on Monica and Steve. Most of her attention was on her watch, waiting for ten o'clock to come around.

She had another entrancing and utterly memorable day. They had breakfast in a nearby cafe and then just walked around the city. Javi was very knowledgeable about his hometown and, she could see, very proud of Barcelona and of his Catalan heritage. He took her on the cable car to Montjuic where they could see over the entire city.

They took the bus back into the center. Susie commented, "You're not going to believe me, but this is the first time I've ever been on a public bus. I use the subway in New York occasionally, but never the buses."

"Oh, I'm not surprised. In most of the US, bus services are terrible. Not enough middle class people use them; and they are the ones who can influence politicians. In European cities there is nowhere to park downtown; so rich and poor, we all use public transport systems, so they are, on the whole, pretty good."

They went to a tiny tapas restaurant for lunch. By now Susie almost took it for granted that Javi would be known everywhere they went. There was always a table available, and the service was always impeccable. And Javi never wrote a check, or showed a credit card. Instead he either simply walked out after saying thanks, or he might sign something. When she asked him, he was very casual about it. Either he had an account, or he was an old friend, or they did business together. Nothing worth talking about really.

In the afternoon, they wandered the side streets, looking into some of the small specialist shops selling paper products, or picture frames, or antiques, or craft supplies.

Susie had a question. "Javi, why are the stores so different here? There are so many small shops and tiny bars and restaurants. In the States we would have more large stores and more chains."

"You know, I noticed that when I was at Harvard, and I had no idea why it was so different. Then I was able to ask an expert, a professor of urban studies. It turns out to be down to property ownership. Most of the small businesses you see around here are in premises that are owned by the shopkeeper or bar owner. And he probably inherited it from his father and grandfather. So he isn't paying rent."

"But why have they not been sold? Property seems very expensive in Barcelona, these little shops must be worth a lot of money."

"Two things. Barcelona property only really became expensive after the Olympics in 1992. Before that, these properties were not very valuable at all. And even today, the average retail property would not bring enough in a sale to live on for the rest of your life. And what would the seller do next? He probably lives above the premises, or around the corner. How would he find another job in the neighborhood? And what about his son or daughter, who expects to inherit the shop and the home one day? Of course, some do sell up and so slowly the city changes, but not too much I hope."

They slowly made their way to Park Güell. As they strolled around, Javi told her something of the story of Gaudi and his wealthy client, Eusebi Güell. He guided her to a sinuous bench that snaked around a terrace, from where they could enjoy another view over the city.

"So Susie, last night I told you my story. What about you? I can't help noticing your wedding ring, but somehow I don't think there is a husband waiting for you in Long Island, I don't believe you would have allowed me to kiss you if there was."

Susie had thought hard about how she was going to answer this question, which she knew was coming.

"It's a long story Javi, and in the end I'm afraid you'll think I'm crazy."

She told him the story, from finding the note in her kitchen, discovering the scale of Andy's crimes, the decision to try to find him, to her arrival in Barcelona. She told him that Sophie and Peter would be arriving in two days and that after her discovery at the yacht club, they had a better idea of where to look for Andy.

"And if you do find him, what then?"

"We threaten him with the police and deportation back to the US. If he won't hand over the money, he'll go to jail for a long time. And comfortable middle class Americans are terrified by the thought of prison. If he does agree, we'll have to hold onto him for a while, to give us time to get hold of his assets, so he can't try to put them out of reach."

"Well, I must say Susie, you are even more interesting than I thought. What a story. It sounds like an airport paperback, to be honest. Beautiful blonde woman with her derring-do sidekicks, tracks down financial fraudster. How does it end do you think?"

"When you say it like that, it does sound ridiculous, I know." Susie responded, somewhat defensively.

"No, please don't misunderstand me. I think your efforts are magnificent. It's a quest. It sounds like the authorities have lost interest. If you don't make the effort, who will?"

"Exactly! That's why I'm here."

"Well, I thought we might do something very low key this evening. I wanted to know if you would like to have dinner at home tonight, with Jordi and me?"

To his surprise, there was a long silence.

"Susie? We can do something else if you prefer."

"Javi, I think you know that I'm attracted to you. We're not children, we're adults, but Jordi is just a boy. I don't want to be part of hurting your son. I'm only here for a few weeks you know."

"Oh Susie, you don't have to worry, Jordi has met some of my friends before. He knows that you're not necessarily going to be here for long. Although, I hope you will be."

And so, she agreed. He told her that he would send a car at eight o'clock, but not to worry if she was late, the driver would wait.

At eight sharp, Susie went down to stand at the door to the street, but the car was already there. She was driven five minutes down towards the waterfront. The car pulled up at a large house behind an ornate cast iron gate. As soon as they stopped, a man appeared from inside and opened the gate. He welcomed her in and guided her to the front door. A young boy was waiting inside the door. He stepped forward as she walked into the hall.

"Good evening, Senyora Smith, I am Jordi."

He was a miniature Javi, with the same strong chin and high cheekbones. He too spoke perfect, unaccented English.

"Good evening Jordi, I'm pleased to meet you. You don't look nearly as horrible as I expected."

He looked at her, startled. Then he laughed. "My father; you should never believe him Senyora Smith, not about me anyway."

"I'm teasing you Jordi, your father is very proud of you. And I am very pleased to meet you. Now should you and I go out for dinner, or shall we go see your father?"

"It would be so much fun to go out and not tell him, but I think we should probably go in."

Javi was waiting in the hall. He kissed her on both cheeks, "I see you are carrying your new bag tonight."

She looked him directly in the eye and said ,"Yes, I've decided it's a keeper after all."

He smiled and nodded in response. "I am very glad."

They ate in the kitchen dining area, a simple dinner of lightly curried fresh seafood with rice followed by a crema catalana.

Afterwards Jordi showed off, making and serving them coffees. They talked about life in America for a while, until Javi decided that it was time for Jordi to go to bed.

"Bon nit, Jordi," Susie succeeded in surprising him.

"Bon nit, Senyora Smith," he replied.

"Please, call me Susie, Jordi."

"Bon nit, Susie."

"Would you like to come into the salon?" asked Javi when he came back downstairs.

As they left the kitchen, Susie glimpsed a very grand dining room through an open door. He led her through the central hall to a large, double height formal room hung with paintings and tapestries.

"It is rather formal, but I wanted you to see something."

He led her over to a large family portrait. A very elderly, very distinguished-looking man with white hair sat erect in a magnificent gilt armchair. His large family was arrayed around him, middle aged children with husbands and wives, she supposed, adult grandchildren and some youngsters

"It was painted in 1991. That is my great-grandfather the year before he died. This was his house. My grandfather and grandmother," he was pointing to various figures in the painting, "my mother and…"

Susie stopped him.

"Wait," she said, taking over, "your father and, here, that's you. Or here maybe?"

Suddenly she wasn't sure.

"Well done, yes, that is my father and that is me," he was pointing to her second guess. "That is my sister Isabella and that is my brother Jordi, who died three years after this was painted. He was a year older than me, he was fourteen when he died, in a sailing accident." A look of sadness crossed his face. "I think of him every day, every time I look at my son."

The family resemblance was strong. When she looked at the painting again, she could see the faint echo of Javi, even in his great-grandfather's lined features. She looked at his brother again.

"Perhaps his spirit lives on, in your Jordi," she suggested.

"I like to think that. Anyway, I wanted you to meet him."

"What a lovely thing to say!" she exclaimed.

She looked at him, and suddenly they were kissing, deeply this time, with passion.

They drew apart, each aware of the intensity of their feelings.

"You know I would like to ask you to stay?"

"It wouldn't be right Javi, I wouldn't want to meet Jordi in the morning, and I don't want to leave like a guilty lover in the night."

"He can stay with Talena and Mateo tomorrow night."

"That would be good." She kissed him again, this time with promise, rather than passion.

"Show me some more." She waved her hand around the room.

"I'll show you more of the family later, let's go next door, it is less formal, and has a surprise."

Susie slipped her arm through his and they went through a set of double pocket doors into a smaller room, with a very different ambiance. She caught her breath. "My goodness," she exclaimed.

The room was hung with six large oil paintings. Susie walked slowly around the room and then approached one in particular.

"Javi, is this...?" Her voice trailed off.

"Yes, it is by Claude Monet. This is the collection of my great-grandfather, Sebastiá Tomás, the man in the painting. He had a good eye. This one too is by Monet, it is one of his last paintings."

"And this?" She pointed.

"Picasso gave this to Sebastiá Tomás's father, they were friends. I think that growing up with this painting gave Sebastiá Tomás his life-long interest in modern art, although he stopped collecting when the Civil War started."

They spent some time looking at the paintings, talking comfortably, easily; both very aware of each other's presence, until it was time for Susie to leave. Javi telephoned for a taxi.

"Each time I see you is very special, you know?" she said to him at the door.

"And for me too, Susie. I'll look forward to seeing you tomorrow. I have meetings during the day I'm afraid, but I could collect you at seven?"

"I'll be waiting; with my toothbrush."

The next morning, Susie did lie in bed for a while, reliving her time in Barcelona. Even if things didn't work out with Javi, *'And face it girl,'* she lectured herself, *'this will be a holiday romance, you're going back to the States in six weeks, come what may,'* even if that was true, she knew she wanted her life to go forward. She was well and truly over Andy and everything he represented. And Jill had pointed out that finding Andy was less important than finding herself.

Last night she had been too excited to simply go to bed. She had called Jill and they had talked for an hour on Skype. She told her all about Javi and their plans for tonight.

"Monica called from her son's house and told me about the elegant Spaniard with the designer bag collection. I'm happy you're having a good time. Just be careful, it's only a holiday romance remember, and remember too, how holiday romances could break your heart when you were fourteen. Don't let it happen this time."

"Oh, he'll break my heart a little, Jill, but I don't mind, it's worth it. This trip has already been a success for me. I'm excited about the future, even if I don't know what it will bring. But don't worry, I still want to carry out the plan and find Andy. The trouble is that there's a limit on what I can do by myself. I'm looking forward to Sophie and Peter arriving and getting back on the hunt for real. Narrowing him down to a particular marina is a good start, I guess. How is everyone?"

"Everyone's fine, Kevin and Lucy have been asking for you, and Alejandra and Charlie have another date tomorrow night. And Frank tells me that Charlie has asked his advice about buying a car. He's driving a twenty-odd year old Ford that is his grandmother's and it seems like he wants to upgrade."

"Charlie must have asked her out all by himself, I haven't talked with him for a few days. Well done, Charlie. I hope he gets a cool car, don't let Frank persuade him into something sensible."

Jill laughed, "Good luck with that thought, honey. 'Sensible' is my husband's middle name."

Susie spent the rest of the morning cleaning the already clean apartment. She changed the bed linen and the towels and prepared bedrooms for Sophie and Peter's arrival the next day. Just as she ran out of things to do, she had an idea. She went online and did a quick Google search 'learn Catalan'. There were lots of online resources and she spent a happy few hours mastering some simple phrases, until it was time to shower, dress, and slip a toothbrush into her purse.

At seven o'clock, Javi picked her up and they drove to his house. As they drove around to the back of the building to the garages, Susie noticed a gardener working in the flowerbeds. Javi followed her gaze.

"There are three staff for the house. The gardener lives up there, above the garage and there is a husband and wife who live over there." He pointed to a separate little cottage. "Apart from looking after anything else, in particular my comfort," he joked, "the insurance company requires someone to be on the premises at all times."

The fact that they both knew how the evening would end, removed any pressure, so they could relax and enjoy just being together.

"I'll show you the rest of the house later, but why don't we have a glass of cava on the terrace and enjoy the last of the sun."

A table had been prepared, with a bottle chilling in an ice bucket and olives in a small crystal bowl.

"Salut! Susie."

"Salut! Javi."

They sat in companionable silence, enjoying the warmth of the sun, the sparkling wine and the presence and promise of each other.

After a while, Susie spoke, "This is lovely wine, very fresh and soft. I like it, what is it?"

"Here, take a look." He handed her the bottle.

The label read *'Cava'* on one line and then *'Sarita Àngel'* in large letters below, and on the next line *'Gran Reserva'*. Along the bottom, in much smaller type, she read *'Elabarador: Domènech S.L. Penedès, España.'*

"This is yours!" she exclaimed.

"My family's," he corrected her. "My father is the President of the company, I run sales and marketing. There are two uncles, an aunt and three cousins in the company. You remember the old man in the painting, my great-grandfather, Sebastiá Tomás? Well, *his* grandfather founded the business in the 1870s."

"So where do your parents live, Javi?"

"In Penedès, in the vineyards, along with my grandparents; although they all have rooms here, for when they come to the city. And I have rooms in the Penedès house."

"The old man, the founder, had a daughter who died when she was only five. Her name was Sarita, which is Sara in Catalan. He named the wine for her."

"You have so much history in your family, you're very lucky."

"I am very lucky, but not all of the history is pleasant, just like Spain, just like Catalunya. But yes, I am lucky. Here I am drinking wine with a beautiful, exciting woman."

He reached across the table and took her hand in his. They sat in silence and watched the last rays of the sun paint the sky with brilliant red streaks and orange flashes. Susie felt peace and serenity wash over her.

"Thank you Javi, thank you for giving me all of this. I feel a little Catalan tonight. You've given me a part of your city, your country, your family. I will take them all with me, when I leave."

"Well, you have certainly taken a part of my family; Jordi is a fan. He told me this morning that you had asked him to dinner. He says he only said no out of pity for me, he didn't want me to know that you liked him better."

They laughed together. "It is true, I did invite him, but he thought we'd better stay with you. He's a lovely boy, you must be very proud."

They went in to have dinner.

"I have to be honest Susie, I don't cook. Anna prepared dinner last night, and she has prepared something for us tonight, let's see what it is, shall we?"

He led her into the formal dining room. Susie's first thought was that there were too many candlesticks on the table; there must have been at least ten, with twenty or thirty candles altogether. There was a note on the table, which Javi picked up and read. He smiled and handed it to Susie. 'No t'oblidis d'encendre les espelmes. Jordi xxxx'

"It means, don't forget to light the candles."

He lit most of the candles, just as Jordi recommended, and the flickering light reflected off the silver and crystal table settings. There were fresh flowers everywhere, and when Javi came back from the kitchen he was carrying two plates of bellota ham and a small basket of bread.

"There is a seafood salad to follow," he told her.

"I bought some of this ham the other day. It's really wonderful, I had never heard of it before."

"I know, we haven't done a great job promoting luxury food and wines from Spain, although things are getting a little better. I've been working with some other producers - of ham, olives, olive oil, cheese and still wines to create a marketing campaign in the US, to promote a range of fine food and wine products. Maybe in a year or so we'll be able to launch. This is my major project these days."

When they had finished their meal it was still only 9.30, but they were both ready. He reached again for her hand, but this time he pulled her gently to her feet and kissed her.

He led her upstairs to his room.

Their lovemaking was everything either had anticipated, and more. At first he was tender; slowly undressing her and delighting in every secret of her body as it was revealed to him. He kissed and caressed every curve and fold until she demanded him inside her. They moved together easily, attuned to each other from the first thrilling moment, until she became more urgent and his thrusts grew deeper as her hips rose to meet him.

Afterwards she lay in his arms, content and secure.

In the middle of the night Susie awoke and, in the faint light of the bedside clock, she saw him looking at her. She reached for his hand, pulled it across her breasts and down between her legs and they made love again, this time slowly and gently.

In the morning they awoke and cuddled. Neither had the slightest feeling of embarrassment or awkwardness.

"I had a lovely, lovely time Javi."

"And thank you Susie, you are very special. I want to see more of you."

She lifted up the sheet, looked at her naked body, and apologized, "There isn't anything else to see I'm afraid, this is all there is."

He laughed. "Very funny. When can I see you, really?"

"I have to take care of Sophie and Peter today and on Sunday. But I could come over later on Sunday evening? And on Monday, we're going to Sitges, but could we perhaps all eat together on Monday evening? I would like them to meet you."

"That all sounds wonderful. When do you have to be at the airport this morning?"

"Not until eleven. Did you have something in mind?"

"Mmmm."

REINFORCEMENTS

Sophie and Peter's flight was on time and they were among the first through to Arrivals. Susie spotted Peter immediately and ran to embrace him, offering both her cheeks to be kissed.

"Very continental," he laughed. "Spain certainly seems to agree with you Susie, you look great."

Susie was about to ask where Sophie was, when she noticed a woman who had stopped a few steps behind Peter. Susie had to look twice, three times.

"Oh my God, Sophie! Is that you? You look … you look fabulous actually. But so different!"

Sophie now had short, peroxide blonde hair. She was wearing a multicolored belted caftan-style dress with a plunging neckline. Her modesty was covered by the collection of six or seven heavy chains she wore around her neck. She hugged Susie, stepped back and gave her a little pirouette.

"I wanted to be a blonde when I was about twelve. And now finally, I am! You look great Susie!"

"I am great, and you look incredible!" she said taking Sophie's arm and guiding them towards the car park. "I am quite wonderful, Sophie. London agreed with me, and Barcelona certainly agrees with me. And I think you'll love it here Peter, everyone is almost as elegant as you. Sophie, just wait until you see the shops, and the people. God, Sophie, I can't believe how different you look. If I hadn't been looking for you, I never would have recognized you."

They drove into the city while Susie brought them up to date. "We're going back to Sitges first thing Monday, you'll love it Peter, it's full of very attractive gay men."

She told them about Javi and that they would be meeting him on Monday evening for dinner.

Sophie had news to share. "I have news for you Susie, and now I see Charlie was unnecessarily worried about telling you about it. Charlie's pretty clever isn't he? You know that photograph of Andy that you sent him? Well, it turns out you can search for someone online using a photo. Charlie did that and he found some images of Andy online, images from after he had run off."

"Really? Where was he?"

"In London. The images came from a site called vk.com. It's a Russian site, their equivalent of Facebook. Andy appears in a few group photos, always with a young Russian woman called Valentina. The photos aren't hers, she and Andy are always among other people. This Valentina has her own page on vk.com, and on Facebook and Twitter for that matter, but she never mentions Andy or uploads any photos of him. Her postings taper off gradually, and finish completely July fifteenth, after that nothing. Her accounts are open and there are quite a few *'where are you?'* kind of messages on her pages, but no responses from her."

"Charlie thinks he may be able to find out where her last few posts were made from. Somehow he knows that they're not from England, but he hasn't yet pinned them down between France and Spain. He thought you might be upset that Andy seems to have a girlfriend, but now I'm thinking, maybe not so much."

"You're right, not so much at all. We're nearly home. Would you like to take a nap, or go out?"

Peter answered first. "If I could have a quick shower, then I'd love to stretch my legs."

Sophie elected to have a nap, after she had called Will.

While Peter had his shower, Susie thought about how lucky she was that he had agreed to help, and about how close the two of them had become in a such a relatively short time.

The week after Sophie had volunteered her son's help back in May, Peter had come to meet Susie for the first time, and to renew his connections with Anne and Jill.

Peter was a talented freelance designer who had completed projects designing private homes, sets for theatre productions, art installations, retail 'experiences'. As he explained to his father, his problem wasn't finding work, but deciding in what direction he should develop. He needed a unique signature to stand out from the many other talented designers in New York. He hadn't found it yet.

Sophie had good reason to be confident that Peter would help in any way he could to find Andy. Only she and her son knew just how badly the episode with Andy had wounded Will. Will's self-esteem had been badly damaged. He understood perfectly well that neither Sophie nor her father, Luis, would have contemplated taking any part in Andy's scheme if he, Will, hadn't recommended it so strongly. He had also seen how Joe and Frank had resisted the same temptation that he had fallen for. And he admitted to himself that deep down, he had known all along that there had to have been something not quite right about Andy's deals; but still he had gone along with him.

The truth was that Will had always harbored feelings of inadequacy because of his abbreviated education. The whole Andy business had made him feel inadequate, guilty and depressed. And his wife and youngest child were completely aware of all of this. And they were determined to help.

Susie and Peter had hit it off immediately at that first meeting. They shared the same sense of humor and discovered that they had the same passion for Broadway musicals.

During the meeting, Peter's phone had beeped with a text alert. He looked at it and swore, "Damn it, Roy has cancelled." He looked up to see everyone looking at him. "Sorry, but the friend I was going to see Cabaret with has called off. Never mind, where were we?"

When the meeting was finished, Susie came up to Peter, "How did you manage to get Cabaret tickets? It's only been open a month."

"I do some work in the theatre, I'm a Broadway dahling, dahling," he laughed. "Hey, do you want to come with me? They're for Wednesday's matinee."

"Are you kidding? Of course, but are you sure?"

"Absolutely, you can buy me dinner after the show."

Cabaret was terrific, and it turned out that Peter could get tickets for almost any current show, on or off-Broadway. They became regular theatergoers together. Susie had spent too many nights at home over the previous six months. Her friends had been great, inviting her to join them at community events and for family dinners, but she felt guilty imposing on them too often. And going out with Peter was fun, and stress free, he wanted her company, nothing more. She got to meet some of his friends, straight and gay, and enjoyed them as well.

In a few short months, Susie and Peter had become fast friends.

Susie walked Peter up the top section of the Ramblas and through Plaça de Catalunya and into Passeig de Gràcia, where they browsed the designer stores, including those where Susie had recently bought her outfit. They were looking at the window display in Jimmy Choo's when the assistant saw Susie and waved. Susie held up her fingers and smiled.

"What was all that about?"

"Girl stuff," Susie answered mysteriously. "Look at the people Peter, what do you see?"

"Well, they're pretty young on the whole, younger than a random crowd in New York."

"Correct, this is a young city. What else strikes you?"

They walked on, Peter scanning the crowds. "A lot of them are very well dressed, is that it? Wait, I know, they *are* very well dressed, but they're also slim, normal, hardly anyone is fat. That's why they look so good."

"Yes, you don't see many overweight people. It took me a while to work it out, something was different, but I couldn't see what it was. The Andersons think it's all about the Mediterranean diet and having hardly any sodas or processed foods. Even the restaurants are different; they're nearly all family-owned, with just the one place, cooking fresh, local food. And of course, the Spanish are all really vain and love looking good and showing off." Susie laughed and continued, "Talking of food, are you hungry?"

"Actually yes, I am."

Susie looked around and led Peter down a side street where they soon found a small tapas restaurant.

"Bona tarda. Que tindrien una taula per a dues persones, si us plau?" *'Good afternoon. Do you have a table for two, please.'*

"Per descomptat senyora, si us plau, segueixi'm." *'Of course, follow me please.'*

"Wow, Susie, you've learned to speak Spanish? Actually, that didn't sound like Spanish."

She laughed, "No Peter, I only learned that phrase yesterday. And it's Catalan, not Spanish. I'll explain in a minute."

"This is a tapas restaurant. Do you see all those little plates? Just point to what you want and the man will bring it in a few minutes. Would you like a beer, or a glass of something?"

They had a very pleasant lunch. Susie filled Peter in with what she had learned about Catalunya and the differences with the rest of Spain.

After lunch, they walked some more until Susie said, "If you're anything like Jill and I were, you guys won't be in the mood for a late dinner; they eat late here, like nine or ten o'clock late. How about we walk back via the market and pick up something for a light snack later?"

"Excellent idea, I am flagging a bit, but I don't want to go to bed too early or I'll be up at dawn."

So that is what they did. Peter was pleasingly amazed by the sights and smells of the market. They bought some food to take home.

Sophie was reading her guidebook when they returned and the three of them took their snacks with a glass of wine on the little balcony. They chatted and enjoyed the sights of the city. Peter went to bed first and Sophie followed an hour later.

While they slept, Susie did an hour or so on her Catalan lessons. She was sorry not to have seen Javi today, but glad Sophie and Peter were here and the search for Andy was back on track. She sent a message to the group confirming that Sophie and Peter were safely installed and then she went to bed and slept soundly. Susie and Peter planned on having an early start in the morning.

Steve Anderson had pointed out that no one wanted to play golf in the afternoon in August when it could easily reach ninety-five degrees. Golfers would look for early tee times, from as early as six o'clock perhaps.

Susie and Peter had decided to try one of the golf clubs early on Sunday morning. They would drive out of the city to the furthest remaining course on the target list. Susie would wait in the car while Peter went in and discreetly looked for any sign of Andy. Sophie had opted out of an early start for her first morning.

They were out of the apartment by 6:15 a.m. and arrived at the golf club at 7:30. Peter went in to the clubhouse and didn't come out for over half an hour.

"Sorry Susie, I met the club bore, at least the English bore. God that man liked to talk! Anyway, no Andy. No new members or ex-pats this year. The club is in trouble and they are trying to recruit, with no luck. They think they are too far out from the city. Personally I think they all want far away from Colonel Blimp back there."

"Never mind, that's one off the list anyway. Let's find somewhere to eat, I'm hungry."

They found a local cafe and had coffee and delicious breakfast pastries. Suitably fortified, they made their way slowly back to the city.

Peter had been thinking. "The soccer season starts next week. I know Andy was a football and baseball guy, but if he's going to live here, I'm betting he starts following soccer. This city is soccer mad, even I know that. I think Sunday lunchtime and afternoon would be the perfect day to sit in your favorite sports bar and watch the match. Today there are previews of the new season, I checked online. So I think I'll take in a couple of sports bars while you spend some time with Mom. What do you think?"

"I think you should. We saw a huge sports bar on the Ramblas last week, that's when I had my bag stolen actually. I'll drive past it and drop you off on the way home. It's easy to walk back to the apartment. Your Mom and I can try another marina then I'll have to leave you guys to go see Javi."

"I'm guessing we shouldn't wait up for you?" he teased her.

"I'll just ignore that remark." Susie replied, digging him in the ribs.

Susie dropped Peter off, parked and went up to the apartment. Sophie was feeling revived and had been out for a walk.

"What a lovely city this is, Susie! I really enjoyed my stroll."

"Shall we go find something for lunch? You must be hungry by now I expect?"

The two women went out and found one of the tapas bars in the area and had lunch. Then they drove to the marina at Port Ginesta. They had no record of Andy or his yacht ever visiting the marina, they would have to expand their search.

By six o'clock they were all back at the apartment, and by seven they were sitting on the balcony with a glass of wine.

"I feel just a little bit guilty leaving you guys."

Sophie preempted her son, "Don't be crazy. It's fantastic that this is happening to you. Enjoy every minute. And don't worry about us. Peter is going to cook for us tonight."

"I am?" Peter demanded.

They all had a good evening. Peter and Sophie actually went out for dinner and got caught up with all their news, while Susie had rather more energetic fun. Still, she was at the apartment at 7:30 in the morning.

As Susie came into the kitchen, Peter looked at her innocently.

"Sleep well?" which earned him another dig in the ribs. Susie was in an even better mood today.

FOUND

Their plan was to drive to Sitges town center and have breakfast. Susie would then walk to the marina, while Sophie and Peter drove on to the golf course.

They walked through Sitges looking for somewhere to eat. They wandered into a small hotel that had a board offering coffee and croissants. When they sat down in the courtyard, Susie realized that she and Sophie were the only females there.

"I hope we're not cramping your style Peter. These guys might think you're straight, you poor thing." She was giggling like a schoolgirl.

"I don't think all this sex is good for you Susie, you're regressing to your childhood."

To prove him right, she flicked a small piece of croissant in his face.

When they were finished, Susie left them and headed for the marina, a twenty minute walk. She was in no great rush, she wasn't sure the Capitania would open before ten. She was walking past the strip of restaurants that lined the marina when her cell rang.

"He's here Susie, I'm in the car park, I'm looking at Andy right now!" It was Sophie, breathless with excitement.

"Are you sure it's him?"

"One hundred percent. They're on their way to the tenth tee right now. Peter says that you should take the train back to town later. We're going to stay here and try to follow him back to the city so we can find out where he lives."

"OK, when do you think he'll finish his round?"

"We think around 11:30, which should get us back to the city by say one o'clock, unless he stays here for a beer, which Peter thinks is quite likely, in which case it could be two or so. Oh, here's Peter."

Sophie heard the car door close.

Peter's voice was animated. "My God, Susie, we've found him! I guess I really never was sure we would, you know. I mean part of me ... well you know. It seemed like a ridiculous quest."

"That's funny, Javi called it a quest as well. I'll get a train and be back well before you. Call me if anything happens, or if there is anything I can do. And well done! I'll talk to Charlie, and we need to tell everyone."

"Slow down, take it easy. It's only just past three in the morning back home, you won't be calling anyone for a while."

They ended the call. Susie could take her time and get back to the city. *We did it, we did it'* she thought, *'now we need to do right by my friends. I'm going to get back every cent.'*

However, there would be some setbacks along the way, starting that morning. Susie caught a train at noon and arrived at Barcelona Sants station at 12:34. She didn't know where she would be meeting Sophie and Peter, so she sat in the coffee bar at the station to wait. Susie had received a text on the train: Andy was having a beer with his foursome. Another text arrived just as she sat down in the bistro: he was leaving. Another text: he was driving a black BMW 650i convertible, plate number 3378 XFW.

At 1:40, Sophie rang Susie. "We lost him. It looks easy in the movies, but as soon as we left the autoroute and hit the city, we lost him in traffic. Sorry Susie."

"Never mind, we can find him again. Let's meet at the apartment, OK?"

"We'll be there in thirty minutes or so."

They were back at the apartment, sitting at the kitchen table.

"Fantastic job finding him, guys." Susie complimented Sophie and Peter.

"In the end it was easy. We were just about to talk to the guy behind the desk about the Monday expat group, when they came in. It seems they take a break after nine holes and come in for a coffee, or a beer. Andy was in the second foursome. He looked right past me Susie! I couldn't believe it. But there wasn't even a flicker of recognition."

Peter took up the story. "Mom headed for the exit and I hung around and ordered a coffee. I heard some banter between Andy and the guy he was playing with, about a lucky shot he had made, the guy called him Andrew several times."

"It's after seven in the morning back home, let's call Jill" Susie couldn't wait to tell someone. She called Jill's number, but Frank answered.

"Good morning Frank, it's Susie. We wanted to share some news. We found Andy, or rather Sophie and Peter found him. He's in Barcelona after all. Can you spread the word to Anne and Ted? Yes, we're all fine. Say hi to Jill, tell her I'll call again soon."

Next Susie sent a text to Charlie asking if it was OK to call, she didn't want to alarm Gran. Within a minute, her phone rang.

"It's OK Susie, We're both up really early. What's up?"

"We've found him Charlie." She explained what had happened and passed on the car registration information. He asked about Valentina.

"Don't worry Charlie, I could care less what he does or who with. By the way, how did the last date with Alejandra go?"

"It was great, I really like her Susie."

"Well, you go ahead and like her Charlie. I hear you're thinking of getting a new car? What are you looking at?"

"Frank had me look at the Ford Focus and Fiesta." Susie's heart sunk a little, "But I've ordered a Miata, it should arrive in a couple of weeks."

"Excellent choice Charlie, well done. Alejandra will love it when you pick her up in your Miata. And if Frank makes any comment, tell him I said he's getting old."

"I would never say that, Susie. Frank is great."

She laughed, "I know he is Charlie. And so are you. Any more news for me?"

"No, I'm glad we can give up on the marinas, it's too difficult. They don't enter most of the data. They scan some of it and hold it locally. To be honest, I don't know why they bother, I can't see what good it does. I'm thinking of getting in touch with someone in Europe to point out how useless it is."

"Good idea. Now Charlie, can you order the things we discussed? You have the address of this apartment, right?"

"Of course, I'll get right on it."

Dinner turned into a celebration. Javi had given Susie the address of the restaurant and they turned up at nine as instructed. The maître d' was expecting them and led them through the dining room, though a set of swing doors and into the kitchen. A few of the staff nodded a greeting, but most were too busy preparing for service. They were taken to a raised alcove with a large table, surrounded on three sides by a red leather banquette. Javi and Jordi were waiting for them.

Susie introduced everyone.

Javi spoke, "I thought you might enjoy watching the chef and his team working through service."

Susie answered for everyone, "It's fantastic Javi, thanks for arranging it."

They were seated in a horseshoe around the table, so everyone had a view of the kitchen. They were not offered menus, but after they had enjoyed an aperitif, cava of course, one of the chefs came to the table, a young woman.

"Good evening, I am Marta, I am responsible for the entrées, the first courses. I will be pleased to have you taste some of my dishes tonight."

She brought over tiny portions of whatever was ordered from the dining room; little fried fish, cold soup, cured ham, salad and much more. After almost an hour of this, another chef appeared before them.

"Hi, I'm John, from Manchester, England as it happens, and I'm handling the fish dishes tonight. We're offering lobster, salmon and sea bass this evening, cooked various ways and with several sauce options. And over there," he pointed to a young man who looked up and smiled at them, "is Marcos, assisting me and Ximena, who is responsible for all meat dishes. Marcos will prepare any vegetables requested tonight."

He raised his voice a little, "Don't expect too much from Marcos, he's from Madrid, and as useless as his football team."

At that there was a general shout from everyone in the kitchen at Marcos's expense.

Of course, they soon saw that Marcos was every bit the master chef. He could have six different vegetables under way at once, every one cooked to perfection and beautifully presented. He was also working on something that they couldn't quite see, but every time there was a lull in service, he would return to whatever extra task was keeping him busy.

For another hour they tasted samples of fish, meat and delicious vegetables.

And then the pastry and dessert chef appeared. Irena was a very striking young woman, close to six feet tall, slim and shapely. "I am Irena, I am from Slovakia and I will be honored to have you try my desserts tonight."

Desserts were sensational. For their table she created miniature towers of pastry with fruit and cream, truffles, minute tarts and tiny ice creams with perfect fruit balls and fancy tuiles.

Peter announced, "This is the first time I wished I wasn't gay, so I could marry that girl."

Finally the executive chef came over to see them. "I hope you have enjoyed our service this evening, it has been our pleasure to have you here."

Peter spoke again, "It was sensational. Everything was perfect, especially Irena's desserts. Can I ask you, they all seem so young, how old are they?"

"You are quite correct, this is an industry for young people. The oldest person here tonight is twenty-nine, apart from me of course. Most are between eighteen and twenty-six. John for example, is twenty-three and has worked in two Michelin restaurants before this."

As he was speaking, Marcos, the vegetable chef, came to the table and handed something to Jordi.

"I would have done Madrid," he said, "but I thought you would prefer this." It was a Barcelona football team logo, carved into a large swede. It was incredibly detailed and brilliantly colored with food dyes to match the team colors. It was amazing.

"Muchas gracias señor. Voy a ser un poco más agradable con el Real Madrid la próxima vez que os ganemos." *'Thank you very much. I will be a little kinder about Real Madrid next time we beat you.'*

Marcos laughed and shook his hand. Susie had noticed that Jordi had thanked him in Spanish, not

Catalan, a very polite and generous thing for an adult to do, never mind a nine-year-old boy.

During the meal they had, of course, all been talking. Susie told Javi about finding Andy and how excited she was. And Sophie and Peter chatted with him and with Jordi at one point or another during the evening. There was lots of laughter and a very relaxed atmosphere the entire evening. In particular, Peter and Jordi had spent a lot of time discussing the merits of both types of football. Susie was delighted to see her friends get on so well with this captivating Spanish family.

Once again, no bill appeared and they simply thanked everyone and left. Both Sophie and Peter tried to intervene, but Javi very kindly assured them that all was well and they should not worry about anything.

Once on the sidewalk, Peter shook hands with Javi and Jordi, and Sophie received kisses on each cheek. They moved slowly away to allow Susie to say her goodnights.

"Thank you, both of you, for entertaining my friends, and for yet another memorable evening. Jordi, look away, I am about to kiss your father." They kissed briefly, but managed to communicate their feelings. "Can I see you tomorrow sometime? I want to ask your advice about something."

"Of course, just call my number. Morning would be best, I have appointments in the afternoon."

"Thank you and again, thank you for tonight, they will talk about this evening for years!"

She turned to say good night to Jordi and was touched when he embraced her and squeezed her tight, "Bona nit, Susie."

She caught up with the others.

"If, by any chance, Javi turns out to be gay, you will let me know, won't you?"

"Peter you are, what's the word, incorrigible."

"What an amazing experience," exclaimed Sophie. "Susie, I feel bad about the bill. There were three of us and I can't begin to think what it all cost, I just assumed we would split it at the end."

"I really wouldn't worry, I've never seen him pay a bill yet. I think tonight I figured it out though. I didn't draw attention to it because Javi didn't, but the cava we drank at the beginning was made by his family. They have been making cava for over 140 years. I think they all exchange favors. Maybe the restaurant wants a special wine or to have a client entertained at the family vineyard, or to be invited to a fashion show that Javi's ex-wife is involved with. I think they respect each other, look after each other and don't take advantage of each other. I bet their families have been friends for years, generations even."

"You know, it would have been special if he *had* bought us all that lovely dinner, but I think it is even more special that he invited us to be a part of his network of friends. I'm pretty sure a case of cava will appear at the owner's home tomorrow. I'm sure if we went back to that restaurant ourselves next week, while we might not eat in the kitchen, we'd get great service, because now we're friends of the family."

Peter had to ask. "Did you just mention Javi's ex-wife, and not choke?"

"It's a long story Peter. Let me tell it to you."

GET READY

At eleven o'clock on Tuesday morning Susie was shown into Javi's office. It was a modestly sized room in a classic Art Nouveau Barcelona building. The company logo was discreetly etched on the glass doors and appeared here and there on handles and other architectural details.

"Good morning, Javi."

He came across the room and kissed her softly on the lips.

"Good day, Susie, this is a pleasant change to my routine."

He led her to the seating area - a sofa and two comfortable armchairs.

"First of all, thank you once again for last night. We're very grateful to be included in your life."

He looked at her, wondering just how wise this young woman was. He was falling in love.

"It was my pleasure Susie, your friends are very nice, and very good friends. And Jordi enjoyed Peter very much."

"Javi, I realize that it would be stupid not to take advantage of you over something. You remember I told you our plan to hold onto my husband until we can take control of his assets? Well, as you know, we've found Andy, and we'll soon know where he lives. We need to keep him somewhere secure for a few weeks while we identify and transfer his assets. I was going to visit some agents to find a remote farm we could rent for a month, but now I think, *'Be smart, ask Javi'.*"

"Very wise Susie, very smart. Let me think for a moment."

He got up and walked to the window and stood looking onto the street, but she could see that his eyes were focused far away. He turned back to her.

"I think I know the place. But first I need to ask if you are quite sure you want to go through with this. You're proposing to kidnap someone, somebody could get hurt; this is a very serious matter Susie."

"I have thought about this a lot, Javi. First of all, we'd only hold him for more than a day or so with his agreement. If he doesn't agree to hand over the money after two days, we'll leave him to the police. We would have effectively carried out a citizen's arrest. I don't think that, in the circumstances, anyone's going to complain too much if we hold him for forty-eight hours before handing him over."

"If he agrees to hand over the assets, he will be agreeing to wait with us for the time it takes for the transfer."

"And as for violence, there won't be any. We have a plan to catch him without using any force at all, and the only weapon we will have, is a Taser, in case he tries to escape in those first one or two days. And while it hurts like hell apparently, it won't do him any permanent damage."

"One more thing. Andy lied to my family, he cheated our friends, he put my special friend Charlie in serious jeopardy, he broke the law, he stole my money and he treated me with complete and utter contempt; and if we don't do this, he will live in luxury, and for the rest of his life."

There was complete silence for a moment or two, and then Javi smiled at her.

"You're very persuasive Susie. OK, I have somewhere that could work for this very well. I wouldn't want you going there in the winter, there's no heating and the roads are treacherous if it has snowed. But now it will be fine, and it is very secluded, but not very comfortable I'm afraid. Why don't I take you up there tomorrow and you can see for yourself?"

"Is there anything you can't manage, Senyor Domènech i Marti?" she was smiling, her eyes sparkling. She felt so good, just knowing this man.

"I don't think I can manage you senyora. By the way, your pronunciation is becoming really very good."

That afternoon, Andy moved into his new apartment.

Susie hurried from Javi's office to meet up with everyone. Sophie and Peter had gone to the airport to pick up the Andersons, who were passing through on their way home. But first they were all having lunch together.

Peter had been away at college when Monica and Steve left Kingsbay, but they had known him all through his high school years. He was close in age to their son and daughter and had been friends with them both. And of course they were still friends with Sophie and Will, even if they hadn't met in person for a few years.

Monica showed him photographs from the last few days.

"Jeffrey looks great, and I'm guessing that's Lisa?"

"Yes, that's his wife, and these are our grandchildren."

Sophie too had lots of catching up to do with her old friends. "It's too bad we're only seeing you for a couple of hours after all these years," she complained.

Monica agreed. "You'll just have to come over again, Sophie. Now you know where Spain is," she teased.

Steve commented, "You guys did great while we were away. I bet his boat is in the marina at Sitges. The guy said he had gone down the coast, and Sitges is the next option after Ginesta."

"You're probably right Steve, but when Sophie called, I was just too excited to go on to the Capitania. I'm not sure I could have composed myself into the grieving sister and daughter at that moment!"

'Well I imagine your friend Charlie will be able to find him soon enough with his car registration details. Anyway, Monica, we need to get going. I want to make it well past Valencia today, so we don't have another long day tomorrow, like we did coming up."

There were lots of hugs, and promises not to let so many years go by next time.

In the evening, Susie and Peter made dinner. Sophie complimented them on their cooking, but pointed out that, for future reference, she preferred her meals to have a minimum of eight different dishes.

Javi called for Susie at ten the following morning. He had warned her to wear comfortable clothes and walking shoes. She had run out to buy a pair of trainers the previous afternoon, she didn't want to be wearing brand new walking shoes if she had to cover any distance, but made a mental note to buy some, if this location worked out.

He set off through the Barcelona traffic, "We'll drive about an hour and a half, more or less west, but because of the mountains, we have to go in a long loop. But some of the countryside is nice, so I hope you'll enjoy the trip."

"Of course I'll enjoy the trip, I'll have my favorite Catalan guide all to myself for hours and hours. What's not to love about that?"

He looked over and smiled at her. *'She is so alive,'* he thought.

They talked the entire journey. He learned more about Susie's childhood, her Catholic high school and college, her passion for ballet and then skiing and about her parents. He laughed at the story of her father and Cliff Walker.

"How he must have enjoyed to be still protecting his little girl," Javi observed, making her rethink her memory of the event.

She told him more about her friends and her life in Kingsbay, although, like so many men before him, he failed to grasp the point of bunco.

"The game doesn't really matter, it's the company and the fun that we like."

"So why not just meet in someone's house to talk and have fun?"

"I don't know why men have so much trouble with this," Susie sighed dramatically.

She told him how much this trip had meant to her, how she was excited now about the future and no longer looking backwards with regrets.

"I know my friends can live without the money, and I know I'm not responsible, but if I can fix this one thing, my old life will be over, completely. Anyway, that's how I feel."

She told him about Charlie, enough for him to get some idea of his amazing online abilities. And about his budding romance with Alejandra.

Eventually they left the main highway behind, for narrow country roads that wound higher and higher up through dense forests. They came to a clearing, and ahead Susie saw a strange sight. A completely abandoned village was scattered on both sides of the road.

"It was destroyed in the Civil War and the people never came back. It is very sad. But it is very quiet. Sometimes walkers take shelter in one of the empty buildings, but there could be weeks between them, and in any case, this is not where we stop."

They drove on another two miles until Javi turned onto a track that Susie would have missed. They bounced down the rutted path for a few hundred yards until Javi pulled up in front of a rundown farmhouse.

"This is it. Come and see."

He led her into the house and she looked around. There was a basic kitchen, with a sink, table, a bottled gas cooker and a few cupboards. Javi turned the faucet and, after a brief delay, clear water poured out.

"It is safe to drink," he said.

Behind the kitchen was a living room, furnished with an ancient sofa and a few chairs. A table stood against a wall, with a bench in front of it. In the corner she saw a wooden staircase. They went upstairs to see the two small bedrooms and a clean, but basic bathroom, with a bathtub with an ugly pink plastic Y-shaped hose that fitted over the hot and cold faucets, though Javi explained again that the house no longer had hot water.

"Welcome to the Hilton!" he announced in a mock TV advert voice. "The beds need mattresses and sheets and everything else. No fabrics can be left here or they will simply rot. There is more to see downstairs."

She followed him back down and out the front door. They walked around the corner to another building. This was even more basic. It consisted of a single room with a toilet in one corner and an old fashioned sink in another. On the opposite wall there was a narrow single bed, again with no mattress. In the center, two wooden chairs faced each other over an old card table. The largest thing in the room was a massive old oak refectory table jammed against a wall. There was a bare lamp hanging from the ceiling. Javi flicked a switch and it came on.

"I meant to show you, there is also electricity in the main house, but no lights. We'll have to bring up some table lamps, I thought you could use the main house and keep your 'guest' in here. I'll send someone up to make this door and window secure and generally tidy both buildings up and make them ready for you. There is no phone of course and," he looked at his cellphone, "no mobile signal."

"I think it will do perfectly. And I won't be alone with him. Ted or Peter will always be here."

Susie had explained that Sophie would be going home in a couple of days, but that Anne and Ted would be arriving the same day to help out.

"Ah, that's good, I did wonder. OK, let's go. It will be ready in a couple of days."

She turned and reached for him. Instead of kissing him, she wrapped her arms around his neck and looked into his eyes "Do you have any idea how it feels to have complete confidence in someone, and so very quickly? To know that you can rely on him, trust him? Not just about practical things either, but about things that matter? That's how I feel about you, Javi."

Javi was overwhelmed. He could think of nothing to say, except that he was falling in love with her, and he wasn't sure she wanted to hear that just yet. So he said nothing. But he held her gaze, and she saw the depth of his feelings. She kissed him, slowly, not closing her eyes and not breaking the connection between them.

After what felt like an eternity, they broke apart, but both knew something had changed.

His voice had a little catch in it for a split second, "It is only noon, come and meet someone, someone very important to me."

They drove down the hill in silence. They continued on the main road, still traveling away from the city. She saw signs for Penedès.

"This is where your vineyards are, isn't it. Oh Javi, we're not going to meet your parents are we? I wouldn't want to meet them looking like this."

"You look perfectly lovely, you always look lovely. But no, my mother would kill me if I arrived unannounced with a new friend. My parents are on vacation at the moment. We are going to visit my great-great aunt, Caterina Chavela. Chavela is an old-fashioned name, like Ethel or Enid in English. She is ninety-eight years old and is well past worrying about what you or anyone else is wearing. She is the youngest sister of Sebastiá Tomás, the man in the painting, so she is my grandfather's aunt, although she is not much older than he is. Her brother was around twenty when she was born. And we will also meet my sister Isabella." He saw the look on her face, "No, don't worry, trust me."

Before they reached the town of Penedès, he turned right and after a few miles, right again. Soon he pulled into a long driveway to a lovely stone house set among well-tended flowerbeds, with two fountains and various ponds. A serenely beautiful young woman close to Susie's age stood up when she heard the sound of their car.

As Javi stepped from the car, the young woman's face broke into an enormous smile and she ran and threw herself into his arms.

"Tià, Tià, estàs aquí! I has vingut amb algú, una dona. Qui és Tià? És maca? T'estimo, Tià." *Tià, Tià you are here! And you have brought someone, a lady. Who is she Tià? Is she nice? I love you, Tià.'*

"Espera que li dic que vingui i te la presento." *'Let me bring her over and you can meet her.'*

He gently prised her arms from his neck and came around the car to Susie. He took her hand.

"I should have mentioned, the family call me Tià. I'll explain later."

"Isabella, this is my very good friend from America. Her name is Susie. Susie, this is my very lovely, but very cheeky sister, Isabella."

Very slowly and deliberately Susie spoke to Isabella, "Estic molt contenta de conèixer-te Isabella. Perdona que tingui aquest accent Català tant dolent." *'I am very pleased to meet you Isabella. Please excuse my terrible accent.'*

Javi looked at her, amazed, and shook his head.

"I speak little English Suzee. Pleased to meet with you. How do you do?"

"Bella, where is Tieta Caterina?"

"In the house Tià. But not sleeping. Come on, let's go in, I want to introduce Suzee."

Isabella ran ahead, excited. They followed her, rather more slowly, into the house.

The old lady was sitting erect in a straight-backed chair. She had a book on her lap. Isabella was beside herself, "Here Suzee, this is Tieta Caterina. She is very old. I love her."

Susie approached the old lady, but before she could say anything, she spoke to her in a soft English voice. "My niece tells me that you are American. I am pleased to meet you."

"And I am very happy to meet you, senyora."

"And where is my nephew? Come here Tià." Javi came to his aunt and went down on one knee before her and embraced her. They exchanged a few quiet words, and then, for Susie's sake, the old lady reverted to English, "Now, what have you been up to?"

They spent almost an hour with her. At one point, a woman came with coffee, and milk for Isabella. Then they could see the old lady tiring and they said their goodbyes.

"I will see you again in how many days, Tià?" Isabella wanted to know.

"I will come and see you at the weekend, Bella, in three or four days. And don't forget, Grandfather Jordi's birthday party is only one week away. Mama and Papa will be there as well."

"Give me a kiss, Tià," she demanded. "You too, Suzee."

They got back in the car and headed for Barcelona.

"In the accident that killed my brother Jordi, Isabella almost drowned. Her brain was deprived of oxygen and, well, she is as she is. She is happy, she loves me, I love her. When my parents are no longer here, she will be with me. Do you understand, Susie?"

"I understand, Javi."

She waited a while and asked, "So explain Tià please."

He laughed. "We Catalans, well all the Spanish really, we have an obsession with names. Do you know what Picasso's name was when he was baptized? Pablo Diego José Francisco de Paula Juan Nepomuceno María de los Remedios Cipriano de la Santísima Trinidad Ruiz y Picasso. How crazy is that? My given names are Sebastiá Xavier. My family always called me Tià. But for some reason, when they introduced me to friends, I was Javi. I have no idea why, perhaps I will ask my mother one day, but probably not. It can be confusing, especially I know to English speakers, who need to hear Tia, for aunt, and Tià for me. And talking of English speakers, when did you learn Catalan? I was astonished when you greeted Isabella."

He looked across and saw her blushing.

"I've been spending one or two hours a day learning. I only have certain phrases, but I'm getting better."

"When did you start?" he asked, quietly.

"On Friday, before I packed my toothbrush," she said, just as softly.

Neither of them spoke as they drove for a few kilometers until Javi pulled off the road at a scenic overlook. He parked the car, came around to open Susie's door, took her hand and helped her out.

He put his hands on her shoulders and looked into her eyes.

"I almost told you earlier, in the hills, but I thought, *'maybe she doesn't need this. In a few weeks she will go back to America, with some happy memories I hope'*. But the fact is that I have fallen in love with you Susie, very much. Please, don't say anything, I just had to tell you."

He held her for a few minutes, then they returned to the car and drove the rest of the way in silence, her hand resting on the back of his neck. He pulled up outside her apartment. She put her hand on his arm to stop him getting out.

"Thank you for what you said Javi. I'm not going to say anything right now except this. I am having the most wonderful time of my life. I feel as though I have been born again into a new world, and you are at the center of it. But, I have all this other stuff to finish, and it feels like too much for me to handle any more right now. So, once again, I have to ask you for a favor. Can we go on a little while longer the way we are? I want to see as much of you and your life as possible, I want to make love to you as often as possible and before too long I want us to talk again. Is that acceptable to you, Javi?"

"More than I would have dared to ask."

"Then will I see you this evening? It must be Talena's turn with Jordi, no?" she smiled at him.

GET SET

Susie flew up the stairs. She tried to stop thinking about what he had said to her, but of course she couldn't stop smiling. She entered the apartment with a light heart.

"Where have you been?" demanded Peter, "We've been calling you for ages. Your man, Charlie, has come through again. Come on, we can Skype him right now."

They sat her in front of her laptop and got Charlie online.

"Hiya Susie, we've been trying to call you."

"Sorry guys, I've been in the mountains. I'll explain later, now what's all the fuss?"

"We've got him Susie, we know his address, his car, his yacht, everything."

"Oh my God, Charlie, how?"

"You were right Susie, he can't live without the Yankees. I thought he might wait for the new season, but this is Derek Jeter's last month as a Yankee, so I guess he just had to watch. He took out a subscription for mlb.com to get the Yankees' games. I've had a trace on new subscriptions from overseas for a few weeks, but he only moved into his apartment yesterday. Thankfully, he didn't waste anytime."

"You're a genius, Charlie!"

"I've emailed you the address and floor plan of his apartment. He took out the subscription in the name of a Panamanian company, which also owns the apartment and his car and his yacht and, I think we'll find, most of his money. Which is awesomely great news for us. Do you know what he called his company Susie? BRI, for Bahía de Reyes Inversiones, which translates to Kingsbay Investments. I'm going to see Jill this evening with all the Panamanian information, just as we agreed. We should plan a call for tomorrow, for when Jill gets home from work. Should I contact Sophie and Anne?"

"Yes please, Charlie. Get a time from Jill and the rest of us will fit in with that. Oh, Charlie, this is great news, we're almost there. And just so you know, I was busy this morning. I was too!" Susie exclaimed after a raised eyebrow and a smirk from Peter.

"We have a house to hold Andy in, for as long as we need to, and it's perfect. Well, it's pretty basic, but it's in the middle of absolutely nowhere. It is something to do with Javi's family. It's ninety minutes drive from here."

Sophie responded, "That's great, one more big item off the list."

"And your packages will be delivered tomorrow, so make sure someone is at home all day," added Charlie.

They signed off until the next day. Sophie announced, "It's a little bit early, but I think we deserve a drink. Cava please, barman."

They toasted Charlie with glasses of the sparkling wine.

Peter observed, "We need to buy in some of Javi's wine, we've been giving business to the competition."

"You're right son, but we're not throwing any away, so he'll have to wait. And Susie, we thought you might want to have Javi to yourself tonight, so we have tickets to see a flamenco performance, it starts at 8:30."

"Thanks Sophie, that's very sweet of you. I'll come back early in the morning and you guys can get out for the day. I'll wait in for the package. But I want you with me tomorrow night, Peter."

"Sure, it'll be fun," Peter replied.

They spent the afternoon rehearsing their plans, which had all of a sudden become more real, and a bit more scary.

"I'm only sorry I won't be here for the end of the story, but I think Will is missing me. Well, I *hope* he is," Sophie laughed.

Susie decided to walk to Javi's house for a change. She loved walking the streets of Barcelona and walking helped her to think. What to do about Javi? She was immensely fond of him, and could easily fall in love with him if she allowed herself. And she had been telling the truth about her total confidence in his strength and competence. Javi was sophisticated well beyond his years. She knew her friends would be amazed to know how young he was. She loved being with Javi and she felt her body respond every time she allowed herself to think about making love with him.

She laughed out loud, drawing some strange looks from passers-by.

Of course she was in love with him.

She arrived at Javi's house, but before she could find a doorbell, the gate was opened by the gardener. Once again, Susie took a deep breath and spoke very slowly, "Bona tarda, em dic Susie, encantada de conèixer-lo. Perdoni, que tingui aquest accent Català tant dolent." *Good afternoon, I am Susie, pleased to meet you. Please excuse my terrible accent.*

He replied in English, in a gruff voice, "Good afternoon."

"Has it been a good year for your garden?"

Forty-five minutes later Susie pushed open the front door.

"Where in God's name have you been?" Javi demanded, "I saw you arrive ages ago. I've been standing here, more or less, forever."

"Jaume wanted to show me the garden."

"Jaume wanted to show you the garden? Jaume is famous for not giving a damn about anyone or anything that isn't a plant. He's only here because he worked for my grandfather!"

He looked at her and started to laugh. Then he couldn't control his laughter and he had to get hold of himself to breathe.

"My family," he tried to talk, "my family will never, never, believe this. Jaume hates everyone. No exceptions. Well, until now anyway."

He kissed her and took her into a room she hadn't seen before, a library full of books. She wanted to look at all the titles, but not right now.

Javi walked over to a well-stocked cocktail bar

"What can I get you?"

"You can get me naked."

He came to her and kissed her and felt her desire, which in turn aroused him. He led her upstairs and slowly undressed her, covering each newly exposed area of skin with his kisses. When she was indeed naked, he lifted her, laid her on the bed and enjoyed looking at her body as he quickly undressed. He started at her foot and slowly traced a path up her long legs with his lips and tongue. It was many, many minutes before he entered and moved inside her.

They made love and talked and made love again. At midnight Susie was wrapped around his back, holding him tight against her breasts. She put her mouth to his ear and gently nibbled him. He could feel her warm breath as she breathed so close to him. She began to stroke his leg under the sheet.

"Javi," she whispered, "would you do something to give me pleasure?"

"I would do anything to please you, my darling."

"Would you get me something to eat before I start on this ear? I'm starving."

The following morning Susie rose early, showered and dressed.

"Get up lazybones, breakfast is ready."

Javi pulled on his dressing gown and followed her downstairs. They sat in the kitchen and Susie explained that they had tracked Andy to his apartment. Their plans were moving ahead.

"You and your friends are kind of spooky, you know? You seem able to do amazing things. What's your secret?"

"We have a secret weapon. I told you about Charlie, he really is amazing at getting information. He tried to explain it to me once. It isn't just knowing all the technical stuff, although that's essential. It's about understanding how the designers think, how they approach problems. He says that every system has a personality, one that comes from the people who build it. He's just really good at getting into their heads and then into their creations."

She kissed him and he thought again how vital, how alive and present she was.

Susie walked quickly back to the apartment. She arrived to find the others sitting down to coffee.

"Good morning all," she announced brightly.

"Good morning, lover girl," Peter smirked.

"You're just jealous. Go get your own."

Sophie and Peter had a full day of sight-seeing planned and would be out most of the day.

By ten o'clock, Susie had the apartment to herself. She dove back into her Catalan lessons and the morning flew by. She had a sandwich for lunch, and was just starting in again, when there was a knock on the door. The delivery guy handed her a large box and went down to street level to get the second package. As soon as he left, Susie opened the packages and spread the contents on the kitchen table.

The first item was the satellite phone with its charger, spare battery and external antenna. This would provide them with phone service in even the remotest parts of the country. There were also handheld radios, each with a charger, spare battery and headset. Then there were the chemicals, two small boxes containing well-packed vials of clear liquids. One was a common date-rape product that caused symptoms similar to being seriously drunk: trouble walking, slurred speech, loss of willpower and memory loss. The second had been recommended by Anne. It was for longer term use and caused drowsiness and a feeling of apathy. Decades ago it was commonly used in mental health hospitals to keep difficult patients constantly docile. The most surprising item was a Taser gun. This particular model apparently had something called Drive Stun capability. She had no idea what this meant.

The second box contained even more ominous items. There were various restraints, from cable ties to handcuffs to leg irons, a length of reasonably light chain, combination padlocks and some plain old ropes. She had no idea where Charlie had found some of these items, although she suspected S&M suppliers might have featured. Everything had been sourced anonymously and shipped through intermediaries, and Susie trusted that Charlie knew exactly what he was doing.

She plugged the phone and radios in to charge and went out and bought a printer/scanner, which she brought back to the apartment and then went back to her lessons.

Sophie and Peter came back late in the afternoon from their exploration of the city. They looked over the delivered items, "We better not be raided by the police," Sophie observed.

She continued, "It was fun speaking Spanish and hearing the differences between my Spanish and the locals. There are a lot of different words, although I was always able to understand what was being said. Even Peter here tried out his Spanish, and I haven't heard him speak it for years."

They prepared and enjoyed a light supper, and at ten o'clock Susie and Peter prepared to go out.

"Good luck, and be careful. I'm going to pack; I'll be waiting for you to come home," said Sophie.

Susie and Peter were heading out to find an escort. They needed to find a very attractive girl who didn't look like a professional. They had decided to visit the lounges in the city's most expensive hotels.

In the event, it turned out to be easy. The very first bar they chose was really busy. There was a group of six or eight pretty girls, apparently single, sitting together drinking sparkling water. They couldn't tell if the girls were professional or not. That's when they realized that it might have been easier if Peter had come by himself; the professionals would have sought him out. Susie decided not to waste time and sent Peter to the men's room, while she went up to the bar. A barman came over immediately.

"I have to arrange a girl for my boss's American client coming in tomorrow," she said, trying to be casual, as if this was the kind of thing she did every day. "The girl I normally use is out of town and I can't get hold of her. Can you recommend someone?"

"Does he want anything special?" enquired the barman, as casually as he might have asked if she wanted an olive in her martini.

"No. Young, but not too young, twenty-four or twenty-six perhaps, blonde, nice figure, the girl next door type would be good."

He thought for a moment. "Jessica might be the answer, and she's English, so no language problem. That's her, over there." He indicated a very attractive young woman Susie would never have taken for a professional. She wasn't with the sparkling water crowd, but had a glass of white wine on the table before her. She was sitting alone, apparently engrossed in the current edition of Vogue.

"Perfect," said Susie.

"I'll bring her over."

"No. Please ask her if I can join her."

He went to the girl's table with a little bowl of salted nuts, put it on her table and had a quick word with her. The girl looked across at Susie and nodded. As Susie passed the barman returning to his station, she placed a 50 euro bill on his tray and asked, "Will that cover a glass of chardonnay?"

She sat opposite the escort and her drink arrived a moment later.

She looked at the girl and reached her hand across the small table, "Susie," she said.

"Jessica; how can I help you?"

"I lied to the barman. I don't have a boss. My husband stole money from me and my friends and then flew across the Atlantic to Barcelona, where he thinks he's safe and can spend our money. We've come to get it back, or hand him over to the police, and we need help. Which we are prepared to pay for."

The girl was surprised. She had had many strange requests in her time, but this was new, even for her.

"What would you want me to do?"

"We want you to pick him up, go back with him to his apartment for wine or champagne, slip a date rape drug that I will give you into his drink, and, when it has taken effect, call me. We will come immediately and take him away. That's it."

"How do you know for sure that he'll be attracted to me and will take me back to his flat?"

"Look at me. He married me, and by the way, he's very handsome and could have easily picked someone else."

Jessica looked at Susie and realized that they were, not exactly alike, but the same type: blonde, tall, shapely and very good looking. Jessica a professional and knew that she was not as stunningly attractive as Susie.

"OK, I see what you mean. You're sure he doesn't have a girlfriend?"

"We're not sure; but anyway, that wouldn't stop him, it didn't before."

"OK Susie, I'm in. When does this have to happen?"

"Well, obviously we can't guarantee where or when he'll be somewhere appropriate for you to meet him, but we're taking a chance that he'll want to go out on Saturday night. One thing I'll say for him, he doesn't drink and drive, so we're hoping he'll walk to a bar, there are several near his apartment apparently. If he gets into a taxi, we're prepared to try to follow him, although that didn't work out so well when we tried it before. I guess what I'm saying is that we would employ you Saturday night, even if it's a bust, in which case we'll try again."

"I never go anywhere with a client unless I've met him in advance, but since I won't be having sex with him, I guess I can go along with this if you guarantee to come and get me, within say, an hour at most."

Jessica continued, "I charge 1000 euros a night Susie, can you afford that?"

"Wow, you girls make good money, but yes we can pay that."

"With your looks, you could make that and more if you ever thought of going professional. Just for reference, it's 3000 if I sleep over."

"Thanks for the compliment, Jessica, but I'll pass."

She told Jessica, Andy's new address. Jessica knew the building and was familiar with two or three upmarket wine bars nearby that would be likely spots for a single guy to go to meet women.

"It's an expensive building, he must have stolen a lot of money. The area attracts quite a few professionals, but also lots of very pretty amateurs hoping to meet a football player or some other eligible man. I'll have a lot of competition."

They agreed to meet on Saturday evening in one of the wine bars Jessica had mentioned.

REUNION

Friday morning at breakfast, the atmosphere in the apartment was tense. The prospect of actually carrying out their plan the following evening was bringing home the reality of what they would be attempting.

Susie mused out loud. "In the worst case scenario, he sees us coming and takes off again, and we don't get another chance. But we'll still have accomplished something. He'll never be able to completely relax again. He'll always be looking over his shoulder, worrying that someone is close behind him."

Peter carried on the thought. "We could go one better. We could print up wanted posters, explaining what Andy did, and distribute them to all the golf courses and marinas in the area. We could make life impossible for him in Barcelona and force him to relocate. And with Charlie's help, we may be able to find him again and do the same thing all over again. We could make his life miserable."

Susie shook her head. "I like the poster idea Peter, but this is it for me. I'm not going to waste my life fixating on Andy, and neither should you. I'm ready to move on. We get him now or we ruin his life in Barcelona and forget him after that. He won't know we've given up, and that's going to have to be enough."

Sophie supported her, "Well said, Susie. If he escapes us, we go with the poster idea and then you all come home. If we catch him, we've agreed a limit of two days to get his agreement to transferring the money, after that you call the cops and the Consulate and come home. The only way you're still here after two days, is if he's agreed and we need time to secure everything."

Susie spoke again, "One last thing. I want to be the only one who uses the Taser, if it gets used at all. We're only going to use it if he tries to hurt someone or if he tries to escape while we're at the farmhouse. If anything goes wrong, I'm most likely to get away with it, if the police ever do get involved. The scorned wife will get more sympathy than any of you guys. However, I've never fired any kind of gun before, so I need to practice. Peter, I think you should volunteer to be my target."

There was a long, silent pause before Susie's laughter exploded. "You should see the look on your face, Peter. There are times when I'd love to zap you with a million volts or whatever it is, but I think this time, I'll just shoot at the box all this stuff came in."

When breakfast was finished, they prepared to split up. Susie was driving to the airport to meet Anne and Ted's flight. A few hours later, Peter would take Sophie to catch her flight home.

But first, Susie had to say goodbye to Sophie.

"I'll never be able to look at you the same way again. I love your new look, but I must say I'm looking forward to seeing you as you again! Thank you so much for coming over to help, it's been fantastic to have you here. We'll keep you posted with every development, promise."

A few minutes later, Susie gave Sophie a final hug and left the apartment.

Anne and Ted were excited when they arrived. Anne had one regret, "I'm so excited to be here for the final chapter, but sorry I don't get to try a complete makeover like Sophie. We saw her the night before she left. Even sitting in her home, I struggled to believe that it was really her."

Ted on the other hand, had grown a full beard, which changed him dramatically, and not for the better, Susie thought. He looked ten years older.

"Well Ted, you sure look..."

"Ancient." Anne finished the sentence for her. "It's coming off as soon as we get home. I've warned him not to get used to not shaving!"

Ted was more focused on action. "So what's been happening while we were in the air, Susie?"

Susie filled them in on recruiting Jessica, and the conversation this morning about what should happen if Andy got spooked and vanished.

Ted was in full agreement with the idea that this was a one-time effort. "I think you're being very wise Susie. You don't want this to become an obsession. Good thinking."

"And talking about obsessions, we're looking forward to meeting your Javi, he sounds dreamy."

"Don't you start Anne; I get enough teasing from Peter. And don't worry, you'll meet Javi soon. Come on, let's go over to Hertz and add you guys to the rental agreement."

By eight o'clock on Saturday night they were all in their assigned places, all incredibly nervous. All that is, except Jessica, who had 1000 euros in her pocketbook, together with the vial of GHB.

They knew from Charlie that, as part of its energy efficiency efforts, the apartment had infrared and motion sensors that turned the lights on and off automatically depending on whether a room was occupied. Peter sat in a newly rented eight-seater Ford van with a clear view of the entrance to Andy's building. Two spaces behind him, Anne and Ted watched from Susie's rental car. They had practiced with all the equipment and had made sure all the batteries were fully charged.

They could see the lights in Andy's apartment go on and off as he moved around, getting ready to go out, they hoped. Sure enough, at 8:50 all the rooms went dark. He was going out. Peter looked up and down the street, there was no sign of a taxi. Three minutes later, Andy appeared from the lobby and walked towards the two parked cars. Peter busied himself looking down at his phone, and Anne and Ted pretended to be kissing as he approached.

When Andy had passed him, Peter left his car and followed him, telephoning Susie as he did.

"He's on the move Susie, walking towards the shopping center. He's turning right, towards you. Be ready to move quickly."

He was silent for a while, and then continued, "No, he's gone into the bar opposite yours, Casa Viniteca. See you in a minute."

Peter quickly went to the bar where the women were waiting. He said hi to Jessica and she left with him to cross the street. They entered the Casa Viniteca at the same time, but not obviously together. Peter casually looked around and spotted

Andy immediately, sitting at the bar. He turned, hoping anyone would think he had looked in vain for his date, and headed back to the door, passing Jessica and whispering *'pale blue shirt at the bar'* as he did. He went back across the street to join Susie.

"This is like being in a movie, isn't it?" he said, collapsing onto the chair vacated by Jessica.

"It is. I've decided I quite like that thought, because in the movies everything always works out. I think you need a drink."

"I think I need ten, but I'll settle for one."

They nursed their drinks for as long as they could, then ordered coffees and made them last. Finally they looked at the bar menu, and ordered non-alcoholic cocktails. They were too nervous for intelligent conversation; Susie made Peter recount every minute of his day sightseeing with Sophie.

At last, Susie's phone rang, it was Ted.

"I think they're coming towards us, there's a couple coming, she's taken his arm ... yes, it's Andy and a pretty blonde. Hey, Susie, she looks a little like you, don't you think? OK, they've gone into his building."

Susie and Peter overpaid their bill and walked quickly to the cars. The plan called for Susie to wait in the car while the others went up to get Andy. If anyone asked, Andy was Peter's boyfriend and Anne and Ted were Peter's parents helping take a drunk Andy home. Susie wasn't happy being the one left behind, but the cover story of parents helping their son was more compelling than anything else they could come up with. Anne would drive the van, with Peter and Ted on either side of Andy, restrained if necessary, in the back. Susie would lead them in the car.

Just like in the movies, it all worked out. Forty minutes after they had gone upstairs, Jessica called Susie. Peter, Ted and Anne immediately went into the apartment block, took the elevator to Andy's floor and walked to his door, where Jessica waited.

"He's on the sofa. I'll hold the elevator for you."

The two men stood over him while Anne ran into the bedroom and quickly searched for papers. Under the bed, she saw the metal briefcase. It was locked, but she guessed that it might hold what they were looking for. She grabbed it and was back with the two men in seconds. They helped a barely conscious Andy to his feet, and supported him as they left the apartment. Anne carefully closed the door behind them.

Ted and Peter, with Andy supported between them, squeezed past Jessica into the elevator and the two women followed them in. Moments later, they were easing Andy into the van.

Jessica gave Susie a wave as she passed her, and she stood watching, as Susie pulled away and the big Ford fell in behind her. He had seemed quite nice, she thought, but she was a professional, well paid to do her job. She looked for a taxi to take her back to the hotel. Perhaps she could earn double money tonight.

Susie found her way back to the farmhouse, even though it was pitch black by the time she turned off the main road. As promised by Javi, it had been made habitable and secure. Beds were made up, there were ample towels, though still no hot water. Javi had organized some basic kitchen equipment, pots, plates and so on and there was food in the cupboards, and coffee and wine on the table.

The lock on the front door had been changed and the outbuilding was now secured with a metal grill over the window and a large hasp and padlock on the door.

They quickly bundled Andy into the outbuilding, which had originally been a cattle byre and later a seasonal farm worker's cottage. Meanwhile, in the main building, Susie opened a bottle of wine, poured some into a glass and added some of the GHB from the second vial. She wanted him out of it a bit longer so they could leave him alone and get themselves sorted out.

She took the drink next door and went over to her husband, as she had to remind herself he still was, and handed him the glass.

"Have a drink Andy."

His speech was still slurred and his eyes unfocused as he tried to look at her. "Jessica, Jess, are you having a drink?"

"Sure, we'll both have a drink."

He drained the glass and was soon snoring loudly. The two men laid him on the bed and, after some discussion, put one of his hands into handcuffs, passed a chain through the other cuff and secured it to one of the many rings set into the wall of the byre, rings that had been used to tie up the cattle. They would give him no more drugs until he completely sobered up and they had questioned him.

They unpacked the Ford into the main house and got everything organized as well as they could. They tried to open the briefcase, but got nowhere with the combination locks. Susie tried every combination she could think of without success. They debated trying to get the right combination out of Andy, but in the end they decided that Peter should take it back to the apartment in the morning, buy an electric drill and force it open. He would then scan anything remotely interesting and email the scans to Charlie and Jill.

They decided to finish the bottle of wine that Susie had opened. She poured them each a glass and was about to suggest a toast, when she had a fit of giggling, which proved to be contagious. Soon all four of them were helplessly laughing, tears running down their faces. They only stopped when they were exhausted.

"What a night: high-class call girls, date rape drugs, handcuffs, midnight kidnapping. They'll never believe this at the next meeting of the Rotary." Ted's comment set them off again.

"Come on Ted, time for bed." Anne announced when the wine was finished.

"I'll come up and get a sheet and a blanket for this sofa," said Peter moving towards the stairs.

"Don't be crazy, you'll sleep with me," Susie replied, "you won't even see what you're missing, I've brought my PJs."

Peter set off back to Barcelona at first light. The others had coffee and already slightly stale bread with jam and then looked at each other.

"OK," said Susie, "let's do it. I've got the Taser, Ted."

They went next door, unlocked the padlock and opened the door. Andy was still asleep. Susie went to move towards him, but Ted stopped her. He went over to Andy and brusquely shook him awake. Andy woke as if from an anesthetic. He looked around in obvious confusion and quickly felt the handcuff on his wrist. Ted had backed away from the bed and was inadvertently blocking Andy's view of Susie. Andy swung his legs to the floor, rubbed his eyes and then ran his fingers through his hair. He looked up at Ted, still with no recognition in his eyes.

"Who are you? Where am I? What the fuck is going on?"

Susie stepped sideways, into his view.

He stared, uncomprehending. He looked around the room once more and rubbed his eyes again. It was almost comical.

"Susie?" His voice was uncertain.

She realized that he was still shaking off the effects of the drugs. She walked over to the sink and poured some water into a glass and brought it over. Again, Ted intercepted her, took the glass and handed it to Andy, who drank it in one long swallow.

"Ted? Is that you? Susie?" A bit stronger this time.

"Yes, Andy, it's us."

"But how? I mean..."

"We tracked you down, Andy. It wasn't so hard, I had a lot of help. You pissed off a lot of people."

He looked like a man in shock, which of course he was.

"Why, I mean, what for? What are you going to do now? The police?"

"That depends on you Andy. What we want, is the money, all of the money you stole, all of the money you made, all of it. We are taking all of your money, Andy, and whatever you've spent it on."

"You're crazy. I'm not giving you my damn money, you must be out of your fucking mind."

"We'll see. First we'll open your briefcase and see what's in there. Then I'll let you know what we need from you. Get some more sleep Andy, someone will bring you some food in a while."

"Did you see his face when Susie mentioned the briefcase? Well done, sweetheart, I think you might have found his secrets." Ted gave Anne a hug.

"Susie, you were absolutely great. You seemed so hard, so confident."

"I'm not the girl he left behind Anne: that's for sure."

Ted took him food at ten o'clock and again at two in the afternoon. Both times Andy asked to see Susie, but she ignored his requests.

"He needs to get it that I have absolutely no feelings for him anymore."

At five o'clock, the satellite phone rang. It was Peter.

"Opening the case was easy enough with the drill. Absolutely everything we need is in there: passport, registration documents for his yacht and the car; ownership papers for a bunch of properties in London, that's where most of the money went; deeds for the apartment, he paid 1.2 million euros for it; bank accounts in various countries and lots of papers about the Panamanian company. It's a goldmine - well done, Anne! I scanned everything and sent emails off hours ago and now Jill is setting up a conference call. She'll text me the phone-in numbers and I'll call you with them shortly."

Fifteen minutes later they dialed the number supplied and were talking with Jill in her office, Charlie at home, Peter in the apartment and them in the middle of nowhere.

Jill's voice conveyed her excitement.

"The briefcase material is absolutely fantastic, well done, whoever got that. And this is going to be much easier than we thought. Absolutely everything, except a Santander account in Barcelona, is in the name of BRI, the Panamanian company. So we don't need to transfer anything except ownership of the company; everything else will flow with that, and we can liquidate it at our leisure. There's maybe 35,000 euros or thereabouts in the Santander account in his own name. Spending money I guess. Charlie will take care of that."

"The Panamanian company is designed for crooks. No one ever sees anyone face-to-face and there are no signatures of the principals anywhere. All you need to sell and transfer the company is a ten digit code and a security word, both a mixture of numbers and letters. You need to enter the code on the web site, and then give the security word over the phone within one hour and the company will be transferred to a new owner instantly. You only get three chances at the code and three at the security word, otherwise you have to wait forty-eight hours and try again. It's beautiful."

"This is great news," Susie commented, then admitting, "I was dreading keeping him secure for two or three weeks."

"Well, as soon as you can get the code and secret word, we can get it done. And once we do it, he can't get it back. We'll have reset our own security. It couldn't have been set up better if we had designed it ourselves. Is there anything else we need to discuss? If not, we'll leave it to you to call us when you have the information. Bye, guys, and well done everyone."

Peter injected a quick comment before Jill could end the call, "I'll drive back down to you guys in the morning, right after I have a nice hot shower. Bye!"

Susie, Anne and Ted were laughing as the call ended.

"He always has the last word," Anne commented, then stopped laughing and looked at the others. "We need a new plan."

They talked for a while, and then the three of them went round to the byre and let themselves in.

"Hello, Andy."

"Hello, Susie. I've been thinking. How about I give everybody back all their money, plus whatever you've spent finding me, and some money for your trouble? Then no one is out of pocket and we can all get on with our lives."

"I'm afraid not, Andy. We want everything. In particular, we want the password and code for the BRI registration." She saw the shock on his face.

"I'm not sure you understand what you're up against. We're going to get the code one way or another. We have all your information and we have experts on the case. But we have a deal to offer you. If you give us the code and password, so we can transfer the company, we'll let you go, as soon as the transfer is done. If you don't, we'll call the Spanish police and the American Consulate"

He looked at her.

"I admit you've changed Susie, but you won't do that. Apart from anything else, you'll get nothing if I'm taken into custody. And once the cops are involved, Will and Ted and the others will all be in the firing line and could be my cellmates. I can't see you risking them."

"You're dead wrong, Andy, the others have been given immunity in return for testifying against you if you're ever brought to trial."

He looked at her steadily, appraising this stranger, who was his wife.

"I don't believe you."

"Anne, would you mind going next door and getting the copy of the immunity letter, and could you bring my laptop and the phone? Thanks."

"I'm going to prove it to you Andy. There's absolutely no reason why we wouldn't hand you over, and about 15 million reasons why we will. There's no chance we're letting you enjoy a life of luxury after what you did, none at all. Just so you understand, we want to ruin you, Andy."

Anne re-appeared, carrying a large envelope, Susie's laptop and the satellite phone. She handed the envelope and the PC to Susie. She had written 'OK' on the front of the envelope.

"Thanks, Anne."

Susie opened the envelope and handed Andy the letter inside. On official looking paper, and addressed to a fictitious law firm, lengthy legalese spelled out the immunity being granted from all lawsuits, subject to full and truthful testimony as outlined in the attached depositions.

"Anyone could have written this, why would I believe this is genuine?"

"We thought you might say that. This is a satellite phone. It allows internet roaming, but it's pretty slow, you'll have to be patient."

She put her laptop on the table. Ted went over to Andy and unlocked his handcuff so he could use both hands to navigate the computer.

"Find the site for the New York District Attorney's office and look at their press releases for June 16th."

They watched as he did what Susie had instructed. The internet connection was painfully slow, but eventually he found the release. It was less legalistic, and there were lots of comments about the fantastic work of the SEC and the DA's office and dire warnings of action against anyone else carrying out fraud, and so on and on, but it was clear enough. They all had immunity.

"We'll give you twenty minutes to think about it Andy, then we'll be back."

"By the way, how is Valentina going to react to the photos we have of you and Jessica, walking arm-in-arm last night?"

Susie didn't know why she threw in that question, but they could all see the reaction it caused. Andy's complexion went white, his eyes flickered from one face to another, but he said nothing. After a moment they left him and secured the door behind them.

As soon as they were back in the main house, Anne commented, "That was weird. He looked like he was going to pass out. Why is he so worried about the Russian girl finding out he's been seeing another woman?"

"I don't know. It is weird. I wonder if she's here in Barcelona. Maybe their relationship is more of a big deal than we thought. What do you think Ted?"

"No idea, Susie. For sure he reacted big time when you mentioned her. I think maybe he's just shaken by how much we know about him. You know, I think that's what it must be. After all, without Charlie we'd have no idea about her."

Back in the byre, Andy was sick with apprehension. If they knew about Valentina then maybe the cops did too. No, they couldn't. Not yet. They'd have come for him. But if the police had him in custody and started checking. *'How the fuck did Susie know about Valentina?'* He couldn't get the thought out of his head. He had to get away, right now.

Back next door, Susie looked at her watch and spoke up, "Come on, Ted, it's time, let's see what he says."

She picked up the Taser and Ted led the way around the corner. Anne followed with a tray holding some fruit, cheese and bread. This would be his last food for the day. Ted unlocked the padlock and was opening the hasp when the door burst open and Andy came rushing out. Ted was surprised and staggered back a few paces, Andy stepped around him and pushed Anne hard, so she fell over on her back. Without a second's hesitation, Susie shot Andy with the Taser and he flopped to the ground, a look of extreme anguish on his face. Susie went over to him and pulled the Taser barbs roughly from his chest. A little blood appeared on his shirt.

Ted reached down and took hold of Andy's ankles and pulled him, none to gently, into the byre and locked him in. He went to check that Anne was not hurt. They were all shaken.

Inside the byre, Andy was in absolute agony. Every muscle had seized up. No-one knew it, but the Taser was faulty. It had discharged all of its energy far too quickly. They would have been unable to shock Andy again as the gun had depleted itself completely in one incredibly strong discharge. Andy had received perhaps five or six times the normal shock level. Instead of taking one or two minutes to wear off, Andy lay incapacitated for a quarter of an hour, before he could painfully drag himself onto his bed.

Ted looked at Susie with admiration. "You were great again Susie. Boy, you women are made for crime."

Peter turned up at ten the next morning and they filled him in on the previous night's developments and their plan for the day.

"Well," he said when they were finished, "you guys go see what he says, after having a few thousand volts shot through him and sleeping on it. I'll wait here, I've thought of a back-up plan."

Susie banged on the locked door and shouted, "Put your hands through the bars of the window, Andy, if you want to eat ever again."

There was a pause and then his hands appeared in view. Ted unlocked and opened the door and Susie and Anne followed him in. Susie had the Taser and Anne was once again carrying a tray. Ted pointed to the table.

"Sit at the table, Andy, I'm going to secure you." The table was massive and rough and stood against a wall. Andy looked at them, especially at Susie holding the Taser. He realized that he was intimidated by his wife; by naive, innocent, malleable Susie. Except this woman before him was unrecognizable as the wife he had walked out on.

"Yes, Andy, I will use it again, try me if you like."

He walked over and sat at the table. Ted secured him once again to the wall with the chain and handcuffs.

"We've brought you some food, but first, what have you decided?"

"I'm not handing everything over, but I will make you a deal. If you give me to the authorities, you'll get nothing. You didn't go to all this trouble just for the satisfaction of putting me away. So here's the deal. I'll give you half. You seem to know a lot already, half is about seven million dollars. You'll give me a receipt acknowledging that you've taken the money so I know you can't come for me again. That's it. Take it or leave it."

They left him locked up again and went next door to discuss what they would do next.

"He has us I think. He's right in what he says," Anne was speaking. "Would you really walk away from seven million dollars, more than enough to make everyone whole again, and much more?"

She had addressed her question to Susie.

"I would walk away in a heartbeat, but it's easy for me to say so, and anyway, it isn't just my decision. We need to discuss this with everyone."

Peter spoke up for the first time. "Hold up, I told you that I had an idea. I don't altogether approve of milking the stereotype of the homosexual sadist, but I'm prepared to make an exception this time, as it's me who gets to do it. Remember, Andy's still never seen me; he has no idea who I am."

He explained his idea.

Ted spoke for everyone, "We've nothing to lose, let's try it."

This time they all went round to the byre, although Peter waited out of sight, just outside the door. Anne had a pen and some paper in her back pocket.

They went in. Andy was still sitting by the table, the chain still through the ring on the wall, restricting his movement. Ted went up to him, bent down and quickly secured him to the leg of the table with the leg irons.

"A bit of overkill, don't you think?"

Peter walked in the door, "Not really, handsome." He put down a bucket of water and a plastic bag he was carrying, and looked at Andy.

Susie spoke. "I hoped that it wouldn't come to this Andy, but you leave us no choice. I don't care about the money enough, to let you go free, and by now, everyone back home has gotten over it as well. This is mostly about making sure you don't get to enjoy it."

She paused, as if steeling herself against something, before continuing, "I'm not sure I could hurt you myself, but even if I could, I don't think I would be very good at it. I think to be good at hurting someone badly, you need to *enjoy* giving pain. I'm sorry Andy, I really am. I wanted to go straight to the police, but the others want to try one more thing first. Then we'll hand you over."

With that, Peter walked over to Susie and took the Taser from her.

"I think the ladies should leave. No need to watch this."

Susie and Anne left, but only to walk around to the open window so they could hear.

Peter walked over to Andy and gently stroked his face and ran his fingers through his hair, as Andy futilely tried to back away from him.

"Very pretty. We can have some fun later if you like, when all this unpleasantness is over."

Peter's voice was conversational, with a slight archness about it. He slid his hand into the front of Andy's shirt and ran his fingers slowly down to his waist, sensually stroking and caressing his skin. Andy was writhing about, trying to get off the chair, but the leg iron now passed around a leg of the table, which was far too heavy for him to move.

With a suddenness that surprised Ted, as well as Andy, Peter ripped Andy's shirt open to just below his chest and pulled the collar down his back to his elbows. Andy was now pinned helpless, with his arms locked beside him. He was clearly terrified.

Peter stepped away and addressed Ted, again as if they were chatting over a beer.

"You see Ted, when Susie zapped him last night, Andy felt a little pain and his muscles froze. But our friends the cops don't always want that. See, I'm changing the setting to Drive Stun. No, I don't know why they call it that either, but there you go. What this does, is cause much more pain, but it doesn't freeze him, so he can tell us what we need to know. Cute, don't you think? And, because I love my work, I've got another wrinkle to increase the fun."

With that, Peter picked a large, filthy, dripping wet sponge out of the bucket and used it to thoroughly wet Andy's chest.

"Improves conductivity, heightens the senses. I *am* an artist aren't I?"

Andy was trembling now, his eyes darting from the Taser to Peter's face to Ted, watching from the side. Ted shrugged his shoulders as if to say, 'Don't ask me for help.'

Peter pulled a roll of packaging tape from the bag on the floor, soaked the sponge once more and taped it to Andy's chest, wrapping the tape round and round his arms, chest and the back of the chair. Suddenly there was a terrible smell in the confined room. Andy had lost control of his body. He started to cry softly. All he could think of was the incredible pain he had felt last night when Susie shot him, and this was going to be much, much worse. He knew he couldn't stand up to this maniac, and then there would be the police, and Valentina.

Peter picked up the Taser again and switched it on. A faint hum could be heard in the silence of the room.

"Let's start, shall we?"

"5-E-0-I-5-S-1-U-1-S"

"Say it again."

"5-E-0-I-5-S-1-U-1-S"

Ted looked out of the door and Anne gave him the thumbs up.

Peter looked back at Andy. Now they needed the secret word. But Andy had passed out. They checked that he was breathing OK and left him sitting there. They left, locking him in again.

No one spoke until they were in the house.

Ted spoke first, "You are one scary, scary person! You had me going in there, I thought you had lost it and were actually going to torture him!"

Peter had a huge sickly grin on his face. "Wasn't I great! I was trying to channel Hannibal Lecter. Christ, I need a drink."

Susie went up and held him. "Have a drink later, honey." Peter was now crying softly.

They gave him some space and after a few minutes, he took a coffee from Anne with thanks.

Susie spoke again. "I think we can try to avoid any more of that. I'm calling Charlie."

Ted looked at his watch. "It's five in the morning for Charlie, Susie."

"I'll call his cell. Gran won't hear it, and Charlie won't mind. I don't want Peter to have to go through that again unless he absolutely has to."

Charlie answered quickly. Susie explained what she wanted to try. She read the code slowly to Charlie who repeated it back to her.

"And I'll need the number to call, Charlie."

"I'll be back in a moment." He hung up.

They watched the phone intently for five minutes, until at last it made its insistent beeping sound.

"Hi Susie, the code was correct. Now, call this number within the hour, it's manned 24/7." She wrote down the international number and called it immediately.

"What account number please?"

"HYT76502D"

"And the one time code?"

"5-E-0-I-5-S-1-U-1-S"

"Thank you, that seems to be in order, I see you used it thirteen minutes ago. And now the security word please, please spell it out."

The others were staring at her.

"S-U-S-I-E."

"That is corr.... I'm sorry, that is incorrect."

"I wasn't finished. S-U-S-I-E-Q."

"That is correct. The transfer will be completed within fifteen minutes. Please submit your new one-time code on our secure website and call this number again with your new security word, as soon as your code is confirmed. Thank you for your business and good day, or good night."

They all looked at Susie for a long minute and then they were in a group hug, dancing around the floor.

"My God, Susie, how did you know?"

"Look Anne, look at his code. It's 'Susie' and our zip code, backwards. He didn't choose it out of affection, but because he was worried he'd forget it, you can be sure he wouldn't want to write it down. I thought the word might have been his social security number, but it was worth a gamble, so Peter didn't have to be Hannibal Lecter again. Come on, let's call everyone, I don't care what time it is!"

They started with Charlie, then woke Jill, and finally Sophie. They reminded Charlie and Jill to set up the new security.

They had done it.

"What are we going to do with him?" Peter asked, turning to Susie.

"Well, first we let him clean himself up, then if you men could take him back to his, actually, our apartment. Give him say, 500 euros to live on and tell him he's got one month and then he has to leave. If he agrees, then at the end of the month, we'll return his passport, give him a one way plane ticket out of Spain to anywhere he wants and $10,000. He'll receive a call in three weeks asking where he wants to go. If he doesn't leave Spain, Peter here will find him and kill him. What do you think?"

Before they could answer, the phone rang. It was Charlie with a request.

The two men went over to the byre once again. Andy was conscious, but still slumped in the chair. Peter went over to remove the tape. Andy flinched.

"It's OK, I'm not going to hurt you. I'm going to untie you, then you can clean yourself up."

Ted walked over to the table, "Here are some clean clothes that I think will more or less fit you."

He laid them on the table. "I'm going to unshackle you now Andy, don't do anything stupid. It's too late anyway. Get cleaned and changed. We'll come back in a few minutes and tell you what's going to happen next."

When they returned, Andy was clean and had changed. His soiled clothes were in the sink, covered with water. They explained what was going to happen and he accepted it all meekly. He seemed like the thing they had read about, but never before seen, a broken man.

"Someone wants to speak to you Andy." Ted said this as he handed the phone to him. Andy lifted the phone to his ear.

"Andy, it's Charlie. You did a terrible thing Andy. I'm going to tell you something, so you'll realize that you can't think of everything and you should never try to do anything bad again. Do you understand?"

Charlie didn't wait for an answer, but continued, "You were never in danger until you did the last trade by yourself, Andy. Did you really think I would do the first trades in my own name? I did more than two hundred different trades in anonymous accounts that vanished as soon as the trades were done. The money was routed through offshore banks. In a million years I would never have been caught, and so neither would you. You didn't have to run Andy, you didn't have to cheat your friends, and you didn't need to betray Susie. Goodbye Andy, and always remember that I'll be watching over Susie and I'll never let anyone hurt her. I found you in Cherbourg, I found Valentina, I found your yacht, and your car and your properties. I even found your mlb subscription. I can always find you Andy. Always."

He ended the call.

Tears were running silently down Andy's face. He spoke one more time, "Can I see Susie?"

Peter looked at him with something close to pity, "She isn't interested in speaking with you Andy. Your old life is over, but you can start again. Let's go, we'll explain everything in the car."

They led him out and took him away.

NEW PLANS

The two women tidied up the house and burned the soiled clothes from the byre. They packed everything they had brought and put it in the Ford. They would think of some safe way to dispose of everything later; a Taser wasn't the kind of thing you handed in to Goodwill or a charity shop.

Anne dropped Susie at Javi's.

"I'll call you later, and I'll see you tomorrow. And Anne, thank you."

"I wouldn't have missed it for the world, sweetie. See you tomorrow."

Jaume let her in, but one look at her face told him that she didn't want to see the flowers today.

She climbed the steps and rang the front door. Javi opened it and saw her standing there, her bag in her hand and a strange look on her face.

Susie looked at him and said, "I have my toothbrush, can I stay?"

And she fell, sobbing, into his arms.

He led her upstairs to his bedroom. He sat her on his bed and left her for a moment, and went into his bathroom. When he returned, he gently undressed her and led her to the bath he was running. He held her hand as she stepped in to the warm water. He soaped her all over, then went around to kneel at the head of the bath. He shampooed, then rinsed her hair.

All the time, they said nothing at all.

Eventually Susie looked at him with a small smile, "These bath salts don't seem like you at all, Javi; an old girlfriend perhaps?"

He laughed, "I have a drawer full of unwanted birthday and Christmas gifts. I can't remember which aunt gave me what, so I can't give them away to anyone, just in case."

He reached down and helped her from the bath. He wrapped her in an enormous bath sheet and patted and gently rubbed her dry. He found his heavy bathrobe and helped her into it, although it swamped her.

Back in the bedroom he sat her on the bed once again, to dry her thick, long hair, finally brushing it back to its normal shine.

"Thank you Javi, that was deliciously lovely. I feel very loved and very cared for."

Back downstairs, they sat in the Impressionist room and watched as the sun, filtered through the thin curtains, illuminated the water lilies, which seemed to move gently on the rippling water. The art, the lovely bath and the presence on the sofa beside her of the man she loved so very much, had calmed her completely. She was able to tell him everything that had happened and what she had decided to do with Andy.

"You and your friends are quite incredible. Europeans think Americans are soft, weak; but I don't know anyone who could have done what you and your friends have accomplished. And you Susie, you are the wisest, bravest, most honest, most compassionate person I have ever known. Which, of course, is why I am in love with you."

"I'm not going back, to America. I'm going to stay here in Spain, in Barcelona. No, don't speak just yet, please. I love you with all my heart, Javi, and I love you here, where you belong, in this place. Part of what I have fallen in love with is just that, you in your world. And I want to become part of your world, but I'm staying here because I choose to. You are not responsible for me, this is my decision, not yours. My old life is over now and I'm free to create a new life here, with or without you. I will not be your burden. Don't invite me into your life because you think you need to take care of me."

"And one last thing, Javi, my darling. If the time comes that we are together, I understand about Isabella, and I willingly accept her and I will love her, as I will love Jordi."

She smiled at him, "You can speak now."

But he didn't speak. He reached for her and held her close and they watched the colors of the water-lilies change as the sun slowly turned red and finally disappeared.

At last, he put his hand under her chin and lifted up her face.

"Wednesday is my grandfather's birthday, and the whole family celebrates it together in Penedès. I would like you to come with me to meet my family, and I would like them to know that you are living here with me now."

"I would like that very, very much Javi, I really would."

"And we should invite your friends. I will call my mother and let her know. She doesn't like surprises."

"Javi, will Talena be there?"

"Of course, she and Mateo are part of my family. Do you mind?"

"Of course not, but a bit like your mother, I don't like some surprises. Now I must call the apartment and let them know about Wednesday. Then I'll get to know that kitchen of yours."

Around ten o'clock that evening, Susie's phone rang.

"Susie, it's Jill. I'm still on a high about everything. I'm so proud of you guys, you did just great. Anyway, I'm too excited to stay here, I'm coming over again. Just for a few days, but I just want to be with you all. I'm flying tonight. Anne and Ted are coming home on Sunday, will you be on the same flight? Maybe we can all travel back together?"

"Oh Jill, that's so fantastic, I love that you're coming here. And we're invited to Javi's grandfather's birthday party on Wednesday, so you'll be able to meet him at last. But about the flight home on Sunday..."

Susie explained her new plan to stay on in Spain. They talked some more and Jill promised to text her flight information.

When Susie and Javi made love that night it was tender and wonderful. They knew they were together now, and not for just a few weeks and it changed everything, again. And Javi noticed that Susie was no longer wearing her wedding ring.

"I'll be out today, but I'll see you for dinner, darling. Is Jordi coming this evening?"

"Yes, but I can ask Talena to keep him."

"No, I think we should have dinner together, please tell Anna, I'll bring home something to cook. I think we should tell Jordi that I will be living here, and before the family party. It should be his news to tell his cousins, not to hear it from others."

"You are ... you are very clever."

Susie rushed over to the apartment, the apartment that was suddenly no longer her temporary home. She hugged her three friends who were still on a high from the day before. She noticed immediately that Ted was already clean-shaven.

"Much better, Ted. How did it go with Andy?" she asked.

"Very easy. I think he's shattered, and not just by Peter here. I don't know what Charlie said to him, but it really seemed to devastate Andy. I don't think we'll have any trouble with him. It really is over. And he signed the papers Bobby sent about the divorce; maybe they'll be useful one day."

"Great. Now you know about the party tomorrow? I thought we could all go together with Javi and Jordi in the Ford before we take it back. That way it'll be easier when we turn up. Anne, I'll show you what I'm wearing tomorrow and you can decide if you want to go shopping later. "

"What about Ted and I?" asked Peter.

"No one cares what you wear, though you might want to smarten up, these are classy people."

She turned to wink at Anne. Now everyone would have new clothes. She continued, "And, are you ready for this? Jill is coming here," she paused for dramatic effect, "this morning!"

Her announcement had just the effect she had hoped for; everyone was excited.

Susie went on. "I have to see someone this morning, so can you guys meet Jill? I have her flight details. We can meet back here for lunch."

Susie and Anne disappeared into Susie's bedroom for a couple of minutes. Anne saw the summer dress that Susie had worn a lifetime ago in London and would wear to the party.

"That settles it, I'm definitely buying a new dress, I have nothing nearly as smart with me."

"We'll shop this afternoon? And would you like to have a manicure if I can arrange last minute appointments for us?"

While the others rushed off to the airport, Susie had a call to make. She went online and found the number for Talena's company. By being polite, persistent and, at the final hurdle, by invoking Javi's name, she was finally connected with the President and CEO of the company.

"Thank you for taking my call. I am Susie Smith, a friend of Javi's and I wondered if you might have time for a coffee today."

"Hello Susie. According to my son, you are much more than just a friend of Javi's."

Susie sensed a smile in her voice, and felt a wave of relief.

"I would love to have a coffee with you. What time would be most convenient?"

"You're the one with a business to run Talena, or should I call you Magdalena? I don't want to cause offense. Please choose a time that suits you."

"Thank you, and please call me Talena, all my friends do. How about 11:30 this morning?"

She gave Susie directions to a cafe near her office. "If you are there before me, give someone my name."

Susie walked into the cafe at 11:30 to be told that Talena was already there. She was guided to a discreet table in an alcove at the very back of the room. Talena stood to greet her. The two women looked at each other and laughed. They were almost exactly the same height and size. But where Susie was a natural strawberry blonde, Talena's hair was raven black.

"I guess he wanted a change." Talena said

"But not too much," Susie added.

The two women were immediately attracted to each other, and knew they would be friends.

"Javi has invited me to the party tomorrow and I thought it would be nice if we met alone before we meet in front of the family. And, you should know that he has asked me to live with him, and I have agreed. And finally, I want to tell your son about that tonight, but I thought I should consult you first."

"I appreciate this very much, Susie. I know that you are not asking my permission, but it is very kind of you to reach out to me. I know it can't have been easy. And I can't think of anyone else who would have done it."

"It wasn't so difficult Talena, Jordi is wonderful and Javi loves you, I knew you would be lovely."

"What a beautiful thing to say! Thank you. I can see why Javi is so smitten. I have one piece of advice, don't wait too long before you take Jordi on that dinner date."

The two striking women talked until Talena suddenly looked at her watch. "I'm afraid I have to run Susie, meetings. Here, please take this card, just let me write something on the back. Take this to El Corte Inglés department store in the square. I've written the name of the head buyer in the designer department. Show this card to any member of staff and they will find her and she will look after your friend. And thank you again for calling me, Susie, I think we will be great friends. See you tomorrow."

She kissed Susie on the cheek, then paused before running off. "His mother can be intimidating. Be yourself, be strong, and don't give her an inch."

Susie asked for the bill and wasn't the least surprised to learn that there wasn't one.

She left to return to the apartment, feeling a little bit more like a local already. While she waited, she called the manicurist and pleaded another emergency, this time invoking the boyfriend's mother. It worked. She *was* a local.

The airport party had arrived at the apartment just ten minutes before Susie arrived. Susie could hear voices as she approached the door to let herself in. As the door opened, the first thing she saw, was Charlie, sitting at the table.

She shrieked his name. "Charlie, Charlie, oh my God." Charlie barely made it to his feet before Susie wrapped him in a hug.

"Charlie, I'm so glad..." Susie choked up and looked for Jill. "Thank you, Jill. This was you wasn't it? What a lovely thing to do."

"Well, after your news yesterday, I thought we better get Charlie over here."

After lunch, Jill opted for a nap and the three men went shopping. Susie and Anne walked to El Cortes Inglés and found the designer department. Anne looked at a couple of price tags.

"Have you seen the prices Susie? Do you want to bankrupt me? Anyway, they'll never have anything to fit me."

"Trust me, I think it will be fine."

She approached a young saleswoman, "Excuse me, I am looking for Senyora Carbonell, perhaps you can help me?"

"Can you tell me what you are looking for? I'm sure I can help you find something."

Susie reached into her Talena bag, produced the card and showed it to the woman.

"This is the Senyora Carbonell I am looking for."

"Just one moment senyora, I will be back immediately."

In a few minutes, a very elegant woman of perhaps fifty came over to them.

"Senyora Smith? Senyora Meier called me a little while ago. Please come with me."

She wanted to know the nature of the occasion, and as soon as Susie mentioned Javi's family party, the lady raised her hand.

"I understand completely. One moment please." She disappeared through a hidden door.

Ten minutes later, two women appeared, each carrying two dresses for Anne's inspection. They were all stylish and most remarkably, looked to be exactly her size. The colors were just right for her slightly tanned complexion, brunette hair and clear blue eyes.

"May I try this one please?"

"A very good choice senyora, please follow me."

Anne returned wearing the selected dress and twirled in front of Susie.

"Oh Anne, it is fabulous, just gorgeous."

"It is, isn't it?"

Just then one of the young women returned with three pairs of shoes. They were identical except for the height of the heels. And of course, the color was perfectly matched to the dress. Anne pointed to the middle pair and the assistant helped her try them on.

"You look a million dollars, Anne, look."

Anne looked in the mirror and let out a little squeal when she saw the flash of red, "These are Christian Louboutins, Susie!"

"I know, please trust me, it's going to be OK."

She turned to the saleswoman. "Senyora will take these. Thank you very much, your taste is impeccable. Perhaps you could give me a card, so I can recommend you to my friends?"

The woman beamed and disappeared with Anne.

A few minutes later, Anne reappeared, closely followed by Senyora Carbonell and the saleswoman, carrying a large El Corte Inglés carrier bag.

"Thank you both very much. I will be seeing Senyora Meier tomorrow at the family event, I will be sure to tell her how well we have been looked after. Thank you. Come on Anne, we have to get to the manicurist."

"It has been our pleasure Senyora, I hope we see you again soon, perhaps something for yourself next time?"

They were in the street before Anne could speak. "Did we just shoplift my outfit?"

Susie laughed, "No, crazy woman. I've been learning how this town works, that is if you're a friend of Javi or Talena."

"What has Talena got to do with anything?"

"That was her card, and this was her favor. We had a coffee this morning."

Anne stared at her, and shook her head. "You belong here Susie. You really do."

Susie didn't get back to Javi's home until almost seven o'clock. After their manicure, she left Anne and ran to the market, desperately trying to think of what to make for dinner. She had explained to Jill and Charlie how important dinner with Jordi was and why she couldn't spend the evening with them.

"I just want you both to know, that I'm never making this again, ever." Susie was facing Javi and Jordi over the kitchen table. "I just ran out of time for anything that takes time."

She went back to the countertop and put a plate before each of them. "OK, you can open your eyes."

"Fantastic!" yelled Jordi, "Thank you Susie, thank you, thank you, thank you!"

Susie smiled, "Well, I guess that's one happy customer. But you and I are sharing Javi, I don't want to turn you into a fat American."

She had made two hamburgers with everything. The burgers were piled high with tomato, cheese, bacon, lettuce and relish, which had been hard to find. The beef was excellent and the butcher had known exactly how to mince it.

To follow, they had New York cheesecake, except that instead of Graham crackers, she had used crushed amaretti biscuits, which she thought was an improvement.

Jordi was first to finish. "Thank you Susie, that was great, really great. When can we have it again?"

"Didn't you hear me? Never again, this is not healthy food."

He came around the table and gave her a hug. She returned his hug and held him gently in front of her.

"Jordi, I think you know that your father and I are very fond of each other. In fact, we love each other, Jordi."

He interrupted her, "Are you going to live with us, Susie?"

"Yes, Jordi, that is what we want. How do you feel about that?"

"Can I have hamburgers on my birthday, for me and my friends?"

"OK, once a year, for your birthday."

She kissed him on the forehead, and said quietly, "Thank you, Jordi."

"I'll go upstairs now, I think I'll call mother with the news."

Susie held him back, "Too late, Jordi, I already told your mother. But no one else in the family knows, you can tell them tomorrow."

He ran to his father and kissed him and headed for the stairs. Suddenly, he stopped and turned to face her again.

"Susie, I don't know if you have bought Grandfather a present, but he told me at Christmas about a cheesecake he and Grandmother once had in America. They both loved it."

He raced up the stairs, leaving them alone.

"I'm not going to ask you when you talked with Talena. Just promise me that you'll never stop surprising me."

She took his hand, "I'll try Javi."

Javi made sure that they were among the first to arrive at the party. As soon as the doors of the van were opened, Jordi took off to find his cousins. Javi led the small group towards the imposing house that dominated the landscape.

Around the house was mostly lawn, with flowerbeds exploding with color, arranged around the driveway and footpaths. To one side of the house was a paddock. Half a dozen horses were visible, contentedly grazing on the luxuriant grasses. In the distance, line after line of vines spilled over softly rounded hills. It was not yet harvest time but the vines were showing their grapes. On the side of the house opposite the paddock, a large marquee had been erected and a few guests were already milling around.

Javi stopped before the covered entrance. "If you don't mind, I should take Susie in to meet my family. Please feel free to wander around and we will find you soon."

He took Susie by the hand and led her into the cool interior. In his other hand he held the handle of a bulky shopping bag.

A young man was standing by the door. "Bon dia, Senyor Domènech, senyora. The family are waiting for you in the salon."

"Just remember, this will be your home, they will be your family." Javi whispered to her.

Two women were sitting together on a brocade sofa. An older man, obviously Javi's grandfather, sat in a formal chair that looked somehow familiar. Javi's father stood facing the doorway. As they came nearer, his father stepped forward. He embraced his son, then turned to Susie.

"You must be Senyora Smith. We have heard a great deal about you, senyora, and all of it extraordinary. I look forward to getting to know you. I am, well you know who I am, I am quite sure; please call me Tomás." He took her hand and kissed it and, as he did so, and to her total astonishment, he looked into her eyes, and winked. "Let me introduce you, my dear."

"Susie, this is my mother, Isabella Justina-Maria, and this is the birthday boy, I think you say, my father Jordi."

Susie again tried to speak clearly and slowly, and hoped that her accent had improved. "Senyor i senyora Domènech, estic molt contenta de conèixer-los. Senyor Domènech, sé que és la seva festa d'aniversari. No sabia ben bé què li podia oferir en un via com avui, però un espia m'ha ajudat. Espero que tots dos en gaudeixin." *I am very pleased to meet you. Mr. Domènech, I know it is your birthday celebration. I had no idea what I could offer you on your birthday, but I had help from a spy. I hope you both enjoy it.'* She reached into the bag and handed over her cheesecake on one of Javi's plates.

"Ah, Susie, young Jordi has been telling stories, I see. We will very much enjoy our cheesecake. You must tell me all about your America. I enjoyed visiting it very much. Thank you, and welcome to our home."

Tomás gently took her elbow, "Susie, may I present my wife, Maria Adriana."

Susie looked at the graceful, elegant woman before her.

"Senyora, by the customs of *my* family, I should also bring you a gift. And my gift is this. I love your son with all my heart. And with my heart, and my mind, and my body, I will try every day to make him happy."

Javi's mother stood and came forward to Susie and embraced her. "Then you will have given me my heart's desire, Susie Smith."

She took Susie's hand and linked it through her arm. "Come and meet our family," and the two women walked into the garden.

Tomás looked at his son, "Don't let this one go, Tiá."

The day passed in a haze. Ted had trouble taking his eyes off Anne, who he thought looked younger and sexier than he remembered. And she was having a ball. Every woman complimented her on her dress, and her shoes. And Ted's admiring glances made her feel fabulous.

"You must be Susie's friend. I recognize that dress, although it has never looked so well as it does on you. I am Talena, I'm delighted to meet you."

"Talena, I can't thank you enough, I've never had so much fun from new clothes. See that man over there? He keeps flirting with me, and I know exactly what's on his mind. I'll introduce you in a moment, that's Ted, my partner."

Talena laughed

"Seriously, Talena, what you did was incredibly generous. I won't forget it, ever."

In the years since her divorce, Talena had remained close to the family, and in particular Isabella, and she was worried about the impact that the news about Susie and Javi might have on the vulnerable young woman. Isabella could be unpredictable; it was impossible to know in advance what might upset her. Talena went to find Javi and Susie.

"Susie, this may sound strange, but I think I would like to be with you when you tell Isabella your news. Otherwise she might think that I would be upset. She knows that Javi and I have been divorced for many years, but I still see her often and she loves my twins. Javi and I have never discussed our divorce in any detail with her and, truthfully, I just don't know how much she understands."

Susie looked across the lawn to where Isabella was happily playing with some of the children of the family. She had grasped immediately what Talena was concerned about.

"I think that's a great idea Talena, and a very generous one. We should have Jordi join us as well; his presence may help reassure Isabella that she has nothing to fear. Javi, why don't you bring them both over, and we can talk with Isabella right now?"

For his part, Peter was captivated by everything about the event. The setting, the house, the food and drink, the people, everything was perfect. He asked someone, a cousin of Javi's he thought, to show him the house. They wandered from room to room. He soon realized that it wasn't the furniture or the art on the walls, lovely though they were; it was the stories that made the house extraordinary.

Everything had a reason for being there. Everything spoke of family, of memorable journeys, adventures, tragedies, love affairs, births and deaths, of favors given and received. The layers of texture had not been bought from a catalog, they had been nurtured and grown.

And in that visit, Peter saw at last, the direction for his professional future.

At three o'clock a bell rang out and everyone headed to the marquee in the garden for the birthday meal. Isabella pushed her way through to her brother and took his arm.

"I want to sit beside you Tiá." Isabella's voice carried across the lawn and her family smiled; she was loved by everyone.

"Of course you will, darling."

"And Suzee will sit on your other side. And then you will be between the two people who love you the most in the whole world."

RESOLUTION

The following morning they were all sitting around the kitchen table.

Anne looked over at Susie, "Yesterday was one of the best days ever. Javi and his family are absolutely delightful and I think I just understood the true meaning of 'sophisticated'."

"I'm so glad you could all meet them, it meant a lot to me. And you know we've all been invited back tomorrow? Not a party this time. Just us. Javi thought we might like a quieter visit after all the people yesterday."

Charlie had an announcement. "Javi's mother is coming here at 11:00."

"I didn't know that, Charlie," replied Susie.

"When she heard that only you and Peter have had any real chance to visit the city, she insisted on showing us some of the sights herself. She's coming in an hour and we're all welcome. She asked me to text her when I know how many we'll be."

Of course they all decided to go along.

At eleven o'clock there was a knock on the door and Maria Adriana ushered them downstairs, where an open-topped mini-coach was waiting, with a young tour guide aboard with headsets for everyone.

They drove past all of the sights: the Gaudi buildings, Montjuic, Park Güell, the Gothic Quarter, the Ramblas and much more. Their guide was excellent and, since they were in no hurry, she had time to explain the background to everything they were seeing. They stopped for a tapas lunch before resuming their tour. During lunch, Maria Adriana answered all of their questions about the city, about Catalonia and its complicated relationship with the rest of Spain. As she listened, Susie realized just how deeply woven Javi's family was with the history of their city and region.

Finally, it was time to board the coach again and the guide addressed them once more.

"Thank you for your attention. We are now approaching the final part of our tour, and I must say that I have never had this opportunity before, so we should thank Senyora Marti i Pellicer, who has somehow arranged this final stop." She nodded at Maria Adriana, before continuing.

"This is Gaudi's masterpiece, the Sagrada Família, the Holy Family Basilica, and for you, there are no other tourists, the basilica officially closed eight minutes ago."

They followed Maria Adriana up to the door, which a security guard unlocked for her. They listened to the guide's explanation of the statuary they could see around the entrance. When they filed through the door, Susie looked up and gasped. She had never imagined such an inspiring, awesome space. She could barely hear the guide, transfixed as she was by the soaring beauty around her. She felt a hand take hers and looked to see Peter, equally overwhelmed by emotion.

"Come over here Susie, Charlie." He led them to the windows on the east side and then turned them around to witness the glory of the west windows, set aflame by the sun, now lower in the sky. They wandered off to explore the amazing structure.

Dinner was in Los Caracoles, a restaurant in the Barri Gòtico. It served good, straightforward food, and it was great fun. They had the mezzanine floor to themselves, overlooking the frenetic kitchen where they could watch the brigade of chefs manage the constant stream of orders. Maria Adriana had excused herself, but Javi, Jordi and Isabella joined them.

At one point, Susie found herself being a spectator, looking at the animated table of her friends and her lover and she felt a strong surge of emotion, a sense of fulfillment and peace. At that moment, Peter happened to be sitting next to her, and so it was he who felt his arm being taken and squeezed.

"I'm really very lucky," she whispered to him. "And take a picture of this in your head, you must tell your mother everything that happened since she left. It's her story too."

The next day was another that the Americans would remember forever. They drove the Ford out to the Penedès house where they were joined once again by Javi, Isabella and Jordi. They broke up into three small groups to be shown around the vineyards, the winemaking area and the wonderful house.

Javi's parents joined them for lunch in the gardens and his father guided them through a tasting of the different styles and vintages of the family wine.

"We sell only our cava," Tomás explained, "but we make still white wines, a rosé and a sweet wine also. But these are only for the family and a few special friends. Some years we also make liqueurs: orange, rose, plum, nut. Never for sale of course."

In the afternoon, they wandered around the grounds, until Peter and Charlie sought out Susie.

"Susie, we wanted to do something to thank Javi for all of the amazing hospitality he and the family have shown us. Do you think you could ask him to join us for a few minutes in one of the rooms in the house?"

Susie decided not to ask what they had in mind, she quite liked this kind of surprise. She went off to find Javi and brought him to the room where Peter and Charlie waited.

Charlie was holding an empty bottle of the family cava.

"Can you see this, Javi? Peter designed it." He pointed to a one-inch square sticker that had been applied to the rear label of the wine.

Peter explained. "Of course this would be printed on your label, and on the labels of your partners in the *España Luxe* project."

Javi looked more closely at the logo. It was a stylized version of the Spanish royal crest, with the words *'España Luxe'* superimposed.

Peter continued, "Susie told us of your idea to have a marketing program to promote high-quality food and drink products from Spain. Of course this is just to give you an idea; in reality someone clever would come up with a better design."

He took the bottle back from Javi and handed it to Charlie.

"That's very nice Peter, but..."

Peter raised a hand. "Please, let Charlie show you what he came up with; it's much more than a logo."

Charlie took out his smartphone and invited Javi and Susie to look at the screen. They could see the label with the logo sticker, as if Charlie was taking a photograph. Suddenly, the screen changed and Talena appeared, talking to them on the screen.

"Hello, my name is Talena. My bags and accessories are recognized throughout the world for their craftsmanship and quality, just like this bottle of cava. This wine has been made by the same family for six generations."

At this point, the image changed to Javi's father, Tomás, and they saw and heard him speaking about the family traditions of wine-making. Talena's voice returned, this time over panoramic shots of green fields, close-ups of grapes, and the golden sparkling wine being poured into a slender crystal flute.

"From planting to harvest to the making of this inimitable wine, nothing is compromised to ensure that you enjoy a truly artisanal product, made with love and care and carrying our guarantee of quality, just like the other products carrying the *España Luxe* label."

"You will now be taken to a web site where you can discover more wonderful products from Spain, and the quality retailers and restaurants in the USA, where you can buy them and try them for yourself. And perhaps you will win the trip of a lifetime, to see for yourself how we pour our souls into every *España Luxe* product. Thank you."

Charlie sat back and looked expectantly at Javi.

For his part, Javi was utterly amazed. "When, how did you do this? How much does this cost?"

Peter answered him.

"Well, you need to understand that Charlie is a genius, which helps. He filmed Talena on Wednesday, he added all the stock images yesterday morning, when we were all still asleep and he filmed your father this morning, without anyone noticing.

And you could put a campaign around this together for less than $100,000. We can give you details of agencies who do this for a living."

Javi sat in silence for a moment, before speaking. "I have already told Susie that she has a remarkable group of friends, who can do the impossible. She also told me that she had a secret weapon. Well, now I know what she meant. That was fantastic, simply amazing. I will discuss it with some of my colleagues immediately; this could save us years, and a lot of money. This project is very important to me. Thank you, both of you, thank you very much. I really appreciate the sentiment and the effort behind this."

They chatted a few minutes more, allowing Charlie to explain a little more about how augmented reality worked. As they left the room to rejoin the others, Susie pushed between Charlie and Peter, put an arm around each of them and squeezed them tight.

"My boys," was all she said. She was wearing an enormous smile.

At six o'clock they returned to their Ford with Peter once again at the wheel. They had just started back towards the city, when Anne called out, "Where's Susie, and Charlie for that matter? We've left them behind."

"No, we haven't, Javi's bringing them back." Peter reassured them.

'

Susie and Charlie were sitting on a bench in Montjuic, high above the city. Javi had dropped them off; they would take a taxi home. As they looked at the city spread out below them, Susie had a flashback to the model town in Dr. Gallo's office in Brooklyn. What would Dr. Gallo think of the end of the story of the pen, she wondered?

"I'm going to stay here Charlie, I'm not coming back."

"I know Susie. It's OK though, we'll see each other now and then."

"Yes, we will Charlie. There will always be a room for you in my house. And now you have a passport, I expect you here often. When you get back, tell Gran everything, all of it. Actually Charlie, how did you get a passport so quickly?"

"I had to put myself at the top of the one hour priority service at JFK. It worked out OK. Gran will be so proud of you, Susie. And so will Alejandra; she's staying with Gran right now, to look after her," he added.

"Do you really like her Charlie? How does she make you feel?"

"I really like her a lot Susie, and she makes me feel ... like me."

"I'll be back for Halloween. I want to bring Jordi and Isabella to see a Kingsbay Halloween."

"I'm going to college in the fall," he announced. "It's Alejandra's idea really. I'm going to study English and history. Alejandra thinks I'd be wasting my time studying computing. She says I can always make money anyway, so I should concentrate on interesting stuff, like history and literature. What do you think, Susie?"

"I think she's a keeper, Charlie."

"Gran really likes her too. It's a pity Gran is too old to travel here now, but I'm going to do something for her while I'm here."

"You know I'm going home with Peter, via Paris? Well, Peter has agreed to come with me and we're going to visit Joe Dawson's grave in Normandy. It's only three hours by train from Paris. I'm going to leave flowers for Gran."

Again, Susie had the sensation of time rushing headlong. It was barely a year since Charlie had told her about Betty and her doomed beau going off to war. Only a year, and so much had happened.

Susie and Charlie sat together peacefully, looking over the city, the brother and sister who weren't. Later, she took him to Lasarte for dinner. Charlie wasn't wearing smart enough clothes for Lasarte, but Javi had said not to worry, they were family.

Susie packed up all of her belongings, and the boxes of materials Charlie had sent. In two days they would give up the apartment. When she was finished, she looked around fondly; it had been her base for the adventure of her life.

Her mind wandered back over the cascade of events, all starting with the would-be bag thief. She wondered briefly how his hand was recovering. Suddenly she realized what she had just thought, that her adventure had started here, in Barcelona, not in Kingsbay or in Brooklyn. Despite a kidnapping, drugs, Tasers, a beautiful escort, recovering everything; despite all of that, her adventure had really been about Barcelona, and her friends and Javi, her love and her future.

They only had one more day left together before they would go their separate ways. They didn't want to go to another restaurant for lunch or dinner, but instead, they asked Javi if he would mind if they made paella on the grill in the garden in the afternoon. Peter and Jordi dragged the reluctant pair of Ted and Charlie to the *Boqueria* to buy the ingredients. They came back enthusing about the fabulous produce they had had to leave behind.

Jordi took charge of directing the men to make the huge platter of prawns, mussels, chicken, peppers and rice. With the sun dropping lower in the sky, they gathered around the table and talked, ate their paella and drank beer and wine.

The Americans were in the Impressionist room. Javi knew that Susie needed some time with her friends, so he and Jordi were clearing up from their meal.

Susie had opened another bottle of Javi's cava and topped up everyone's glass. Charlie had propped his laptop on the table and had reached Sophie on Skype. It wasn't as good as her being there, but it was the best they could do.

Susie proposed a toast. "Here's to the greatest friends a girl could have. Thanks to you, I've started my new life and I couldn't be more excited. I'll never be able to repay you, but thank you from the bottom of my heart. To my friends."

They chinked glasses and drank some wine.

"Well," said Anne, "I don't want to steal your thunder, Susie, but my life is about to change as well. Ted has asked me to marry him, and this time I've said yes!"

Of course they all had to come around and hug them both. Ted looked at Susie, "And you'll have to come back for the wedding, you and Javi."

They chatted and reminisced. It had been quite an adventure and there were lots of details to be relived. Charlie was, as always, quiet, but they didn't allow him to be silent. Anne in particular, wanted the inside scoop on his romance with Alejandra. Charlie wouldn't be drawn, except to allow that he had enjoyed her reaction the first time he pulled up in his new red Miata.

Jill interceded, "Alejandra has never looked happier in all the years we've known her, and, while I won't betray any confidences, I will say that she is looking forward to you coming home Charlie."

To save Charlie's blushes, Sophie redirected their attention to herself. Over the computer's speakers, they heard her reveal, "This trip has meant a lot to my family, it has been great for two of my men. I don't know if you all realize just how badly Andy's betrayal affected Will, but I can tell you it's a huge weight off his shoulders that Luis will get his money back. And he is so proud that his son, his gay son, was so strong."

A single tear rolled down Sophie's cheek, but she brushed it quickly away as she continued, "And my wonderful son has been energized by Barcelona and, I must say Susie, by your Javi's family and their lovely homes. He knows now what he wants to do with his life."

Susie had put her arm around Peter as his mother talked. "In the end, Peter saved the day, and it was very hard for him."

For a few moments they all sat with their own thoughts.

"I've had a lot of time to think about everything," continued Susie, "and here is what I believe we should do. We can't keep the money: it's the product of dishonesty and we did nothing for it. But, we should give everyone back whatever they invested in Andy's schemes. Then we should pay everyone back the money we've had to spend. I would like to give something to Peter here, maybe invest in his new business, when he sets one up. And I thought we could send round trip tickets to Monica and Steve, to bring them from their home to New York for a vacation. Is that OK so far?"

Every head was nodding.

Susie looked straight at Charlie. "And with the millions of dollars left, I would like us to create the Joe Dawson Scholarship Fund, which will finance grants for poor American students to have a study year in Europe. The rest of you should ask Charlie who Joe Dawson was. We all will be the trustees. And once a year, the trustees will have to meet, here, in my Barcelona home."

On Sunday they were all at the airport. Peter and Charlie were going to Paris, and Jill, Anne and Ted were heading home. Jill was sent off with gifts for Kevin and Lucy, including the two caricatures Susie had commissioned from their photographs.

The flight to Paris was the last to leave. Charlie and Susie had said everything they needed to say to each other on Friday night, so they simply hugged, and Susie managed not to cry. Peter stepped forward and took both of Susie's hands in his own.

"Now that we've slept together I feel kind of responsible for you. I think I'll have to come back soon to keep an eye on you." His expression changed and became serious, "Really, Susie, I want to come back and study this city some more, I know I can learn a lot here."

Just when Susie thought Peter was leaving on a serious note, he wrapped his arms around her and looked into her eyes, "See you around, kid. And remember, we'll always have Penedès."

GAPS

Exactly one week after the Kingsbay group boarded their planes, and two weeks before his deadline for leaving, there was a knock on Andy's apartment door. He was still recovering from his ordeal in the hills, still trying to come to terms with the complete collapse of his dreams.

He opened the door to a powerfully built man standing with a gun pointed straight at his face. Andy froze. For some reason, he noticed that the man was wearing black gloves, had vivid blue eyes and had extremely short hair.

The man waved his free hand to indicate that Andy should walk back into the room. The hand with the gun hadn't wavered so much as a hair's breadth. The man followed Andy in, closing the door carefully behind him. He motioned to the sofa and Andy sat down. The gun was still aimed at his face.

"Are you Andrew Smith, yes or no?" He had a thick accent that Andy couldn't quite place, but it was something from a movie he had seen.

"Yes," he managed to answer, through dry lips.

"Do you know Valentina Sokolov? Yes or no?"

A shard of ice penetrated Andy's belly.

"I do, or I did, but I haven't..."

The man made a show of doing something to the gun; releasing the safety catch, Andy assumed.

"I said yes or no, asshole. Do you know where she is?"

"No, I don't."

The man knew Andy was lying; he had played out scenes like this many times before.

He lowered the gun, and calmly shot Andy in the thigh. The weapon made almost no noise.

Andy screamed and the man whipped the gun across his face.

"Shut up. What happened to Valentina Sokolov, where is she?"

Andy thought he might pass out from the pain. He was clutching his leg as hard as he could to slow the bleeding, but knew he needed to get to a doctor quickly. He saw blood from his damaged face, drip onto his trouser leg.

"It was an accident, she fell overboard," he squeezed the words out, now unable to hold back tears of pain and fear.

The man thought Andy was probably lying, but he had spent too much time on this fucking job already. Anyway, no one cared, the girl was dead either way.

"Mr. Petrov sends his regards, but he doesn't allow people to steal his property."

Andy barely registered the impact, as the bullet smashed into his forehead, and he was dead by the time his head came to rest on the back of the sofa, his eyes staring sightlessly at the ceiling.

As instructed, the man took from his pocket, a small figure from a nesting Russian doll set and carefully placed it directly on top of the neat hole in Andy's head.

Weeks later, the information about the doll would be leaked to the media, and the people who Mr. Petrov wanted to know, would understand.

In his $50 million house in Kensington Palace Road in London, Mr. Petrov had a very private study. Only certain people, including each of his mistresses, ever saw the inside of this room. One wall displayed a collection of priceless medieval Byzantine icons.

The opposite wall held a single shelf displaying a beautiful antique Russian nesting doll set, with the individual dolls arrayed from left to right in decreasing size. There had originally been thirty dolls, but there were obvious gaps in the series; spaces where once there had been exquisite painted figures.

Now there were eight gaps.

As Mr. Petrov explained to the select visitors to this room, mistresses left when Mr. Petrov decided they should. And, as his executioner had truthfully told Andy, no one stole Anatoly Petrov's property.

THE AUTHOR

Brian McPhee lived in Glasgow, Scotland until he was 21, when he moved to London. In his early 40s, after a year in Manhattan and Long Island, he moved with his wife and daughter to a wonderful community near Annapolis, Maryland. For several years the family kept their motor yacht in Sitges, near Barcelona.

They hold UK and US passports.

He and his wife currently live in Monpazier in south-west France.

BUNCO is his first novel.

WORDS FOR THE WISE, a collection of quotations, specifically selected for students, is available on Amazon.

A COLD DISH AND OTHER TALES, a collection of short stories, will be available on Amazon in June 2017.

21592806R00282

Printed in Great Britain
by Amazon